WEE WILLIE WINKIE

UNDER THE DEODARS
THE PHANTOM 'RICKSHAW
AND OTHER STORIES

BY

RUDYARD KIPLING

ISBN (cased) 0 333 32775 6
ISBN (paper) 0 333 32776 4

MACMILLAN LONDON LIMITED
London and Basingstoke

Associated companies in Auckland, Dallas,
Delhi, Dublin, Hong Kong, Johannesburg,
Lagos, Manzini, Melbourne, Nairobi,
New York, Singapore, Tokyo, Washington
and Zaria

First edition 1895
Reprinted 1896, 1898
Edition de Luxe 1898
Uniform edition 1899, 1901
Library edition 1947, 1951, 1963
Centenary edition 1965, 1969
Centenary edition (n.s.) 1982
Paperback edition 1982

Printed in Great Britain by
St. Edmundsbury Press
Bury St. Edmunds, Suffolk

CONTENTS

UNDER THE DEODARS

And since he cannot spend nor use aright
   The little time here given him in trust,
But wasteth it in weary undelight
   Of foolish toil and trouble, strife and lust,
He naturally clamours to inherit
The Everlasting Future that his merit
   May have full scope—as surely is most just.

The City of Dreadful Night.

The Education of Otis Yeere

I

In the pleasant orchard-closes
  'God bless all our gains,' say we ;
But 'May God bless all our losses,'
  Better suits with our degree.

The Lost Bower.

THIS is the history of a failure ; but the woman
who failed said that it might be an instructive tale
to put into print for the benefit of the younger
generation. The younger generation does not
want instruction, being perfectly willing to instruct
if any one will listen to it. None the less, here
begins the story where every right-minded story
should begin, that is to say at Simla, where all
things begin and many come to an evil end.

The mistake was due to a very clever woman
making a blunder and not retrieving it. Men are
licensed to stumble, but a clever woman's mistake
is outside the regular course of Nature and Providence ; since all good people know that a woman
is the only infallible thing in this world, except
Government Paper of the '79 issue, bearing interest

at four and a half per cent. Yet, we have to remember that six consecutive days of rehearsing the leading part of *The Fallen Angel*, at the New Gaiety Theatre where the plaster is not yet properly dry, might have brought about an unhingement of spirits which, again, might have led to eccentricities.

Mrs. Hauksbee came to 'The Foundry' to tiffin with Mrs. Mallowe, her one bosom friend, for she was in no sense 'a woman's woman.' And it was a woman's tiffin, the door shut to all the world; and they both talked *chiffons*, which is French for Mysteries.

'I've enjoyed an interval of sanity,' Mrs. Hauksbee announced, after tiffin was over and the two were comfortably settled in the little writing-room that opened out of Mrs. Mallowe's bedroom.

'My dear girl, what has *he* done?' said Mrs. Mallowe sweetly. It is noticeable that ladies of a certain age call each other 'dear girl,' just as commissioners of twenty-eight years' standing address their equals in the Civil List as 'my boy.'

'There's no *he* in the case. Who am I that an imaginary man should be always credited to me? Am I an Apache?'

'No, dear, but somebody's scalp is generally drying at your wigwam-door. Soaking rather.'

This was an allusion to the Hawley Boy, who was in the habit of riding all across Simla in the Rains, to call on Mrs. Hauksbee. That lady laughed.

'For my sins, the Aide at Tyrconnel last night told me off to The Mussuck. Hsh! Don't laugh. One of my most devoted admirers. When the

duff came—some one really ought to teach them
to make puddings at Tyrconnel—The Mussuck
was at liberty to attend to me.'

'Sweet soul! I know his appetite,' said Mrs.
Mallowe. 'Did he, oh *did* he, begin his wooing?'

'By a special mercy of Providence, *no*. He
explained his importance as a Pillar of the Empire.
I didn't laugh.'

'Lucy, I don't believe you.'

'Ask Captain Sangar; he was on the other side.
Well, as I was saying, The Mussuck dilated.'

'I think I can see him doing it,' said Mrs.
Mallowe pensively, scratching her fox-terrier's
ears.

'I was properly impressed. Most properly. I
yawned openly. "Strict supervision, and play
them off one against the other," said The Mussuck,
shovelling down his ice by *tureenfuls*, I assure
you. "*That*, Mrs. Hauksbee, is the secret of our
Government."'

Mrs. Mallowe laughed long and merrily. 'And
what did you say?'

'Did you ever know me at loss for an answer
yet? I said: "So I have observed in my dealings
with you." The Mussuck swelled with pride.
He is coming to call on me to-morrow. The
Hawley Boy is coming too.'

'"Strict supervision and play them off one
against the other. *That*, Mrs. Hauksbee, is the
secret of *our* Government." And I daresay if we
could get to The Mussuck's heart, we should find
that he considers himself a man of the world.'

'As he is of the other two things. I like The

Mussuck, and I won't have you call him names. He amuses me.'

'He has reformed you, too, by what appears. Explain the interval of sanity, and hit Tim on the nose with the paper-cutter, please. That dog is too fond of sugar. Do you take milk in yours?'

'No, thanks. Polly, I'm wearied of this life. It's hollow.'

'Turn religious, then. I always said that Rome would be your fate.'

'Only exchanging half-a-dozen *attachés* in red for one in black, and if I fasted, the wrinkles would come, and never, *never* go. Has it ever struck you, dear, that I'm getting old?'

'Thanks for your courtesy. I'll return it. Ye-es, we are both not exactly—how shall I put it?'

'What we have been. "I feel it in my bones," as Mrs. Crossley says. Polly, I've wasted my life.'

'As how?'

'Never mind how. I feel it. I want to be a Power before I die.'

'Be a Power then. You've wits enough for anything—and beauty!'

Mrs. Hauksbee pointed a teaspoon straight at her hostess. 'Polly, if you heap compliments on me like this, I shall cease to believe that you're a woman. Tell me how I am to be a Power.'

'Inform The Mussuck that he is the most fascinating and slimmest man in Asia, and he'll tell you anything and everything you please.'

'Bother The Mussuck! I mean an intellectual Power—not a gas-power. Polly, I'm going to start a *salon*.'

Mrs. Mallowe turned lazily on the sofa and rested her head on her hand. 'Hear the words of the Preacher, the son of Baruch,' she said.

'*Will* you talk sensibly?'

'I will, dear, for I see that you are going to make a mistake.'

'I never made a mistake in my life—at least, never one that I couldn't explain away afterwards.'

'Going to make a mistake,' went on Mrs. Mallowe composedly. 'It is impossible to start a *salon* in Simla. A bar would be much more to the point.'

'Perhaps, but why? It seems so easy.'

'Just what makes it so difficult. How many clever women are there in Simla?'

'Myself and yourself,' said Mrs. Hauksbee, without a moment's hesitation.

'Modest woman! Mrs. Feardon would thank you for that. And how many clever men?'

'Oh — er — hundreds,' said Mrs. Hauksbee vaguely.

'What a fatal blunder! Not one. They are all bespoke by the Government. Take my husband, for instance. Jack *was* a clever man, though I say so who shouldn't. Government has eaten him up. All his ideas and powers of conversation—he really used to be a good talker, even to his wife, in the old days—are taken from him by this—this kitchen-sink of a Government. That's the case with every man up here who is at work. I don't suppose a Russian convict under the knout is able to amuse the rest of his gang; and all our men-folk here are gilded convicts.'

'But there are scores——'

'I know what you're going to say. Scores of idle men up on leave. I admit it, but they are all of two objectionable sets. The Civilian who'd be delightful if he had the military man's knowledge of the world and style, and the military man who'd be adorable if he had the Civilian's culture.'

'Detestable word! *Have* Civilians culchaw? I never studied the breed deeply.'

'Don't make fun of Jack's Service. Yes. They're like the teapoys in the Lakka Bazar—good material but not polished. They can't help themselves, poor dears. A Civilian only begins to be tolerable after he has knocked about the world for fifteen years.'

'And a military man?'

'When he has had the same amount of service. The young of both species are horrible. You would have scores of them in your *salon*.'

'I would *not!*' said Mrs. Hauksbee fiercely. 'I would tell the bearer to *darwaza band* them. I'd put their own colonels and commissioners at the door to turn them away. I'd give them to the Topsham Girl to play with.'

'The Topsham Girl would be grateful for the gift. But to go back to the *salon*. Allowing that you had gathered all your men and women together, what would you do with them? Make them talk? They would all with one accord begin to flirt. Your *salon* would become a glorified Peliti's—a "Scandal Point" by lamplight.'

'There's a certain amount of wisdom in that view.'

'There's all the wisdom in the world in it. Surely, twelve Simla seasons ought to have taught you that you can't focus anything in India ; and a *salon*, to be any good at all, must be permanent. In two seasons your roomful would be scattered all over Asia. We are only little bits of dirt on the hillsides—here one day and blown down the *khud* the next. We have lost the art of talking—at least our men have. We have no cohesion——'

'George Eliot in the flesh,' interpolated Mrs. Hauksbee wickedly.

'And collectively, my dear scoffer, we, men and women alike, have *no* influence. Come into the verandah and look at the Mall !'

The two looked down on the now rapidly filling road, for all Simla was abroad to steal a stroll between a shower and a fog.

'How do you propose to fix that river ? Look ! There's The Mussuck—head of goodness knows what. He is a power in the land, though he *does* eat like a costermonger. There's Colonel Blone, and General Grucher, and Sir Dugald Delane, and Sir Henry Haughton, and Mr. Jellalatty. All Heads of Departments, and all powerful.'

'And all my fervent admirers,' said Mrs. Hauksbee piously. 'Sir Henry Haughton raves about me. But go on.'

'One by one, these men are worth something. Collectively, they're just a mob of Anglo-Indians. Who cares for what Anglo-Indians say ? Your *salon* won't weld the Departments together and make you mistress of India, dear. And these creatures won't talk administrative " shop " in a

crowd—your *salon*—because they are so afraid of
the men in the lower ranks overhearing it. They
have forgotten what of Literature and Art they
ever knew, and the women——'

'Can't talk about anything except the last
Gymkhana, or the sins of their last nurse. I was
calling on Mrs. Derwills this morning.'

'You admit that? They can talk to the
subalterns though, and the subalterns can talk to
them. Your *salon* would suit their views admirably, if you respected the religious prejudices of
the country and provided plenty of *kala juggahs*.'

'Plenty of *kala juggahs*. Oh my poor little
idea! *Kala juggahs* in a *salon*! But who made
you so awfully clever?'

'Perhaps I've tried myself; or perhaps I know
a woman who has. I have preached and expounded
the whole matter and the conclusion thereof——'

'You needn't go on. "Is Vanity." Polly, I
thank you. These vermin'—Mrs. Hauksbee
waved her hand from the verandah to two men in
the crowd below who had raised their hats to her
—'these vermin shall not rejoice in a new Scandal
Point or an extra Peliti's. I will abandon the
notion of a *salon*. It did seem so tempting, though.
But what shall I do? I must do something.'

'Why? Are not Abana and Pharpar——'

'Jack has made you nearly as bad as himself!
I want to, of course. I'm tired of everything and
everybody, from a moonlight picnic at Seepee to
the blandishments of The Mussuck.'

'Yes—that comes, too, sooner or later. Have
you nerve enough to make your bow yet?'

Mrs. Hauksbee's mouth shut grimly. Then she laughed. 'I think I see myself doing it. Big pink placards on the Mall : "Mrs. Hauksbee ! Positively her last appearance on *any* stage ! This is to give notice !" No more dances ; no more rides ; no more luncheons ; no more theatricals with supper to follow ; no more sparring with one's dearest, dearest friend ; no more fencing with an inconvenient man who hasn't wit enough to clothe what he's pleased to call his sentiments in passable speech ; no more parading of The Mussuck while Mrs. Tarkass calls all round Simla, spreading horrible stories about me ! No more of anything that is thoroughly wearying, abominable, and detestable, but, all the same, makes life worth the having. Yes ! I see it all ! Don't interrupt, Polly, I'm inspired. A mauve and white striped "cloud" round my excellent shoulders, a seat in the fifth row of the Gaiety, and *both* horses sold. Delightful vision ! A comfortable arm-chair, situated in three different draughts, at every ball-room ; and nice, large, sensible shoes for all the couples to stumble over as they go into the verandah ! Then at supper. Can't you imagine the scene ? The greedy mob gone away. Reluctant subaltern, pink all over like a newly-powdered baby,—they really ought to *tan* subalterns before they are exported, Polly,—sent back by the hostess to do his duty. Slouches up to me across the room, tugging at a glove two sizes too large for him—I *hate* a man who wears gloves like overcoats —and trying to look as if he'd thought of it from the first. "May I ah-have the pleasure 'f takin'

you 'nt' supper?" Then I get up with a hungry
smile. Just like this.'

'Lucy, how *can* you be so absurd?'

'And sweep out on his arm. So! After supper
I shall go away early, you know, because I shall be
afraid of catching cold. No one will look for my
'rickshaw. *Mine*, so please you! I shall stand,
always with that mauve and white "cloud" over
my head, while the wet soaks into my dear, old,
venerable feet, and Tom swears and shouts for the
mem-sahib's gharri. Then home to bed at half-
past eleven! Truly excellent life—helped out by
the visits of the *Padri*, just fresh from burying
somebody down below there.' She pointed through
the pines toward the Cemetery, and continued
with vigorous dramatic gesture—

'Listen! I see it all—down, down even to the
stays! *Such* stays! Six-eight a pair, Polly, with
red flannel—or list, is it?—that they put into the
tops of those fearful things. I can draw you a
picture of them.'

'Lucy, for Heaven's sake, don't go waving
your arms about in that idiotic manner! Recollect
every one can see you from the Mall.'

'Let them see! They'll think I am rehearsing
for *The Fallen Angel*. Look! There's the Mussuck. How badly he rides. There!'

She blew a kiss to the venerable Indian adminis-
trator with infinite grace.

'Now,' she continued, 'he'll be chaffed about
that at the Club in the delicate manner those brutes
of men affect, and the Hawley Boy will tell me
all about it—softening the details for fear of

shocking me. That boy is too good to live, Polly. I've serious thoughts of recommending him to throw up his commission and go into the Church. In his present frame of mind he would obey me. Happy, happy child!'

'Never again,' said Mrs. Mallowe, with an affectation of indignation, 'shall you tiffin here! "Lucindy your behaviour is scand'lus."'

'All your fault,' retorted Mrs. Hauksbee, 'for suggesting such a thing as my abdication. No! *jamais!* nevaire! I will act, dance, ride, frivol, talk scandal, dine out, and appropriate the legitimate captives of any woman I choose, until I d-r-r-rop, or a better woman than I puts me to shame before all Simla,—and it's dust and ashes in my mouth while I'm doing it!'

She swept into the drawing-room. Mrs. Mallowe followed and put an arm round her waist.

'I'm *not!*' said Mrs. Hauksbee defiantly, rummaging for her handkerchief. 'I've been dining out the last ten nights, and rehearsing in the afternoon. You'd be tired yourself. It's only because I'm tired.'

Mrs. Mallowe did not offer Mrs. Hauksbee any pity or ask her to lie down, but gave her another cup of tea, and went on with the talk.

'I've been through that too, dear,' she said.

'I remember,' said Mrs. Hauksbee, a gleam of fun on her face. 'In '84, wasn't it? You went out a great deal less next season.'

Mrs. Mallowe smiled in a superior and Sphinx-like fashion.

'I became an Influence,' said she.

'Good gracious, child, you didn't join the Theosophists and kiss Buddha's big toe, did you? I tried to get into their set once, but they cast me out for a sceptic—without a chance of improving my poor little mind, too.'

'No, I didn't Theosophilander. Jack says——'

'Never mind Jack. What a husband says is known before. What did you do?'

'I made a lasting impression.'

'So have I—for four months. But that didn't console me in the least. I hated the man. *Will* you stop smiling in that inscrutable way and tell me what you mean?'

Mrs. Mallowe told.

.   .   .   .   .

'And—you—mean—to—say that it is absolutely Platonic on both sides?'

'Absolutely, or I should never have taken it up.'

'And his last promotion was due to you?'

Mrs. Mallowe nodded.

'And you warned him against the Topsham Girl?'

Another nod.

'And told him of Sir Dugald Delane's private memo about him?'

A third nod.

'*Why?*'

'What a question to ask a woman! Because it amused me at first. I am proud of my property now. If I live, he shall continue to be successful. Yes, I will put him upon the straight road to Knighthood, and everything else that a man values. The rest depends upon himself.'

' Polly, you are a most extraordinary woman.'

' Not in the least. I'm concentrated, that's all. You diffuse yourself, dear ; and though all Simla knows your skill in managing a team——'

' Can't you choose a prettier word ? '

' *Team*, of half-a-dozen, from The Mussuck to the Hawley Boy, you gain nothing by it. Not even amusement.'

' And you ? '

' Try my recipe. Take a man, not a boy, mind, but an almost mature, unattached man, and be his guide, philosopher, and friend. You'll find it *the* most interesting occupation that you ever embarked on. It can be done—you needn't look like that—because I've done it.'

' There's an element of risk about it that makes the notion attractive. I'll get such a man and say to him, " Now, understand that there must be no flirtation. Do exactly what I tell you, profit by my instruction and counsels, and all will yet be well." Is that the idea ? '

' More or less,' said Mrs. Mallowe, with an unfathomable smile. ' But be sure he understands.'

II

Dribble-dribble—trickle-trickle—
What a lot of raw dust !
My dollie's had an accident
And out came all the sawdust !
Nursery Rhyme.

So Mrs. Hauksbee, in 'The Foundry' which overlooks Simla Mall, sat at the feet of Mrs. Mallowe and gathered wisdom. The end of the Conference was the Great Idea upon which Mrs. Hauksbee so plumed herself.

'I warn you,' said Mrs. Mallowe, beginning to repent of her suggestion, 'that the matter is not half so easy as it looks. Any woman—even the Topsham Girl—can catch a man, but very, *very* few know how to manage him when caught.'

'My child,' was the answer, 'I've been a female St. Simon Stylites looking down upon men for these — these years past. Ask The Mussuck whether I can manage them.'

Mrs. Hauksbee departed humming, '*I'll go to him and say to him in manner most ironical.*' Mrs. Mallowe laughed to herself. Then she grew suddenly sober. 'I wonder whether I've done well in advising that amusement? Lucy's a clever woman, but a thought too careless.'

A week later the two met at a Monday Pop. 'Well?' said Mrs. Mallowe.

'I've caught him!' said Mrs. Hauksbee : her eyes were dancing with merriment.

'Who is it, mad woman? I'm sorry I ever spoke to you about it.'

'Look between the pillars. In the third row ; fourth from the end. You can see his face now. Look!'

'Otis Yeere! Of *all* the improbable and impossible people! I don't believe you.'

'Hsh! Wait till Mrs. Tarkass begins murdering Milton Wellings ; and I'll tell you all about it. *S-s-ss!* That woman's voice always reminds me of an Underground train coming into Earl's Court with the brakes on. Now listen. It is *really* Otis Yeere.'

'So I see, but does it follow that he is your property!'

'He *is !* By right of trove. I found him, lonely and unbefriended, the very next night after our talk, at the Dugald Delanes' *burra-khana*. I liked his eyes, and I talked to him. Next day he called. Next day we went for a ride together, and to-day he's tied to my 'rickshaw-wheels hand and foot. You'll see when the concert's over. He doesn't know I'm here yet.'

'Thank goodness you haven't chosen a boy. What are you going to do with him, assuming that you've got him?'

'Assuming, indeed! Does a woman—do *I*—

ever make a mistake in that sort of thing? First'
—Mrs. Hauksbee ticked off the items ostentatiously
on her little gloved fingers—'First, my dear, I
shall dress him properly. At present his raiment
is a disgrace, and he wears a dress-shirt like a
crumpled sheet of the *Pioneer*. Secondly, after
I have made him presentable, I shall form his
manners—his morals are above reproach.'

'You seem to have discovered a great deal
about him considering the shortness of your
acquaintance.'

'Surely *you* ought to know that the first proof
a man gives of his interest in a woman is by talking to her about his own sweet self. If the woman
listens without yawning, he begins to like her. If
she flatters the animal's vanity, he ends by adoring
her.'

'In some cases.'

'Never mind the exceptions. I know which
one you are thinking of. Thirdly, and lastly,
after he is polished and made pretty, I shall, as
you said, be his guide, philosopher, and friend,
and he shall become a success—as great a success
as your friend. I always wondered how that man
got on. *Did* The Mussuck come to you with
the Civil List and, dropping on one knee—no,
two knees, *à la Gibbon*—hand it to you and say,
"Adorable angel, choose your friend's appointment"?'

'Lucy, your long experiences of the Military
Department have demoralised you. One doesn't
do that sort of thing on the Civil Side.'

'No disrespect meant to Jack's Service, my

dear. I only asked for information. Give me three months, and see what changes I shall work in my prey.'

'Go your own way since you must. But I'm sorry that I was weak enough to suggest the amusement.'

' " I am all discretion, and may be trusted to an in-fin-ite extent," ' quoted Mrs. Hauksbee from *The Fallen Angel;* and the conversation ceased with Mrs. Tarkass's last, long-drawn war-whoop.

Her bitterest enemies—and she had many— could hardly accuse Mrs. Hauksbee of wasting her time. Otis Yeere was one of those wandering 'dumb' characters, foredoomed through life to be nobody's property. Ten years in Her Majesty's Bengal Civil Service, spent, for the most part, in undesirable Districts, had given him little to be proud of, and nothing to bring confidence. Old enough to have lost the first fine careless rapture that showers on the immature 'Stunt imaginary Commissionerships and Stars, and sends him into the collar with coltish earnestness and abandon; too young to be yet able to look back upon the progress he had made, and thank Providence that under the conditions of the day he had come even so far, he stood upon the dead-centre of his career. And when a man stands still he feels the slightest impulse from without. Fortune had ruled that Otis Yeere should be, for the first part of his service, one of the rank and file who are ground up in the wheels of the Administration; losing heart and soul, and mind and strength, in the process. Until steam replaces manual power in the working of the Empire, there must always be this percentage—must always be the men who are used up, expended, in the mere mechanical routine. For these promotion is far off and the mill-grind of every day very instant. The Secretariats know them only by name; they are not the picked men of the Districts with Divisions and Collectorates awaiting them. They are simply the rank and file—the food for fever—sharing with the *ryot* and the plough-bullock the honour of being the plinth on which the State rests. The older ones have lost their aspirations; the younger are putting theirs aside with a sigh. Both learn to endure patiently until the end of the day. Twelve years in the rank and file, men say, will sap the hearts of the bravest and dull the wits of the most keen.

Out of this life Otis Yeere had fled for a few months; drifting, in the hope of a little masculine society, into Simla. When his leave was over he would return to his swampy, sour-green, under-manned Bengal district; to the native Assistant, the native Doctor, the native Magistrate, the steaming, sweltering Station, the ill-kempt City, and the undisguised insolence of the Municipality that babbled away the lives of men. Life was cheap, however. The soil spawned humanity, as it bred frogs in the Rains, and the gap of the sickness of one season was filled to overflowing by the fecundity of the next. Otis was unfeignedly thankful to lay down his work for a little while and escape from the seething, whining, weakly hive, impotent to help itself, but strong in its power to cripple, thwart, and annoy the sunken-eyed man who, by official irony, was said to be 'in charge' of it.

.   .   .   .   .

'I knew there were women-dowdies in Bengal. They come up here sometimes. But I didn't know that there were men-dowds, too.'

Then, for the first time, it occurred to Otis Yeere that his clothes wore rather the mark of the ages. It will be seen that his friendship with Mrs. Hauksbee had made great strides.

As that lady truthfully says, a man is never so happy as when he is talking about himself. From Otis Yeere's lips Mrs. Hauksbee, before long, learned everything that she wished to know about the subject of her experiment : learned what manner of life he had led in what she vaguely called 'those awful cholera districts'; learned, too, but this knowledge came later, what manner of life he had purposed to lead and what dreams he had dreamed in the year of grace '77, before the reality had knocked the heart out of him. Very pleasant are the shady bridle-paths round Prospect Hill for the telling of such confidences.

'Not yet,' said Mrs. Hauksbee to Mrs. Mallowe. 'Not yet. I must wait until the man is properly dressed, at least. Great heavens, is it possible that he doesn't know what an honour it is to be taken up by *Me!*'

Mrs. Hauksbee did not reckon false modesty as one of her failings.

'Always with Mrs. Hauksbee!' murmured Mrs. Mallowe, with her sweetest smile, to Otis.

'Oh you men, you men! Here are our Punjabis growling because you've monopolised the nicest woman in Simla. They'll tear you to pieces on the Mall, some day, Mr. Yeere.'

Mrs. Mallowe rattled downhill, having satisfied herself, by a glance through the fringe of her sunshade, of the effect of her words.

The shot went home. Of a surety Otis Yeere was somebody in this bewildering whirl of Simla—had monopolised the nicest woman in it, and the Punjabis were growling. The notion justified a mild glow of vanity. He had never looked upon his acquaintance with Mrs. Hauksbee as a matter for general interest.

The knowledge of envy was a pleasant feeling to the man of no account. It was intensified later in the day when a luncher at the Club said spitefully, 'Well, for a debilitated Ditcher, Yeere, you *are* going it. Hasn't any kind friend told you that she's the most dangerous woman in Simla ?'

Yeere chuckled and passed out. When, oh, when would his new clothes be ready? He descended into the Mall to inquire ; and Mrs. Hauksbee, coming over the Church Ridge in her 'rickshaw, looked down upon him approvingly. 'He's learning to carry himself as if he were a man, instead of a piece of furniture,—and,' she screwed up her eyes to see the better through the sunlight— 'he *is* a man when he holds himself like that. O blessed Conceit, what should we be without you?'

With the new clothes came a new stock of self-confidence. Otis Yeere discovered that he could enter a room without breaking into a gentle perspiration—could cross one, even to talk to Mrs. Hauksbee, as though rooms were meant to be crossed. He was for the first time in nine years proud of himself, and contented with his life, satisfied with his new clothes, and rejoicing in the friendship of Mrs. Hauksbee.

'Conceit is what the poor fellow wants,' she said in confidence to Mrs. Mallowe. 'I believe they must use Civilians to plough the fields with in Lower Bengal. You see I have to begin from the very beginning—haven't I? But you'll admit, won't you, dear, that he is immensely improved since I took him in hand. Only give me a little more time and he won't know himself.'

Indeed, Yeere was rapidly beginning to forget what he had been. One of his own rank and file put the matter brutally when he asked Yeere, in reference to nothing, 'And who has been making *you* a Member of Council, lately? You carry the side of half-a-dozen of 'em.'

'I—I'm awf'ly sorry. I didn't mean it, you know,' said Yeere apologetically.

'There'll be no holding you,' continued the old stager grimly. 'Climb down, Otis—climb down, and get all that beastly affectation knocked out of you with fever! Three thousand a month wouldn't support it.'

Yeere repeated the incident to Mrs. Hauksbee. He had come to look upon her as his Mother Confessor.

'And you apologised!' she said. 'Oh, shame! I *hate* a man who apologises. Never apologise for what your friend called "side." *Never!* It's a man's business to be insolent and overbearing until he meets with a stronger. Now, you bad boy, listen to me.'

Simply and straightforwardly, as the 'rickshaw loitered round Jakko, Mrs. Hauksbee preached to Otis Yeere the Great Gospel of Conceit, illustrating it with living pictures encountered during their Sunday afternoon stroll.

'Good gracious!' she ended with the personal argument, 'you'll apologise next for being my *attaché!*'

'Never!' said Otis Yeere. 'That's another thing altogether. I shall always be——'

'What's coming?' thought Mrs. Hauksbee.

'Proud of that,' said Otis.

'Safe for the present,' she said to herself.

'But I'm afraid I have grown conceited. Like Jeshurun, you know. When he waxed fat, then he kicked. It's the having no worry on one's mind and the Hill air, I suppose.'

'Hill air, indeed!' said Mrs. Hauksbee to herself. 'He'd have been hiding in the Club till the last day of his leave, if I hadn't discovered him.' And aloud——

'Why shouldn't you be? You have every right to.'

'I! Why?'

'Oh, hundreds of things. I'm not going to waste this lovely afternoon by explaining; but I know you have. What was that heap of manuscript you showed me about the grammar of the aboriginal—what's their names?'

'*Gullals.* A piece of nonsense. I've far too

much work to do to bother over *Gullals* now. You should see my District. Come down with your husband some day and I'll show you round. Such a lovely place in the Rains! A sheet of water with the railway-embankment and the snakes sticking out, and, in the summer, green flies and green squash. The people would die of fear if you shook a dogwhip at 'em. But they know you're forbidden to do that, so they conspire to make your life a burden to you. My District's worked by some man at Darjiling, on the strength of a native pleader's false reports. Oh, it's a heavenly place!'

Otis Yeere laughed bitterly.

'There's not the least necessity that you should stay in it. Why do you?'

'Because I must. How'm I to get out of it?'

'How! In a hundred and fifty ways. If there weren't so many people on the road I'd like to box your ears. Ask, my dear boy, *ask!* Look! There is young Hexarly with six years' service and half your talents. He asked for what he wanted, and he got it. See, down by the Convent! There's McArthurson, who has come to his present position by asking—sheer, downright asking—after he had pushed himself out of the rank and file. One man is as good as another in your service—believe me. I've seen Simla for more seasons than I care to think about. Do you suppose men are chosen for appointments because of their special fitness *beforehand?* You have all passed a high test—what do you call it?—in the beginning, and, except for the few who have gone

altogether to the bad, you can all work hard.
Asking does the rest. Call it cheek, call it insolence, call it anything you like, but *ask !* Men
argue—yes, I know what men say—that a man,
by the mere audacity of his request, *must* have
some good in him. A weak man doesn't say :
" Give me this and that." He whines : " Why
haven't I been given this and that ? " If you were
in the Army, I should say learn to spin plates or
play a tambourine with your toes. As it is—*ask !*
You belong to a Service that ought to be able to
command the Channel Fleet, or set a leg at twenty
minutes' notice, and *yet* you hesitate over asking
to escape from a squashy green district where you
admit you are not master. Drop the Bengal
Government altogether. Even Darjiling is a little
out-of-the-way hole. I was there once, and the
rents were extortionate. Assert yourself. Get
the Government of India to take you over. Try
to get on the Frontier, where *every* man has a
grand chance if he can trust himself. *Go* somewhere ! *Do* something ! You have twice the wits
and three times the presence of the men up here,
and, and '—Mrs. Hauksbee paused for breath ;
then continued—'and in *any* way you look at it,
you *ought* to. *You* who could go so far ! '

'I don't know,' said Yeere, rather taken aback
by the unexpected eloquence. 'I haven't such a
good opinion of myself.'

It was not strictly Platonic, but it was Policy.
Mrs. Hauksbee laid her hand lightly upon the
ungloved paw that rested on the turned-back 'rickshaw hood, and, looking the man full in the face,

said tenderly, almost too tenderly, '*I* believe in you if you mistrust yourself. Is that enough, my friend ?'

'It is enough,' answered Otis very solemnly.

He was silent for a long time, redreaming the dreams that he had dreamed eight years ago, but through them all ran, as sheet-lightning through golden cloud, the light of Mrs. Hauksbee's violet eyes.

Curious and impenetrable are the mazes of Simla life—the only existence in this desolate land worth the living. Gradually it went abroad among men and women, in the pauses between dance, play, and Gymkhana, that Otis Yeere, the man with the newly-lit light of self-confidence in his eyes, had 'done something decent' in the wilds whence he came. He had brought an erring Municipality to reason, appropriated the funds on his own responsibility, and saved the lives of hundreds. He knew more about the *Gullals* than any living man. Had a vast knowledge of the aboriginal tribes ; was, in spite of his juniority, the greatest authority on the aboriginal *Gullals*. No one quite knew who or what the *Gullals* were till The Mussuck, who had been calling on Mrs. Hauksbee, and prided himself upon picking people's brains, explained they were a tribe of ferocious hillmen, somewhere near Sikkim, whose friendship even the Great Indian Empire would find it worth her while to secure. Now we know that Otis Yeere had showed Mrs. Hauksbee his MS. notes of six years' standing on these same *Gullals*. He had told her, too, how, sick and shaken with the fever their negligence had bred, crippled by the loss of his pet clerk, and savagely angry at the desolation in his charge, he had once damned the collective eyes of his 'intelligent local board' for a set of *haramzadas*. Which act of 'brutal and tyrannous oppression' won him a Reprimand Royal from the Bengal Government; but in the anecdote as amended for Northern consumption we find no record of this. Hence we are forced to conclude that Mrs. Hauksbee edited his reminiscences before sowing them in idle ears, ready, as she well knew, to exaggerate good or evil. And Otis Yeere bore himself as befitted the hero of many tales.

'You can talk to *me* when you don't fall into a brown study. Talk now, and talk your brightest and best,' said Mrs. Hauksbee.

Otis needed no spur. Look to a man who has the counsel of a woman of or above the world to back him. So long as he keeps his head, he can meet both sexes on equal ground—an advantage never intended by Providence, who fashioned Man on one day and Woman on another, in sign that neither should know more than a very little of the other's life. Such a man goes far, or, the counsel being withdrawn, collapses suddenly while his world seeks the reason.

Generalled by Mrs. Hauksbee, who, again, had all Mrs. Mallowe's wisdom at her disposal, proud of himself and, in the end, believing in himself because he was believed in, Otis Yeere stood ready for any fortune that might befall, certain that it would be good. He would fight for his own hand, and intended that this second struggle should lead to better issue than the first helpless surrender of the bewildered 'Stunt.

What might have happened it is impossible to say. This lamentable thing befell, bred directly by a statement of Mrs. Hauksbee that she would spend the next season in Darjiling.

'Are you certain of that?' said Otis Yeere.

'Quite. We're writing about a house now.'

Otis Yeere 'stopped dead,' as Mrs. Hauksbee put it in discussing the relapse with Mrs. Mallowe.

'He has behaved,' she said angrily, 'just like Captain Kerrington's pony—only Otis is a donkey —at the last Gymkhana. Planted his forefeet and refused to go on another step. Polly, my man's going to disappoint me. What shall I do?'

As a rule, Mrs. Mallowe does not approve of staring, but on this occasion she opened her eyes to the utmost.

'You have managed cleverly so far,' she said. 'Speak to him, and ask him what he means.'

'I will—at to-night's dance.'

'No—o, not at a dance,' said Mrs. Mallowe cautiously. 'Men are never themselves quite at dances. Better wait till to-morrow morning.'

'Nonsense. If he's going to 'vert in this insane way there isn't a day to lose. Are you going? No? Then sit up for me, there's a dear. I shan't stay longer than supper under any circumstances.'

Mrs. Mallowe waited through the evening, looking long and earnestly into the fire, and sometimes smiling to herself.

.   .   .   .   .

'Oh! oh! oh! The man's an idiot! A

raving, positive idiot! I'm sorry I ever saw him!'

Mrs. Hauksbee burst into Mrs. Mallowe's house, at midnight, almost in tears.

'What in the world has happened?' said Mrs. Mallowe, but her eyes showed that she had guessed an answer.

'Happened! Everything has happened! He was there. I went to him and said, "Now, what does this nonsense mean?" Don't laugh, dear, I can't bear it. But you know what I mean I said. Then it was a square, and I sat it out with him and wanted an explanation, and *he* said—Oh! I haven't patience with such idiots! You know what I said about going to Darjiling next year? It doesn't matter to me *where* I go. I'd have changed the Station and lost the rent to have saved this. He said, in so many words, that he wasn't going to try to work up any more, because —because he would be shifted into a province away from Darjiling, and his own District, where these creatures are, is within a day's journey——'

'Ah—hh!' said Mrs. Mallowe, in a tone of one who has successfully tracked an obscure word through a large dictionary.

'Did you ever *hear* of anything so mad—so absurd? And he had the ball at his feet. He had only to kick it! I would have made him *anything*! Anything in the wide world. He could have gone to the world's end. I would have helped him. I made him, didn't I, Polly? Didn't I *create* that man? Doesn't he owe everything to me? And to reward me, just when everything was nicely arranged, by this lunacy that spoilt everything !'

'Very few men understand your devotion thoroughly.'

'Oh, Polly, *don't* laugh at me ! I give men up from this hour. I could have killed him then and there. What *right* had this man—this *Thing* I had picked out of his filthy paddy-fields—to make love to me ?'

'He did that, did he ?'

'He did. I don't remember half he said, I was so angry. Oh, but such a funny thing happened ! I can't help laughing at it now, though I felt nearly ready to cry with rage. He raved and I stormed —I'm afraid we must have made an awful noise in our *kala juggah*. Protect my character, dear, if it's all over Simla by to-morrow—and then he bobbed forward in the middle of this insanity —I *firmly* believe the man's demented—and kissed me.'

'Morals above reproach,' purred Mrs. Mallowe.

'So they were—so they are ! It was the most absurd kiss. I don't believe he'd ever kissed a woman in his life before. I threw my head back, and it was a sort of slidy, pecking dab, just on the end of the chin—here.' Mrs. Hauksbee tapped her masculine little chin with her fan. 'Then, of course, I was *furiously* angry, and told him that he was no gentleman, and I was sorry I'd ever met him, and so on. He was crushed so easily then I couldn't be *very* angry. Then I came away straight to you.'

'Was this before or after supper ?'

'Oh! before—oceans before. Isn't it perfectly disgusting?'

'Let me think. I withhold judgment till to-morrow. Morning brings counsel.'

But morning brought only a servant with a dainty bouquet of Annandale roses for Mrs. Hauksbee to wear at the dance at Viceregal Lodge that night.

'He doesn't seem to be very penitent,' said Mrs. Mallowe. 'What's the *billet-doux* in the centre?'

Mrs. Hauksbee opened the neatly-folded note, —another accomplishment that she had taught Otis,—read it, and groaned tragically.

'Last wreck of a feeble intellect! Poetry! Is it his own, do you think? Oh, that I ever built my hopes on such a maudlin idiot!'

'No. It's a quotation from Mrs. Browning, and in view of the facts of the case, as Jack says, uncommonly well chosen. Listen—

> Sweet, thou hast trod on a heart,
>   Pass! There's a world full of men;
> And women as fair as thou art
>   Must do such things now and then.
>
> Thou only hast stepped unaware—
>   Malice not one can impute;
> And why should a heart have been there,
>   In the way of a fair woman's foot?

'I didn't—I didn't—I didn't!'—said Mrs. Hauksbee angrily, her eyes filling with tears; 'there was no malice at all. Oh, it's *too* vexatious!'

'You've misunderstood the compliment,' said Mrs. Mallowe. 'He clears you completely and—ahem—I should think by this, that *he* has cleared completely too. My experience of men is that when they begin to quote poetry they are going to flit. Like swans singing before they die, you know.'

'Polly, you take my sorrows in a most unfeeling way.'

'Do I? Is it so terrible? If he's hurt your vanity, I should say that you've done a certain amount of damage to his heart.'

'Oh, you can never tell about a man!' said Mrs. Hauksbee.

At the Pit's Mouth

Men say it was a stolen tide—
 The Lord that sent it He knows all,
But in mine ear will aye abide
 The message that the bells let fall,
And awesome bells they were to me,
That in the dark rang, 'Enderby.'

Jean Ingelow.

ONCE upon a time there was a Man and his Wife and a Tertium Quid.

All three were unwise, but the Wife was the unwisest. The Man should have looked after his Wife, who should have avoided the Tertium Quid, who, again, should have married a wife of his own, after clean and open flirtations, to which nobody can possibly object, round Jakko or Observatory Hill. When you see a young man with his pony in a white lather and his hat on the back of his head, flying downhill at fifteen miles an hour to meet a girl who will be properly surprised to meet him, you naturally approve of that young man, and wish him Staff appointments, and take an interest in his welfare, and, as the proper time comes, give them sugar-tongs or side-saddles according to your means and generosity.

The Tertium Quid flew downhill on horseback, but it was to meet the Man's Wife ; and when he flew uphill it was for the same end. The Man was in the Plains, earning money for his Wife to spend on dresses and four-hundred-rupee bracelets, and inexpensive luxuries of that kind. He worked very hard, and sent her a letter or a post-card daily. She also wrote to him daily, and said that she was longing for him to come up to Simla. The Tertium Quid used to lean over her shoulder and laugh as she wrote the notes. Then the two would ride to the Post-office together.

Now, Simla is a strange place and its customs are peculiar ; nor is any man who has not spent at least ten seasons there qualified to pass judgment on circumstantial evidence, which is the most untrustworthy in the Courts. For these reasons, and for others which need not appear, I decline to state positively whether there was anything irretrievably wrong in the relations between the Man's Wife and the Tertium Quid. If there was, and hereon you must form your own opinion, it was the Man's Wife's fault. She was kittenish in her manners, wearing generally an air of soft and fluffy innocence. But she was deadlily learned and evil-instructed ; and, now and again, when the mask dropped, men saw this, shuddered and— almost drew back. Men are occasionally particular, and the least particular men are always the most exacting.

Simla is eccentric in its fashion of treating friendships. Certain attachments which have set and crystallised through half-a-dozen seasons acquire almost the sanctity of the marriage bond, and are revered as such. Again, certain attachments equally old, and, to all appearance, equally venerable, never seem to win any recognised official status; while a chance-sprung acquaintance, not two months born, steps into the place which by right belongs to the senior. There is no law reducible to print which regulates these affairs.

Some people have a gift which secures them infinite toleration, and others have not. The Man's Wife had not. If she looked over the garden wall, for instance, women taxed her with stealing their husbands. She complained pathetically that she was not allowed to choose her own friends. When she put up her big white muff to her lips, and gazed over it and under her eyebrows at you as she said this thing, you felt that she had been infamously misjudged, and that all the other women's instincts were all wrong; which was absurd. She was not allowed to own the Tertium Quid in peace; and was so strangely constructed that she would not have enjoyed peace had she been so permitted. She preferred some semblance of intrigue to cloak even her most commonplace actions.

After two months of riding, first round Jakko, then Elysium, then Summer Hill, then Observatory Hill, then under Jutogh, and lastly up and down the Cart Road as far as the Tara Devi gap in the dusk, she said to the Tertium Quid, 'Frank, people say we are too much together, and people are so horrid.'

The Tertium Quid pulled his moustache, and

replied that horrid people were unworthy of the consideration of nice people.

'But they have done more than talk—they have written—written to my hubby—I'm sure of it,' said the Man's Wife, and she pulled a letter from her husband out of her saddle-pocket and gave it to the Tertium Quid.

It was an honest letter, written by an honest man, then stewing in the Plains on two hundred rupees a month (for he allowed his wife eight hundred and fifty), and in a silk banian and cotton trousers. It said that, perhaps, she had not thought of the unwisdom of allowing her name to be so generally coupled with the Tertium Quid's ; that she was too much of a child to understand the dangers of that sort of thing ; that he, her husband, was the last man in the world to interfere jealously with her little amusements and interests, but that it would be better were she to drop the Tertium Quid quietly and for her husband's sake. The letter was sweetened with many pretty little pet names, and it amused the Tertium Quid considerably. He and She laughed over it, so that you, fifty yards away, could see their shoulders shaking while the horses slouched along side by side.

Their conversation was not worth reporting. The upshot of it was that, next day, no one saw the Man's Wife and the Tertium Quid together. They had both gone down to the Cemetery, which, as a rule, is only visited officially by the inhabitants of Simla.

A Simla funeral with the clergyman riding, the

mourners riding, and the coffin creaking as it swings between the bearers, is one of the most depressing things on this earth, particularly when the procession passes under the wet, dank dip beneath the Rockcliffe Hotel, where the sun is shut out, and all the hill streams are wailing and weeping together as they go down the valleys.

Occasionally folk tend the graves, but we in India shift and are transferred so often that, at the end of the second year, the Dead have no friends —only acquaintances who are far too busy amusing themselves up the hill to attend to old partners. The idea of using a Cemetery as a rendezvous is distinctly a feminine one. A man would have said simply, 'Let people talk. We'll go down the Mall.' A woman is made differently, especially if she be such a woman as the Man's Wife. She and the Tertium Quid enjoyed each other's society among the graves of men and women whom they had known and danced with aforetime.

They used to take a big horse-blanket and sit on the grass a little to the left of the lower end, where there is a dip in the ground, and where the occupied graves stop short and the ready-made ones are not ready. Each well-regulated Indian Cemetery keeps half-a-dozen graves permanently open for contingencies and incidental wear and tear. In the Hills these are more usually baby's size, because children who come up weakened and sick from the Plains often succumb to the effects of the Rains in the Hills or get pneumonia from their *ayahs* taking them through damp pine-woods after the sun has set. In Cantonments, of course, the man's size is more in request ; these arrangements varying with the climate and population.

One day when the Man's Wife and the Tertium Quid had just arrived in the Cemetery, they saw some coolies breaking ground. They had marked out a full-size grave, and the Tertium Quid asked them whether any *Sahib* was sick. They said that they did not know ; but it was an order that they should dig a *Sahib's* grave.

'Work away,' said the Tertium Quid, 'and let's see how it's done.'

The coolies worked away, and the Man's Wife and the Tertium Quid watched and talked for a couple of hours while the grave was being deepened. Then a coolie, taking the earth in baskets as it was thrown up, jumped over the grave.

'That's queer,' said the Tertium Quid. 'Where's my ulster ? '

'What's queer ? ' said the Man's Wife.

'I have got a chill down my back—just as if a goose had walked over my grave.'

'Why do you look at the thing, then ? ' said the Man's Wife. 'Let us go.'

The Tertium Quid stood at the head of the grave, and stared without answering for a space. Then he said, dropping a pebble down, 'It is nasty —and cold : horribly cold. I don't think I shall come to the Cemetery any more. I don't think grave-digging is cheerful.'

The two talked and agreed that the Cemetery was depressing. They also arranged for a ride next day out from the Cemetery through the Mashobra Tunnel up to Fagoo and back, because all the world was going to a garden-party at Viceregal Lodge, and all the people of Mashobra would go too.

Coming up the Cemetery road, the Tertium Quid's horse tried to bolt uphill, being tired with standing so long, and managed to strain a back sinew.

'I shall have to take the mare to-morrow,' said the Tertium Quid, 'and she will stand nothing heavier than a snaffle.'

They made their arrangements to meet in the Cemetery, after allowing all the Mashobra people time to pass into Simla.   That night it rained heavily, and, next day, when the Tertium Quid came to the trysting-place, he saw that the new grave had a foot of water in it, the ground being a tough and sour clay.

''Jove !   That looks beastly,' said the Tertium Quid.   'Fancy being boarded up and dropped into that well !'

They then started off to Fagoo, the mare playing with the snaffle and picking her way as though she were shod with satin, and the sun shining divinely. The road below Mashobra to Fagoo is officially styled the Himalayan-Thibet road ; but in spite of its name it is not much more than six feet wide in most places, and the drop into the valley below may be anything between one and two thousand feet.

'Now we're going to Thibet,' said the Man's Wife merrily, as the horses drew near to Fagoo. She was riding on the cliff-side.

'Into Thibet,' said the Tertium Quid, 'ever so

far from people who say horrid things, and hubbies who write stupid letters. With you—to the end of the world!'

A coolie carrying a log of wood came round a corner, and the mare went wide to avoid him—forefeet in and haunches out, as a sensible mare should go.

'To the world's end,' said the Man's Wife, and looked unspeakable things over her near shoulder at the Tertium Quid.

He was smiling, but, while she looked, the smile froze stiff as it were on his face, and changed to a nervous grin—the sort of grin men wear when they are not quite easy in their saddles. The mare seemed to be sinking by the stern, and her nostrils cracked while she was trying to realise what was happening. The rain of the night before had rotted the drop-side of the Himalayan-Thibet Road, and it was giving way under her. 'What are you doing?' said the Man's Wife. The Tertium Quid gave no answer. He grinned nervously and set his spurs into the mare, who rapped with her forefeet on the road, and the struggle began. The Man's Wife screamed, 'Oh, Frank, get off!'

But the Tertium Quid was glued to the saddle—his face blue and white—and he looked into the Man's Wife's eyes. Then the Man's Wife clutched at the mare's head and caught her by the nose instead of the bridle. The brute threw up her head and went down with a scream, the Tertium Quid upon her, and the nervous grin still set on his face.

The Man's Wife heard the tinkle-tinkle of little

stones and loose earth falling off the roadway, and the sliding roar of the man and horse going down. Then everything was quiet, and she called on Frank to leave his mare and walk up. But Frank did not answer. He was underneath the mare, nine hundred feet below, spoiling a patch of Indian corn.

As the revellers came back from Viceregal Lodge in the mists of the evening, they met a temporarily insane woman, on a temporarily mad horse, swinging round the corners, with her eyes and her mouth open, and her head like the head of a Medusa. She was stopped by a man at the risk of his life, and taken out of the saddle, a limp heap, and put on the bank to explain herself. This wasted twenty minutes, and then she was sent home in a lady's 'rickshaw, still with her mouth open and her hands picking at her riding-gloves.

She was in bed through the following three days, which were rainy ; so she missed attending the funeral of the Tertium Quid, who was lowered into eighteen inches of water, instead of the twelve to which he had first objected.

A Wayside Comedy

Because to every purpose there is time and judgment, therefore
the misery of man is great upon him.—*Eccles*. viii. 6.

FATE and the Government of India have turned
the Station of Kashima into a prison ; and, because
there is no help for the poor souls who are now
lying there in torment, I write this story, praying
that the Government of India may be moved to
scatter the European population to the four winds.

Kashima is bounded on all sides by the rock-
tipped circle of the Dosehri hills.   In Spring, it is
ablaze with roses ; in Summer, the roses die and the
hot winds blow from the hills ; in Autumn, the
white mists from the *jhils* cover the place as with
water, and in Winter the frosts nip everything
young and tender to earth-level.   There is but one
view in Kashima—a stretch of perfectly flat pasture
and plough-land, running up to the gray-blue
scrub of the Dosehri hills.

There are no amusements, except snipe and
tiger shooting ; but the tigers have been long since
hunted from their lairs in the rock-caves, and the
snipe only come once a year.   Narkarra—one
hundred and forty-three miles by road—is the

nearest station to Kashima. But Kashima never goes to Narkarra, where there are at least twelve English people. It stays within the circle of the Dosehri hills.

All Kashima acquits Mrs. Vansuythen of any intention to do harm; but all Kashima knows that she, and she alone, brought about their pain.

Boulte, the Engineer, Mrs. Boulte, and Captain Kurrell know this. They are the English population of Kashima, if we except Major Vansuythen, who is of no importance whatever, and Mrs. Vansuythen, who is the most important of all.

You must remember, though you will not understand, that all laws weaken in a small and hidden community where there is no public opinion. When a man is absolutely alone in a Station he runs a certain risk of falling into evil ways. This risk is multiplied by every addition to the population up to twelve—the Jury-number. After that, fear and consequent restraint begin, and human action becomes less grotesquely jerky.

There was deep peace in Kashima till Mrs. Vansuythen arrived. She was a charming woman, every one said so everywhere; and she charmed every one. In spite of this, or, perhaps, because of this, since Fate is so perverse, she cared only for one man, and he was Major Vansuythen. Had she been plain or stupid, this matter would have been intelligible to Kashima. But she was a fair woman, with very still gray eyes, the colour of a lake just before the light of the sun touches it. No man who had seen those eyes could, later on, explain what fashion of woman she was to look upon. The eyes dazzled him. Her own sex said that she was 'not bad-looking, but spoilt by pretending to be so grave.' And yet her gravity was natural. It was not her habit to smile. She merely went through life, looking at those who passed; and the women objected while the men fell down and worshipped.

She knows and is deeply sorry for the evil she has done to Kashima; but Major Vansuythen cannot understand why Mrs. Boulte does not drop in to afternoon tea at least three times a week. 'When there are only two women in one Station, they ought to see a great deal of each other,' says Major Vansuythen.

Long and long before ever Mrs. Vansuythen came out of those far-away places where there is society and amusement, Kurrell had discovered that Mrs. Boulte was the one woman in the world for him and—you dare not blame them. Kashima was as out of the world as Heaven or the Other Place, and the Dosehri hills kept their secret well. Boulte had no concern in the matter. He was in camp for a fortnight at a time. He was a hard, heavy man, and neither Mrs. Boulte nor Kurrell pitied him. They had all Kashima and each other for their very, very own; and Kashima was the Garden of Eden in those days. When Boulte returned from his wanderings he would slap Kurrell between the shoulders and call him 'old fellow,' and the three would dine together. Kashima was happy then when the judgment of God seemed almost as distant as Narkarra or the railway that ran down to the sea. But the Government sent

Major Vansuythen to Kashima, and with him came his wife.

The etiquette of Kashima is much the same as that of a desert island. When a stranger is cast away there, all hands go down to the shore to make him welcome. Kashima assembled at the masonry platform close to the Narkarra Road, and spread tea for the Vansuythens. That ceremony was reckoned a formal call, and made them free of the Station, its rights and privileges. When the Vansuythens settled down they gave a tiny house-warming to all Kashima ; and that made Kashima free of their house, according to the immemorial usage of the Station.

Then the Rains came, when no one could go into camp, and the Narkarra Road was washed away by the Kasun River, and in the cup-like pastures of Kashima the cattle waded knee-deep. The clouds dropped down from the Dosehri hills and covered everything.

At the end of the Rains Boulte's manner towards his wife changed and became demonstratively affectionate. They had been married twelve years, and the change startled Mrs. Boulte, who hated her husband with the hate of a woman who has met with nothing but kindness from her mate, and, in the teeth of this kindness, has done him a great wrong. Moreover, she had her own trouble to fight with—her watch to keep over her own property, Kurrell. For two months the Rains had hidden the Dosehri hills and many other things besides ; but, when they lifted, they showed Mrs. Boulte that her man among men, her Ted—

for she called him Ted in the old days when Boulte was out of earshot—was slipping the links of the allegiance.

'The Vansuythen Woman has taken him,' Mrs. Boulte said to herself; and when Boulte was away, wept over her belief, in the face of the over-vehement blandishments of Ted. Sorrow in Kashima is as fortunate as Love because there is nothing to weaken it save the flight of Time. Mrs. Boulte had never breathed her suspicion to Kurrell because she was not certain; and her nature led her to be very certain before she took steps in any direction. That is why she behaved as she did.

Boulte came into the house one evening, and leaned against the door-posts of the drawing-room, chewing his moustache. Mrs. Boulte was putting some flowers into a vase. There is a pretence of civilisation even in Kashima.

'Little woman,' said Boulte quietly, 'do you care for me?'

'Immensely,' said she, with a laugh. 'Can you ask it?'

'But I'm serious,' said Boulte. '*Do* you care for me?'

Mrs. Boulte dropped the flowers, and turned round quickly. 'Do you want an honest answer?'

'Ye-es, I've asked for it.'

Mrs. Boulte spoke in a low, even voice for five minutes, very distinctly, that there might be no misunderstanding her meaning. When Samson broke the pillars of Gaza, he did a little thing, and one not to be compared to the deliberate pulling down of a woman's homestead about her own ears.

There was no wise female friend to advise Mrs. Boulte, the singularly cautious wife, to hold her hand. She struck at Boulte's heart, because her own was sick with suspicion of Kurrell, and worn out with the long strain of watching alone through the Rains. There was no plan or purpose in her speaking. The sentences made themselves; and Boulte listened, leaning against the door-post with his hands in his pockets. When all was over, and Mrs. Boulte began to breathe through her nose before breaking out into tears, he laughed and stared straight in front of him at the Dosehri hills.

'Is that all?' he said. 'Thanks, I only wanted to know, you know.'

'What are you going to do?' said the woman, between her sobs.

'Do! Nothing. What should I do? Kill Kurrell, or send you Home, or apply for leave to get a divorce? It's two days' *dâk* into Narkarra.' He laughed again and went on: 'I'll tell you what *you* can do. You can ask Kurrell to dinner to-morrow—no, on Thursday, that will allow you time to pack—and you can bolt with him. I give you my word I won't follow.'

He took up his helmet and went out of the room, and Mrs. Boulte sat till the moonlight streaked the floor, thinking and thinking and thinking. She had done her best upon the spur of the moment to pull the house down; but it would not fall. Moreover, she could not understand her husband, and she was afraid. Then the folly of her useless truthfulness struck her, and she was ashamed to write to Kurrell, saying, 'I have gone mad and told everything. My husband says that I am free to elope with you. Get a *dâk* for Thursday, and we will fly after dinner.' There was a cold-bloodedness about that procedure which did not appeal to her. So she sat still in her own house and thought.

At dinner-time Boulte came back from his walk, white and worn and haggard, and the woman was touched at his distress. As the evening wore on she muttered some expression of sorrow, something approaching to contrition. Boulte came out of a brown study and said, ' Oh, *that!* I wasn't thinking about that. By the way, what does Kurrell say to the elopement? '

' I haven't seen him,' said Mrs. Boulte. ' Good God, is that all? '

But Boulte was not listening and her sentence ended in a gulp.

The next day brought no comfort to Mrs. Boulte, for Kurrell did not appear, and the new life that she, in the five minutes' madness of the previous evening, had hoped to build out of the ruins of the old, seemed to be no nearer.

Boulte ate his breakfast, advised her to see her Arab pony fed in the verandah, and went out. The morning wore through, and at mid-day the tension became unendurable. Mrs. Boulte could not cry. She had finished her crying in the night, and now she did not want to be left alone. Perhaps the Vansuythen Woman would talk to her; and, since talking opens the heart, perhaps there might be some comfort to be found in her company. She was the only other woman in the Station.

In Kashima there are no regular calling-hours. Every one can drop in upon every one else at pleasure. Mrs. Boulte put on a big *terai* hat, and walked across to the Vansuythens' house to borrow last week's *Queen*. The two compounds touched, and instead of going up the drive, she crossed through the gap in the cactus-hedge, entering the house from the back. As she passed through the dining-room, she heard, behind the *purdah* that cloaked the drawing-room door, her husband's voice, saying—

'But on my Honour! On my Soul and Honour, I tell you she doesn't care for me. She told me so last night. I would have told you then if Vansuythen hadn't been with you. If it is for *her* sake that you'll have nothing to say to me, you can make your mind easy. It's Kurrell——'

'What?' said Mrs. Vansuythen, with a hysterical little laugh. 'Kurrell! Oh, it can't be! You two must have made some horrible mistake. Perhaps you—you lost your temper, or misunderstood, or something. Things *can't* be as wrong as you say.'

Mrs. Vansuythen had shifted her defence to avoid the man's pleading, and was desperately trying to keep him to a side-issue.

'There must be some mistake,' she insisted, ' and it can be all put right again.'

Boulte laughed grimly.

'It can't be Captain Kurrell! He told me that he had never taken the least—the least interest in your wife, Mr. Boulte. Oh, *do* listen! He said

he had not.   He swore he had not,' said Mrs.
Vansuythen.

The *purdah* rustled, and the speech was cut
short by the entry of a little thin woman, with big
rings round her eyes.   Mrs. Vansuythen stood up
with a gasp.

'What was that you said?' asked Mrs. Boulte.
'Never mind that man.   What did Ted say to
you?   What did he say to you?   What did he
say to you?'

Mrs. Vansuythen sat down helplessly on the
sofa, overborne by the trouble of her questioner.

'He said—I can't remember exactly what he
said—but I understood him to say—that is——
But, really, Mrs. Boulte, isn't it rather a strange
question?'

'*Will* you tell me what he said?' repeated
Mrs. Boulte.   Even a tiger will fly before a bear
robbed of her whelps, and Mrs. Vansuythen was
only an ordinarily good woman.   She began in a
sort of desperation : 'Well, he said that he never
cared for you at all, and, of course, there was not
the least reason why he should have; and—and—
that was all.'

'You said he *swore* he had not cared for me.
Was that true?'

'Yes,' said Mrs. Vansuythen very softly.

Mrs. Boulte wavered for an instant where she
stood, and then fell forward fainting.

'What did I tell you?' said Boulte, as though
the conversation had been unbroken.   'You can
see for yourself.   She cares for *him*.'   The light
began to break into his dull mind, and he

went on—'And he—what was *he* saying to you?'

But Mrs. Vansuythen, with no heart for explanations or impassioned protestations, was kneeling over Mrs. Boulte.

'Oh, you brute!' she cried. 'Are *all* men like this? Help me to get her into my room—and her face is cut against the table. Oh, *will* you be quiet, and help me to carry her? I hate you, and I hate Captain Kurrell. Lift her up carefully, and now—go! Go away!'

Boulte carried his wife into Mrs. Vansuythen's bedroom, and departed before the storm of that lady's wrath and disgust, impenitent and burning with jealousy. Kurrell had been making love to Mrs. Vansuythen—would do Vansuythen as great a wrong as he had done Boulte, who caught himself considering whether Mrs. Vansuythen would faint if she discovered that the man she loved had forsworn her.

In the middle of these meditations, Kurrell came cantering along the road and pulled up with a cheery 'Good-mornin'. 'Been mashing Mrs. Vansuythen as usual, eh? Bad thing for a sober, married man, that. What will Mrs. Boulte say?'

Boulte raised his head and said slowly,—'Oh, you liar!' Kurrell's face changed. 'What's that?' he asked quickly.

'Nothing much,' said Boulte. 'Has my wife told you that you two are free to go off whenever you please? She has been good enough to explain the situation to me. You've been a true friend to me, Kurrell—old man—haven't you?'

Kurrell groaned, and tried to frame some sort of idiotic sentence about being willing to give 'satisfaction.' But his interest in the woman was dead, had died out in the Rains, and, mentally, he was abusing her for her amazing indiscretion. It would have been so easy to have broken off the thing gently and by degrees, and now he was saddled with——Boulte's voice recalled him.

'I don't think I should get any satisfaction from killing you, and I'm pretty sure you'd get none from killing me.'

Then in a querulous tone, ludicrously disproportioned to his wrongs, Boulte added—

''Seems rather a pity that you haven't the decency to keep to the woman, now you've got her. You've been a true friend to *her* too, haven't you?'

Kurrell stared long and gravely. The situation was getting beyond him.

'What do you mean?' he said.

Boulte answered, more to himself than the questioner: 'My wife came over to Mrs. Vansuythen's just now; and it seems you'd been telling Mrs. Vansuythen that you'd never cared for Emma. I suppose you lied, as usual. What had Mrs. Vansuythen to do with you, or you with her? Try to speak the truth for once in a way.'

Kurrell took the double insult without wincing, and replied by another question: 'Go on. What happened?'

'Emma fainted,' said Boulte simply. 'But, look here, what had you been saying to Mrs. Vansuythen?'

Kurrell laughed. Mrs. Boulte had, with un-bridled tongue, made havoc of his plans; and he could at least retaliate by hurting the man in whose eyes he was humiliated and shown dis-honourable.

'Said to her? What *does* a man tell a lie like that for? I suppose I said pretty much what you've said, unless I'm a good deal mistaken.'

'I spoke the truth,' said Boulte, again more to himself than Kurrell. 'Emma told me she hated me. She has no right in me.'

'No! I suppose not. You're only her husband, y'know. And what did Mrs. Van-suythen say after you had laid your disengaged heart at her feet?'

Kurrell felt almost virtuous as he put the question.

'I don't think that matters,' Boulte replied; 'and it doesn't concern you.'

'But it does! I tell you it does'—began Kurrell shamelessly.

The sentence was cut by a roar of laughter from Boulte's lips. Kurrell was silent for an instant, and then he, too, laughed—laughed long and loudly, rocking in his saddle. It was an un-pleasant sound—the mirthless mirth of these men on the long white line of the Narkarra Road. There were no strangers in Kashima, or they might have thought that captivity within the Dosehri hills had driven half the European popula-tion mad. The laughter ended abruptly, and Kurrell was the first to speak.

'Well, what are you going to do?'

Boulte looked up the road, and at the hills. 'Nothing,' said he quietly; 'what's the use? It's too ghastly for anything. We must let the old life go on. I can only call you a hound and a liar, and I can't go on calling you names for ever. Besides which, I don't feel that I'm much better. We can't get out of this place. What *is* there to do?'

Kurrell looked round the rat-pit of Kashima and made no reply. The injured husband took up the wondrous tale.

'Ride on, and speak to Emma if you want to. God knows *I* don't care what you do.'

He walked forward, and left Kurrell gazing blankly after him. Kurrell did not ride on either to see Mrs. Boulte or Mrs. Vansuythen. He sat in his saddle and thought, while his pony grazed by the roadside.

The whir of approaching wheels roused him. Mrs. Vansuythen was driving home Mrs. Boulte, white and wan, with a cut on her forehead.

'Stop, please,' said Mrs. Boulte, 'I want to speak to Ted.'

Mrs. Vansuythen obeyed, but as Mrs. Boulte leaned forward, putting her hand upon the splash-board of the dog-cart, Kurrell spoke.

'I've seen your husband, Mrs. Boulte.'

There was no necessity for any further explanation. The man's eyes were fixed, not upon Mrs. Boulte, but her companion. Mrs. Boulte saw the look.

'Speak to him!' she pleaded, turning to the woman at her side. 'Oh, speak to him! Tell him what you told me just now. Tell him you hate him. Tell him you hate him!'

She bent forward and wept bitterly, while the *sais*, impassive, went forward to hold the horse. Mrs. Vansuythen turned scarlet and dropped the reins. She wished to be no party to such unholy explanations.

'I've nothing to do with it,' she began coldly; but Mrs. Boulte's sobs overcame her, and she addressed herself to the man. 'I don't know what I am to say, Captain Kurrell. I don't know what I can call you. I think you've—you've behaved abominably, and she has cut her forehead terribly against the table.'

'It doesn't hurt. It isn't anything,' said Mrs. Boulte feebly. '*That* doesn't matter. Tell him what you told me. Say you don't care for him. Oh, Ted, *won't* you believe her?'

'Mrs. Boulte has made me understand that you were—that you were fond of her once upon a time,' went on Mrs. Vansuythen.

'Well!' said Kurrell brutally. 'It seems to me that Mrs. Boulte had better be fond of her own husband first.'

'Stop!' said Mrs. Vansuythen. 'Hear me first. I don't care—I don't want to know anything about you and Mrs. Boulte; but I want *you* to know that I hate you, that I think you are a cur, and that I'll never, *never* speak to you again. Oh, I don't dare to say what I think of you, you —— man!'

'I want to speak to Ted,' moaned Mrs. Boulte, but the dog-cart rattled on, and Kurrell was left on the road, shamed, and boiling with wrath against Mrs. Boulte.

He waited till Mrs. Vansuythen was driving back to her own house, and, she being freed from the embarrassment of Mrs. Boulte's presence, learned for the second time her opinion of himself and his actions.

In the evenings it was the wont of all Kashima to meet at the platform on the Narkarra Road, to drink tea and discuss the trivialities of the day. Major Vansuythen and his wife found themselves alone at the gathering-place for almost the first time in their remembrance ; and the cheery Major, in the teeth of his wife's remarkably reasonable suggestion that the rest of the Station might be sick, insisted upon driving round to the two bungalows and unearthing the population.

'Sitting in the twilight !' said he, with great indignation, to the Boultes. 'That'll never do ! Hang it all, we're one family here ! You *must* come out, and so must Kurrell. I'll make him bring his banjo.'

So great is the power of honest simplicity and a good digestion over guilty consciences that all Kashima did turn out, even down to the banjo; and the Major embraced the company in one expansive grin. As he grinned, Mrs. Vansuythen raised her eyes for an instant and looked at all Kashima. Her meaning was clear. Major Vansuythen would never know anything. He was to be the outsider in that happy family whose cage was the Dosehri hills.

'You're singing villainously out of tune.

Kurrell,' said the Major truthfully. 'Pass me that banjo.'

And he sang in excruciating-wise till the stars came out and all Kashima went to dinner.

.   .   .   .

That was the beginning of the New Life of Kashima—the life that Mrs. Boulte made when her tongue was loosened in the twilight.

Mrs. Vansuythen has never told the Major ; and since he insists upon keeping up a burdensome geniality, she has been compelled to break her vow of not speaking to Kurrell. This speech, which must of necessity preserve the semblance of politeness and interest, serves admirably to keep alight the flame of jealousy and dull hatred in Boulte's bosom, as it awakens the same passions in his wife's heart. Mrs. Boulte hates Mrs. Vansuythen because she has taken Ted from her, and, in some curious fashion, hates her because Mrs. Vansuythen—and here the wife's eyes see far more clearly than the husband's—detests Ted. And Ted—that gallant captain and honourable man—knows now that it is possible to hate a woman once loved, to the verge of wishing to silence her for ever with blows. Above all, is he shocked that Mrs. Boulte cannot see the error of her ways.

Boulte and he go out tiger-shooting together in all friendship. Boulte has put their relationship on a most satisfactory footing.

'You're a blackguard,' he says to Kurrell, 'and I've lost any self-respect I may ever have had ; but when you're with me, I can feel certain that you are not with Mrs. Vansuythen, or making Emma miserable.'

Kurrell endures anything that Boulte may say to him. Sometimes they are away for three days together, and then the Major insists upon his wife going over to sit with Mrs. Boulte ; although Mrs. Vansuythen has repeatedly declared that she prefers her husband's company to any in the world. From the way in which she clings to him, she would certainly seem to be speaking the truth.

But of course, as the Major says, 'in a little Station we must all be friendly.'

The Hill of Illusion

What rendered vain their deep desire ?
A God, a God their severance ruled,
And bade between their shores to be
The unplumbed, salt, estranging sea.
Matthew Arnold.

HE. Tell your *jhampanies* not to hurry so, dear. They forget I'm fresh from the Plains.

SHE. Sure proof that *I* have not been going out with any one. Yes, they *are* an untrained crew. Where do we go ?

HE. As usual—to the world's end. No, Jakko.

SHE. Have your pony led after you, then. It's a long round.

HE. And for the last time, thank Heaven !

SHE. Do you mean *that* still ? I didn't dare to write to you about it—all these months.

HE. Mean it ! I've been shaping my affairs to that end since Autumn. What makes you speak as though it had occurred to you for the first time ?

SHE. I ? Oh! I don't know. I've had long enough to think, too.

He. And you've changed your mind?

She. No. You ought to know that I am a miracle of constancy. What are your—arrangements?

He. *Ours*, Sweetheart, please.

She. Ours, be it then. My poor boy, how the prickly heat has marked your forehead! Have you ever tried sulphate of copper in water?

He. It'll go away in a day or two up here. The arrangements are simple enough. Tonga in the early morning—reach Kalka at twelve—Umballa at seven—down, straight by night train, to Bombay, and then the steamer of the 21st for Rome. That's my idea. The Continent and Sweden—a ten-week honeymoon.

She. Ssh! Don't talk of it in that way. It makes me afraid. Guy, how long have we two been insane?

He. Seven months and fourteen days, I forget the odd hours exactly, but I'll think.

She. I only wanted to see if you remembered. Who are those two on the Blessington Road?

He. Eabrey and the Penner Woman. What do they matter to *us?* Tell me everything that you've been doing and saying and thinking.

She. Doing little, saying less, and thinking a great deal. I've hardly been out at all.

He. That was wrong of you. You haven't been moping?

She. Not very much. Can you wonder that I'm disinclined for amusement?

He. Frankly, I do. Where was the difficulty?

She. In this only. The more people I know

and the more I'm known here, the wider spread will be the news of the crash when it comes. I don't like that.

He. Nonsense. We shall be out of it.

She. You think so?

He. I'm sure of it, if there is any power in steam or horse-flesh to carry us away. Ha! ha!

She. And the *fun* of the situation comes in— where, my Lancelot?

He. Nowhere, Guinevere. I was only thinking of something.

She. They say men have a keener sense of humour than women. Now *I* was thinking of the scandal.

He. Don't think of anything so ugly. We shall be beyond it.

She. It will be there all the same—in the mouths of Simla—telegraphed over India, and talked of at the dinners—and when He goes out they will stare at Him to see how he takes it. And we shall be dead, Guy dear—dead and cast into the outer darkness where there is——

He. Love at least. Isn't that enough?

She. I have said so.

He. And you think so still?

She. What do *you* think?

He. What have I *done*? It means equal ruin to me, as the world reckons it—outcasting, the loss of my appointment, the breaking off my life's work. I pay my price.

She. And are you so much above the world that you can afford to pay it. Am I?

He. My Divinity—what else?

SHE. A very ordinary woman, I'm afraid, but so far, respectable. How d'you do, Mrs. Middleditch? Your husband? I think he's riding down to Annandale with Colonel Statters. Yes, isn't it divine after the rain?—Guy, how long am I to be allowed to bow to Mrs. Middleditch? Till the 17th?

HE. Frowsy Scotchwoman! What is the use of bringing her into the discussion? You were saying?

SHE. Nothing. Have you ever seen a man hanged?

HE. Yes. Once.

SHE. What was it for?

HE. Murder, of course.

SHE. Murder. Is *that* so great a sin after all? I wonder how he felt before the drop fell.

HE. I don't think he felt much. What a gruesome little woman it is this evening! You're shivering. Put on your cape, dear.

SHE. I think I will. Oh! Look at the mist coming over Sanjaoli; and I thought we should have sunshine on the Ladies' Mile! Let's turn back.

HE. What's the good? There's a cloud on Elysium Hill, and that means it's foggy all down the Mall. We'll go on. It'll blow away before we get to the Convent, perhaps. 'Jove! It *is* chilly.

SHE. You feel it, fresh from below. Put on your ulster. What do you think of my cape?

HE. Never ask a man his opinion of a woman's dress when he is desperately and abjectly in love with the wearer. Let me look. Like everything else of yours it's perfect. Where did you get it from?

SHE. He gave it me, on Wednesday—our wedding-day, you know.

HE. The Deuce He did! He's growing generous in his old age. D'you like all that frilly, bunchy stuff at the throat? I don't.

SHE. Don't you?

> Kind Sir, o' your courtesy,
>   As you go by the town, Sir,
> 'Pray you o' your love for me,
>   Buy me a russet gown, Sir.

HE. I won't say : 'Keek into the draw-well, Janet, Janet.' Only wait a little, darling, and you shall be stocked with russet gowns and everything else.

SHE. And when the frocks wear out you'll get me new ones—and everything else?

HE. Assuredly.

SHE. I wonder!

HE. Look here, Sweetheart, I didn't spend two days and two nights in the train to hear you wonder. I thought we'd settled all that at Shaifazehat.

SHE (*dreamily*). At Shaifazehat? Does the Station go on still? That was ages and *ages* ago. It must be crumbling to pieces. All except the Amirtollah *kutcha* road. I don't believe *that* could crumble till the Day of Judgment.

HE. You think so? What *is* the mood now?

SHE. I can't tell. How cold it is! Let us get on quickly.

He. 'Better walk a little. Stop your *jhampanies* and get out. What's the matter with you this evening, dear?

She. Nothing. You must grow accustomed to my ways. If I'm boring you I can go home. Here's Captain Congleton coming, I daresay he'll be willing to escort me.

He. Goose! Between *us*, too! *Damn* Captain Congleton.

She. Chivalrous Knight. Is it your habit to swear much in talking? It jars a little, and you might swear at me.

He. My angel! I didn't know what I was saying; and you changed so quickly that I couldn't follow. I'll apologise in dust and ashes.

She. There'll be enough of those later on—— Good-night, Captain Congleton. Going to the singing-quadrilles already? What dances am I giving you next week? No! You must have written them down wrong. Five and Seven, *I* said. If you've made a mistake, I certainly don't intend to suffer for it. You must alter your programme.

He. I thought you told me that you had not been going out much this season?

She. Quite true, but when I do I dance with Captain Congleton. He dances very nicely.

He. And sit out with him, I suppose?

She. Yes. Have you any objection? Shall I stand under the chandelier in future?

He. What does he talk to you about?

She. What do men talk about when they sit out?

He. Ugh! Don't! Well, now I'm up, you

must dispense with the fascinating Congleton for a while.   I don't like him.

SHE (*after a pause*).   Do you know what you have said?

HE.   'Can't say that I do exactly.   I'm not in the best of tempers.

SHE.   So I see,—and feel.   My true and faithful lover, where is your eternal constancy,' 'unalterable trust,' and 'reverent devotion'?   I remember those phrases; you seem to have forgotten them.   I mention a man's name——

HE.   A good deal more than that.

SHE.   Well, speak to him about a dance—perhaps the last dance that I shall ever dance in my life before I,—before I go away ; and you at once distrust and insult me.

HE.   I never said a word.

SHE.   How much did you imply?   Guy, is *this* amount of confidence to be our stock to start the new life on?

HE.   No, of course not.   I didn't mean that. On my word and honour, I didn't.   Let it pass, dear.   Please let it pass.

SHE.   This once—yes—and a second time, and again and again, all through the years when I shall be unable to resent it.   You want too much, my Lancelot, and,—you know too much.

HE.   How do you mean?

SHE.   That is a part of the punishment.   There *cannot* be perfect trust between us.

HE.   In Heaven's name, why not?

SHE.   Hush !   The Other Place is quite enough.   Ask yourself.

He. I don't follow.

She. You trust me so implicitly that when I look at another man——Never mind. Guy, have you ever made love to a girl—a *good* girl?

He. Something of the sort. Centuries ago —in the Dark Ages, before I ever met you, dear.

She. Tell me what you said to her.

He. What does a man say to a girl? I've forgotten.

She. *I* remember. He tells her that he trusts her and worships the ground she walks on, and that he'll love and honour and protect her till her dying day ; and so she marries in that belief. At least, I speak of one girl who was *not* protected.

He. Well, and then?

She. And then, Guy, and then, that girl needs *ten* times the love and trust and honour— yes, *honour*—that was enough when she was only a mere wife if—if—the other life she chooses to lead is to be made even bearable. Do you understand?

He. Even bearable ! It'll be Paradise.

She. Ah ! Can you give me all I've asked for—not now, nor a few months later, but when you begin to think of what you might have done if you had kept your own appointment and your caste here—when you begin to look upon me as a drag and a burden? I shall want it most then, Guy, for there will be no one in the wide world but you.

He. You're a little over-tired to-night, Sweetheart, and you're taking a stage view of the situation.　After the necessary business in the Courts, the road is clear to——

SHE.　'The holy state of matrimony!'　Ha! ha! ha!

HE.　Ssh!　Don't laugh in that horrible way!

SHE.　I—I—c-c-c-can't help it!　Isn't it too absurd!　Ah!　Ha! ha! ha!　Guy, stop me quick or I shall—l-l-laugh till we get to the Church.

HE.　For goodness sake, stop!　Don't make an exhibition of yourself.　What *is* the matter with you?

SHE.　N-nothing.　I'm better now.

HE.　That's all right.　One moment, dear. There's a little wisp of hair got loose from behind your right ear and it's straggling over your cheek. So!

SHE.　Thank'oo.　I'm 'fraid my hat's on one side, too.

HE.　What do you wear these huge dagger bonnet-skewers for?　They're big enough to kill a man with.

SHE.　Oh!　don't kill *me*, though.　You're sticking it into my head!　Let *me* do it.　You men are so clumsy.

HE.　Have you had many opportunities of comparing us—in this sort of work?

SHE.　Guy, what is my name?

HE.　Eh!　I don't follow.

SHE.　Here's my card-case.　Can you read?

HE.　Yes.　Well?

SHE.　Well, that answers your question.　You know the other's man's name.　Am I sufficiently humbled, or would you like to ask me if there is any one else?

HE. I see now. My darling, I never meant that for an instant. I was only joking. There! Lucky there's no one on the road. They'd be scandalised.

SHE. They'll be more scandalised before the end.

HE. Do-on't! I don't like you to talk in that way.

SHE. Unreasonable man! Who asked me to face the situation and accept it?—Tell me, do I look like Mrs. Penner? *Do* I look like a naughty woman! *Swear* I don't! Give me your word of honour, my *honourable* friend, that I'm not like Mrs. Buzgago. That's the way she stands, with her hands clasped at the back of her head. D'you like that?

HE. Don't be affected.

SHE. I'm not. I'm Mrs. Buzgago. Listen!

> Pendant une anne' toute entière
> Le régiment n'a pas r'paru.
> Au Ministère de la Guerre
> On le r'porta comme perdu.
>
> On se r'noncait à r'trouver sa trace,
> Quand un matin subitement,
> On le vit r'paraître sur la place,
> L'Colonel toujours en avant.

That's the way she rolls her r's. *Am* I like her?

HE. No, but I object when you go on like an actress and sing stuff of that kind. Where in the

world did you pick up the *Chanson du Colonel?*
It isn't a drawing-room song. It isn't proper.

She. Mrs. Buzgago taught it me. She is both
drawing-room and proper, and in another month
she'll shut her drawing-room to me, and, thank
God, she isn't as improper as I am. Oh, Guy,
Guy! I wish I was like some women and had no
scruples about—What is it Keene says?—'Wearing
a corpse's hair and being false to the bread they
eat.'

He. I am only a man of limited intelligence,
and, just now, very bewildered. When you have
quite finished flashing through all your moods tell
me, and I'll try to understand the last one.

She. Moods, Guy! I haven't any. I'm
sixteen years old and you're just twenty, and
you've been waiting for two hours outside the
school in the cold. And now I've met you, and
now we're walking home together. Does *that* suit
you, My Imperial Majesty?

He. No. We aren't children. Why can't
you be rational?

She. He asks me that when I'm going to
commit suicide for his sake, and, and—I don't
want to be French and rave about my mother, but
have I ever told you that I have a mother, and a
brother who was my pet before I married? He's
married now. Can't you imagine the pleasure
that the news of the elopement will give him?
Have *you* any people at Home, Guy, to be pleased
with your performances?

He. One or two. One can't make omelets
without breaking eggs.

SHE (*slowly*).   I don't see the necessity——

HE.   Hah!   What do you mean?

SHE.   Shall I speak the truth?

HE.   Under the circumstances, perhaps it *would* be as well.

SHE.   Guy, I'm afraid.

HE.   I thought we'd settled all that.   What of?

SHE.   Of you.

HE.   Oh, damn it all!   The old business! This is *too* bad!

SHE.   Of *you.*

HE.   And what now?

SHE.   What do you think of me?

HE.   Beside the question altogether.   What do you intend to do?

SHE.   I daren't risk it.   I'm afraid.   If I could only cheat——

HE.   *À la Buzgago?*   No, *thanks.*   That's the one point on which I have any notion of Honour. I won't eat his salt and steal too.   I'll loot openly or not at all.

SHE.   I never meant anything else.

HE.   Then, why in the world do you pretend not to be willing to come?

SHE.   It's *not* pretence, Guy.   I *am* afraid.

HE.   Please explain.

SHE.   It can't last, Guy.   It can't last.   You'll get angry, and then you'll swear, and then you'll get jealous, and then you'll mistrust me—you do *now*—and you yourself will be the best reason for doubting.   And I—what shall *I* do?   I shall be no better than Mrs. Buzgago found out—no better than any one. And you'll *know* that. Oh, Guy, can't you *see?*

HE. I see that you are desperately unreasonable, little woman.

SHE. There! The moment I begin to object, you get angry. What will you do when I am only your property—stolen property? It can't be, Guy. It can't be! I thought it could, but it *can't*. You'll get tired of me.

HE. I tell you I shall *not*. Won't anything make you understand that?

SHE. There, can't you see? If you speak to me like that now, you'll call me horrible names later, if I don't do everything as you like. And if you were cruel to me, Guy, where should I go?—where should I go? I can't trust you. Oh! I *can't* trust you!

HE. I suppose I ought to say that I *can* trust you. I've ample reason.

SHE. *Please* don't, dear. It hurts as much as if you hit me.

HE. It isn't exactly pleasant for *me*.

SHE. I can't help it. I wish I were dead! I can't trust you, and I don't trust myself. Oh, Guy, let it die away and be forgotten!

HE. Too late now. I don't understand you—I won't—and I can't trust myself to talk this evening. May I call to-morrow?

SHE. Yes. ·*No!* Oh, give me time! The day after. I get into my 'rickshaw here and meet Him at Peliti's. You ride.

HE. I'll go on to Peliti's too. I think I want a drink. My world's knocked about my ears and the stars are falling. Who are those brutes howling in the Old Library?

SHE. They're rehearsing the singing-quadrilles for the Fancy Ball. Can't you hear Mrs. Buzgago's voice? She has a solo. It's quite a new idea. Listen!

MRS. BUZGAGO (*in the Old Library, con. molt. exp.*).

> See-saw! Margery Daw!
> Sold her bed to lie upon straw.
> Wasn't she a silly slut
> To sell her bed and lie upon dirt?

Captain Congleton, I'm going to alter that to 'flirt.' It sounds better.

HE. No, I've changed my mind about the drink. Good-night, little lady. I shall see you to-morrow?

SHE. Ye—es. Good-night, Guy. *Don't* be angry with me.

HE. Angry! You *know* I trust you absolutely. Good-night and—God bless you!

(*Three seconds later. Alone.*) Hmm! I'd give something to discover whether there's another man at the back of all this.

A Second-Rate Woman

Est fuga, volvitur rota,
  On we drift : where looms the dim port ?
One Two Three Four Five contribute their quota :
  Something is gained if one caught but the import,
Show it us, Hugues of Saxe-Gotha.
                            Master Hugues of Saxe-Gotha.

'DRESSED ! Don't tell me that woman ever dressed in her life. She stood in the middle of the room while her *ayah*—no, her husband—it *must* have been a man—threw her clothes at her. She then did her hair with her fingers, and rubbed her bonnet in the flue under the bed. I *know* she did, as well as if I had assisted at the orgy. Who is she ?' said Mrs. Hauksbee.

'Don't !' said Mrs. Mallowe feebly. 'You make my head ache. I'm miserable to-day. Stay me with *fondants*, comfort me with chocolates, for I am——Did you bring anything from Peliti's ? '

'Questions to begin with. You shall have the sweets when you have answered them. Who and what is the creature ? There were at least half-a-dozen men round her, and she appeared to be going to sleep in their midst.'

'Delville,' said Mrs. Mallowe, ' " Shady "

Delville, to distinguish her from Mrs. Jim of that ilk. She dances as untidily as she dresses, I believe, and her husband is somewhere in Madras. Go and call, if you are so interested.'

'What have I to do with Shigramitish women? She merely caught my attention for a minute, and I wondered at the attraction that a dowd has for a certain type of man. I expected to see her walk out of her clothes—until I looked at her eyes.'

'Hooks and eyes, surely,' drawled Mrs. Mallowe.

'Don't be clever, Polly. You make my head ache. And round this hayrick stood a crowd of men—a positive crowd!'

'Perhaps *they* also expected——

'Polly, don't be Rabelaisian!'

Mrs. Mallowe curled herself up comfortably on the sofa, and turned her attention to the sweets. She and Mrs. Hauksbee shared the same house at Simla; and these things befell two seasons after the matter of Otis Yeere, which has been already recorded.

Mrs. Hauksbee stepped into the verandah and looked down upon the Mall, her forehead puckered with thought.

'Hah!' said Mrs. Hauksbee shortly. 'Indeed!'

'What is it?' said Mrs. Mallowe sleepily.

'That dowd and The Dancing Master—to whom I object.'

'Why to The Dancing Master? He is a middle-aged gentleman, of reprobate and romantic tendencies, and tries to be a friend of mine.'

'Then make up your mind to lose him. Dowds

cling by nature, and I should imagine that this animal—how terrible her bonnet looks from above!—is specially clingsome.'

'She is welcome to The Dancing Master so far as I am concerned. I never could take an interest in a monotonous liar. The frustrated aim of his life is to persuade people that he is a bachelor.'

'O-oh! I think I've met that sort of man before. And isn't he?'

'No. He confided that to me a few days ago. Ugh! Some men ought to be killed.'

'What happened then?'

'He posed as the horror of horrors—a misunderstood man. Heaven knows the *femme incomprise* is sad enough and bad enough—but the other thing!'

'And so fat too! *I* should have laughed in his face. Men seldom confide in me. How is it they come to you?'

'For the sake of impressing me with their careers in the past. Protect me from men with confidences!'

'And yet you encourage them?'

'What can I do? They talk, I listen, and they vow that I am sympathetic. I know I always profess astonishment even when the plot is—of the most old possible.'

'Yes. Men are so unblushingly explicit if they are once allowed to talk, whereas women's confidences are full of reservations and fibs, except——'

'When they go mad and babble of the Unutterabilities after a week's acquaintance. Really, if you come to consider, we know a great deal more of men than of our own sex.'

'And the extraordinary thing is that men will never believe it. They say we are trying to hide something.'

'They are generally doing that on their own account. Alas! These chocolates pall upon me, and I haven't eaten more than a dozen. I think I shall go to sleep.'

'Then you'll get fat, dear. If you took more exercise and a more intelligent interest in your neighbours you would——'

'Be as much loved as Mrs. Hauksbee. You're a darling in many ways, and I like you—you are not a woman's woman—but *why* do you trouble yourself about mere human beings ? '

'Because in the absence of angels, who I am sure would be horribly dull, men and women are the most fascinating things in the whole wide world, lazy one. I am interested in The Dowd— I am interested in The Dancing Master—I am interested in the Hawley Boy—and I am interested in *you.*'

'Why couple me with the Hawley Boy ? He is your property.'

'Yes, and in his own guileless speech, I'm making a good thing out of him. When he is slightly more reformed, and has passed his Higher Standard, or whatever the authorities think fit to exact from him, I shall select a pretty little girl, the Holt girl, I think, and '—here she waved her hands airily—'" whom Mrs. Hauksbee hath joined together let no man put asunder." That's all.'

'And when you have yoked May Holt with the most notorious detrimental in Simla, and earned the undying hatred of Mamma Holt, what will you do with me, Dispenser of the Destinies of the Universe?'

Mrs. Hauksbee dropped into a low chair in front of the fire, and, chin in hand, gazed long and steadfastly at Mrs. Mallowe.

'I do not know,' she said, shaking her head, '*what* I shall do with you, dear. It's obviously impossible to marry you to some one else—your husband would object and the experiment might not be successful after all. I think I shall begin by preventing you from—what is it?—"sleeping on ale-house benches and snoring in the sun."'

'Don't! I don't like your quotations. They are so rude. Go to the Library and bring me new books.'

'While you sleep? *No!* If you don't come with me I shall spread your newest frock on my 'rickshaw-bow, and when any one asks me what I am doing, I shall say that I am going to Phelps's to get it let out. I shall take care that Mrs. MacNamara sees me. Put your things on, there's a good girl.'

Mrs. Mallowe groaned and obeyed, and the two went off to the Library, where they found Mrs. Delville and the man who went by the nick-name of The Dancing Master. By that time Mrs. Mallowe was awake and eloquent.

'That is the Creature!' said Mrs. Hauksbee, with the air of one pointing out a slug in the road.

'No,' said Mrs. Mallowe. 'The man is the

Creature. Ugh! Good-evening, Mr. Bent. I thought you were coming to tea this evening.'

'Surely it was for to-morrow, was it not?' answered The Dancing Master. 'I understood . . . I fancied . . . I'm so sorry . . . How very unfortunate!' . . .

But Mrs. Mallowe had passed on.

'For the practised equivocator you said he was,' murmured Mrs. Hauksbee, 'he strikes *me* as a failure. Now wherefore should he have preferred a walk with The Dowd to tea with us? Elective affinities, I suppose—both grubby. Polly, I'd never forgive that woman as long as the world rolls.'

'I forgive every woman everything,' said Mrs. Mallowe. 'He will be a sufficient punishment for her. What a common voice she has!'

Mrs. Delville's voice was not pretty, her carriage was even less lovely, and her raiment was strikingly neglected. All these things Mrs. Mallowe noticed over the top of a magazine.

'Now *what* is there in her?' said Mrs. Hauksbee. 'Do you see what I meant about the clothes falling off? If I were a man I would perish sooner than be seen with that rag-bag. And yet, she has good eyes, but—Oh!'

'What is it?'

'She doesn't know how to use them! On my honour, she does not. Look! Oh look! Untidiness I can endure, but ignorance never! The woman's a fool.'

'Hsh! She'll hear you.'

'All the women in Simla are fools. She'll

think I mean some one else. Now she's going out. What a thoroughly objectionable couple she and The Dancing Master make! Which reminds me. Do you suppose they'll ever dance together?'

'Wait and see. I don't envy her the conversation of The Dancing Master—loathly man! His wife ought to be up here before long?'

'Do you know anything about him?'

'Only what he told me. It may be all a fiction. He married a girl bred in the country, I think, and, being an honourable, chivalrous soul, told me that he repented his bargain and sent her to her mother as often as possible—a person who has lived in the Doon since the memory of man and goes to Mussoorie when other people go Home. The wife is with her at present. So he says.'

'Babies?'

'One only, but he talks of his wife in a revolting way. I hated him for it. *He* thought he was being epigrammatic and brilliant.'

'That is a vice peculiar to men. I dislike him because he is generally in the wake of some girl, disappointing the Eligibles. He will persecute May Holt no more, unless I am much mistaken.'

'No. I think Mrs. Delville may occupy his attention for a while.'

'Do you suppose she knows that he is the head of a family?'

'Not from his lips. He swore me to eternal secrecy. Wherefore I tell you. Don't you know that type of man?'

'Not intimately, thank goodness! As a general rule, when a man begins to abuse his wife to me, I find that the Lord gives me wherewith to answer him according to his folly; and we part with a coolness between us. I laugh.'

'I'm different. I've no sense of humour.'

'Cultivate it, then. It has been my mainstay for more years than I care to think about. A well-educated sense of humour will save a woman when Religion, Training, and Home influences fail; and we may all need salvation sometimes.'

'Do you suppose that the Delville woman has humour?'

'Her dress bewrays her. How can a Thing who wears her *supplément* under her left arm have any notion of the fitness of things—much less their folly? If she discards The Dancing Master after having once seen him dance, I may respect her. Otherwise——'

'But are we not both assuming a great deal too much, dear? You saw the woman at Peliti's— half an hour later you saw her walking with The Dancing Master—an hour later you met her here at the Library.'

'Still with The Dancing Master, remember.'

'Still with The Dancing Master, I admit, but why on the strength of that should you imagine——'

'I imagine nothing. I have no imagination. I am only convinced that The Dancing Master is attracted to The Dowd because he is objectionable in every way and she in every other. If I know the man as you have described him, he holds his wife in slavery at present.'

'She is twenty years younger than he.'

'Poor wretch! And, in the end, after he has posed and swaggered and lied—he has a mouth under that ragged moustache simply made for lies —he will be rewarded according to his merits.'

'I wonder what those really are,' said Mrs. Mallowe.

But Mrs. Hauksbee, her face close to the shelf of the new books, was humming softly : '*What shall he have who killed the Deer ?*' She was a lady of unfettered speech.

One month later she announced her intention of calling upon Mrs. Delville. Both Mrs. Hauksbee and Mrs. Mallowe were in morning wrappers, and there was a great peace in the land.

'I should go as I was,' said Mrs. Mallowe. 'It would be a delicate compliment to her style.'

Mrs. Hauksbee studied herself in the glass.

'Assuming for a moment that she ever darkened these doors, I should put on this robe, after all the others, to show her what a morning-wrapper ought to be. It might enliven her. As it is, I shall go in the dove-coloured—sweet emblem of youth and innocence—and shall put on my new gloves.'

'If you really are going, dirty tan would be too good ; and you know that dove-colour spots with the rain.'

'I care not. I may make her envious. At least I shall try, though one cannot expect very much from a woman who puts a lace tucker into her habit.'

'Just Heavens ! When did she do that ? '

'Yesterday—riding with The Dancing Master.

I met them at the back of Jakko, and the rain had made the lace lie down. To complete the effect, she was wearing an unclean *terai* with the elastic under her chin. I felt almost too well content to take the trouble to despise her.'

'The Hawley Boy was riding with you. What did he think?'

'Does a boy ever notice these things? Should I like him if he did? He stared in the rudest way, and just when I thought he had seen the elastic, he said, "There's something very taking about that face." I rebuked him on the spot. I don't approve of boys being taken by faces.'

'Other than your own. I shouldn't be in the least surprised if the Hawley Boy immediately went to call.'

'I forbade him. Let her be satisfied with The Dancing Master, and his wife when she comes up. I'm rather curious to see Mrs. Bent and the Delville woman together.'

Mrs. Hauksbee departed and, at the end of an hour, returned slightly flushed.

'There is no limit to the treachery of youth! I *ordered* the Hawley Boy, as he valued my patronage, not to call. The first person I stumble over—literally stumble over—in her poky, dark little drawing-room is, of course, the Hawley Boy. She kept us waiting ten minutes, and then emerged as though she had been tipped out of the dirty-clothes-basket. You know my way, dear, when I am at all put out. I was Superior, *crrrrushingly* Superior! 'Lifted my eyes to Heaven, and had heard of nothing—'dropped my eyes on the carpet and "really didn't know"—'played with my card-case and "supposed so." The Hawley Boy giggled like a girl, and I had to freeze him with scowls between the sentences.'

'And she?'

'She sat in a heap on the edge of a couch, and managed to convey the impression that she was suffering from stomach-ache, at the very least. It was all I could do not to ask after her symptoms. When I rose, she grunted just like a buffalo in the water—too lazy to move.'

'Are you certain?——'

'Am I blind, Polly? Laziness, sheer laziness, nothing else—or her garments were only constructed for sitting down in. I stayed for a quarter of an hour trying to penetrate the gloom, to guess what her surroundings were like, while she stuck out her tongue.'

'Lu—*cy* !'

'Well—I'll withdraw the tongue, though I'm sure if she didn't do it when I was in the room, she did the minute I was outside. At any rate, she lay in a lump and grunted. Ask the Hawley Boy, dear. I believe the grunts were meant for sentences, but she spoke so indistinctly that I can't swear to it.'

'You are incorrigible, simply.'

'I am *not* ! Treat me civilly, give me peace with honour, don't put the only available seat facing the window, and a child may eat jam in my lap before Church. But I resent being grunted at. Wouldn't you? Do you suppose that she communicates her views on life and love to The Dancing Master in a set of modulated "Grmphs" ?'

'You attach too much importance to The Dancing Master.'

'He came as we went, and The Dowd grew almost cordial at the sight of him. He smiled greasily, and moved about that darkened dog-kennel in a suspiciously familiar way.'

'Don't be uncharitable. Any sin but that I'll forgive.'

'Listen to the voice of History. I am only describing what I saw. He entered, the heap on the sofa revived slightly, and the Hawley Boy and I came away together. *He* is disillusioned, but I felt it my duty to lecture him severely for going there. And that's all.'

'Now for Pity's sake leave the wretched creature and The Dancing Master alone. They never did you any harm.'

'No harm? To dress as an example and a stumbling-block for half Simla, and then to find this Person who is dressed by the hand of God— not that I wish to disparage *Him* for a moment, but you know the *tikka dhurzie* way He attires those lilies of the field—this Person draws the eyes of men—and some of them nice men? It's almost enough to make one discard clothing. I told the Hawley Boy so.'

'And what did that sweet youth do?'

'Turned shell-pink and looked across the far blue hills like a distressed cherub. *Am* I talking wildly, Polly? Let me say my say, and I shall be calm. Otherwise I may go abroad and disturb Simla with a few original reflections. Excepting always your own sweet self, there isn't a single woman in the land who understands me when I am—what's the word?'

'*Tête-fêlée*,' suggested Mrs. Mallowe.

'Exactly! And now let us have tiffin. The demands of Society are exhausting, and as Mrs. Delville says——' Here Mrs. Hauksbee, to the horror of the *khitmatgars*, lapsed into a series of grunts, while Mrs. Mallowe stared in lazy surprise.

'"God gie us a guid conceit of oorselves,"' said Mrs. Hauksbee piously, returning to her natural speech. 'Now, in any other woman that would have been vulgar. I am consumed with curiosity to see Mrs. Bent. I expect complications.'

'Woman of one idea,' said Mrs. Mallowe shortly; 'all complications are as old as the hills! I have lived through or near all—*all*—ALL!'

'And yet do not understand that men and women never behave twice alike. I am old who was young—if ever I put my head in your lap, you dear, big sceptic, you will learn that my parting is gauze—but never, no never, have I lost my interest in men and women. Polly, I shall see this business out to the bitter end.'

'I am going to sleep,' said Mrs. Mallowe calmly. 'I never interfere with men or women unless I am compelled,' and she retired with dignity to her own room.

Mrs. Hauksbee's curiosity was not long left ungratified, for Mrs. Bent came up to Simla a few days after the conversation faithfully reported above, and pervaded the Mall by her husband's side.

'Behold!' said Mrs. Hauksbee, thoughtfully rubbing her nose. 'That is the last link of the chain, if we omit the husband of the Delville, whoever he may be. Let me consider. The Bents and the Delvilles inhabit the same hotel; and the Delville is detested by the Waddy—do you know the Waddy?—who is almost as big a dowd. The Waddy also abominates the male Bent, for which, if her other sins do not weigh too heavily, she will eventually go to Heaven.'

'Don't be irreverent,' said Mrs. Mallowe, 'I like Mrs. Bent's face.'

'I am discussing the Waddy,' returned Mrs. Hauksbee loftily. 'The Waddy will take the female Bent apart, after having borrowed—yes!— everything that she can, from hairpins to babies' bottles. Such, my dear, is life in a hotel. The Waddy will tell the female Bent facts and fictions about The Dancing Master and The Dowd.'

'Lucy, I should like you better if you were not always looking into people's back-bedrooms.'

'Anybody can look into their front drawing-rooms; and remember whatever I do, and whatever I look, I never talk—as the Waddy will. Let us hope that The Dancing Master's greasy smile and manner of the pedagogue will soften the heart of that cow, his wife. If mouths speak truth, I should think that little Mrs. Bent could get very angry on occasion.'

'But what reason has she for being angry?'

'What reason! The Dancing Master in himself is a reason. How does it go? "If in his life some trivial errors fall, Look in his face and you'll believe them all." I am prepared to credit *any* evil of The Dancing Master, because I hate him so. And The Dowd is so disgustingly badly dressed——'

'That she, too, is capable of every iniquity? I always prefer to believe the best of everybody. It saves so much trouble.'

'Very good. I prefer to believe the worst. It saves useless expenditure of sympathy. And you may be quite certain that the Waddy believes with me.'

Mrs. Mallowe sighed and made no answer.

The conversation was holden after dinner while Mrs. Hauksbee was dressing for a dance.

'I am too tired to go,' pleaded Mrs. Mallowe, and Mrs. Hauksbee left her in peace till two in the morning, when she was aware of emphatic knocking at her door.

'Don't be *very* angry, dear,' said Mrs. Hauksbee. 'My idiot of an *ayah* has gone home, and, as I hope to sleep to-night, there isn't a soul in the place to unlace me.'

'Oh, this is too bad!' said Mrs. Mallowe sulkily.

''Cant help it. I'm a lone, lorn grass-widow, dear, but I will *not* sleep in my stays. And such news too! Oh, *do* unlace me, there's a darling! The Dowd—The Dancing Master—I and the Hawley Boy—You know the North verandah?'

'How can I do anything if you spin round like this?' protested Mrs. Mallowe, fumbling with the knot of the laces.

'Oh, I forget. I must tell my tale without

the aid of your eyes. Do you know you've lovely eyes, dear? Well, to begin with, I took the Hawley Boy to a *kala juggah*.'

' Did he want much taking? '

' Lots! There was an arrangement of loose-boxes in *kanats*, and *she* was in the next one talking to *him*.'

' Which? How? Explain.'

' You know what I mean—The Dowd and The Dancing Master. We could hear every word, and we listened shamelessly—'specially the Hawley Boy. Polly, I quite love that woman ! '

' This is interesting. There ! Now turn round. What happened? '

' One moment. Ah—h ! Blessed relief. I've been looking forward to taking them off for the last half-hour—which is ominous at my time of life. But, as I was saying, we listened and heard The Dowd drawl worse than ever. She drops her final g's like a barmaid or a blue-blooded Aide-de-Camp. " Look he-ere, you're gettin' too fond o' me," she said, and The Dancing Master owned it was so in language that nearly made me ill. The Dowd reflected for a while. Then we heard her say, " Look he-ere, Mister Bent, why are you such an aw-ful liar? " I nearly exploded while The Dancing Master denied the charge. It seems that he never told her he was a married man.'

' I said he wouldn't.'

' And she had taken this to heart, on personal grounds, I suppose. She drawled along for five minutes, reproaching him with his perfidy, and grew quite motherly. " Now you've got a nice little wife of your own—you have," she said. "She's ten times too good for a fat old man like you, and, look he-ere, you never told me a word about her, and I've been thinkin' about it a good deal, and I think you're a liar." Wasn't that delicious? The Dancing Master maundered and raved till the Hawley Boy suggested that he should burst in and beat him. His voice runs up into an impassioned squeak when he is afraid. The Dowd must be an extraordinary woman. She explained that had he been a bachelor she might not have objected to his devotion ; but since he was a married man and the father of a very nice baby, she considered him a hypocrite, and this she repeated twice. She wound up her drawl with : "An' I'm tellin' you this because your wife is angry with me, an' I hate quarrellin' with any other woman, an' I like your wife. You know how you have behaved for the last six weeks. You shouldn't have done it, indeed you shouldn't. You're too old an' too fat." Can't you imagine how The Dancing Master would wince at that ! "Now go away," she said. " I don't want to tell you what I think of you, because I think you are not nice. I'll stay he-ere till the next dance begins." Did you think that the creature had so much in her ? '

' I never studied her as closely as you did. It sounds unnatural. What happened ? '

' The Dancing Master attempted blandishment, reproof, jocularity, and the style of the Lord High Warden, and I had almost to pinch the Hawley Boy to make him keep quiet. She grunted at the end of each sentence and, in the end, *he* went away swearing to himself, quite like a man in a novel. He looked more objectionable than ever. I laughed. I love that woman—in spite of her clothes. And now I'm going to bed. What do you think of it?'

'I shan't begin to think till the morning,' said Mrs. Mallowe, yawning. 'Perhaps she spoke the truth. They do fly into it by accident sometimes.'

Mrs. Hauksbee's account of her eavesdropping was an ornate one, but truthful in the main. For reasons best known to herself, Mrs. 'Shady' Delville had turned upon Mr. Bent and rent him limb from limb, casting him away limp and disconcerted ere she withdrew the light of her eyes from him permanently. Being a man of resource, and anything but pleased in that he had been called both old and fat, he gave Mrs. Bent to understand that he had, during her absence in the Doon, been the victim of unceasing persecution at the hands of Mrs. Delville, and he told the tale so often and with such eloquence that he ended in believing it, while his wife marvelled at the manners and customs of 'some women.' When the situation showed signs of languishing, Mrs. Waddy was always on hand to wake the smouldering fires of suspicion in Mrs. Bent's bosom and to contribute generally to the peace and comfort of the hotel. Mr. Bent's life was not a happy one, for if Mrs. Waddy's story were true, he was, argued his wife, untrustworthy to the last degree. If his own statement was true, his charms of manner and conversation were so great that he needed constant surveillance. And he received it, till he repented genuinely of his marriage and neglected his personal appearance. Mrs. Delville alone in the hotel was unchanged. She removed her chair some six paces towards the head of the table, and occasionally in the twilight ventured on timid overtures of friendship to Mrs. Bent, which were repulsed.

'She does it for my sake,' hinted the virtuous Bent.

'A dangerous and designing woman,' purred Mrs. Waddy.

Worst of all, every other hotel in Simla was full !

.   .   .   .

'Polly, are you afraid of diphtheria?'

'Of nothing in the world except small-pox. Diphtheria kills, but it doesn't disfigure. Why do you ask?'

'Because the Bent baby has got it, and the whole hotel is upside down in consequence. The Waddy has "set her five young on the rail" and fled. The Dancing Master fears for his precious throat, and that miserable little woman, his wife, has no notion of what ought to be done. She wanted to put it into a mustard bath — for croup!'

'Where did you learn all this?'

'Just now, on the Mall. Dr. Howlen told me. The manager of the hotel is abusing the Bents, and the Bents are abusing the manager. They *are* a feckless couple.'

'Well. What's on your mind?'

'This ; and I know it's a grave thing to ask.

Would you seriously object to my bringing the child over here, with its mother?'

'On the most strict understanding that we see nothing of The Dancing Master.'

'He will be only too glad to stay away. Polly, you're an angel. The woman really is at her wits' end.'

'And you know nothing about her, careless, and would hold her up to public scorn if it gave you a minute's amusement. Therefore you risk your life for the sake of her brat. No, Loo, *I'm* not the angel. I shall keep to my rooms and avoid her. But do as you please—only tell me why you do it.'

Mrs. Hauksbee's eyes softened ; she looked out of the window and back into Mrs. Mallowe's face.

'I don't know,' said Mrs. Hauksbee simply.

'You dear!'

'Polly!—and for aught you knew you might have taken my fringe off. Never do that again without warning. Now we'll get the rooms ready. I don't suppose I shall be allowed to circulate in society for a month.'

'And I also. Thank goodness I shall at last get all the sleep I want.'

Much to Mrs. Bent's surprise she and the baby were brought over to the house almost before she knew where she was. Bent was devoutly and un-disguisedly thankful, for he was afraid of the infection, and also hoped that a few weeks in the hotel alone with Mrs. Delville might lead to explanations. Mrs. Bent had thrown her jealousy to the winds in her fear for her child's life.

'We can give you good milk,' said Mrs. Hauksbee to her, 'and our house is much nearer to the Doctor's than the hotel, and you won't feel as though you were living in a hostile camp. Where is the dear Mrs. Waddy? She seemed to be a particular friend of yours.'

'They've all left me,' said Mrs. Bent bitterly. 'Mrs. Waddy went first. She said I ought to be ashamed of myself for introducing diseases there, and I am *sure* it wasn't my fault that little Dora——'

'How nice!' cooed Mrs. Hauksbee. 'The Waddy is an infectious disease herself—"more quickly caught than the plague and the taker runs presently mad." I lived next door to her at the Elysium, three years ago. Now see, you won't give us the *least* trouble, and I've ornamented all the house with sheets soaked in carbolic. It smells comforting, doesn't it? Remember I'm always in call, and my *ayah's* at your service when yours goes to her meals, and—and—if you cry I'll *never* forgive you.'

Dora Bent occupied her mother's unprofitable attention through the day and the night. The Doctor called thrice in the twenty-four hours, and the house reeked with the smell of the Condy's Fluid, chlorine-water, and carbolic acid washes. Mrs. Mallowe kept to her own rooms—she considered that she had made sufficient concessions in the cause of humanity—and Mrs. Hauksbee was more esteemed by the Doctor as a help in the sick-room than the half-distraught mother.

'I know nothing of illness,' said Mrs. Hauksbee

to the Doctor. 'Only tell me what to do, and I'll do it.'

'Keep that crazy woman from kissing the child, and let her have as little to do with the nursing as you possibly can,' said the Doctor; 'I'd turn her out of the sick-room, but that I honestly believe she'd die of anxiety. She is less than no good, and I depend on you and the *ayahs*, remember.'

Mrs. Hauksbee accepted the responsibility, though it painted olive hollows under her eyes and forced her to her oldest dresses. Mrs. Bent clung to her with more than childlike faith.

'I *know* you'll make Dora well, won't you?' she said at least twenty times a day; and twenty times a day Mrs. Hauksbee answered valiantly, 'Of course I will.'

But Dora did not improve, and the Doctor seemed to be always in the house.

'There's some danger of the thing taking a bad turn,' he said; 'I'll come over between three and four in the morning to-morrow.'

'Good gracious!' said Mrs. Hauksbee. 'He never told me what the turn would be! My education has been horribly neglected; and I have only this foolish mother-woman to fall back upon.'

The night wore through slowly, and Mrs. Hauksbee dozed in a chair by the fire. There was a dance at the Viceregal Lodge, and she dreamed of it till she was aware of Mrs. Bent's anxious eyes staring into her own.

'Wake up! Wake up! Do something!' cried Mrs. Bent piteously. 'Dora's choking to death! Do you mean to let her die?'

Mrs. Hauksbee jumped to her feet and bent over the bed. The child was fighting for breath, while the mother wrung her hands despairingly.

'Oh, what can I do? What can you do? She won't stay still! I can't hold her. Why didn't the Doctor say this was coming?' screamed Mrs. Bent. '*Won't* you help me? She's dying!'

'I — I've never seen a child die before!' stammered Mrs. Hauksbee feebly, and then—let none blame her weakness after the strain of long watching—she broke down, and covered her face with her hands. The *ayahs* on the threshold snored peacefully.

There was a rattle of 'rickshaw wheels below, the clash of an opening door, a heavy step on the stairs, and Mrs. Delville entered to find Mrs. Bent screaming for the Doctor as she ran round the room. Mrs. Hauksbee, her hands to her ears, and her face buried in the chintz of a chair, was quivering with pain at each cry from the bed, and murmuring, 'Thank God, I never bore a child! Oh! thank God, I never bore a child!'

Mrs. Delville looked at the bed for an instant, took Mrs. Bent by the shoulders, and said quietly, 'Get me some caustic. Be quick.'

The mother obeyed mechanically. Mrs. Delville had thrown herself down by the side of the child and was opening its mouth.

'Oh, you're killing her!' cried Mrs. Bent. 'Where's the Doctor? Leave her alone!'

Mrs. Delville made no reply for a minute, but busied herself with the child.

'Now the caustic, and hold a lamp behind my

shoulder. *Will* you do as you are told? The acid-bottle, if you don't know what I mean,' she said.

A second time Mrs. Delville bent over the child. Mrs. Hauksbee, her face still hidden, sobbed and shivered. One of the *ayahs* staggered sleepily into the room, yawning: '*Doctor Sahib* come.'

Mrs. Delville turned her head.

'You're only just in time,' she said. 'It was chokin' her when I came, an' I've burnt it.'

'There was no sign of the membrane getting to the air-passages after the last steaming. It was the general weakness I feared,' said the Doctor half to himself, and he whispered as he looked, 'You've done what I should have been afraid to do without consultation.'

'She was dyin',' said Mrs. Delville, under her breath. 'Can you do anythin'? What a mercy it was I went to the dance!'

Mrs. Hauksbee raised her head.

'Is it all over?' she gasped. 'I'm useless— I'm worse than useless! What are *you* doing here?'

She stared at Mrs. Delville, and Mrs. Bent, realising for the first time who was the Goddess from the Machine, stared also.

Then Mrs. Delville made explanation, putting on a dirty long glove and smoothing a crumpled and ill-fitting ball-dress.

'I was at the dance, an' the Doctor was tellin' me about your baby bein' so ill. So I came away early, an' your door was open, an' I—I—lost my

boy this way six months ago, an' I've been tryin'
to forget it ever since, an' I—I—I am very sorry
for intrudin' an' anythin' that has happened.'

Mrs. Bent was putting out the Doctor's eye
with a lamp as he stooped over Dora.

'Take it away,' said the Doctor. 'I think the
child will do, thanks to you, Mrs. Delville. *I*
should have come too late, but, I assure you '—he
was addressing himself to Mrs. Delville—'I had
not the faintest reason to expect *this*. The
membrane must have grown like a mushroom.
Will one of you help me, please ?'

He had reason for the last sentence. Mrs.
Hauksbee had thrown herself into Mrs. Delville's
arms, where she was weeping bitterly, and Mrs.
Bent was unpicturesquely mixed up with both,
while from the tangle came the sound of many
sobs and much promiscuous kissing.

'Good gracious ! I've spoilt all your beautiful
roses !' said Mrs. Hauksbee, lifting her head from
the lump of crushed gum and calico atrocities on
Mrs. Delville's shoulder and hurrying to the
Doctor.

Mrs. Delville picked up her shawl, and slouched
out of the room, mopping her eyes with the glove
that she had not put on.

'I always said she was more than a woman,'
sobbed Mrs. Hauksbee hysterically, 'and *that*
proves it !'

.   .   .   .   .   .

Six weeks later Mrs. Bent and Dora had
returned to the hotel. Mrs. Hauksbee had come
out of the Valley of Humiliation, had ceased to

reproach herself for her collapse in an hour of need, and was even beginning to direct the affairs of the world as before.

'So nobody died, and everything went off as it should, and I kissed The Dowd, Polly. I feel so old. Does it show in my face?'

'Kisses don't as a rule, do they? Of course you know what the result of The Dowd's providential arrival has been.'

'They ought to build her a statue—only no sculptor dare copy those skirts.'

'Ah!' said Mrs. Mallowe quietly. 'She has found another reward. The Dancing Master has been smirking through Simla, giving every one to understand that she came because of her undying love for him—for him—to save *his* child, and all Simla naturally believes this.'

'But Mrs. Bent——'

'Mrs. Bent believes it more than any one else. She won't speak to The Dowd now. *Isn't* The Dancing Master an angel?'

Mrs. Hauksbee lifted up her voice and raged till bed-time. The doors of the two rooms stood open.

'Polly,' said a voice from the darkness, 'what did that American-heiress-globe-trotter girl say last season when she was tipped out of her 'rickshaw turning a corner? Some absurd adjective that made the man who picked her up explode.'

'"Paltry,"' said Mrs. Mallowe. 'Through her nose—like this—"Ha-ow pahltry!"'

'Exactly,' said the voice. 'Ha-ow pahltry it all is!'

'Which?'

'Everything. Babies, Diphtheria, Mrs. Bent and The Dancing Master, I whooping in a chair, and The Dowd dropping in from the clouds.   I wonder what the motive was—*all* the motives.'

'Um!'

'What do *you* think?'

'Don't ask me.   Go to sleep.

Only a Subaltern

. . . Not only to enforce by command, but to encourage by example the energetic discharge of duty and the steady endurance of the difficulties and privations inseparable from Military Service.—*Bengal Army Regulations.*

THEY made Bobby Wick pass an examination at Sandhurst. He was a gentleman before he was gazetted, so, when the Empress announced that 'Gentleman-Cadet Robert Hanna Wick' was posted as Second Lieutenant to the Tyneside Tail Twisters at Krab Bokhar, he became an officer *and* a gentleman, which is an enviable thing; and there was joy in the house of Wick where Mamma Wick and all the little Wicks fell upon their knees and offered incense to Bobby by virtue of his achievements.

Papa Wick had been a Commissioner in his day, holding authority over three millions of men in the Chota-Buldana Division, building great works for the good of the land, and doing his best to make two blades of grass grow where there was but one before. Of course, nobody knew anything about this in the little English village where he was just 'old Mr. Wick,' and had forgotten that he was a Companion of the Order of the Star of India.

He patted Bobby on the shoulder and said : ' Well done, my boy ! '

There followed, while the uniform was being prepared, an interval of pure delight, during which Bobby took brevet-rank as a ' man ' at the women-swamped tennis-parties and tea-fights of the village, and, I daresay, had his joining-time been extended, would have fallen in love with several girls at once. Little country villages at Home are very full of nice girls, because all the young men come out to India to make their fortunes.

' India,' said Papa Wick, ' is the place. I've had thirty years of it and, begad, I'd like to go back again. When you join the Tail Twisters you'll be among friends, if every one hasn't forgotten Wick of Chota-Buldana, and a lot of people will be kind to you for our sakes. The mother will tell you more about outfit than I can ; but remember this. Stick to your Regiment, Bobby—stick to your Regiment. You'll see men all round you going into the Staff Corps, and doing every possible sort of duty but regimental, and you may be tempted to follow suit. Now so long as you keep within your allowance, and I haven't stinted you there, stick to the Line, the whole Line, and nothing but the Line. Be careful how you back another young fool's bill, and if you fall in love with a woman twenty years older than yourself, don't tell *me* about it, that's all.'

With these counsels, and many others equally valuable, did Papa Wick fortify Bobby ere that

last awful night at Portsmouth when the Officers'
Quarters held more inmates than were provided
for by the Regulations, and the liberty-men of the
ships fell foul of the drafts for India, and the
battle raged from the Dockyard Gates even to the
slums of Longport, while the drabs of Fratton
came down and scratched the faces of the Queen's
Officers.

Bobby Wick, with an ugly bruise on his freckled
nose, a sick and shaky detachment to manoeuvre
inship, and the comfort of fifty scornful females to
attend to, had no time to feel home-sick till the
Malabar reached mid-Channel, when he doubled his
emotions with a little guard-visiting and a great
many other matters.

The Tail Twisters were a most particular
Regiment. Those who knew them least said that
they were eaten up with ' side.' But their reserve
and their internal arrangements generally were
merely protective diplomacy. Some five years
before, the Colonel commanding had looked into
the fourteen fearless eyes of seven plump and
juicy subalterns who had all applied to enter the
Staff Corps, and had asked them why the three
stars should he, a colonel of the Line, command a
dashed nursery for double-dashed bottle-suckers
who put on condemned tin spurs and rode
qualified mokes at the hiatused heads of forsaken
Black Regiments. He was a rude man and a
terrible. Wherefore the remnant took measures
[with the half-butt as an engine of public opinion]
till the rumour went abroad that young men who
used the Tail Twisters as a crutch to the Staff

Corps had many and varied trials to endure.
However, a regiment had just as much right to its
own secrets as a woman.

When Bobby came up from Deolali and took
his place among the Tail Twisters, it was gently
but firmly borne in upon him that the Regiment
was his father and his mother and his indissolubly
wedded wife, and that there was no crime under
the canopy of heaven blacker than that of bringing
shame on the Regiment, which was the best-
shooting, best-drilled, best-set-up, bravest, most
illustrious, and in all respects most desirable
Regiment within the compass of the Seven Seas.
He was taught the legends of the Mess Plate, from
the great grinning Golden Gods that had come out
of the Summer Palace in Pekin to the silver-
mounted markhor-horn snuff-mull presented by
the last C. O. [he who spake to the seven
subalterns]. And every one of those legends told
him of battles fought at long odds, without fear
as without support ; of hospitality catholic as an
Arab's ; of friendships deep as the sea and steady
as the fighting-line ; of honour won by hard roads
for honour's sake ; and of instant and unquestioning
devotion to the Regiment—the Regiment that
claims the lives of all and lives for ever.

More than once, too, he came officially into contact with the Regimental colours, which looked like
the lining of a bricklayer's hat on the end of a
chewed stick. Bobby did not kneel and worship
them, because British subalterns are not constructed
in that manner. Indeed, he condemned them for
their weight at the very moment that they

were filling with awe and other more noble sentiments.

But best of all was the occasion when he moved
with the Tail Twisters in review order at the
breaking of a November day. Allowing for duty-
men and sick, the Regiment was one thousand and
eighty strong, and Bobby belonged to them ; for
was he not a Subaltern of the Line—the whole
Line, and nothing but the Line—as the tramp of
two thousand one hundred and sixty sturdy
ammunition boots attested ? He would not have
changed places with Deighton of the Horse Battery,
whirling by in a pillar of cloud to a chorus of
'Strong right ! Strong left !' or Hogan-Yale of
the White Hussars, leading his squadron for all it
was worth, with the price of horseshoes thrown in ;
or 'Tick' Boileau, trying to live up to his fierce
blue and gold turban while the wasps of the Bengal
Cavalry stretched to a gallop in the wake of the
long, lollopping Walers of the White Hussars.

They fought through the clear cool day, and
Bobby felt a little thrill run down his spine when
he heard the *tinkle-tinkle-tinkle* of the empty
cartridge-cases hopping from the breech-blocks
after the roar of the volleys ; for he knew that he
should live to hear that sound in action. The
review ended in a glorious chase across the plain—
batteries thundering after cavalry to the huge
disgust of the White Hussars, and the Tyneside
Tail Twisters hunting a Sikh Regiment, till the
lean lathy Singhs panted with exhaustion. Bobby
was dusty and dripping long before noon, but his
enthusiasm was merely focused—not diminished.

He returned to sit at the feet of Revere, his
'skipper,' that is to say, the Captain of his Company,
and to be instructed in the dark art and mystery of
managing men, which is a very large part of the
Profession of Arms.

'If you haven't a taste that way,' said Revere
between his puffs of his cheroot, 'you'll never be
able to get the hang of it, but remember, Bobby, 't
isn't the best drill, though drill is nearly everything,
that hauls a Regiment through Hell and out on the
other side. It's the man who knows how to handle
men—goat-men, swine-men, dog-men, and so on.'

'Dormer, for instance,' said Bobby, 'I think he
comes under the head of fool-men. He mopes
like a sick owl.'

'That's where you make your mistake, my son.
Dormer isn't a fool *yet*, but he's a dashed dirty
soldier, and his room corporal makes fun of his
socks before kit-inspection. Dormer, being two-
thirds pure brute, goes into a corner and growls.'

'How do you know?' said Bobby admiringly.

'Because a Company commander has to know
these things—because, if he does *not* know, he may
have crime—ay, murder—brewing under his very
nose and yet not see that it's there. Dormer is
being badgered out of his mind—big as he is—and
he hasn't intellect enough to resent it. He's taken
to quiet boozing, and, Bobby, when the butt of a
room goes on the drink, or takes to moping by
himself, measures are necessary to pull him out of
himself.'

'What measures? 'Man can't run round
coddling his men for ever.'

'No. The men would precious soon show him that he was not wanted. You've got to——'

Here the Colour-Sergeant entered with some papers ; Bobby reflected for a while as Revere looked through the Company forms.

'Does Dormer do anything, Sergeant?' Bobby asked with the air of one continuing an interrupted conversation.

'No, sir. Does 'is dooty like a hortomato,' said the Sergeant, who delighted in long words. 'A dirty soldier and 'e's under full stoppages for new kit. It's covered with scales, sir.'

'Scales? What scales?'

'Fish-scales, sir. 'E's always pokin' in the mud by the river an' a-cleanin' them *muchly*-fish with 'is thumbs.' Revere was still absorbed in the Company papers, and the Sergeant, who was sternly fond of Bobby, continued—''E generally goes down there when 'e's got 'is skinful, beggin' your pardon, sir, an' they *do* say that the more lush—in-*he*-briated 'e is, the more fish 'e catches. They call 'im the Looney Fishmonger in the Comp'ny, sir.'

Revere signed the last paper and the Sergeant retreated.

'It's a filthy amusement,' sighed Bobby to himself. Then aloud to Revere : 'Are you really worried about Dormer?'

'A little. You see he's never mad enough to send to hospital, or drunk enough to run in, but at any minute he may flare up, brooding and sulking as he does. He resents any interest being shown in him, and the only time I took him out shooting he all but shot *me* by accident.'

'I fish,' said Bobby with a wry face. 'I hire a country-boat and go down the river from Thursday to Sunday, and the amiable Dormer goes with me —if you can spare us both.'

'You blazing young fool!' said Revere, but his heart was full of much more pleasant words.

Bobby, the Captain of a *dhoni*, with Private Dormer for mate, dropped down the river on Thursday morning—the Private at the bow, the Subaltern at the helm. The Private glared uneasily at the Subaltern, who respected the reserve of the Private.

After six hours, Dormer paced to the stern, saluted, and said—'Beg y' pardon, sir, but *was* you ever on the Durh'm Canal?'

'No,' said Bobby Wick. 'Come and have some tiffin.'

They ate in silence. As the evening fell, Private Dormer broke forth, speaking to himself—

'Hi was on the Durh'm Canal, jes' such a night, come next week twelve month, a-trailin' *of* my toes in the water.' He smoked and said no more till bedtime.

The witchery of the dawn turned the gray river-reaches to purple, gold, and opal; and it was as though the lumbering *dhoni* crept across the splendours of a new heaven.

Private Dormer popped his head out of his blanket and gazed at the glory below and around.

'Well—damn—my eyes!' said Private Dormer in an awed whisper. 'This 'ere is like a bloomin' gallantry-show!' For the rest of the day he was dumb, but achieved an ensanguined filthiness through the cleaning of big fish.

The boat returned on Saturday evening. Dormer had been struggling with speech since noon. As the lines and luggage were being disembarked, he found tongue.

'Beg y' pardon, sir,' he said, 'but would you—would you min' shakin' 'ands with me, sir?'

'Of course not,' said Bobby, and he shook accordingly. Dormer returned to barracks and Bobby to mess.

'He wanted a little quiet and some fishing, I think,' said Bobby. 'My aunt, but he's a filthy sort of animal! Have you ever seen him clean " them *muchly*-fish with 'is thumbs "?'

'Anyhow,' said Revere three weeks later, 'he's doing his best to keep his things clean.'

When the spring died, Bobby joined in the general scramble for Hill leave, and to his surprise and delight secured three months.

'As good a boy as I want,' said Revere the admiring skipper.

'The best of the batch,' said the Adjutant to the Colonel. 'Keep back that young skrim-shanker Porkiss, sir, and let Revere make him sit up.'

So Bobby departed joyously to Simla Pahar with a tin box of gorgeous raiment.

''Son of Wick—old Wick of Chota-Buldana? Ask him to dinner, dear,' said the aged men.

'What a nice boy!' said the matrons and the maids.

'First-class place, Simla. Oh, ri—ipping!' said

Bobby Wick, and ordered new white cord breeches on the strength of it.

'We're in a bad way,' wrote Revere to Bobby at the end of two months. 'Since you left, the Regiment has taken to fever and is fairly rotten with it—two hundred in hospital, about a hundred in cells—drinking to keep off fever—and the Companies on parade fifteen file strong at the outside. There's rather more sickness in the out-villages than I care for, but then I'm so blistered with prickly-heat that I'm ready to hang myself. What's the yarn about your mashing a Miss Haverley up there? Not serious, I hope? You're over-young to hang millstones round your neck, and the Colonel will turf you out of that in double-quick time if you attempt it.'

It was not the Colonel that brought Bobby out of Simla, but a much-more-to-be-respected Commandant. The sickness in the out-villages spread, the Bazar was put out of bounds, and then came the news that the Tail Twisters must go into camp. The message flashed to the Hill stations.—'Cholera—Leave stopped—Officers recalled.' Alas for the white gloves in the neatly-soldered boxes, the rides and the dances and picnics that were to be, the loves half spoken, and the debts unpaid! Without demur and without question, fast as tonga could fly or pony gallop, back to their Regiments and their Batteries, as though they were hastening to their weddings, fled the subalterns.

Bobby received his orders on returning from a dance at Viceregal Lodge where he had—— But only the Haverley girl knows what Bobby had said, or how many waltzes he had claimed for the next ball. Six in the morning saw Bobby at the Tonga Office in the drenching rain, the whirl of the last waltz still in his ears, and an intoxication due neither to wine nor waltzing in his brain.

'Good man !' shouted Deighton of the Horse Battery through the mist. 'Whar you raise dat tonga ? I'm coming with you. Ow ! But I've a head and a half. *I* didn't sit out all night. They say the Battery's awful bad,' and he hummed dolorously—

> Leave the what at the what's-its-name,
> Leave the flock without shelter,
> Leave the corpse uninterred,
> Leave the bride at the altar !

' My faith !   It'll be more bally corpse than bride, though, this journey. Jump in, Bobby. Get on, *Coachwan !* '

On the Umballa platform waited a detachment of officers discussing the latest news from the stricken cantonment, and it was here that Bobby learned the real condition of the Tail Twisters.

'They went into camp,' said an elderly Major recalled from the whist-tables at Mussoorie to a sickly Native Regiment, 'they went into camp with two hundred and ten sick in carts. Two hundred and ten fever cases only, and the balance looking like so many ghosts with sore eyes. A Madras Regiment could have walked through 'em.'

' But they were as fit as be-damned when I left them !' said Bobby.

' Then you'd better make them as fit as be-damned when you rejoin,' said the Major brutally.

Bobby pressed his forehead against the rain-splashed window-pane as the train lumbered across the sodden Doab, and prayed for the health of the Tyneside Tail Twisters.   Naini Tal had sent down her contingent with all speed ; the lathering ponies of the Dalhousie Road staggered into Pathankot, taxed to the full stretch of their strength ; while from cloudy Darjiling the Calcutta Mail whirled up the last straggler of the little army that was to fight a fight in which was neither medal nor honour for the winning, against an enemy none other than ' the sickness that destroyeth in the noonday.'

And as each man reported himself, he said : ' This is a bad business,' and went about his own forthwith, for every Regiment and Battery in the cantonment was under canvas, the sickness bearing them company.

Bobby fought his way through the rain to the Tail Twisters' temporary mess, and Revere could have fallen on the boy's neck for the joy of seeing that ugly, wholesome phiz once more.

' Keep 'em amused and interested,' said Revere. ' They went on the drink, poor fools, after the first two cases, and there was no improvement. Oh, it's good to have you back, Bobby ! Porkiss is a—never mind.'

Deighton came over from the Artillery camp to attend a dreary mess dinner, and contributed to the general gloom by nearly weeping over the condition of his beloved Battery. Porkiss so far forgot himself as to insinuate that the presence of the officers could do no earthly good, and that the

best thing would be to send the entire Regiment
into hospital and 'let the doctors look after them.'
Porkiss was demoralised with fear, nor was his peace
of mind restored when Revere said coldly : 'Oh!
The sooner *you* go out the better, if that's your
way of thinking. Any public school could send
us fifty *good* men in your place, but it takes time,
time, Porkiss, and money, and a certain amount of
trouble, to make a Regiment. 'S'pose *you're* the
person we go into camp for, eh ? '

Whereupon Porkiss was overtaken with a great
and chilly fear which a drenching in the rain did
not allay, and, two days later, quitted this world for
another where, men do fondly hope, allowances
are made for the weaknesses of the flesh. The
Regimental Sergeant-Major looked wearily across
the Sergeants' Mess tent when the news was announced.

' There goes the worst of them,' he said. 'It'll
take the best, and then, please God, it'll stop.'
The Sergeants were silent till one said : ' It
couldn't be *him !* ' and all knew of whom Travis
was thinking.

Bobby Wick stormed through the tents of his
Company, rallying, rebuking, mildly, as is consistent
with the Regulations, chaffing the faint-hearted ;
hailing the sound into the watery sunlight when
there was a break in the weather, and bidding them
be of good cheer for their trouble was nearly at an
end ; scuttling on his dun pony round the outskirts
of the camp, and heading back men who, with the
innate perversity of British soldiers, were always
wandering into infected villages, or drinking deeply

from rain-flooded marshes ; comforting the panic-stricken with rude speech, and more than once tending the dying who had no friends—the men without 'townies'; organising, with banjos and burnt cork, Sing-songs which should allow the talent of the Regiment full play ; and generally, as he explained, 'playing the giddy garden-goat all round.'

'You're worth half-a-dozen of us, Bobby,' said Revere in a moment of enthusiasm.   'How the devil do you keep it up ?'

Bobby made no answer, but had Revere looked into the breast-pocket of his coat he might have seen there a sheaf of badly-written letters which perhaps accounted for the power that possessed the boy.   A letter came to Bobby every other day. The spelling was not above reproach, but the sentiments must have been most satisfactory, for on receipt Bobby's eyes softened marvellously, and he was wont to fall into a tender abstraction for a while ere, shaking his cropped head, he charged into his work.

By what power he drew after him the hearts of the roughest, and the Tail Twisters counted in their ranks some rough diamonds indeed, was a mystery to both skipper and C. O., who learned from the regimental chaplain that Bobby was considerably more in request in the hospital tents than the Reverend John Emery.

'The men seem fond of you.   Are you in the hospitals much ?' said the Colonel, who did his daily round and ordered the men to get well with a hardness that did not cover his bitter grief.

'A little, sir,' said Bobby.

''Shouldn't go there too often if I were you. They say it's not contagious, but there's no use in running unnecessary risks. We can't afford to have you down, y'know.'

Six days later, it was with the utmost difficulty that the post-runner plashed his way out to the camp with the mail-bags, for the rain was falling in torrents. Bobby received a letter, bore it off to his tent, and, the programme for the next week's Sing-song being satisfactorily disposed of, sat down to answer it. For an hour the unhandy pen toiled over the paper, and where sentiment rose to more than normal tide-level, Bobby Wick stuck out his tongue and breathed heavily. He was not used to letter-writing.

'Beg y' pardon, sir,' said a voice at the tent door ; 'but Dormer's 'orrid bad, sir, an' they've taken him orf, sir.'

'Damn Private Dormer and you too !' said Bobby Wick, running the blotter over the half-finished letter. 'Tell him I'll come in the morning.'

''E's awful bad, sir,' said the voice hesitatingly. There was an undecided squelching of heavy boots.

'Well?' said Bobby impatiently.

'Excusin' 'imself before 'and for takin' the liberty, 'e says it would be a comfort for to assist 'im, sir, if——'

'*Tattoo lao !* Get my pony ! Here, come in out of the rain till I'm ready. What blasted nuisances you are ! That's brandy. Drink some ; you want it. Hang on to my stirrup and tell me if I go too fast.'

Strengthened by a four-finger 'nip' which he swallowed without a wink, the Hospital Orderly kept up with the slipping, mud-stained, and very disgusted pony as it shambled to the hospital tent.

Private Dormer was certainly ' 'orrid bad.' He had all but reached the stage of collapse and was not pleasant to look upon.

'What's this, Dormer?' said Bobby, bending over the man. 'You're not going out this time. You've got to come fishing with me once or twice more yet.'

The blue lips parted and in the ghost of a whisper said,—'Beg y' pardon, sir, disturbin' of you now, but would you min' 'oldin' my 'and, sir?'

Bobby sat on the side of the bed, and the icy cold hand closed on his own like a vice, forcing a lady's ring which was on the little finger deep into the flesh. Bobby set his lips and waited, the water dripping from the hem of his trousers. An hour passed and the grasp of the hand did not relax, nor did the expression of the drawn face change. Bobby with infinite craft lit himself a cheroot with the left hand, his right arm was numbed to the elbow, and resigned himself to a night of pain.

Dawn showed a very white-faced Subaltern sitting on the side of a sick man's cot, and a Doctor in the doorway using language unfit for publication.

'Have you been here all night, you young ass?' said the Doctor.

'There or thereabouts,' said Bobby ruefully. 'He's frozen on to me.'

Dormer's mouth shut with a click. He turned

his head and sighed. The clinging hand opened, and Bobby's arm fell useless at his side.

'He'll do,' said the Doctor quietly. 'It must have been a toss-up all through the night. 'Think you're to be congratulated on this case.'

'Oh, bosh!' said Bobby. 'I thought the man had gone out long ago—only—only I didn't care to take my hand away. Rub my arm down, there's a good chap. What a grip the brute has! I'm chilled to the marrow!' He passed out of the tent shivering.

Private Dormer was allowed to celebrate his repulse of Death by strong waters. Four days later he sat on the side of his cot and said to the patients mildly : 'I'd 'a' liken to 'a' spoken to 'im —so I should.'

But at that time Bobby was reading yet another letter—he had the most persistent correspondent of any man in camp—and was even then about to write that the sickness had abated, and in another week at the outside would be gone. He did not intend to say that the chill of a sick man's hand seemed to have struck into the heart whose capacities for affection he dwelt on at such length. He did intend to enclose the illustrated programme of the forthcoming Sing-song whereof he was not a little proud. He also intended to write on many other matters which do not concern us, and doubtless would have done so but for the slight feverish headache which made him dull and unresponsive at mess.

'You are overdoing it, Bobby,' said his skipper. ''Might give the rest of us credit of doing a little

work.   You go on as if you were the whole Mess
rolled into one.   Take it easy.'

'I will,' said Bobby.   'I'm feeling done up,
somehow.'   Revere looked at him anxiously and
said nothing.

There was a flickering of lanterns about the
camp that night, and a rumour that brought men
out of their cots to the tent doors, a paddling of
the naked feet of doolie-bearers and the rush of a
galloping horse.

'Wot's up?' asked twenty tents; and through
twenty tents ran the answer—'Wick, 'e's down.'

They brought the news to Revere and he
groaned.   'Any one but Bobby and I shouldn't
have cared!   The Sergeant-Major was right.'

'Not going out this journey,' gasped Bobby, as
he was lifted from the doolie.   'Not going out
this journey.'   Then with an air of supreme con-
viction—'I *can't*, you see.'

'Not if I can do anything!' said the Surgeon-
Major, who had hastened over from the mess
where he had been dining.

He and the Regimental Surgeon fought together
with Death for the life of Bobby Wick.   Their
work was interrupted by a hairy apparition in a blue-
gray dressing-gown who stared in horror at the bed
and cried—'Oh, my Gawd!   It can't be *'im!*' until
an indignant Hospital Orderly whisked him away.

If care of man and desire to live could have
done aught, Bobby would have been saved.   As it
was, he made a fight of three days, and the
Surgeon-Major's brow uncreased.   'We'll save
him yet,' he said; and the Surgeon, who, though

he ranked with the Captain, had a very youthful
heart, went out upon the word and pranced joyously in the mud.

'Not going out this journey,' whispered Bobby
Wick gallantly, at the end of the third day.

'Bravo!' said the Surgeon-Major.   'That's
the way to look at it, Bobby.'

As evening fell a gray shade gathered round
Bobby's mouth, and he turned his face to the tent
wall wearily.   The Surgeon-Major frowned.

'I'm awfully tired,' said Bobby, very faintly.
'What's the use of bothering me with medicine ?
I—don't—want—it.   Let me alone.'

The desire for life had departed, and Bobby
was content to drift away on the easy tide of Death.

'It's no good,' said the Surgeon-Major.   'He
doesn't want to live.   He's meeting it, poor
child.'   And he blew his nose.

Half a mile away the regimental band was
playing the overture to the Sing-song, for the men
had been told that Bobby was out of danger.   The
clash of the brass and the wail of the horns reached
Bobby's ears.

> Is there a single joy or pain,
> That I should never kno—ow ?
> You do not love me, 'tis in vain,
> Bid me good-bye and go !

An expression of hopeless irritation crossed the
boy's face, and he tried to shake his head.

The Surgeon-Major bent down—'What is it,
Bobby ?'—'Not that waltz,' muttered Bobby.
'That's our own—our very ownest own. . . .
Mummy dear.'

With this he sank into the stupor that gave place to death early next morning.

Revere, his eyes red at the rims and his nose very white, went into Bobby's tent to write a letter to Papa Wick which should bow the white head of the ex-Commissioner of Chota-Buldana in the keenest sorrow of his life.   Bobby's little store of papers lay in confusion on the table, and among them a half-finished letter.   The last sentence ran: ' So you see, darling, there is really no fear, because as long as I know you care for me and I care for you, nothing can touch me.'

Revere stayed in the tent for an hour.   When he came out his eyes were redder than ever.

.   .   .   .   .

Private Conklin sat on a turned-down bucket, and listened to a not unfamiliar tune.   Private Conklin was a convalescent and should have been tenderly treated.

' Ho! ' said Private Conklin.   ' There's another bloomin' orf'cer da—ed.'

The bucket shot from under him, and his eyes filled with a smithyful of sparks.   A tall man in a blue-gray bedgown was regarding him with deep disfavour.

' You ought to take shame for yourself, Conky! Orf'cer ?—Bloomin' orf'cer ?   I'll learn you to misname the likes of 'im.   Hangel !   *Bloomin'* Hangel!   That's wot 'e is ! '

And the Hospital Orderly was so satisfied with the justice of the punishment that he did not even order Private Dormer back to his cot.

THE PHANTOM 'RICKSHAW

AND OTHER TALES

The Phantom 'Rickshaw

May no ill dreams disturb my rest,
Nor Powers of Darkness me molest.
                                    Evening Hymn.

ONE of the few advantages that India has over
England is a great Knowability. After five years'
service a man is directly or indirectly acquainted
with the two or three hundred Civilians in his
Province, all the Messes of ten or twelve Regiments
and Batteries, and some fifteen hundred other
people of the non-official caste. In ten years his
knowledge should be doubled, and at the end of
twenty he knows, or knows something about,
every Englishman in the Empire, and may travel
anywhere and everywhere without paying hotel-
bills.

Globe-trotters who expect entertainment as a
right, have, even within my memory, blunted this
open-heartedness, but none the less to-day, if you
belong to the Inner Circle and are neither a Bear
nor a Black Sheep, all houses are open to you, and
our small world is very, very kind and helpful.

Rickett of Kamartha stayed with Polder of
Kumaon some fifteen years ago. He meant to

stay two nights, but was knocked down by rheumatic fever, and for six weeks disorganised Polder's establishment, stopped Polder's work, and nearly died in Polder's bedroom. Polder behaves as though he had been placed under eternal obligation by Rickett, and yearly sends the little Ricketts a box of presents and toys. It is the same everywhere. The men who do not take the trouble to conceal from you their opinion that you are an incompetent ass, and the women who blacken your character and misunderstand your wife's amusements, will work themselves to the bone in your behalf if you fall sick or into serious trouble.

Heatherlegh, the Doctor, kept, in addition to his regular practice, a hospital on his private account—an arrangement of loose boxes for Incurables, his friend called it—but it was really a sort of fitting-up shed for craft that had been damaged by stress of weather. The weather in India is often sultry, and since the tale of bricks is always a fixed quantity, and the only liberty allowed is permission to work overtime and get no thanks, men occasionally break down and become as mixed as the metaphors in this sentence.

Heatherlegh is the dearest doctor that ever was, and his invariable prescription to all his patients is, 'Lie low, go slow, and keep cool.' He says that more men are killed by overwork than the importance of this world justifies. He maintains that overwork slew Pansay, who died under his hands about three years ago. He has, of course, the right to speak authoritatively, and he laughs at my theory that there was a crack in Pansay's head and a little bit of the Dark World came through and pressed him to death. 'Pansay went off the handle,' says Heatherlegh, 'after the stimulus of long leave at Home. He may or he may not have behaved like a blackguard to Mrs. Keith-Wessington. My notion is that the work of the Katabundi Settlement ran him off his legs, and that he took to brooding and making much of an ordinary P. & O. flirtation. He certainly was engaged to Miss Mannering, and she certainly broke off the engagement. Then he took a feverish chill and all that nonsense about ghosts developed. Overwork started his illness, kept it alight, and killed him, poor devil. Write him off to the System that uses one man to do the work of two and a half men.'

I do not believe this. I used to sit up with Pansay sometimes when Heatherlegh was called out to patients and I happened to be within claim. The man would make me most unhappy by describing, in a low, even voice, the procession that was always passing at the bottom of his bed. He had a sick man's command of language. When he recovered I suggested that he should write out the whole affair from beginning to end, knowing that ink might assist him to ease his mind.

He was in a high fever while he was writing, and the blood-and-thunder Magazine diction he adopted did not calm him. Two months afterwards he was reported fit for duty, but, in spite of the fact that he was urgently needed to help an undermanned Commission stagger through a deficit, he preferred to die ; vowing at the last that he was hag-ridden. I got his manuscript before he died, and this is his version of the affair, dated 1885, exactly as he wrote it :—

My doctor tells me that I need rest and change of air. It is not improbable that I shall get both ere long—rest that neither the red-coated messenger nor the mid-day gun can break, and change of air far beyond that which any homeward-bound steamer can give me. In the meantime I am resolved to stay where I am ; and, in flat defiance of my doctor's orders, to take all the world into my confidence. You shall learn for yourselves the precise nature of my malady, and shall, too, judge for yourselves whether any man born of woman on this weary earth was ever so tormented as I.

Speaking now as a condemned criminal might speak ere the drop-bolts are drawn, my story, wild and hideously improbable as it may appear, demands at least attention. That it will ever receive credence I utterly disbelieve. Two months ago I should have scouted as mad or drunk the man who had dared tell me the like. Two months ago I was the happiest man in India. To-day, from Peshawar to the sea, there is no one more wretched. My doctor and I are the only two who know this. His explanation is, that my brain, digestion, and eyesight are all slightly affected ; giving rise to my frequent and persistent ' delusions.' Delusions, indeed ! I call him a fool ; but he attends me still with the same

unwearied smile, the same bland professional
manner, the same neatly-trimmed red whiskers,
till I begin to suspect that I am an ungrateful,
evil-tempered invalid. But you shall judge for
yourselves.

Three years ago it was my fortune—my great
misfortune—to sail from Gravesend to Bombay,
on return from long leave, with one Agnes Keith-
Wessington, wife of an officer on the Bombay
side. It does not in the least concern you to
know what manner of woman she was. Be
content with the knowledge that, ere the voyage
had ended, both she and I were desperately and
unreasoningly in love with one another. Heaven
knows that I can make the admission now without
one particle of vanity. In matters of this sort
there is always one who gives and another who
accepts. From the first day of our ill-omened
attachment, I was conscious that Agnes's passion
was a stronger, a more dominant, and—if I may
use the expression—a purer sentiment than mine.
Whether she recognised the fact then, I do not
know. Afterwards it was bitterly plain to both
of us.

Arrived at Bombay in the spring of the year,
we went our respective ways, to meet no more for
the next three or four months, when my leave and
her love took us both to Simla. There we spent
the season together ; and there my fire of straw
burnt itself out to a pitiful end with the closing
year. I attempt no excuse. I make no apology.
Mrs. Wessington had given up much for my
sake, and was prepared to give up all. From

my own lips, in August 1882, she learnt that I was sick of her presence, tired of her company, and weary of the sound of her voice.   Ninety-nine women out of a hundred would have wearied of me as I wearied of them ; seventy-five of that number would have promptly avenged themselves by active and obtrusive flirtation with other men. Mrs. Wessington was the hundredth.   On her neither my openly - expressed aversion nor the cutting brutalities with which I garnished our interviews had the least effect.

'Jack, darling !' was her one eternal cuck'oo cry : 'I'm sure it's all a mistake—a hideous mistake ; and we'll be good friends again some day. *Please* forgive me, Jack, dear.'

I was the offender, and I knew it.   That know-ledge transformed my pity into passive endurance, and, eventually, into blind hate—the same instinct, I suppose, which prompts a man to savagely stamp on the spider he has but half killed.   And with this hate in my bosom the season of 1882 came to an end.

Next year we met again at Simla—she with her monotonous face and timid attempts at reconcilia-tion, and I with loathing of her in every fibre of my frame.   Several times I could not avoid meet-ing her alone ; and on each occasion her words were identically the same.   Still the unreasoning wail that it was all a 'mistake' ; and still the hope of eventually 'making friends.'   I might have seen, had I cared to look, that that hope only was keeping her alive.   She grew more wan and thin month by month.   You will agree with me, at least, that such conduct would have driven any one to despair. It was uncalled for ; childish ; unwomanly. I maintain that she was much to blame. And again, sometimes, in the black, fever-stricken night-watches, I have begun to think that I might have been a little kinder to her. But that really *is* a 'delusion.' I could not have continued pretending to love her when I didn't ; could I ? It would have been unfair to us both.

Last year we met again—on the same terms as before. The same weary appeals, and the same curt answers from my lips. At least I would make her see how wholly wrong and hopeless were her attempts at resuming the old relationship. As the season wore on, we fell apart—that is to say, she found it difficult to meet me, for I had other and more absorbing interests to attend to. When I think it over quietly in my sick-room, the season of 1884 seems a confused nightmare wherein light and shade were fantastically intermingled : my courtship of little Kitty Mannering ; my hopes, doubts, and fears ; our long rides together ; my trembling avowal of attachment ; her reply ; and now and again a vision of a white face flitting by in the 'rickshaw with the black and white liveries I once watched for so earnestly ; the wave of Mrs. Wessington's gloved hand ; and, when she met me alone, which was but seldom, the irksome monotony of her appeal. I loved Kitty Mannering ; honestly, heartily loved her, and with my love for her grew my hatred for Agnes. In August Kitty and I were engaged. The next day I met those accursed 'magpie' *jhampanies* at the back of Jakko, and, moved by some passing sentiment of pity, stopped to tell Mrs. Wessington everything. She knew it already.

'So I hear you're engaged, Jack, dear.' Then, without a moment's pause : 'I'm sure it's all a mistake—a hideous mistake. We shall be as good friends some day, Jack, as we ever were.'

My answer might have made even a man wince. It cut the dying woman before me like the blow of a whip. 'Please forgive me, Jack ; I didn't mean to make you angry ; but it's true, it's true ! '

And Mrs. Wessington broke down completely. I turned away and left her to finish her journey in peace, feeling, but only for a moment or two, that I had been an unutterably mean hound. I looked back, and saw that she had turned her 'rickshaw with the idea, I suppose, of overtaking me.

The scene and its surroundings were photographed on my memory. The rain-swept sky (we were at the end of the wet weather), the sodden, dingy pines, the muddy road, and the black powder-riven cliffs formed a gloomy background against which the black and white liveries of the *jhampanies*, the yellow-panelled 'rickshaw, and Mrs. Wessington's down-bowed golden head stood out clearly. She was holding her handkerchief in her left hand and was leaning back exhausted against the 'rickshaw cushions. I turned my horse up a bypath near the Sanjowlie Reservoir and literally ran away. Once I fancied I heard a faint call of 'Jack ! ' This may have been imagination. I never stopped to verify it. Ten minutes later I came across Kitty on horseback ; and, in the delight of a long ride with her, forgot all about the interview.

A week later Mrs. Wessington died, and the inexpressible burden of her existence was removed from my life. I went Plainsward perfectly happy. Before three months were over I had forgotten all about her, except that at times the discovery of some of her old letters reminded me unpleasantly of our bygone relationship. By January I had disinterred what was left of our correspondence from among my scattered belongings and had burnt it. At the beginning of April of this year, 1885, I was at Simla—semi-deserted Simla—once more, and was deep in lover's talks and walks with Kitty. It was decided that we should be married at the end of June. You will understand, therefore, that, loving Kitty as I did, I am not saying too much when I pronounce myself to have been, at that time, the happiest man in India.

Fourteen delightful days passed almost before I noticed their flight. Then, aroused to the sense of what was proper among mortals circumstanced as we were, I pointed out to Kitty that an engagement ring was the outward and visible sign of her dignity as an engaged girl ; and that she must forthwith come to Hamilton's to be measured for one. Up to that moment, I give you my word, we had completely forgotten so trivial a matter. To Hamilton's we accordingly went on the 15th of April 1885. Remember that—whatever my doctor may say to the contrary—I was then in perfect health, enjoying a well-balanced mind and

an *absolutely* tranquil spirit.   Kitty and I entered
Hamilton's shop together, and there, regardless of
the order of affairs, I measured Kitty for the ring
in the presence of the amused assistant.   The ring
was a sapphire with two diamonds.   We then rode
out down the slope that leads to the Combermere
Bridge and Peliti's shop.

While my Waler was cautiously feeling his way
over the loose shale, and Kitty was laughing and
chattering at my side,—while all Simla, that is to
say as much of it as had then come from the
Plains, was grouped round the Reading-room and
Peliti's verandah,—I was aware that some one,
apparently at a vast distance, was calling me by
my Christian name.   It struck me that I had
heard the voice before, but when and where I
could not at once determine.   In the short space
it took to cover the road between the path from
Hamilton's shop and the first plank of the
Combermere Bridge I had thought over half-a-
dozen people who might have committed such a
solecism, and had eventually decided that it must
have been some singing in my ears.   Immediately
opposite Peliti's shop my eye was arrested by the
sight of four *jhampanies* in 'magpie' livery, pulling a yellow-panelled, cheap, bazar 'rickshaw.   In
a moment my mind flew back to the previous
season and Mrs. Wessington with a sense of irritation and disgust.   Was it not enough that the
woman was dead and done with, without her
black and white servitors reappearing to spoil the
day's happiness?   Whoever employed them now
I thought I would call upon, and ask as a personal

favour to change her *jhampanies'* livery. I would hire the men myself, and, if necessary, buy their coats from off their backs. It is impossible to say here what a flood of undesirable memories their presence evoked.

'Kitty,' I cried, 'there are poor Mrs. Wessington's *jhampanies* turned up again! I wonder who has them now?'

Kitty had known Mrs. Wessington slightly last season, and had always been interested in the sickly woman.

'What? Where?' she asked. 'I can't see them anywhere.'

Even as she spoke, her horse, swerving from a laden mule, threw himself directly in front of the advancing 'rickshaw. I had scarcely time to utter a word of warning when, to my unutterable horror, horse and rider passed *through* men and carriage as if they had been thin air.

'What's the matter?' cried Kitty; 'what made you call out so foolishly, Jack? If I *am* engaged I don't want all creation to know about it. There was lots of space between the mule and the verandah; and, if you think I can't ride—— There!'

Whereupon wilful Kitty set off, her dainty little head in the air, at a hand-gallop in the direction of the Band-stand; fully expecting, as she herself afterwards told me, that I should follow her. What was the matter? Nothing indeed. Either that I was mad or drunk, or that Simla was haunted with devils. I reined in my impatient cob, and turned round. The 'rickshaw had turned too, and now stood immediately facing me, near the left railing of the Combermere Bridge.

'Jack! Jack, darling!' (There was no mistake about the words this time : they rang through my brain as if they had been shouted in my ear.) 'It's some hideous mistake, I'm sure. *Please* forgive me, Jack, and let's be friends again.'

The 'rickshaw-hood had fallen back, and inside, as I hope and pray daily for the death I dread by night, sat Mrs. Keith-Wessington, handkerchief in hand, and golden head bowed on her breast.

How long I stared motionless I do not know. Finally, I was aroused by my syce taking the Waler's bridle and asking whether I was ill. From the horrible to the commonplace is but a step. I tumbled off my horse and dashed, half fainting, into Peliti's for a glass of cherry-brandy. There two or three couples were gathered round the coffee-tables discussing the gossip of the day. Their trivialities were more comforting to me just then than the consolations of religion could have been. I plunged into the midst of the conversation at once ; chatted, laughed, and jested with a face (when I caught a glimpse of it in a mirror) as white and drawn as that of a corpse. Three or four men noticed my condition ; and, evidently setting it down to the results of over-many pegs, charitably endeavoured to draw me apart from the rest of the loungers. But I refused to be led away. I wanted the company of my kind—as a child rushes into the midst of the dinner-party after a fright in the dark. I must have talked for about ten minutes or so, though it seemed an eternity to me, when I heard Kitty's clear voice outside inquiring for me. In another minute she had entered the shop, prepared to upbraid me for failing so signally in my duties. Something in my face stopped her.

'Why, Jack,' she cried, 'what *have* you been doing? What *has* happened? Are you ill?' Thus driven into a direct lie, I said that the sun had been a little too much for me. It was close upon five o'clock of a cloudy April afternoon, and the sun had been hidden all day. I saw my mistake as soon as the words were out of my mouth; attempted to recover it; blundered hopelessly, and followed Kitty in a regal rage out of doors, amid the smiles of my acquaintances. I made some excuse (I have forgotten what) on the score of my feeling faint; and cantered away to my hotel, leaving Kitty to finish the ride by herself.

In my room I sat down and tried calmly to reason out the matter. Here was I, Theobald Jack Pansay, a well-educated Bengal Civilian in the year of grace 1885, presumably sane, certainly healthy, driven in terror from my sweetheart's side by the apparition of a woman who had been dead and buried eight months ago. These were facts that I could not blink. Nothing was farther from my thought than any memory of Mrs. Wessington when Kitty and I left Hamilton's shop. Nothing was more utterly commonplace than the stretch of wall opposite Peliti's. It was broad daylight. The road was full of people; and yet here, look you, in defiance of every law of probability, in direct outrage of Nature's ordinance, there had appeared to me a face from the grave.

Kitty's Arab had gone *through* the 'rickshaw : so that my first hope that some woman marvellously like Mrs. Wessington had hired the carriage and the coolies with their old livery was lost. Again and again I went round this treadmill of thought ; and again and again gave up baffled and in despair. The voice was as inexplicable as the apparition. I had originally some wild notion of confiding it all to Kitty ; of begging her to marry me at once, and in her arms defying the ghostly occupant of the 'rickshaw. ' After all,' I argued, ' the presence of the 'rickshaw is in itself enough to prove the existence of a spectral illusion. One may see ghosts of men and women, but surely never coolies and carriages. The whole thing is absurd. Fancy the ghost of a hillman ! '

Next morning I sent a penitent note to Kitty, imploring her to overlook my strange conduct of the previous afternoon. My Divinity was still very wroth, and a personal apology was necessary. I explained, with a fluency born of night - long pondering over a falsehood, that I had been attacked with a sudden palpitation of the heart—the result of indigestion. This eminently practical solution had its effect ; and Kitty and I rode out that afternoon with the shadow of my first lie dividing us.

Nothing would please her save a canter round Jakko. With my nerves still unstrung from the previous night I feebly protested against the notion, suggesting Observatory Hill, Jutogh, the Boileaugunge road—anything rather than the Jakko round. Kitty was angry and a little hurt; so I yielded from fear of provoking further misunderstanding, and we set out together towards Chota Simla. We walked a greater part of the way, and, according to our custom, cantered from a mile or so below the Convent to the stretch of level road by the Sanjowlie Reservoir. The wretched horses appeared to fly, and my heart beat quicker and quicker as we neared the crest of the ascent. My mind had been full of Mrs. Wessington all the afternoon; and every inch of the Jakko road bore witness to our old-time walks and talks. The boulders were full of it; the pines sang it aloud overhead; the rain-fed torrents giggled and chuckled unseen over the shameful story; and the wind in my ears chanted the iniquity aloud.

As a fitting climax, in the middle of the level men call the Ladies' Mile the Horror was awaiting me. No other 'rickshaw was in sight—only the four black and white *jhampanies*, the yellow-panelled carriage, and the golden head of the woman within—all apparently just as I had left them eight months and one fortnight ago! For an instant I fancied that Kitty *must* see what I saw—we were so marvellously sympathetic in all things. Her next words undeceived me—'Not a soul in sight! Come along, Jack, and I'll race you to the Reservoir buildings!' Her wiry little Arab was off like a bird, my Waler following close behind, and in this order we dashed under the cliffs. Half a minute brought us within fifty yards of the 'rickshaw. I pulled my Waler and

fell back a little.   The 'rickshaw was directly in
the middle of the road ; and once more the Arab
passed through it, my horse following.   'Jack !
Jack dear !   *Please* forgive me,' rang with a wail
in my ears, and, after an interval : 'It's all a
mistake, a hideous mistake ! '

I spurred my horse like a man possessed.
When I turned my head at the Reservoir works
the black and white liveries were still waiting—
patiently waiting—under the gray hillside, and the
wind brought me a mocking echo of the words I
had just heard.   Kitty bantered me a good deal on
my silence throughout the remainder of the ride.
I had been talking up till then wildly and at
random.   To save my life I could not speak afterwards naturally, and from Sanjowlie to the Church
wisely held my tongue.

I was to dine with the Mannerings that night,
and had barely time to canter home to dress.   On
the road to Elysium Hill I overheard two men
talking together in the dusk.—'It's a curious
thing,' said one, 'how completely all trace of it
disappeared.   You know my wife was insanely
fond of the woman ('never could see anything in
her myself), and wanted me to pick up her old
'rickshaw and coolies if they were to be got for
love or money.   Morbid sort of fancy I call it ;
but I've got to do what the *Memsahib* tells me.
Would you believe that the man she hired it from
tells me that all four of the men—they were
brothers—died of cholera on the way to Hardwar,
poor devils ; and the 'rickshaw has been broken
up by the man himself.   'Told me he never used a

dead *Memsahib's* 'rickshaw.   'Spoilt his luck.
Queer notion, wasn't it ?   Fancy poor little Mrs.
Wessington spoiling any one's luck except her
own !'   I laughed aloud at this point ; and my
laugh jarred on me as I uttered it.   So there *were*
ghosts of 'rickshaws after all, and ghostly employ-
ments in the other world !   How much did Mrs.
Wessington give her men ?   What were their
hours ?   Where did they go ?

And for visible answer to my last question I
saw the infernal Thing blocking my path in the
twilight.   The dead travel fast, and by short cuts
unknown to ordinary coolies.   I laughed aloud a
second time and checked my laughter suddenly,
for I was afraid I was going mad.   Mad to a
certain extent I must have been, for I recollect that
I reined in my horse at the head of the 'rickshaw,
and politely wished Mrs. Wessington 'Good-
evening.'   Her answer was one I knew only too
well.   I listened to the end ; and replied that I
had heard it all before, but should be delighted if
she had anything further to say.   Some malignant
devil stronger than I must have entered into me
that evening, for I have a dim recollection of
talking the commonplaces of the day for five
minutes to the Thing in front of me.

' Mad as a hatter, poor devil—or drunk.   Max,
try and get him to come home.'

Surely *that* was not Mrs. Wessington's voice !
The two men had overheard me speaking to the
empty air, and had returned to look after me.
They were very kind and considerate, and from
their words evidently gathered that I was extremely

drunk.   I thanked them confusedly and cantered
away to my hotel, there changed, and arrived at
the Mannerings' ten minutes late.   I pleaded the
darkness of the night as an excuse ; was rebuked
by Kitty for my unlover-like tardiness ; and sat
down.

The conversation had already become general ;
and, under cover of it, I was addressing some tender
small talk to my sweetheart when I was aware that
at the farther end of the table a short, red-
whiskered man was describing, with much broidery,
his encounter with a mad unknown that evening.

A few sentences convinced me that he was
repeating the incident of half an hour ago.   In the
middle of the story he looked round for applause,
as professional story-tellers do, caught my eye, and
straightway collapsed.   There was a moment's
awkward silence, and the red-whiskered man
muttered something to the effect that he had 'forgotten the rest,' thereby sacrificing a reputation as
a good story-teller which he had built up for six
seasons past.   I blessed him from the bottom of
my heart, and—went on with my fish.

In the fulness of time that dinner came to an
end ; and with genuine regret I tore myself away
from Kitty—as certain as I was of my own
existence that It would be waiting for me outside
the door.   The red-whiskered man, who had been
introduced to me as Dr. Heatherlegh of Simla,
volunteered to bear me company as far as our roads
lay together.   I accepted his offer with gratitude.

My instinct had not deceived me.   It lay in
readiness in the Mall, and, in what seemed devilish

mockery of our ways, with a lighted head-lamp. The red-whiskered man went to the point at once, in a manner that showed he had been thinking over it all dinner-time.

' I say, Pansay, what the deuce was the matter with you this evening on the Elysium Road? ' The suddenness of the question wrenched an answer from me before I was aware.

' That ! ' said I, pointing to It.

' *That* may be either D. T. or Eyes for aught I know. Now you don't liquor. I saw as much at dinner, so it can't be D. T. There's nothing whatever where you're pointing, though you're sweating and trembling with fright like a scared pony. Therefore, I conclude that it's Eyes. And I ought to understand all about them. Come along home with me. I'm on the Blessington lower road.'

To my intense delight the 'rickshaw, instead of waiting for us kept about twenty yards ahead—and this, too, whether we walked, trotted, or cantered. In the course of that long night ride I had told my companion almost as much as I have told you here.

' Well, you've spoilt one of the best tales I've ever laid tongue to,' said he, ' but I'll forgive you for the sake of what you've gone through. Now come home and do what I tell you ; and when I've cured you, young man, let this be a lesson to you to steer clear of women and indigestible food till the day of your death.'

The 'rickshaw kept steady in front ; and my red-whiskered friend seemed to derive great pleasure from my account of its exact whereabouts.

'Eyes, Pansay—all Eyes, Brain, and Stomach.
And the greatest of these three is Stomach. You've
too much conceited Brain, too little Stomach, and
thoroughly unhealthy Eyes. Get your Stomach
straight and the rest follows. And all that's
French for a liver pill. I'll take sole medical
charge of you from this hour! for you're too
interesting a phenomenon to be passed over.'

By this time we were deep in the shadow of the
Blessington lower road, and the 'rickshaw came to
a dead stop under a pine-clad, overhanging shale
cliff. Instinctively I halted too, giving my reason.
Heatherlegh rapped out an oath.

'Now, if you think I'm going to spend a cold
night on the hillside for the sake of a Stomach-
cum-Brain-*cum*-Eye illusion—— Lord, ha' mercy!
What's that?'

There was a muffled report, a blinding smother
of dust just in front of us, a crack, the noise of
rent boughs, and about ten yards of the cliff-side—
pines, undergrowth, and all—slid down into the
road below, completely blocking it up. The up-
rooted trees swayed and tottered for a moment
like drunken giants in the gloom, and then fell
prone among their fellows with a thunderous crash.
Our two horses stood motionless and sweating with
fear. As soon as the rattle of falling earth and
stone had subsided, my companion muttered:
'Man, if we'd gone forward we should have been
ten feet deep in our graves by now. "There are
more things in heaven and earth". . . Come
home, Pansay, and thank God. I want a peg
badly.'

We retraced our way over the Church Ridge, and I arrived at Dr. Heatherlegh's house shortly after midnight.

His attempts towards my cure commenced almost immediately, and for a week I never left his sight. Many a time in the course of that week did I bless the good-fortune which had thrown me in contact with Simla's best and kindest doctor. Day by day my spirits grew lighter and more equable. Day by day, too, I became more and more inclined to fall in with Heatherlegh's 'spectral illusion' theory, implicating eyes, brain, and stomach. I wrote to Kitty, telling her that a slight sprain caused by a fall from my horse kept me indoors for a few days ; and that I should be recovered before she had time to regret my absence.

Heatherlegh's treatment was simple to a degree. It consisted of liver pills, cold-water baths, and strong exercise, taken in the dusk or at early dawn —for, as he sagely observed : 'A man with a sprained ankle doesn't walk a dozen miles a day, and your young woman might be wondering if she saw you.'

At the end of the week, after much examination of pupil and pulse, and strict injunctions as to diet and pedestrianism, Heatherlegh dismissed me as brusquely as he had taken charge of me. Here is his parting benediction : 'Man, I certify to your mental cure, and that's as much as to say I've cured most of your bodily ailments. Now, get your traps out of this as soon as you can ; and be off to make love to Miss Kitty.'

I was endeavouring to express my thanks for his kindness. He cut me short.

'Don't think I did this because I like you. I gather that you've behaved like a blackguard all through. But, all the same, you're a phenomenon, and as queer a phenomenon as you are a blackguard. No!'—checking me a second time—'not a rupee, please. Go out and see if you can find the eyes-brain-and-stomach business again. I'll give you a lakh for each time you see it.'

Half an hour later I was in the Mannerings' drawing-room with Kitty—drunk with the intoxication of present happiness and the foreknowledge that I should never more be troubled with Its hideous presence. Strong in the sense of my new-found security, I proposed a ride at once ; and, by preference, a canter round Jakko.

Never had I felt so well, so overladen with vitality and mere animal spirits, as I did on the afternoon of the 30th of April. Kitty was delighted at the change in my appearance, and complimented me on it in her delightfully frank and outspoken manner. We left the Mannerings' house together, laughing and talking, and cantered along the Chota Simla road as of old.

I was in haste to reach the Sanjowlie Reservoir and there make my assurance doubly sure. The horses did their best, but seemed all too slow to my impatient mind. Kitty was astonished at my boisterousness. 'Why, Jack!' she cried at last, 'you are behaving like a child. What are you doing?'

We were just below the Convent, and from

sheer wantonness I was making my Waler plunge and curvet across the road as I tickled it with the loop of my riding-whip.

'Doing?' I answered; 'nothing, dear. That's just it. If you'd been doing nothing for a week except lie up, you'd be as riotous as I.

> 'Singing and murmuring in your feastful mirth,
> Joying to feel yourself alive;
> Lord over Nature, Lord of the visible Earth,
> Lord of the senses five.'

My quotation was hardly out of my lips before we had rounded the corner above the Convent, and a few yards farther on could see across to Sanjowlie. In the centre of the level road stood the black and white liveries, the yellow-panelled 'rickshaw, and Mrs. Keith-Wessington. I pulled up, looked, rubbed my eyes, and, I believe, must have said something. The next thing I knew was that I was lying face downward on the road, with Kitty kneeling above me in tears.

'Has it gone, child!' I gasped. Kitty only wept more bitterly.

'Has what gone, Jack dear? what does it all mean? There must be a mistake somewhere, Jack. A hideous mistake.' Her last words brought me to my feet—mad—raving for the time being.

'Yes, there *is* a mistake somewhere,' I repeated, 'a hideous mistake. Come and look at It.'

I have an indistinct idea that I dragged Kitty by the wrist along the road up to where It stood, and implored her for pity's sake to speak to It; to tell It that we were betrothed; that neither Death nor Hell could break the tie between us: and

Kitty only knows how much more to the same effect. Now and again I appealed passionately to the Terror in the 'rickshaw to bear witness to all I had said, and to release me from a torture that was killing me. As I talked I suppose I must have told Kitty of my old relations with Mrs. Wessington, for I saw her listen intently with white face and blazing eyes.

'Thank you, Mr. Pansay,' she said, 'that's *quite* enough. *Syce ghora láo.*'

The syces, impassive as Orientals always are, had come up with the recaptured horses; and as Kitty sprang into her saddle I caught hold of her bridle, entreating her to hear me out and forgive. My answer was the cut of her riding-whip across my face from mouth to eye, and a word or two of farewell that even now I cannot write down. So I judged, and judged rightly, that Kitty knew all; and I staggered back to the side of the 'rickshaw. My face was cut and bleeding, and the blow of the riding-whip had raised a livid blue wheal on it. I had no self-respect. Just then, Heatherlegh, who must have been following Kitty and me at a distance, cantered up.

'Doctor,' I said, pointing to my face, 'here's Miss Mannering's signature to my order of dismissal and——I'll thank you for that lakh as soon as convenient.'

Heatherlegh's face, even in my abject misery, moved me to laughter.

'I'll stake my professional reputation——' he began.

'Don't be a fool,' I whispered. 'I've lost

my life's happiness and you'd better take me home.'

As I spoke the 'rickshaw was gone. Then I lost all knowledge of what was passing. The crest of Jakko seemed to heave and roll like the crest of a cloud and fall in upon me.

Seven days later (on the 7th of May, that is to say) I was aware that I was lying in Heatherlegh's room as weak as a little child. Heatherlegh was watching me intently from behind the papers on his writing-table. His first words were not encouraging ; but I was too far spent to be much moved by them.

'Here's Miss Kitty has sent back your letters. You corresponded a good deal, you young people. Here's a packet that looks like a ring, and a cheerful sort of a note from Mannering Papa, which I've taken the liberty of reading and burning. The old gentleman's not pleased with you.'

'And Kitty ?' I asked dully.

'Rather more drawn than her father from what she says. By the same token you must have been letting out any number of queer reminiscences just before I met you. 'Says that a man who would have behaved to a woman as you did to Mrs. Wessington ought to kill himself out of sheer pity for his kind. She's a hot-headed little virago, your mash. 'Will have it too that you were suffering from D. T. when that row on the Jakko road turned up. 'Says she'll die before she ever speaks to you again.'

I groaned and turned over on the other side.

'Now you've got your choice, my friend. This engagement has to be broken off; and the Mannerings don't want to be too hard on you. Was it broken through D. T. or epileptic fits? Sorry I can't offer you a better exchange unless you'd prefer hereditary insanity. Say the word and I'll tell 'em it's fits. All Simla knows about that scene on the Ladies' Mile. Come! I'll give you five minutes to think over it.'

During those five minutes I believe that I explored thoroughly the lowest circles of the Inferno which it is permitted man to tread on earth. And at the same time I myself was watching myself faltering through the dark labyrinths of doubt, misery, and utter despair. I wondered, as Heatherlegh in his chair might have wondered, which dreadful alternative I should adopt. Presently I heard myself answering in a voice that I hardly recognised—

'They're confoundedly particular about morality in these parts. Give 'em fits, Heatherlegh, and my love. Now let me sleep a bit longer.'

Then my two selves joined, and it was only I (half-crazed, devil-driven I) that tossed in my bed tracing step by step the history of the past month.

'But I am in Simla,' I kept repeating to myself. 'I, Jack Pansay, am in Simla, and there are no ghosts here. It's unreasonable of that woman to pretend there are. Why couldn't Agnes have left me alone? I never did her any harm. It might just as well have been me as Agnes. Only I'd never have come back on purpose to kill *her*. Why can't I be left alone—left alone and happy?'

It was high noon when I first awoke; and the sun was low in the sky before I slept—slept as the tortured criminal sleeps on his rack, too worn to feel further pain.

Next day I could not leave my bed. Heatherlegh told me in the morning that he had received an answer from Mr. Mannering, and that, thanks to his (Heatherlegh's) friendly offices, the story of my affliction had travelled through the length and breadth of Simla, where I was on all sides much pitied.

'And that's rather more than you deserve,' he concluded pleasantly, 'though the Lord knows you've been going through a pretty severe mill. Never mind; we'll cure you yet, you perverse phenomenon.'

I declined firmly to be cured. 'You've been much too good to me already, old man,' said I; 'but I don't think I need trouble you further.'

In my heart I knew that nothing Heatherlegh could do would lighten the burden that had been laid upon me.

With that knowledge came also a sense of hopeless, impotent rebellion against the unreasonableness of it all. There were scores of men no better than I whose punishments had at least been reserved for another world; and I felt that it was bitterly, cruelly unfair that I alone should have been singled out for so hideous a fate. This mood would in time give place to another where it seemed that the 'rickshaw and I were the only realities in a world of shadows; that Kitty was a ghost; that Mannering, Heatherlegh, and all the

other men and women I knew were all ghosts ;
and the great gray hills themselves but vain
shadows devised to torture me.   From mood to
mood I tossed backwards and forwards for seven
weary days ; my body growing daily stronger and
stronger, until the bedroom looking-glass told me
that I had returned to everyday life, and was
as other men once more.   Curiously enough my
face showed no signs of the struggle I had gone
through.   It was pale indeed, but as expressionless
and commonplace as ever.   I had expected some
permanent alteration — visible evidence of the
disease that was eating me away.   I found nothing.

On the 15th of May I left Heatherlegh's house
at eleven o'clock in the morning ; and the instinct
of the bachelor drove me to the Club.   There I
found that every man knew my story as told by
Heatherlegh, and was, in clumsy fashion, abnormally
kind and attentive.   Nevertheless I recognised that
for the rest of my natural life I should be among
but not of my fellows ; and I envied very bitterly
indeed the laughing coolies on the Mall below.   I
lunched at the Club, and at four o'clock wandered
aimlessly down the Mall in the vague hope of meeting Kitty.   Close to the Band-stand the black and
white liveries joined me ; and I heard Mrs. Wessington's old appeal at my side.   I had been expecting
this ever since I came out, and was only surprised
at her delay.   The phantom 'rickshaw and I went
side by side along the Chota Simla road in silence.
Close to the bazar, Kitty and a man on horseback
overtook and passed us.   For any sign she gave
I might have been a dog in the road.   She did not

even pay me the compliment of quickening her pace, though the rainy afternoon had served for an excuse.

So Kitty and her companion, and I and my ghostly Light-o'-Love, crept round Jakko in couples. The road was streaming with water; the pines dripped like roof-pipes on the rocks below, and the air was full of fine driving rain. Two or three times I found myself saying to myself almost aloud : ' I'm Jack Pansay on leave at Simla —*at Simla!* Everyday, ordinary Simla. I mustn't forget that—I mustn't forget that.' Then I would try to recollect some of the gossip I had heard at the Club : the prices of So-and-So's horses—anything, in fact, that related to the workaday Anglo-Indian world I knew so well. I even repeated the multiplication-table rapidly to myself, to make quite sure that I was not taking leave of my senses. It gave me much comfort, and must have prevented my hearing Mrs. Wessington for a time.

Once more I wearily climbed the Convent slope and entered the level road. Here Kitty and the man started off at a canter, and I was left alone with Mrs. Wessington. ' Agnes,' said I, ' will you put back your hood and tell me what it all means?' The hood dropped noiselessly, and I was face to face with my dead and buried mistress. She was wearing the dress in which I had last seen her alive ; carried the same tiny handkerchief in her right hand, and the same card-case in her left. (A woman eight months dead with a card-case !) I had to pin myself down to the multiplication-table, and to set both hands on the stone parapet of the road, to assure myself that that at least was real.

'Agnes,' I repeated, 'for pity's sake tell me what it all means.' Mrs. Wessington leaned forward, with that odd, quick turn of the head I used to know so well, and spoke.

If my story had not already so madly overleaped the bounds of all human belief I should apologise to you now. As I know that no one—no, not even Kitty, for whom it is written as some sort of justification of my conduct—will believe me, I will go on. Mrs. Wessington spoke, and I walked with her from the Sanjowlie road to the turning below the Commander-in-Chief's house as I might walk by the side of any living woman's 'rickshaw, deep in conversation. The second and most tormenting of my moods of sickness had suddenly laid hold upon me, and, like the Prince in Tennyson's poem, 'I seemed to move amid a world of ghosts.' There had been a garden-party at the Commander-in-Chief's, and we two joined the crowd of homeward-bound folk. As I saw them it seemed that *they* were the shadows—impalpable fantastic shadows—that divided for Mrs. Wessington's 'rickshaw to pass through. What we said during the course of that weird interview I cannot—indeed, I dare not —tell. Heatherlegh's comment would have been a short laugh and a remark that I had been 'mashing a brain-eye-and-stomach chimera.' It was a ghastly and yet in some indefinable way a marvellously dear experience. Could it be possible, I wondered, that I was in this life to woo a second time the woman I had killed by my own neglect and cruelty?

I met Kitty on the homeward road—a shadow among shadows.

If I were to describe all the incidents of the next fortnight in their order, my story would never come to an end, and your patience would be exhausted. Morning after morning and evening after evening the ghostly 'rickshaw and I used to wander through Simla together. Wherever I went there the four black and white liveries followed me and bore me company to and from my hotel. At the Theatre I found them amid the crowd of yelling *jhampanies*; outside the Club verandah, after a long evening of whist; at the Birthday Ball, waiting patiently for my reappearance; and in broad daylight when I went calling. Save that it cast no shadow, the 'rickshaw was in every respect as real to look upon as one of wood and iron. More than once, indeed, I have had to check myself from warning some hard-riding friend against cantering over it. More than once I have walked down the Mall deep in conversation with Mrs. Wessington, to the unspeakable amazement of the passers-by.

Before I had been out and about a week I learned that the 'fit' theory had been discarded in favour of insanity. However, I made no change in my mode of life. I called, rode, and dined out as freely as ever. I had a passion for the society of my kind which I had never felt before; I hungered to be among the realities of life; and at the same time I felt vaguely unhappy when I had been separated too long from my ghostly companion. It would be almost impossible to describe my varying moods from the 15th of May up to to-day.

The presence of the 'rickshaw filled me by turns with horror, blind fear, a dim sort of pleasure, and utter despair. I dared not leave Simla; and I knew that my stay there was killing me. I knew, moreover, that it was my destiny to die slowly and a little every day. My only anxiety was to get the penance over as quietly as might be. Alternately I hungered for a sight of Kitty, and watched her outrageous flirtations with my successor—to speak more accurately, my successors—with amused interest. She was as much out of my life as I was out of hers. By day I wandered with Mrs. Wessington almost content. By night I implored Heaven to let me return to the world as I used to know it. Above all these varying moods lay the sensation of dull, numbing wonder that the seen and the Unseen should mingle so strangely on this earth to hound one poor soul to its grave.

August 27.—Heatherlegh has been indefatigable in his attendance on me; and only yesterday told me that I ought to send in an application for sick leave. An application to escape the company of a phantom! A request that the Government would graciously permit me to get rid of five ghosts and an airy 'rickshaw by going to England! Heatherlegh's proposition moved me to almost hysterical laughter. I told him that I should await the end quietly at Simla; and I am sure that the end is not far off. Believe me that I dread its advent more than any word can say; and I torture myself nightly with a thousand speculations as to the manner of my death.

Shall I die in my bed decently and as an English gentleman should die ; or, in one last walk on the Mall, will my soul be wrenched from me to take its place for ever and ever by the side of that ghastly phantasm ?   Shall I return to my old lost allegiance in the next world, or shall I meet Agnes loathing her and bound to her side through all eternity?   Shall we two hover over the scene of our lives till the end of Time ?   As the day of my death draws nearer, the intense horror that all living flesh feels toward escaped spirits from beyond the grave grows more and more powerful. It is an awful thing to go down quick among the dead with scarcely one-half of your life completed. It is a thousand times more awful to wait as I do in your midst, for I know not what unimaginable terror.   Pity me, at least on the score of my ' delusion,' for I know you will never believe what I have written here.   Yet as surely as ever a man was done to death by the Powers of Darkness I am that man.

In justice, too, pity her.   For as surely as ever woman was killed by man, I killed Mrs. Wessington.   And the last portion of my punishment is even now upon me.

My Own True Ghost Story

As I came through the Desert thus it was—
As I came through the Desert.
                    The City of Dreadful Night.

THIS story deals entirely with ghosts. There are, in India, ghosts who take the form of fat, cold, pobby corpses, and hide in trees near the roadside till a traveller passes. Then they drop upon his neck and remain. There are also terrible ghosts of women who have died in childbed. These wander along the pathways at dusk, or hide in the crops near a village, and call seductively. But to answer their call is death in this world and the next. Their feet are turned backwards that all sober men may recognise them. There are ghosts of little children who have been thrown into wells. These haunt well-curbs and the fringes of jungles, and wail under the stars, or catch women by the wrist and beg to be taken up and carried. These and the corpse-ghosts, however, are only vernacular articles and do not attack Sahibs. No native ghost has yet been authentically reported to have frightened an Englishman ; but many English ghosts have scared the life out of both white and black.

Nearly every other Station owns a ghost. There

are said to be two at Simla, not counting the woman
who blows the bellows at Syree dâk-bungalow on
the Old Road ; Mussoorie has a house haunted by
a very lively Thing ; a White Lady is supposed
to do night-watchman round a house in Lahore ;
Dalhousie says that one of her houses 'repeats' on
autumn evenings all the incidents of a horrible
horse-and-precipice accident ; Murree has a merry
ghost, and, now that she has been swept by cholera,
will have room for a sorrowful one ; there are
Officers' Quarters in Mian Mir whose doors open
without reason, and whose furniture is guaranteed
to creak, not with the heat of June, but with the
weight of Invisibles who come to lounge in the
chairs ; Peshawar possesses houses that none will
willingly rent ; and there is something—not fever
—wrong with a big bungalow in Allahabad. The
older Provinces simply bristle with haunted houses,
and march phantom armies along their main
thoroughfares.

Some of the dâk-bungalows on the Grand
Trunk Road have handy little cemeteries in their
compound—witnesses to the 'changes and chances
of this mortal life' in the days when men drove
from Calcutta to the North-West. These bungalows are objectionable places to put up in. They
are generally very old, always dirty, while the
khansamah is as ancient as the bungalow. He
either chatters senilely, or falls into the long trances
of age. In both moods he is useless. If you get
angry with him, he refers to some Sahib dead and
buried these thirty years, and says that when he
was in that Sahib's service not a *khansamah* in the

Province could touch him. Then he jabbers and mows and trembles and fidgets among the dishes, and you repent of your irritation.

Not long ago it was my business to live in dâk-bungalows. I never inhabited the same house for three nights running, and grew to be learned in the breed. I lived in Government-built ones with red brick walls and rail ceilings, an inventory of the furniture posted in every room, and an excited cobra on the threshold to give welcome. I lived in ' converted ' ones—old houses officiating as dâk-bungalows—where nothing was in its proper place and there was not even a fowl for dinner. I lived in second-hand palaces where the wind blew through open-work marble tracery just as uncomfortably as through a broken pane. I lived in dâk-bunga-lows where the last entry in the visitors' book was fifteen months old, and where they slashed off the curry-kid's head with a sword. It was my good luck to meet all sorts of men, from sober travel-ling missionaries and deserters flying from British Regiments, to drunken loafers who threw whisky bottles at all who passed ; and my still greater good fortune just to escape a maternity case. Seeing that a fair proportion of the tragedy of our lives in India acted itself in dâk-bungalows, I wondered that I had met no ghosts. A ghost that would voluntarily hang about a dâk-bungalow would be mad, of course ; but so many men have died mad in dâk-bungalows that there must be a fair per-centage of lunatic ghosts.

In due time I found my ghost, or ghosts rather, for there were two of them.

We will call the bungalow Katmal dâk-bungalow ; but *that* was the smallest part of the horror. A man with a sensitive hide has no right to sleep in dâk-bungalows. He should marry. Katmal dâk-bungalow was old and rotten and unrepaired. The floor was of worn brick, the walls were filthy, and the windows were nearly black with grime. It stood on a bypath largely used by native Sub-Deputy Assistants of all kinds, from Finance to Forests ; but real Sahibs were rare. The *khansamah*, who was bent nearly double with old age, said so.

When I arrived, there was a fitful, undecided rain on the face of the land, accompanied by a restless wind, and every gust made a noise like the rattling of dry bones in the stiff toddy-palms outside. The *khansamah* completely lost his head on my arrival. He had served a Sahib once. Did I know that Sahib? He gave me the name of a well-known man who has been buried for more than a quarter of a century, and showed me an ancient daguerreotype of that man in his prehistoric youth. I had seen a steel engraving of him at the head of a double volume of Memoirs a month before, and I felt ancient beyond telling.

The day shut in and the *khansamah* went to get me food. He did not go through the pretence of calling it ' *khana*,' — man's victuals. He said '*ratub*,' and that means, among other things, 'grub' —dog's rations. There was no insult in his choice of the term. He had forgotten the other word, I suppose.

While he was cutting up the dead bodies of animals, I settled myself down, after exploring the

dâk-bungalow. There were three rooms besides
my own, which was a corner kennel, each giving
into the other through dingy white doors fastened
with long iron bars. The bungalow was a very
solid one, but the partition-walls of the rooms were
almost jerry-built in their flimsiness. Every step
or bang of a trunk echoed from my room down
the other three, and every footfall came back
tremulously from the far walls. For this reason
I shut the door. There were no lamps—only
candles in long glass shades. An oil wick was set
in the bathroom.

For bleak, unadulterated misery that dâk-
bungalow was the worst of the many that I had
ever set foot in. There was no fireplace, and the
windows would not open ; so a brazier of char-
coal would have been useless. The rain and the
wind splashed and gurgled and moaned round the
house, and the toddy-palms rattled and roared.
Half-a-dozen jackals went through the compound
singing, and a hyena stood afar off and mocked
them. A hyena would convince a Sadducee of the
Resurrection of the Dead—the worst sort of Dead.
Then came the *ratub*—a curious meal, half native
and half English in composition—with the old
khansamah babbling behind my chair about dead-
and-gone English people, and the wind-blown
candles playing shadow-bo-peep with the bed and
the mosquito-curtains. It was just the sort of
dinner and evening to make a man think of every
single one of his past sins, and of all the others
that he intended to commit if he lived.

Sleep, for several hundred reasons, was not

easy. The lamp in the bathroom threw the most absurd shadows into the room, and the wind was beginning to talk nonsense.

Just when the reasons were drowsy with blood-sucking I heard the regular —'Let-us-take-and-heave-him-over' grunt of doolie-bearers in the compound. First one doolie came in, then a second, and then a third. I heard the doolies dumped on the ground, and the shutter in front of my door shook.

'That's some one trying to come in,' I said. But no one spoke, and I persuaded myself that it was the gusty wind. The shutter of the room next to mine was attacked, flung back, and the inner door opened. 'That's some Sub-Deputy Assistant,' I said, 'and he has brought his friends with him. Now they'll talk and spit and smoke for an hour.'

But there were no voices and no footsteps. No one was putting his luggage into the next room. The door shut, and I thanked Providence that I was to be left in peace. But I was curious to know where the doolies had gone. I got out of bed and looked into the darkness. There was never a sign of a doolie. Just as I was getting into bed again, I heard, in the next room, the sound that no man in his senses can possibly mistake — the whir of a billiard ball down the length of the slate when the striker is stringing for break. No other sound is like it. A minute afterwards there was another whir, and I got into bed. I was not frightened — indeed I was not. I was very curious to know what had become of the doolies. I jumped into bed for that reason.

Next minute I heard the double click of a cannon, and my hair sat up. It is a mistake to say that hair stands up. The skin of the head tightens, and you can feel a faint, prickly bristling all over the scalp. That is the hair sitting up.

There was a whir and a click, and both sounds could only have been made by one thing—a billiard ball. I argued the matter out at great length with myself; and the more I argued the less probable it seemed that one bed, one table, and two chairs—all the furniture of the room next to mine—could so exactly duplicate the sounds of a game of billiards. After another cannon, a three-cushion one to judge by the whir, I argued no more. I had found my ghost, and would have given worlds to have escaped from that dâk-bungalow. I listened, and with each listen the game grew clearer. There was whir on whir and click on click. Sometimes there was a double click and a whir and another click. Beyond any sort of doubt, people were playing billiards in the next room. And the next room was not big enough to hold a billiard table!

Between the pauses of the wind I heard the game go forward—stroke after stroke. I tried to believe that I could not hear voices; but that attempt was a failure.

Do you know what fear is? Not ordinary fear of insult, injury, or death, but abject, quivering dread of something that you cannot see—fear that dries the inside of the mouth and half of the throat

—fear that makes you sweat on the palms of the hands, and gulp in order to keep the uvula at work? This is a fine Fear—a great cowardice, and must be felt to be appreciated. The very improbability of billiards in a dâk-bungalow proved the reality of the thing. No man—drunk or sober —could imagine a game at billiards, or invent the spitting crack of a 'screw cannon.'

A severe course of dâk-bungalows has this disadvantage—it breeds infinite credulity. If a man said to a confirmed dâk-bungalow-haunter : 'There is a corpse in the next room, and there's a mad girl in the next one, and the woman and man on that camel have just eloped from a place sixty miles away,' the hearer would not disbelieve, because he would know that nothing is too wild, grotesque, or horrible to happen in a dâk-bungalow.

This credulity, unfortunately, extends to ghosts. A rational person fresh from his own house would have turned on his side and slept. I did not. So surely as I was given up for a dry carcase by the scores of things in the bed, because the bulk of my blood was in my heart, so surely did I hear every stroke of a long game at billiards played in the echoing room behind the iron-barred door. My dominant fear was that the players might want a marker. It was an absurd fear ; because creatures who could play in the dark would be above such superfluities. I only know that that was my terror ; and it was real.

After a long, long while the game stopped, and the door banged. I slept because I was dead tired.

Otherwise I should have preferred to have kept awake. Not for everything in Asia would I have dropped the door-bar and peered into the dark of the next room.

When the morning came I considered that I had done well and wisely, and inquired for the means of departure.

'By the way, *khansamah*,' I said, 'what were those three doolies doing in my compound in the night?'

'There were no doolies,' said the *khansamah*.

I went into the next room, and the daylight streamed through the open door. I was immensely brave. I would, at that hour, have played Black Pool with the owner of the big Black Pool down below.

'Has this place always been a dâk-bungalow?' I asked.

'No,' said the *khansamah*. 'Ten or twenty years ago, I have forgotten how long, it was a billiard room.'

'A what!'

'A billiard room for the Sahibs who built the Railway. I was *khansamah* then in the big house where all the Railway-Sahibs lived, and I used to come across with brandy-*shrab*. These three rooms were all one, and they held a big table on which the Sahibs played every evening. But the Sahibs are all dead now, and the Railway runs, you say, nearly to Kabul.'

'Do you remember anything about the Sahibs?'

'It is long ago, but I remember that one Sahib, a fat man, and always angry, was playing here one

night, and he said to me : " Mangal Khan, brandy-
pani do," and I filled the glass, and he bent over
the table to strike, and his head fell lower and
lower till it hit the table, and his spectacles came
off, and when we—the Sahibs and I myself—ran
to lift him he was dead. I helped to carry him
out. Aha, he was a strong Sahib ! But he is
dead, and I, old Mangal Khan, am still living, by
your favour.'

That was more than enough ! I had my ghost
—a first-hand, authenticated article. I would write
to the Society for Psychical Research — I would
paralyse the Empire with the news ! But I would,
first of all, put eighty miles of assessed crop-land
between myself and that dâk-bungalow before
nightfall. The Society might send their regular
agent to investigate later on.

I went into my own room and prepared to
pack, after noting down the facts of the case. As
I smoked I heard the game begin again,— with
a miss in balk this time, for the whir was a short
one.

The door was open, and I could see into the
room. *Click — click !* That was a cannon. I
entered the room without fear, for there was
sunlight within and a fresh breeze without. The
unseen game was going on at a tremendous rate.
And well it might, when a restless little rat was
running to and fro inside the dingy ceiling-cloth,
and a piece of loose window-sash was making fifty
breaks off the window-bolt as it shook in the
breeze !

Impossible to mistake the sound of billiard balls !

Impossible to mistake the whir of a ball over the slate ! But I was to be excused. Even when I shut my enlightened eyes the sound was marvellously like that of a fast game.

Entered angrily the faithful partner of my sorrows, Kadir Baksh.

' This bungalow is very bad and low-caste ! No wonder the Presence was disturbed and is speckled. Three sets of doolie-bearers came to the bungalow late last night when I was sleeping outside, and said that it was their custom to rest in the rooms set apart for the English people ! What honour has the *khansamah*? They tried to enter, but I told them to go. No wonder, if these *Oorias* have been here, that the Presence is sorely spotted. It is shame, and the work of a dirty man ! '

Kadir Baksh did not say that he had taken from each gang two annas for rent in advance, and then, beyond my earshot, had beaten them with the big green umbrella whose use I could never before divine. But Kadir Baksh has no notions of morality.

There was an interview with the *khansamah*, but as he promptly lost his head, wrath gave place to pity, and pity led to a long conversation, in the course of which he put the fat Engineer-Sahib's tragic death in three separate stations—two of them fifty miles away. The third shift was to Calcutta, and there the Sahib died while driving a dog-cart.

I did not go away as soon as I intended. I stayed for the night, while the wind and the rat and the sash and the window-bolt played a ding-dong ' hundred and fifty up.' Then the wind ran out and the billiards stopped, and I felt that I had ruined my one genuine ghost story.

Had I only ceased investigating at the proper time I could have made *anything* out of it.

That was the bitterest thought of all.

The Strange Ride of Morrowbie Jukes

Alive or dead—there is no other way.—Native Proverb

THERE is no invention about this tale. Jukes by
accident stumbled upon a village that is well known
to exist, though he is the only Englishman who has
been there. A somewhat similar institution used
to flourish on the outskirts of Calcutta, and there is
a story that if you go into the heart of Bikanir, which
is in the heart of the Great Indian Desert, you shall
come across, not a village, but a town where the
Dead who did not die, but may not live, have estab-
lished their headquarters. And, since it is perfectly
true that in the same Desert is a wonderful city
where all the rich money-lenders retreat after they
have made their fortunes (fortunes so vast that the
owners cannot trust even the strong hand of the
Government to protect them, but take refuge in the
waterless sands), and drive sumptuous C-spring
barouches, and buy beautiful girls, and decorate
their palaces with gold and ivory and Minton tiles
and mother-o'-pearl, I do not see why Jukes's tale
should not be true. He is a Civil Engineer, with

a head for plans and distances and things of that kind, and he certainly would not take the trouble to invent imaginary traps. He could earn more by doing his legitimate work. He never varies the tale in the telling, and grows very hot and indignant when he thinks of the disrespectful treatment he received. He wrote this quite straightforwardly at first, but he has touched it up in places and introduced Moral Reflections : thus :—

In the beginning it all arose from a slight attack of fever. My work necessitated my being in camp for some months between Pakpattan and Mubarakpur—a desolate sandy stretch of country as every one who has had the misfortune to go there may know. My coolies were neither more nor less exasperating than other gangs, and my work demanded sufficient attention to keep me from moping, had I been inclined to so unmanly a weakness.

On the 23rd December 1884 I felt a little feverish. There was a full moon at the time, and, in consequence, every dog near my tent was baying it. The brutes assembled in twos and threes and drove me frantic. A few days previously I had shot one loud-mouthed singer and suspended his carcase *in terrorem* about fifty yards from my tent-door, but his friends fell upon, fought for, and ultimately devoured the body ; and, as it seemed to me, sang their hymns of thanksgiving afterwards with renewed energy.

The light-headedness which accompanies fever acts differently on different men. My irritation gave way, after a short time, to a fixed determination to slaughter one huge black and white beast who had been foremost in song and first in flight throughout the evening. Thanks to a shaking hand and a giddy head I had already missed him twice with both barrels of my shot-gun, when it struck me that my best plan would be to ride him down in the open and finish him off with a hog-spear. This, of course, was merely the semi-delirious notion of a fever-patient ; but I remember that it struck me at the time as being eminently practical and feasible.

I therefore ordered my groom to saddle Pornic and bring him round quietly to the rear of my tent. When the pony was ready, I stood at his head prepared to mount and dash out as soon as the dog should again lift up his voice. Pornic, by the way, had not been out of his pickets for a couple of days ; the night air was crisp and chilly ; and I was armed with a specially long and sharp pair of persuaders with which I had been rousing a sluggish cob that afternoon. You will easily believe, then, that when he was let go he went quickly. In one moment, for the brute bolted as straight as a die, the tent was left far behind, and we were flying over the smooth sandy soil at racing speed. In another we had passed the wretched dog, and I had almost forgotten why it was that I had taken horse and hog-spear.

The delirium of fever and the excitement of rapid motion through the air must have taken away the remnant of my senses. I have a faint recollection of standing upright in my stirrups, and of brandishing my hog-spear at the great white moon that looked down so calmly on my mad gallop ; and of shouting challenges to the camelthorn bushes as they whizzed past. Once or twice, I believe, I swayed forward on Pornic's neck, and literally hung on by my spurs—as the marks next morning showed.

The wretched beast went forward like a thing possessed, over what seemed to be a limitless expanse of moonlit sand. Next, I remember, the ground rose suddenly in front of us, and as we topped the ascent I saw the waters of the Sutlej shining like a silver bar below. Then Pornic blundered heavily on his nose, and we rolled together down some unseen slope.

I must have lost consciousness, for when I recovered I was lying on my stomach in a heap of soft white sand, and the dawn was beginning to break dimly over the edge of the slope down which I had fallen. As the light grew stronger I saw I was at the bottom of a horseshoe-shaped crater of sand, opening on one side directly on to the shoals of the Sutlej. My fever had altogether left me, and, with the exception of a slight dizziness in the head, I felt no bad effects from the fall overnight.

Pornic, who was standing a few yards away, was naturally a good deal exhausted, but had not hurt himself in the least. His saddle, a favourite polo one, was much knocked about, and had been twisted under his belly. It took me some time to put him to rights, and in the meantime I had ample opportunities of observing the spot into which I had so foolishly dropped.

At the risk of being considered tedious, I must

describe it at length ; inasmuch as an accurate mental picture of its peculiarities will be of material assistance in enabling the reader to understand what follows.

Imagine then, as I have said before, a horseshoe-shaped crater of sand with steeply-graded sand walls about thirty-five feet high. (The slope, I fancy, must have been about 65°.) This crater enclosed a level piece of ground about fifty yards long by thirty at its broadest part, with a rude well in the centre. Round the bottom of the crater, about three feet from the level of the ground proper, ran a series of eighty-three semicircular, ovoid, square, and multi-lateral holes, all about three feet at the mouth. Each hole on inspection showed that it was carefully shored internally with drift-wood and bamboos, and ever the mouth a wooden drip-board projected, like the peak of a jockey's cap, for two feet. No sign of life was visible in these tunnels, but a most sickening stench pervaded the entire amphitheatre—a stench fouler than any which my wanderings in Indian villages have introduced me to.

Having remounted Pornic, who was as anxious as I to get back to camp, I rode round the base of the horseshoe to find some place whence an exit would be practicable. The inhabitants, whoever they might be, had not thought fit to put in an appearance, so I was left to my own devices. My first attempt to ' rush ' Pornic up the steep sand-banks showed me that I had fallen into a trap exactly on the same model as that which the ant-lion sets for its prey. At each step the shifting sand poured down from above in tons, and rattled on the drip-boards of the

holes like small shot.   A couple of ineffectual
charges sent us both rolling down to the bottom,
half choked with the torrents of sand ; and I was
constrained to turn my attention to the river-bank.

Here everything seemed easy enough.   The
sand-hills ran down to the river edge, it is true, but
there were plenty of shoals and shallows across
which I could gallop Pornic, and find my way back
to *terra firma* by turning sharply to the right or
the left.   As I led Pornic over the sands I was
startled by the faint pop of a rifle across the river ;
and at the same moment a bullet dropped with
a sharp ' *whit* ' close to Pornic's head.

There was no mistaking the nature of the missile
—a regulation Martini-Henry ' picket.'   About five
hundred yards away a country-boat was anchored in
mid-stream ; and a jet of smoke drifting away from
its bows in the still morning air showed me whence
the delicate attention had come.   Was ever a
respectable gentleman in such an *impasse ?*   The
treacherous sand-slope allowed no escape from a
spot which I had visited most involuntarily, and a
promenade on the river frontage was the signal for a
bombardment from some insane native in a boat.
I'm afraid that I lost my temper very much indeed.

Another bullet reminded me that I had better
save my breath to cool my porridge ; and I retreated
hastily up the sands and back to the horseshoe,
where I saw that the noise of the rifle had drawn
sixty-five human beings from the badger-holes which
I had up till that point supposed to be untenanted.
I found myself in the midst of a crowd of spectators
—about forty men, twenty women, and one child

who could not have been more than five years old.
They were all scantily clothed in that salmon-
coloured cloth which one associates with Hindu
mendicants, and, at first sight, gave me the impression
of a band of loathsome *fakirs*.   The filth and re-
pulsiveness of the assembly were beyond all descrip-
tion, and I shuddered to think what their life in the
badger-holes must be.

Even in these days, when local self-government
has destroyed the greater part of a native's respect for
a Sahib, I have been accustomed to a certain amount
of civility from my inferiors, and on approaching
the crowd naturally expected that there would be
some recognition of my presence.   As a matter of
fact there was, but it was by no means what I had
looked for.

The ragged crew actually laughed at me—such
laughter I hope I may never hear again.   They
cackled, yelled, whistled, and howled as I walked
into their midst ; some of them literally throwing
themselves down on the ground in convulsions of
unholy mirth.   In a moment I had let go Pornic's
head, and, irritated beyond expression at the
morning's adventure, commenced cuffing those
nearest to me with all the force I could.   The
wretches dropped under my blows like ninepins, and
the laughter gave place to wails for mercy ; while
those yet untouched clasped me round the knees,
imploring me in all sorts of uncouth tongues to spare
them.

In the tumult, and just when I was feeling very
much ashamed of myself for having thus easily given
way to my temper, a thin high voice murmured in

English from behind my shoulder : 'Sahib ! Sahib !
Do you not know me? Sahib, it is Gunga Dass,
the telegraph-master.'

I spun round quickly and faced the speaker.

Gunga Dass (I have, of course, no hesitation in
mentioning the man's real name) I had known four
years before as a Deccanee Brahmin lent by the
Punjab Government to one of the Khalsia States.
He was in charge of a branch telegraph-office there,
and when I had last met him was a jovial, full-
stomached, portly Government servant with a
marvellous capacity for making bad puns in English
—a peculiarity which made me remember him
long after I had forgotten his services to me in his
official capacity. It is seldom that a Hindu makes
English puns.

Now, however, the man was changed beyond
all recognition. Caste-mark, stomach, slate-
coloured continuations, and unctuous speech were
all gone. I looked at a withered skeleton,
turbanless and almost naked, with long matted
hair and deep-set codfish-eyes. But for a crescent-
shaped scar on the left cheek—the result of an
accident for which I was responsible—I should
never have known him. But it was indubitably
Gunga Dass, and—for this I was thankful—an
English-speaking native who might at least tell me
the meaning of all that I had gone through that day.

The crowd retreated to some distance as I
turned towards the miserable figure, and ordered
him to show me some method of escaping from
the crater. He held a freshly-plucked crow in his
hand, and in reply to my question climbed slowly

to a platform of sand which ran in front of the holes, and commenced lighting a fire there in silence. Dried bents, sand-poppies, and drift-wood burn quickly; and I derived much consolation from the fact that he lit them with an ordinary sulphur match. When they were in a bright glow and the crow was neatly spitted in front thereof, Gunga Dass began without a word of preamble :—

'There are only two kinds of men, Sar—the alive and the dead. When you are dead you are dead, but when you are alive you live.' (Here the crow demanded his attention for an instant as it twirled before the fire in danger of being burnt to a cinder.) 'If you die at home and do not die when you come to the ghât to be burnt you come here.'

The nature of the reeking village was made plain now, and all that I had known or read of the grotesque and the horrible paled before the fact just communicated by the ex-Brahmin. Sixteen years ago, when I first landed in Bombay, I had been told by a wandering Armenian of the existence, somewhere in India, of a place to which such Hindus as had the misfortune to recover from trance or catalepsy were conveyed and kept, and I recollect laughing heartily at what I was then pleased to consider a traveller's tale. Sitting at the bottom of the sand-trap, the memory of Watson's Hotel, with its swinging punkahs, white-robed servants, and the sallow-faced Armenian, rose up in my mind as vividly as a photograph, and I burst into a loud fit of laughter. The contrast was too absurd !

Gunga Dass, as he bent over the unclean bird, watched me curiously. Hindus seldom laugh, and his surroundings were not such as to move him that way. He removed the crow solemnly from the wooden spit and as solemnly devoured it. Then he continued his story, which I give in his own words :—

'In epidemics of the cholera you are carried to be burnt almost before you are dead. When you come to the riverside the cold air, perhaps, makes you alive, and then, if you are only little alive, mud is put on your nose and mouth and you die conclusively. If you are rather more alive, more mud is put ; but if you are too lively they let you go and take you away. I was too lively, and made protestation with anger against the indignities that they endeavoured to press upon me. In those days I was Brahmin and proud man. Now I am dead man and eat'—here he eyed the well-gnawed breast-bone with the first sign of emotion that I had seen in him since we met— 'crows, and—other things. They took me from my sheets when they saw that I was too lively and gave me medicines for one week, and I survived successfully. Then they sent me by rail from my place to Okara Station, with a man to take care of me ; and at Okara Station we met two other men, and they conducted we three on camels, in the night, from Okara Station to this place, and they propelled me from the top to the bottom, and the other two succeeded, and I have been here ever since two and a half years. Once I was Brahmin and proud man, and now I eat crows.'

'There is no way of getting out?'

'None of what kind at all. When I first came I made experiments frequently, and all the others also, but we have always succumbed to the sand which is precipitated upon our heads.'

'But surely,' I broke in at this point, 'the river-front is open, and it is worth while dodging the bullets; while at night——'

I had already matured a rough plan of escape which a natural instinct of selfishness forbade me sharing with Gunga Dass. He, however, divined my unspoken thought almost as soon as it was formed; and, to my intense astonishment, gave vent to a long low chuckle of derision—the laughter, be it understood, of a superior or at least of an equal.

'You will not'—he had dropped the Sir after his first sentence—'make any escape that way. But you can try. I have tried. Once only.'

The sensation of nameless terror which I had in vain attempted to strive against overmastered me completely. My long fast—it was now close upon ten o'clock, and I had eaten nothing since tiffin on the previous day—combined with the violent agitation of the ride had exhausted me, and I verily believe that, for a few minutes, I acted as one mad. I hurled myself against the sand-slope. I ran round the base of the crater, blaspheming and praying by turns. I crawled out among the sedges of the river-front, only to be driven back each time in an agony of nervous dread by the rifle-bullets which cut up the sand round me—for I dared not face the death of a mad dog among that hideous crowd—and so fell, spent and raving, at the curb of the well. No one had taken the slightest notice of an exhibition which makes me blush hotly even when I think of it now.

Two or three men trod on my panting body as they drew water, but they were evidently used to this sort of thing, and had no time to waste upon me. Gunga Dass, indeed, when he had banked the embers of his fire with sand, was at some pains to throw half a cupful of fetid water over my head, an attention for which I could have fallen on my knees and thanked him, but he was laughing all the while in the same mirthless, wheezy key that greeted me on my first attempt to force the shoals. And so, in a half-fainting state, I lay till noon. Then, being only a man after all, I felt hungry, and said as much to Gunga Dass, whom I had begun to regard as my natural protector. Following the impulse of the outer world when dealing with natives, I put my hand into my pocket and drew out four annas. The absurdity of the gift struck me at once, and I was about to replace the money.

Gunga Dass, however, cried : 'Give me the money, all you have, or I will get help, and we will kill you !'

A Briton's first impulse, I believe, is to guard the contents of his pockets ; but a moment's thought showed me the folly of differing with the one man who had it in his power to make me comfortable ; and with whose help it was possible that I might eventually escape from the crater. I gave him all the money in my possession, Rs.9-8-5

—nine rupees, eight annas, and five pie—for I always keep small change as *bakshish* when I am in camp. Gunga Dass clutched the coins, and hid them at once in his ragged loin-cloth, looking round to assure himself that no one had observed us.

'*Now* I will give you something to eat,' said he.

What pleasure my money could have given him I am unable to say ; but inasmuch as it did please him I was not sorry that I had parted with it so readily, for I had no doubt that he would have had me killed if I had refused. One does not protest against the doings of a den of wild beasts ; and my companions were lower than any beasts. While I ate what Gunga Dass had provided, a coarse *chapatti* and a cupful of the foul well-water, the people showed not the faintest sign of curiosity —that curiosity which is so rampant, as a rule, in an Indian village.

I could even fancy that they despised me. At all events they treated me with the most chilling indifference, and Gunga Dass was nearly as bad. I plied him with questions about the terrible village, and received extremely unsatisfactory answers. So far as I could gather, it had been in existence from time immemorial—whence I concluded that it was at least a century old—and during that time no one had ever been known to escape from it. [I had to control myself here with both hands, lest the blind terror should lay hold of me a second time and drive me raving round. the crater.] Gunga Dass took a malicious pleasure in emphasising this point and in watching me wince.

Nothing that I could do would induce him to tell me who the mysterious 'They' were.

'It is so ordered,' he would reply, 'and I do not yet know any one who has disobeyed the orders.'

'Only wait till my servants find that I am missing,' I retorted, 'and I promise you that this place shall be cleared off the face of the earth, and I'll give you a lesson in civility, too, my friend.'

'Your servants would be torn in pieces before they came near this place; and, besides, you are dead, my dear friend. It is not your fault, of course, but none the less you are dead *and* buried.'

At irregular intervals supplies of food, I was told, were dropped down from the land side into the amphitheatre, and the inhabitants fought for them like wild beasts. When a man felt his death coming on he retreated to his lair and died there. The body was sometimes dragged out of the hole and thrown on to the sand, or allowed to rot where it lay.

The phrase 'thrown on to the sand' caught my attention, and I asked Gunga Dass whether this sort of thing was not likely to breed a pestilence.

'That,' said he, with another of his wheezy chuckles, 'you may see for yourself subsequently. You will have much time to make observations.'

Whereat, to his great delight, I winced once more and hastily continued the conversation: 'And how do you live here from day to day? What do you do?' The question elicited exactly the same answer as before—coupled with the information that 'this place is like your European heaven ; there is neither marrying nor giving in marriage.'

Gunga Dass had been educated at a Mission School, and, as he himself admitted, had he only changed his religion 'like a wise man,' might have avoided the living grave which was now his portion. But as long as I was with him I fancy he was happy.

Here was a Sahib, a representative of the dominant race, helpless as a child and completely at the mercy of his native neighbours. In a deliberate lazy way he set himself to torture me as a schoolboy would devote a rapturous half-hour to watching the agonies of an impaled beetle, or as a ferret in a blind burrow might glue himself comfortably to the neck of a rabbit. The burden of his conversation was that there was no escape 'of no kind whatever,' and that I should stay here till I died and was 'thrown on to the sand.' If it were possible to forejudge the conversation of the Damned on the advent of a new soul in their abode, I should say that they would speak as Gunga Dass did to me throughout that long afternoon. I was powerless to protest or answer ; all my energies being devoted to a struggle against the inexplicable terror that threatened to over-whelm me again and again. I can compare the feeling to nothing except the struggles of a man against the overpowering nausea of the Channel passage—only my agony was of the spirit and infinitely more terrible.

As the day wore on, the inhabitants began to

appear in full strength to catch the rays of the afternoon sun, which were now sloping in at the mouth of the crater. They assembled by little knots, and talked among themselves without even throwing a glance in my direction. About four o'clock, so far as I could judge, Gunga Dass rose and dived into his lair for a moment, emerging with a live crow in his hands. The wretched bird was in a most draggled and deplorable condition, but seemed to be in no way afraid of its master. Advancing cautiously to the river-front, Gunga Dass stepped from tussock to tussock until he had reached a smooth patch of sand directly in the line of the boat's fire. The occupants of the boat took no notice. Here he stopped, and, with a couple of dexterous turns of the wrist, pegged the bird on its back with outstretched wings. As was only natural, the crow began to shriek at once and beat the air with its claws. In a few seconds the clamour had attracted the attention of a bevy of wild crows on a shoal a few hundred yards away, where they were discussing something that looked like a corpse. Half-a-dozen crows flew over at once to see what was going on, and also, as it proved, to attack the pinioned bird. Gunga Dass, who had lain down on a tussock, motioned to me to be quiet, though I fancy this was a needless precaution. In a moment, and before I could see how it happened, a wild crow, which had grappled with the shrieking and helpless bird, was entangled in the latter's claws, swiftly disengaged by Gunga Dass, and pegged down beside its companion in adversity.

Curiosity, it seemed, overpowered the rest of the flock, and almost before Gunga Dass and I had time to withdraw to the tussock, two more captives were struggling in the upturned claws of the decoys. So the chase—if I can give it so dignified a name—continued until Gunga Dass had captured seven crows. Five of them he throttled at once, reserving two for further operations another day. I was a good deal impressed by this, to me, novel method of securing food, and complimented Gunga Dass on his skill.

'It is nothing to do,' said he. 'To-morrow you must do it for me. You are stronger than I am.'

This calm assumption of superiority upset me not a little, and I answered peremptorily : 'Indeed, you old ruffian? What do you think I have given you money for ? '

'Very well,' was the unmoved reply. 'Perhaps not to-morrow, nor the day after, nor subsequently; but in the end, and for many years, you will catch crows and eat crows, and you will thank your European God that you have crows to catch and eat.'

I could have cheerfully strangled him for this, but judged it best under the circumstances to smother my resentment. An hour later I was eating one of the crows ; and, as Gunga Dass had said, thanking my God that I had a crow to eat. Never as long as I live shall I forget that evening meal. The whole population were squatting on the hard sand platform opposite their dens, huddled over tiny fires of refuse and dried rushes. Death,

having once laid his hand upon these men and
forborne to strike, seemed to stand aloof from
them now; for most of our company were old
men, bent and worn and twisted with years, and
women aged to all appearance as the Fates themselves. They sat together in knots and talked—
God only knows what they found to discuss—in
low equable tones, curiously in contrast to the
strident babble with which natives are accustomed
to make day hideous. Now and then an access of
that sudden fury which had possessed me in the
morning would lay hold on a man or woman; and
with yells and imprecations the sufferer would
attack the steep slope until, baffled and bleeding,
he fell back on the platform incapable of moving a
limb. The others would never even raise their
eyes when this happened, as men too well aware of
the futility of their fellows' attempts and wearied
with their useless repetition. I saw four such out-
bursts in the course of that evening.

Gunga Dass took an eminently business-like
view of my situation, and while we were dining—I
can afford to laugh at the recollection now, but it
was painful enough at the time—propounded the
terms on which he would consent to 'do' for me.
My nine rupees eight annas, he argued, at the rate
of three annas a day, would provide me with food
for fifty-one days, or about seven weeks; that is
to say, he would be willing to cater for me for that
length of time. At the end of it I was to look
after myself. For a further consideration—*videlicet*
my boots—he would be willing to allow me to
occupy the den next to his own, and would supply

me with as much dried grass for bedding as he could spare.

'Very well, Gunga Dass,' I replied; 'to the first terms I cheerfully agree, but, as there is nothing on earth to prevent my killing you as you sit here and taking everything that you have' (I thought of the two invaluable crows at the time), 'I flatly refuse to give you my boots and shall take whichever den I please.'

The stroke was a bold one, and I was glad when I saw that it had succeeded. Gunga Dass changed his tone immediately, and disavowed all intention of asking for my boots. At the time it did not strike me as at all strange that I, a Civil Engineer, a man of thirteen years' standing in the Service, and, I trust, an average Englishman, should thus calmly threaten murder and violence against the man who had, for a consideration it is true, taken me under his wing. I had left the world, it seemed, for centuries. I was as certain then as I am now of my own existence, that in the accursed settlement there was no law save that of the strongest; that the living dead men had thrown behind them every canon of the world which had cast them out; and that I had to depend for my own life on my strength and vigilance alone. The crew of the ill-fated *Mignonette* are the only men who would understand my frame of mind. 'At present,' I argued to myself, 'I am strong and a match for six of these wretches. It is imperatively necessary that I should, for my own sake, keep both health and strength until the hour of my release comes— if it ever does.'

Fortified with these resolutions, I ate and drank as much as I could, and made Gunga Dass understand that I intended to be his master, and that the least sign of insubordination on his part would be visited with the only punishment I had it in my power to inflict — sudden and violent death. Shortly after this I went to bed. That is to say, Gunga Dass gave me a double armful of dried bents which I thrust down the mouth of the lair to the right of his, and followed myself, feet foremost; the hole running about nine feet into the sand with a slight downward inclination, and being neatly shored with timbers. From my den, which faced the river-front, I was able to watch the waters of the Sutlej flowing past under the light of a young moon and compose myself to sleep as best I might.

The horrors of that night I shall never forget. My den was nearly as narrow as a coffin, and the sides had been worn smooth and greasy by the contact of innumerable naked bodies, added to which it smelt abominably. Sleep was altogether out of the question to one in my excited frame of mind. As the night wore on, it seemed that the entire amphitheatre was filled with legions of unclean devils that, trooping up from the shoals below, mocked the unfortunates in their lairs.

Personally I am not of an imaginative temperament — very few Engineers are — but on that occasion I was as completely prostrated with nervous terror as any woman. After half an hour or so, however, I was able once more to calmly review my chances of escape. Any exit by the steep sand walls was, of course, impracticable. I had been thoroughly convinced of this some time before. It was possible, just possible, that I might, in the uncertain moonlight, safely run the gauntlet of the rifle shots. The place was so full of terror for me that I was prepared to undergo any risk in leaving it. Imagine my delight, then, when after creeping stealthily to the river-front I found that the infernal boat was not there. My freedom lay before me in the next few steps!

By walking out to the first shallow pool that lay at the foot of the projecting left horn of the horseshoe, I could wade across, turn the flank of the crater, and make my way inland. Without a moment's hesitation I marched briskly past the tussocks where Gunga Dass had snared the crows, and out in the direction of the smooth white sand beyond. My first step from the tufts of dried grass showed me how utterly futile was any hope of escape; for, as I put my foot down, I felt an indescribable drawing, sucking motion of the sand below. Another moment and my leg was swallowed up nearly to the knee. In the moonlight the whole surface of the sand seemed to be shaken with devilish delight at my disappointment. I struggled clear, sweating with terror and exertion, back to the tussocks behind me and fell on my face.

My only means of escape from the semicircle was protected by a quicksand!

How long I lay I have not the faintest idea; but I was roused at last by the malevolent chuckle of Gunga Dass at my ear. 'I would advise you, Protector of the Poor' (the ruffian was speaking

English) 'to return to your house. It is unhealthy to lie down here. Moreover, when the boat returns you will most certainly be rifled at.' He stood over me in the dim light of the dawn, chuckling and laughing to himself. Suppressing my first impulse to catch the man by the neck and throw him on to the quicksand, I rose sullenly and followed him to the platform below the burrows.

Suddenly, and futilely as I thought while I spoke, I asked : 'Gunga Dass, what is the good of the boat if I can't get out *anyhow?*' I recollect that even in my deepest trouble I had been speculating vaguely on the waste of ammunition in guarding an already well-protected foreshore.

Gunga Dass laughed again and made answer : 'They have the boat only in daytime. It is for the reason that *there is a way*. I hope we shall have the pleasure of your company for much longer time. It is a pleasant spot when you have been here some years and eaten roast crow long enough.'

I staggered, numbed and helpless, towards the fetid burrow allotted to me, and fell asleep. An hour or so later I was awakened by a piercing scream—the shrill, high-pitched scream of a horse in pain. Those who have once heard that will never forget the sound. I found some little difficulty in scrambling out of the burrow. When I was in the open, I saw Pornic, my poor old Pornic, lying dead on the sandy soil. How they had killed him I cannot guess. Gunga Dass explained that horse was better than crow, and 'greatest good of greatest number is political

maxim.   We are now Republic, Mister Jukes, and
you are entitled to a fair share of the beast.   If
you like, we will pass a vote of thanks.   Shall I
propose ? '

Yes, we were a Republic indeed !   A Republic
of wild beasts penned at the bottom of a pit, to
eat and fight and sleep till we died.   I attempted
no protest of any kind, but sat down and stared at
the hideous sight in front of me.   In less time
almost than it takes me to write this, Pornic's
body was divided, in some unclean way or other ;
the men and women had dragged the fragments on
to the platform and were preparing their morning
meal.   Gunga Dass cooked mine.   The almost
irresistible impulse to fly at the sand walls until I
was wearied laid hold of me afresh, and I had to
struggle against it with all my might.   Gunga
Dass was offensively jocular till I told him that if
he addressed another remark of any kind whatever
to me I should strangle him where he sat.   This
silenced him till the silence became insupportable,
and I bade him say something.

'You will live here till you die like the other
Feringhi,' he said coolly, watching me over the
fragment of gristle that he was gnawing.

'What other Sahib, you swine?   Speak at once,
and don't stop to tell me a lie.'

'He is over there,' answered Gunga Dass, pointing to a burrow-mouth about four doors to the
left of my own.   'You can see for yourself.   He
died in the burrow as you will die, and I will die,
and as all these men and women and the one child
will also die.'

'For pity's sake tell me all you know about him. Who was he? When did he come, and when did he die?'

This appeal was a weak step on my part. Gunga Dass only leered and replied: 'I will not —unless you give me something first.'

Then I recollected where I was, and struck the man between the eyes, partially stunning him. He stepped down from the platform at once, and, cringing and fawning and weeping and attempting to embrace my feet, led me round to the burrow which he had indicated.

'I know nothing whatever about the gentleman. Your God be my witness that I do not. He was as anxious to escape as you were, and he was shot from the boat, though we all did all things to prevent him from attempting. He was shot here.' Gunga Dass laid his hand on his lean stomach and bowed to the earth.

'Well, and what then? Go on!'

'And then — and then, Your Honour, we carried him into his house and gave him water, and put wet cloths on the wound, and he laid down in his house and gave up the ghost.'

'In how long? In how long?'

'About half an hour after he received his wound. I call Vishnu to witness,' yelled the wretched man, 'that I did everything for him. Everything which was possible, that I did!'

He threw himself down on the ground and clasped my ankles. But I had my doubts about Gunga Dass's benevolence, and kicked him off as he lay protesting.

' I believe you robbed him of everything he had. But I can find out in a minute or two. How long was the Sahib here ? '

' Nearly a year and a half. I think he must have gone mad. But hear me swear, Protector of the Poor ! Won't Your Honour hear me swear that I never touched an article that belonged to him ? What is Your Worship going to do ? '

I had taken Gunga Dass by the waist and had hauled him on to the platform opposite the deserted burrow. As I did so I thought of my wretched fellow-prisoner's unspeakable misery among all these horrors for eighteen months, and the final agony of dying like a rat in a hole, with a bullet-wound in the stomach. Gunga Dass fancied I was going to kill him and howled pitifully. The rest of the population, in the plethora that follows a full flesh meal, watched us without stirring.

' Go inside, Gunga Dass,' said I, ' and fetch it out.'

I was feeling sick and faint with horror now. Gunga Dass nearly rolled off the platform and howled aloud.

' But I am Brahmin, Sahib—a high-caste Brahmin. By your soul, by your father's soul, do not make me do this thing ! '

' Brahmin or no Brahmin, by my soul and my father's soul, in you go ! ' I said, and, seizing him by the shoulders, I crammed his head into the mouth of the burrow, kicked the rest of him in, and, sitting down, covered my face with my hands.

At the end of a few minutes I heard a rustle and a creak ; then Gunga Dass in a sobbing, chok-

ing whisper speaking to himself ; then a soft thud
—and I uncovered my eyes.

The dry sand had turned the corpse entrusted
to its keeping into a yellow-brown mummy. I
told Gunga Dass to stand off while I examined it.
The body—clad in an olive-green hunting-suit
much stained and worn, with leather pads on the
shoulders—was that of a man between thirty and
forty, above middle height, with light sandy hair,
long moustache, and a rough unkempt beard.
The left canine of the upper jaw was missing, and
a portion of the lobe of the right ear was gone.
On the second finger of the left hand was a ring—
a shield-shaped bloodstone set in gold, with a
monogram that might have been either ' B. K.' or
' B. L.' On the third finger of the right hand was
a silver ring in the shape of a coiled cobra, much
worn and tarnished. Gunga Dass deposited a
handful of trifles he had picked out of the burrow
at my feet, and, covering the face of the body with
my handkerchief, I turned to examine these. I
give the full list in the hope that it may lead to
the identification of the unfortunate man :—

1. Bowl of a briarwood pipe, serrated at the
edge ; much worn and blackened ; bound with
string at the screw.

2. Two patent-lever keys ; wards of both
broken.

3. Tortoise-shell-handled penknife, silver or
nickel, name-plate marked with monogram ' B. K.'

4. Envelope, postmark undecipherable, bearing
a Victorian stamp, addressed to ' Miss Mon——'
(rest illegible)—' ham '—' nt.'

5. Imitation crocodile-skin notebook with pencil. First forty-five pages blank ; four and a half illegible ; fifteen others filled with private memoranda relating chiefly to three persons—a Mrs. L. Singleton, abbreviated several times to 'Lot Single,' 'Mrs. S. May,' and 'Garmison,' referred to in places as 'Jerry' or 'Jack.'

6. Handle of small-sized hunting-knife. Blade snapped short. Buck's horn, diamond-cut, with swivel and ring on the butt ; fragment of cotton cord attached.

It must not be supposed that I inventoried all these things on the spot as fully as I have here written them down. The notebook first attracted my attention, and I put it in my pocket with a view to studying it later on. The rest of the articles I conveyed to my burrow for safety's sake, and there, being a methodical man, I inventoried them. I then returned to the corpse and ordered Gunga Dass to help me to carry it out to the river-front. While we were engaged in this, the exploded shell of an old brown cartridge dropped out of one of the pockets and rolled at my feet. Gunga Dass had not seen it ; and I fell to thinking that a man does not carry exploded cartridge-cases, especially 'browns,' which will not bear loading twice, about with him when shooting. In other words, that cartridge-case had been fired inside the crater. Consequently there must be a gun some-where. I was on the verge of asking Gunga Dass, but checked myself, knowing that he would lie. We laid the body down on the edge of the quick-sand by the tussocks. It was my intention to push

it out and let it be swallowed up—the only possible
mode of burial that I could think of. I ordered
Gunga Dass to go away.

Then I gingerly put the corpse out on the
quicksand. In doing so—it was lying face downward—I tore the frail and rotten khaki shooting-
coat open, disclosing a hideous cavity in the back.
I have already told you that the dry sand had, as
it were, mummified the body. A moment's glance
showed that the gaping hole had been caused by a
gunshot wound ; the gun must have been fired
with the muzzle almost touching the back. The
shooting-coat, being intact, had been drawn over
the body after death, which must have been
instantaneous. The secret of the poor wretch's
death was plain to me in a flash. Some one of the
crater, presumably Gunga Dass, must have shot
him with his own gun—the gun that fitted the
brown cartridges. He had never attempted to
escape in the face of the rifle-fire from the boat.

I pushed the corpse out hastily, and saw it sink
from sight literally in a few seconds. I shuddered
as I watched. In a dazed, half-conscious way I
turned to peruse the notebook. A stained and
discoloured slip of paper had been inserted between
the binding and the back, and dropped out as I
opened the pages. This is what it contained :
'*Four out from crow-clump; three left; nine out;
two right; three back; two left; fourteen out; two
left; seven out; one left; nine back; two right;
six back; four right; seven back.*' The paper had
been burnt and charred at the edges. What it
meant I could not understand. I sat down on the

dried bents turning it over and over between my fingers, until I was aware of Gunga Dass standing immediately behind me with glowing eyes and outstretched hands.

'Have you got it?' he panted. 'Will you not let me look at it also? I swear that I will return it.'

'Got what? Return what?' I asked.

'That which you have in your hands. It will help us both.' He stretched out his long bird-like talons, trembling with eagerness.

'I could never find it,' he continued. 'He had secreted it about his person. Therefore I shot him, but nevertheless I was unable to obtain it.'

Gunga Dass had quite forgotten his little fiction about the rifle-bullet. I heard him calmly. Morality is blunted by consorting with the Dead who are alive.

'What on earth are you raving about? What is it you want me to give you?'

'The piece of paper in the notebook. It will help us both. Oh, you fool! You fool! Can you not see what it will do for us? We shall escape!'

His voice rose almost to a scream, and he danced with excitement before me. I own I was moved at the chance of getting away.

'Do you mean to say that this slip of paper will help us? What does it mean?'

'Read it aloud! Read it aloud! I beg and I pray to you to read it aloud.'

I did so. Gunga Dass listened delightedly, and drew an irregular line in the sand with his fingers.

'See now! It was the length of his gun-barrels without the stock. I have those barrels. Four gun-barrels out from the place where I caught crows. Straight out; do you mind me? Then three left. Ah! Now well I remember how that man worked it out night after night. Then nine out, and so on. Out is always straight before you across the quicksand to the north. He told me so before I killed him.'

'But if you knew all this why didn't you get out before?'

'I did *not* know it. He told me that he was working it out a year and a half ago, and how he was working it out night after night when the boat had gone away, and he could get out near the quicksand safely. Then he said that we would get away together. But I was afraid that he would leave me behind one night when he had worked it all out, and so I shot him. Besides, it is not advisable that the men who once get in here should escape. Only I, and *I* am a Brahmin.'

The hope of escape had brought Gunga Dass's caste back to him. He stood up, walked about, and gesticulated violently. Eventually I managed to make him talk soberly, and he told me how this Englishman had spent six months night after night in exploring, inch by inch, the passage across the quicksand; how he had declared it to be simplicity itself up to within about twenty yards of the river bank after turning the flank of the left horn of the horseshoe. This much he had evidently not completed when Gunga Dass shot him with his own gun.

In my frenzy of delight at the possibilities of escape I recollect shaking hands wildly with Gunga Dass, after we had decided that we were to make an attempt to get away that very night.   It was weary work waiting throughout the afternoon.

About ten o'clock, as far as I could judge, when the moon had just risen above the lip of the crater, Gunga Dass made a move for his burrow to bring out the gun-barrels whereby to measure our path. All the other wretched inhabitants had retired to their lairs long ago.   The guardian boat drifted down-stream some hours before, and we were utterly alone by the crow-clump.   Gunga Dass, while carrying the gun-barrels, let slip the piece of paper which was to be our guide.   I stooped down hastily to recover it, and, as I did so, I was aware that the creature was aiming a violent blow at the back of my head with the gun-barrels.   It was too late to turn round.   I must have received the blow somewhere on the nape of my neck, for I fell senseless at the edge of the quicksand.

When I recovered consciousness the moon was going down, and I was sensible of intolerable pain in the back of my head.   Gunga Dass had dis-appeared and my mouth was full of blood.   I lay down again and prayed that I might die without more ado.   Then the unreasoning fury which I have before mentioned laid hold upon me, and I staggered inland towards the walls of the crater. It seemed that some one was calling to me in a whisper—'Sahib! Sahib! Sahib!' exactly as my bearer used to call me in the mornings.   I fancied that I was delirious until a handful of sand fell at

my feet.   Then I looked up and saw a head peering
down into the amphitheatre—the head of Dunnoo,
my dog-boy, who attended to my collies.   As soon
as he had attracted my attention, he held up his
hand and showed a rope.   I motioned, staggering
to and fro the while, that he should throw it down.
It was a couple of leather punkah-ropes knotted
together, with a loop at one end.   I slipped the
loop over my head and under my arms ; heard
Dunnoo urge something forward ; was conscious
that I was being dragged, face downward, up the
steep sand-slope, and the next instant found myself
choked and half-fainting on the sand-hills overlooking the crater.   Dunnoo, with his face ashy
gray in the moonlight, implored me not to stay,
but to get back to my tent at once.

It seems that he had tracked Pornic's footprints
fourteen miles across the sands to the crater; had
returned and told my servants, who flatly refused
to meddle with any one, white or black, once fallen
into the hideous Village of the Dead ; whereupon
Dunnoo had taken one of my ponies and a couple
of punkah ropes, returned to the crater, and hauled
me out as I have described.

The Man who would be King

Brother to a Prince and fellow to a beggar if he be found worthy

THE Law, as quoted, lays down a fair conduct of life, and one not easy to follow. I have been fellow to a beggar again and again under circumstances which prevented either of us finding out whether the other was worthy. I have still to be brother to a Prince, though I once came near to kinship with what might have been a veritable King, and was promised the reversion of a Kingdom—army, law-courts, revenue, and policy all complete. But, to-day, I greatly fear that my King is dead, and if I want a crown I must go hunt it for myself.

The beginning of everything was in a railway train upon the road to Mhow from Ajmir. There had been a Deficit in the Budget, which necessitated travelling, not Second-class, which is only half as dear as First-class, but by Intermediate, which is very awful indeed. There are no cushions in the Intermediate class, and the population are either Intermediate, which is Eurasian, or native, which for a long night journey is nasty, or Loafer, which is amusing though intoxicated. Intermediates do not buy from refreshment-rooms. They carry their food in bundles and pots, and buy sweets from the native sweetmeat-sellers, and drink the road-side water. That is why in the hot weather Intermediates are taken out of the carriages dead, and in all weathers are most properly looked down upon.

My particular Intermediate happened to be empty till I reached Nasirabad, when a big black-browed gentleman in shirt-sleeves entered, and, following the custom of Intermediates, passed the time of day. He was a wanderer and a vagabond like myself, but with an educated taste for whisky. He told tales of things he had seen and done, of out-of-the-way corners of the Empire into which he had penetrated, and of adventures in which he risked his life for a few days' food.

'If India was filled with men like you and me, not knowing more than the crows where they'd get their next day's rations, it isn't seventy millions of revenue the land would be paying—it's seven hundred millions,' said he ; and as I looked at his mouth and chin I was disposed to agree with him..

We talked politics—the politics of Loaferdom, that sees things from the underside where the lath and plaster is not smoothed off—and we talked postal arrangements because my friend wanted to send a telegram back from the next station to Ajmir, the turning-off place from the Bombay to the Mhow line as you travel westward. My friend had no money beyond eight annas, which he wanted for dinner, and I had no money at all, owing to the hitch in the Budget before mentioned. Further, I was going into a wilderness where, though I should resume touch with the Treasury, there were no telegraph offices. I was, therefore, unable to help him in any way.

'We might threaten a Station-master, and make him send a wire on tick,' said my friend, 'but that'd mean inquiries for you and for me, and *I*'ve got my hands full these days. Did you say you are travelling back along this line within any days?'

'Within ten,' I said.

'Can't you make it eight?' said he. 'Mine is rather urgent business.'

'I can send your telegram within ten days if that will serve you,' I said.

'I couldn't trust the wire to fetch him now I think of it. It's this way. He leaves Delhi on the 23rd for Bombay. That means he'll be running through Ajmir about the night of the 23rd.'

'But I'm going into the Indian Desert,' I explained.

'Well *and* good,' said he. 'You'll be changing at Marwar Junction to get into Jodhpore territory— you must do that—and he'll be coming through Marwar Junction in the early morning of the 24th by the Bombay Mail. Can you be at Marwar Junction on that time? 'Twon't be inconveniencing you because I know that there's precious few pickings to be got out of these Central India States —even though you pretend to be correspondent of the *Backwoodsman*.'

'Have you ever tried that trick?' I asked.

'Again and again, but the Residents find you out, and then you get escorted to the Border before you've time to get your knife into them. But about

my friend here. I *must* give him a word o' mouth
to tell him what's come to me or else he won't know
where to go. I would take it more than kind of you
if you was to come out of Central India in time to
catch him at Marwar Junction, and say to him :
" He has gone South for the week." He'll know
what that means. He's a big man with a red beard,
and a great swell he is. You'll find him sleeping
like a gentleman with all his luggage round him in
a Second-class compartment. But don't you be
afraid. Slip down the window, and say : " He has
gone South for the week," and he'll tumble. It's
only cutting your time of stay in those parts by two
days. I ask you as a stranger—going to the West,'
he said with emphasis.

'Where have *you* come from ? ' said I.

'From the East,' said he. 'and I am hoping that
you will give him the message on the Square—for
the sake of my Mother as well as your own.'

Englishmen are not usually softened by appeals
to the memory of their mothers, but for certain
reasons, which will be fully apparent, I saw fit to
agree.

'It's more than a little matter,' said he, 'and
that's why I asked you to do it—and now I know
that I can depend on you doing it. A Second-class
carriage at Marwar Junction, and a red-haired man
asleep in it. You'll be sure to remember. I get
out at the next station, and I must hold on there till
he comes or sends me what I want.'

'I'll give the message if I catch him,' I said,
'and for the sake of your Mother as well as mine
I'll give you a word of advice. Don't try to run the

Central India States just now as the correspondent of the *Backwoodsman*. There's a real one knocking about here, and it might lead to trouble.'

'Thank you,' said he simply, 'and when will the swine be gone? I can't starve because he's ruining my work. I wanted to get hold of the Degumber Rajah down here about his father's widow, and give him a jump.'

'What did he do to his father's widow, then?'

'Filled her up with red pepper and slippered her to death as she hung from a beam. I found that out myself, and I'm the only man that would dare going into the State to get hush-money for it. They'll try to poison me, same as they did in Chortumna when I went on the loot there. But you'll give the man at Marwar Junction my message?'

He got out at a little roadside station, and I reflected. I had heard, more than once, of men personating correspondents of newspapers and bleeding small Native States with threats of exposure, but I had never met any of the caste before. They led a hard life, and generally die with great suddenness. The Native States have a wholesome horror of English newspapers which may throw light on their peculiar methods of government, and do their best to choke correspondents with champagne, or drive them out of their mind with four-in-hand barouches. They do not understand that nobody cares a straw for the internal administration of Native States so long as oppression and crime are kept within decent limits, and the ruler is not drugged, drunk, or diseased from one end of the

year to the other. They are the dark places of
the earth, full of unimaginable cruelty, touching the
Railway and the Telegraph on one side, and, on
the other, the days of Harun-al-Raschid. When I
left the train I did business with divers Kings, and
in eight days passed through many changes of life.
Sometimes I wore dress-clothes and consorted with
Princes and Politicals, drinking from crystal and
eating from silver. Sometimes I lay out upon the
ground and devoured what I could get, from a
plate made of leaves, and drank the running water,
and slept under the same rug as my servant. It
was all in the day's work.

Then I headed for the Great Indian Desert upon
the proper date, as I had promised, and the night
Mail set me down at Marwar Junction, where a
funny, little, happy-go-lucky, native-managed railway runs to Jodhpore. The Bombay Mail from
Delhi makes a short halt at Marwar. She arrived
as I got in, and I had just time to hurry to her
platform and go down the carriages. There was
only one Second-class on the train. I slipped the
window and looked down upon a flaming red beard,
half covered by a railway rug. That was my man,
fast asleep, and I dug him gently in the ribs. He
woke with a grunt, and I saw his face in the light
of the lamps. It was a great and shining face.

'Tickets again?' said he.

'No,' said I. 'I am to tell you that he is gone
South for the week. He has gone South for the
week!'

The train had begun to move out. The red
man rubbed his eyes. 'He has gone South for

the week,' he repeated. 'Now that's just like his impidence. Did he say that I was to give you anything? 'Cause I won't.'

'He didn't,' I said, and dropped away, and watched the red lights die out in the dark. It was horribly cold because the wind was blowing off the sands. I climbed into my own train—not an Intermediate Carriage this time—and went to sleep.

If the man with the beard had given me a rupee I should have kept it as a memento of a rather curious affair. But the consciousness of having done my duty was my only reward.

Later on I reflected that two gentlemen like my friends could not do any good if they for-gathered and personated correspondents of news-papers, and might, if they black-mailed one of the little rat-trap states of Central India or Southern Rajputana, get themselves into serious difficulties. I therefore took some trouble to describe them as accurately as I could remember to people who would be interested in deporting them; and suc-ceeded, so I was later informed, in having them headed back from the Degumber borders.

Then I became respectable, and returned to an Office where there were no Kings and no incidents outside the daily manufacture of a newspaper. A newspaper office seems to attract every conceivable sort of person, to the prejudice of discipline. Zenana-mission ladies arrive, and beg that the Editor will instantly abandon all his duties to describe a Christian prize-giving in a back-slum of a perfectly inaccessible village; Colonels who have been overpassed for command sit down and sketch the outline of a series of ten, twelve, or twenty-four leading articles on Seniority *versus* Selection ; Missionaries wish to know why they have not been permitted to escape from their regular vehicles of abuse and swear at a brother-missionary under special patronage of the editorial We ; stranded theatrical companies troop up to explain that they cannot pay for their advertisements, but on their return from New Zealand or Tahiti will do so with interest ; inventors of patent punkah-pulling machines, carriage couplings, and unbreakable swords and axle-trees, call with specifications in their pockets and hours at their disposal ; tea-companies enter and elaborate their prospectuses with the office pens ; secretaries of ball-committees clamour to have the glories of their last dance more fully described ; strange ladies rustle in and say, ' I want a hundred lady's cards printed *at once*, please,' which is manifestly part of an Editor's duty ; and every dissolute ruffian that ever tramped the Grand Trunk Road makes it his business to ask for employment as a proof-reader. And, all the time, the telephone-bell is ringing madly, and Kings are being killed on the Continent, and Empires are saying, ' You're another,' and Mister Gladstone is calling down brimstone upon the British Dominions, and the little black copy-boys are whining, ' *kaa-pi chay-ha-yeh* ' (copy wanted) like tired bees, and most of the paper is as blank as Modred's shield.

But that is the amusing part of the year. There are six other months when none ever comes to call, and the thermometer walks inch by inch up to the top of the glass, and the office is darkened to just above reading-light, and the press-machines are red-hot of touch, and nobody writes anything but accounts of amusements in the Hill-stations or obituary notices. Then the telephone becomes a tinkling terror, because it tells you of the sudden deaths of men and women that you knew intimately, and the prickly-heat covers you with a garment, and you sit down and write: ' A slight increase of sickness is reported from the Khuda Janta Khan District. The outbreak is purely sporadic in its nature, and, thanks to the energetic efforts of the District authorities, is now almost at an end. It is, however, with deep regret we record the death, etc.'

Then the sickness really breaks out, and the less recording and reporting the better for the peace of the subscribers. But the Empires and the Kings continue to divert themselves as selfishly as before, and the Foreman thinks that a daily paper really ought to come out once in twenty-four hours, and all the people at the Hill-stations in the middle of their amusements say: ' Good gracious! Why can't the paper be sparkling? I'm sure there's plenty going on up here.'

That is the dark half of the moon, and, as the advertisements say, ' must be experienced to be appreciated.'

It was in that season, and a remarkably evil season, that the paper began running the last issue of the week on Saturday night, which is to say Sunday morning, after the custom of a London paper. This was a great convenience, for immediately after the paper was put to bed, the dawn would lower the thermometer from 96° to almost 84° for half an hour, and in that chill—you have no idea how cold is 84° on the grass until you begin to pray for it—a very tired man could get off to sleep ere the heat roused him.

One Saturday night it was my pleasant duty to put the paper to bed alone. A King or courtier or a courtesan or a Community was going to die or get a new Constitution, or do something that was important on the other side of the world, and the paper was to be held open till the latest possible minute in order to catch the telegram.

It was a pitchy black night, as stifling as a June night can be, and the *loo*, the red-hot wind from the westward, was booming among the tinder-dry trees and pretending that the rain was on its heels. Now and again a spot of almost boiling water would fall on the dust with the flop of a frog, but all our weary world knew that was only pretence. It was a shade cooler in the press-room than the office, so I sat there, while the type ticked and clicked, and the night-jars hooted at the windows, and the all but naked compositors wiped the sweat from their foreheads, and called for water. The thing that was keeping us back, whatever it was, would not come off, though the *loo* dropped and the last type was set, and the whole round earth stood still in the choking heat, with its finger on its lip, to wait the event. I drowsed, and wondered whether the telegraph was a blessing, and whether this dying man, or struggling people, might be aware of the inconvenience the delay was causing. There was no special reason beyond the heat and worry to make tension, but, as the clock-hands crept up to three o'clock, and the machines spun their fly-wheels two or three times to see that all was in order before I said the word that would set them off, I could have shrieked aloud.

Then the roar and rattle of the wheels shivered the quiet into little bits. I rose to go away, but two men in white clothes stood in front of me. The first one said : 'It's him !' The second said : 'So it is !' And they both laughed almost as loudly as the machinery roared, and mopped their foreheads. 'We seed there was a light burning across the road, and we were sleeping in that ditch there for coolness, and I said to my friend here, The office is open. Let's come along and speak to him as turned us back from the Degumber State,' said the smaller of the two. He was the man I had met in the Mhow train, and his fellow was the red-bearded man of Marwar Junction. There was no mistaking the eyebrows of the one or the beard of the other.

I was not pleased, because I wished to go to sleep, not to squabble with loafers. 'What do you want?' I asked.

'Half an hour's talk with you, cool and comfortable, in the office,' said the red-bearded man. 'We'd *like* some drink—the Contrack doesn't begin yet, Peachey, so you needn't look— but what we really want is advice. We don't want money. We ask you as a favour, because

we found out you did us a bad turn about Degumber State.'

I led from the press-room to the stifling office
with the maps on the walls, and the red-haired
man rubbed his hands. 'That's something like,'
said he. 'This was the proper shop to come to.
Now, Sir, let me introduce to you Brother Peachey
Carnehan, that's him, and Brother Daniel Dravot,
that is *me*, and the less said about our professions
the better, for we have been most things in our
time. Soldier, sailor, compositor, photographer,
proof-reader, street-preacher, and correspondents
of the *Backwoodsman* when we thought the paper
wanted one. Carnehan is sober, and so am I.
Look at us first, and see that's sure. It will save
you cutting into my talk. We'll take one of
your cigars apiece, and you shall see us light up.'

I watched the test. The men were absolutely
sober, so I gave them each a tepid whisky and
soda.

'Well *and* good,' said Carnehan of the eyebrows, wiping the froth from his moustache.
'Let me talk now, Dan. We have been all over
India, mostly on foot. We have been boiler-
fitters, engine-drivers, petty contractors, and all
that, and we have decided that India isn't big
enough for such as us.'

They certainly were too big for the office.
Dravot's beard seemed to fill half the room and
Carnehan's shoulders the other half, as they sat on
the big table. Carnehan continued: 'The country
isn't half worked out because they that governs it
won't let you touch it. They spend all their

blessed time in governing it, and you can't lift a
spade, nor chip a rock, nor look for oil, nor anything like that, without all the Government saying, "Leave it alone, and let us govern." Therefore, such *as* it is, we will let it alone, and go away
to some other place where a man isn't crowded
and can come to his own. We are not little men,
and there is nothing that we are afraid of except
Drink, and we have signed a Contrack on that.
Therefore, we are going away to be Kings.'

'Kings in our own right,' muttered Dravot.

'Yes, of course,' I said. 'You've been tramping
in the sun, and it's a very warm night, and hadn't
you better sleep over the notion? Come to-
morrow.'

'Neither drunk nor sunstruck,' said Dravot.
'We have slept over the notion half a year, and
require to see Books and Atlases, and we have
decided that there is only one place now in the
world that two strong men can Sar-a-*whack*.
They call it Kafiristan. By my reckoning it's the
top right-hand corner of Afghanistan, not more than
three hundred miles from Peshawar. They have
two-and-thirty heathen idols there, and we'll be
the thirty-third and fourth. It's a mountaineous
country, and the women of those parts are very
beautiful.'

'But that is provided against in the Contrack,'
said Carnehan. 'Neither Woman nor Liqu-or,
Daniel.'

'And that's all we know, except that no one
has gone there, and they fight, and in any place
where they fight a man who knows how to drill

men can always be a King. We shall go to those
parts and say to any King we find—" D'you want
to vanquish your foes?" and we will show him
how to drill men ; for that we know better than
anything else. Then we will subvert that King
and seize his Throne and establish a Dy-nasty.'

'You'll be cut to pieces before you're fifty miles
across the Border,' I said. 'You have to travel
through Afghanistan to get to that country. It's
one mass of mountains and peaks and glaciers, and
no Englishman has been through it. The people
are utter brutes, and even if you reached them
you couldn't do anything.'

'That's more like,' said Carnehan. 'If you
could think us a little more mad we would be
more pleased. We have come to you to know
about this country, to read a book about it, and to
be shown maps. We want you to tell us that we
are fools and to show us your books.' He turned
to the bookcases.

'Are you at all in earnest?' I said.

'A little,' said Dravot sweetly. 'As big a map
as you have got, even if it's all blank where
Kafiristan is, and any books you've got. We can
read, though we aren't very educated.'

I uncased the big thirty-two-miles-to-the-inch
map of India, and two smaller Frontier maps,
hauled down volume INF-KAN of the *Encyclopædia Britannica*, and the men consulted them.

'See here!' said Dravot, his thumb on the map.
'Up to Jagdallak, Peachey and me know the
road. We was there with Roberts' Army. We'll
have to turn off to the right at Jagdallak through

Laghmann territory. Then we get among the hills—fourteen thousand feet—fifteen thousand—it will be cold work there, but it don't look very far on the map.'

I handed him Wood on the *Sources of the Oxus.* Carnehan was deep in the *Encyclopædia.*

'They're a mixed lot,' said Dravot reflectively ; 'and it won't help us to know the names of their tribes. The more tribes the more they'll fight, and the better for us. From Jagdallak to Ashang H'mm !'

'But all the information about the country is as sketchy and inaccurate as can be,' I protested. 'No one knows anything about it really. Here's the file of the *United Services' Institute.* Read what Bellew says.'

'Blow Bellew !' said Carnehan. 'Dan, they're a stinkin' lot of heathens, but this book here says they think they're related to us English.'

I smoked while the men poured over Raverty, Wood, the maps, and the *Encyclopædia.*

'There is no use your waiting,' said Dravot politely. 'It's about four o'clock now. We'll go before six o'clock if you want to sleep, and we won't steal any of the papers. Don't you sit up. We're two harmless lunatics, and if you come to-morrow evening down to the Serai we'll say good-bye to you.'

'You *are* two fools,' I answered. 'You'll be turned back at the Frontier or cut up the minute you set foot in Afghanistan. Do you want any money or a recommendation down-country ? I can help you to the chance of work next week.'

'Next week we shall be hard at work ourselves, thank you,' said Dravot. 'It isn't so easy being a King as it looks. When we've got our Kingdom in going order we'll let you know, and you can come up and help us to govern it.'

'Would two lunatics make a contrack like that?' said Carnehan, with subdued pride, showing me a greasy half-sheet of notepaper on which was written the following. I copied it, then and there, as a curiosity—

This Contract between me and you persuing witnesseth in the name of God—Amen and so forth.

> *(One)* *That me and you will settle this matter together; i.e. to be Kings of Kafiristan.*
> *(Two)* *That you and me will not, while this matter is being settled, look at any Liquor, nor any Woman black, white, or brown, so as to get mixed up with one or the other harmful.*
> *(Three)* *That we conduct ourselves with Dignity and Discretion, and if one of us gets into trouble the other will stay by him.*
> *Signed by you and me this day.*
> *Peachey Taliaferro Carnehan.*
> *Daniel Dravot.*
> *Both Gentlemen at Large.*

'There was no need for the last article,' said Carnehan, blushing modestly ; 'but it looks regular. Now you know the sort of men that loafers are—we *are* loafers, Dan, until we get out of India—and *do* you think that we would sign a

Contrack like that unless we was in earnest? We have kept away from the two things that make life worth having.'

'You won't enjoy your lives much longer if you are going to try this idiotic adventure. Don't set the office on fire,' I said, 'and go away before nine o'clock.'

I left them still poring over the maps and making notes on the back of the 'Contrack.' 'Be sure to come down to the Serai to-morrow,' were their parting words.

The Kumharsen Serai is the great four-square sink of humanity where the strings of camels and horses from the North load and unload. All the nationalities of Central Asia may be found there, and most of the folk of India proper. Balkh and Bokhara there meet Bengal and Bombay, and try to draw eye-teeth. You can buy ponies, turquoises, Persian pussy-cats, saddle-bags, fat-tailed sheep and musk in the Kumharsen Serai, and get many strange things for nothing. In the afternoon I went down to see whether my friends intended to keep their word or were lying there drunk.

A priest attired in fragments of ribbons and rags stalked up to me, gravely twisting a child's paper whirligig. Behind him was his servant bending under the load of a crate of mud toys. The two were loading up two camels, and the inhabitants of the Serai watched them with shrieks of laughter.

'The priest is mad,' said a horse-dealer to me. 'He is going up to Kabul to sell toys to the Amir. He will either be raised to honour or have his head cut off. He came in here this morning and has been behaving madly ever since.'

'The witless are under the protection of God,' stammered a flat-cheeked Usbeg in broken Hindi. 'They foretell future events.'

'Would they could have foretold that my caravan would have been cut up by the Shinwaris almost within shadow of the Pass!' grunted the Eusufzai agent of a Rajputana trading-house whose goods had been diverted into the hands of other robbers just across the Border, and whose misfortunes were the laughing-stock of the bazar. 'Ohé, priest, whence come you and whither do you go?'

'From Roum have I come,' shouted the priest, waving his whirligig; 'from Roum, blown by the breath of a hundred devils across the sea! O thieves, robbers, liars, the blessing of Pir Khan on pigs, dogs, and perjurers! Who will take the Protected of God to the North to sell charms that are never still to the Amir? The camels shall not gall, the sons shall not fall sick, and the wives shall remain faithful while they are away, of the men who give me place in their caravan. Who will assist me to slipper the King of the Roos with a golden slipper with a silver heel? The protection of Pir Khan be upon his labours!' He spread out the skirts of his gaberdine and pirouetted between the lines of tethered horses.

'There starts a caravan from Peshawar to Kabul in twenty days, *Huzrut*,' said the Eusufzai trader. 'My camels go therewith. Do thou also go and bring us good luck.'

'I will go even now!' shouted the priest. 'I will depart upon my winged camels, and be at Peshawar in a day! Ho! Hazar Mir Khan,' he yelled to his servant, 'drive out the camels, but let me first mount my own.'

He leaped on the back of his beast as it knelt, and, turning round to me, cried : 'Come thou also, Sahib, a little along the road, and I will sell thee a charm—an amulet that shall make thee King of Kafiristan.'

Then the light broke upon me, and I followed the two camels out of the Serai till we reached open road and the priest halted.

'What d'you think o' that?' said he in English. 'Carnehan can't talk their patter, so I've made him my servant. He makes a handsome servant. 'Tisn't for nothing that I've been knocking about the country for fourteen years. Didn't I do that talk neat? We'll hitch on to a caravan at Peshawar till we get to Jagdallak, and then we'll see if we can get donkeys for our camels, and strike into Kafiristan. Whirligigs for the Amir, O Lor! Put your hand under the camel-bags and tell me what you feel.'

I felt the butt of a Martini, and another and another.

'Twenty of 'em,' said Dravot placidly. 'Twenty of 'em and ammunition to correspond, under the whirligigs and the mud dolls.'

'Heaven help you if you are caught with those things!' I said. 'A Martini is worth her weight in silver among the Pathans.'

'Fifteen hundred rupees of capital—every rupee

we could beg, borrow, or steal—are invested on these two camels,' said Dravot. 'We won't get caught. We're going through the Khaiber with a regular caravan. Who'd touch a poor mad priest?'

'Have you got everything you want?' I asked, overcome with astonishment.

'Not yet, but we shall soon. Give us a memento of your kindness, *Brother*. You did me a service, yesterday, and that time in Marwar. Half my Kingdom shall you have, as the saying is.' I slipped a small charm compass from my watch-chain and handed it up to the priest.

'Good-bye,' said Dravot, giving me hand cautiously. 'It's the last time we'll shake hands with an Englishman these many days. Shake hands with him, Carnehan,' he cried, as the second camel passed me.

Carnehan leaned down and shook hands. Then the camels passed away along the dusty road, and I was left alone to wonder. My eye could detect no failure in the disguises. The scene in the Serai proved that they were complete to the native mind. There was just the chance, therefore, that Carnehan and Dravot would be able to wander through Afghanistan without detection. But, beyond, they would find death—certain and awful death.

Ten days later a native correspondent giving me the news of the day from Peshawar, wound up his letter with : 'There has been much laughter here on account of a certain mad priest who is going in his estimation to sell petty gauds and insignificant trinkets which he ascribes as great charms to H.H.

the Amir of Bokhara. He passed through Peshawar
and associated himself to the Second Summer caravan that goes to Kabul. The merchants are pleased
because through superstition they imagine that such
mad fellows bring good fortune.'

The two, then, were beyond the Border. I
would have prayed for them, but, that night, a real
King died in Europe, and demanded an obituary
notice.

.   .   .   .   .

The wheel of the world swings through the
same phases again and again. Summer passed and
winter thereafter, and came and passed again. The
daily paper continued and I with it, and upon the
third summer there fell a hot night, a night-issue,
and a strained waiting for something to be telegraphed from the other side of the world, exactly
as had happened before. A few great men had
died in the past two years, the machines worked
with more clatter, and some of the trees in the
office garden were a few feet taller. But that was
all the difference.

I passed over to the press-room, and went
through just such a scene as I have already described. The nervous tension was stronger than it
had been two years before, and I felt the heat more
acutely. At three o'clock I cried, ' Print off,' and
turned to go, when there crept to my chair what
was left of a man. He was bent into a circle, his
head was sunk between his shoulders, and he
moved his feet one over the other like a bear. I
could hardly see whether he walked or crawled—
this rag-wrapped, whining cripple who addressed

me by name, crying that he was come back. 'Can you give me a drink?' he whimpered. 'For the Lord's sake give me a drink!'

I went back to the office, the man following with groans of pain, and I turned up the lamp.

'Don't you know me?' he gasped, dropping into a chair, and he turned his drawn face, surmounted by a shock of gray hair, to the light.

I looked at him intently. Once before had I seen eyebrows that met over the nose in an inch-broad black band, but for the life of me I could not tell where.

'I don't know you,' I said, handing him the whisky. 'What can I do for you?'

He took a gulp of the spirit raw, and shivered in spite of the suffocating heat.

'I've come back,' he repeated; 'and I was the King of Kafiristan — me and Dravot — crowned Kings we was! In this office we settled it — you setting there and giving us the books. I am Peachey — Peachey Taliaferro Carnehan, and you've been setting here ever since — O Lord!'

I was more than a little astonished, and expressed my feelings accordingly.

'It's true,' said Carnehan, with a dry cackle, nursing his feet, which were wrapped in rags. 'True as gospel. Kings we were, with crowns upon our heads — me and Dravot — poor Dan — oh, poor, poor Dan, that would never take advice, not though I begged of him!'

'Take the whisky,' I said, 'and take your own time. Tell me all you can recollect of everything from beginning to end. You got across the Border

on your camels, Dravot dressed as a mad priest
and you his servant. Do you remember that?'

'I ain't mad—yet, but I shall be that way soon.
Of course I remember. Keep looking at me, or
maybe my words will go all to pieces. Keep looking at me in my eyes and don't say anything.'

I leaned forward and looked into his face as
steadily as I could. He dropped one hand upon
the table and I grasped it by the wrist. It was
twisted like a bird's claw, and upon the back was a
ragged red diamond-shaped scar.

'No, don't look there. Look at *me*,' said
Carnehan. 'That comes afterwards, but for the
Lord's sake don't distrack me. We left with that
caravan, me and Dravot playing all sorts of antics
to amuse the people we were with. Dravot used
to make us laugh in the evenings when all the
people was cooking their dinners—cooking their
dinners, and . . . what did they do then? They
lit little fires with sparks that went into Dravot's
beard, and we all laughed—fit to die. Little red
fires they was, going into Dravot's big red beard
—so funny.' His eyes left mine and he smiled
foolishly.

'You went as far as Jagdallak with that
caravan,' I said at a venture, 'after you had lit
those fires. To Jagdallak, where you turned off
to try to get into Kafiristan.'

'No, we didn't neither. What are you talking
about? We turned off before Jagdallak, because
we heard the roads was good. But they wasn't
good enough for our two camels — mine and
Dravot's. When we left the caravan, Dravot

took off all his clothes and mine too, and said we would be heathen, because the Kafirs didn't allow Mohammedans to talk to them. So we dressed betwixt and between, and such a sight as Daniel Dravot I never saw yet nor expect to see again. He burned half his beard, and slung a sheep-skin over his shoulder, and shaved his head into patterns. He shaved mine, too, and made me wear outrageous things to look like a heathen. That was in a most mountaineous country, and our camels couldn't go along any more because of the mountains. They were tall and black, and coming home I saw them fight like wild goats—there are lots of goats in Kafiristan. And these mountains, they never keep still, no more than the goats. Always fighting they are, and don't let you sleep at night.'

'Take some more whisky,' I said very slowly. 'What did you and Daniel Dravot do when the camels could go no farther because of the rough roads that led into Kafiristan?'

'What did which do? There was a party called Peachey Taliaferro Carnehan that was with Dravot. Shall I tell you about him? He died out there in the cold. Slap from the bridge fell old Peachey, turning and twisting in the air like a penny whirligig that you can sell to the Amir.— No; they was two for three-ha'pence, those whirligigs, or I am much mistaken and woful sore. . . . And then these camels were no use, and Peachey said to Dravot—"For the Lord's sake let's get out of this before our heads are chopped off," and with that they killed the camels all among the mountains, not having anything in particular to eat, but first they took off the boxes with the guns and the ammunition, till two men came along driving four mules. Dravot up and dances in front of them, singing—"Sell me four mules." Says the first man—"If you are rich enough to buy, you are rich enough to rob;" but before ever he could put his hand to his knife, Dravot breaks his neck over his knee, and the other party runs away. So Carnehan loaded the mules with the rifles that was taken off the camels, and together we starts forward into those bitter cold mountaineous parts, and never a road broader than the back of your hand.'

He paused for a moment, while I asked him if he could remember the nature of the country through which he had journeyed.

'I am telling you as straight as I can, but my head isn't as good as it might be. They drove nails through it to make me hear better how Dravot died. The country was mountaineous and the mules were most contrary, and the inhabitants was dispersed and solitary. They went up and up, and down and down, and that other party, Carnehan, was imploring of Dravot not to sing and whistle so loud, for fear of bringing down the tremenjus avalanches. But Dravot says that if a King couldn't sing it wasn't worth being King, and whacked the mules over the rump, and never took no heed for ten cold days. We came to a big level valley all among the mountains, and the mules were near dead, so we killed them, not having anything in special for them or us to eat.

We sat upon the boxes, and played odd and even with the cartridges that was jolted out.

'Then ten men with bows and arrows ran down that valley, chasing twenty men with bows and arrows, and the row was tremenjus. They was fair men—fairer than you or me—with yellow hair and remarkable well built. Says Dravot, unpacking the guns—"This is the beginning of the business. We'll fight for the ten men," and with that he fires two rifles at the twenty men, and drops one of them at two hundred yards from the rock where he was sitting. The other men began to run, but Carnehan and Dravot sits on the boxes picking them off at all ranges, up and down the valley. Then we goes up to the ten men that had run across the snow too, and they fires a footy little arrow at us. Dravot he shoots above their heads and they all falls down flat. Then he walks over them and kicks them, and then he lifts them up and shakes hands all round to make them friendly like. He calls them and gives them the boxes to carry, and waves his hand for all the world as though he was King already. They takes the boxes and him across the valley and up the hill into a pine wood on the top, where there was half-a-dozen big stone idols. Dravot he goes to the biggest—a fellow they call Imbra—and lays a rifle and a cartridge at his feet, rubbing his nose respectful with his own nose, patting him on the head, and saluting in front of it. He turns round to the men and nods his head, and says—"That's all right. I'm in the know too, and all these old jim-jams are

my friends." Then he opens his mouth and
points down it, and when the first man brings
him food, he says—"No"; and when the second
man brings him food he says—"No"; but when
one of the old priests and the boss of the village
brings him food, he says—"Yes," very haughty,
and eats it slow. That was how he came to our
first village, without any trouble, just as though
we had tumbled from the skies. But we tumbled
from one of those damned rope-bridges, you see,
and—you couldn't expect a man to laugh much
after that?'

'Take some more whisky and go on,' I said.
'That was the first village you came into. How
did you get to be King?'

'I wasn't King,' said Carnehan. 'Dravot he
was the King, and a handsome man he looked
with the gold crown on his head and all. Him
and the other party stayed in that village, and
every morning Dravot sat by the side of old
Imbra, and the people came and worshipped.
That was Dravot's order. Then a lot of men
came into the valley, and Carnehan and Dravot
picks them off with the rifles before they knew
where they was, and runs down into the valley and
up again the other side and finds another village,
same as the first one, and the people all falls down
flat on their faces, and Dravot says—"Now what
is the trouble between you two villages?" and the
people points to a woman, as fair as you or me,
that was carried off, and Dravot takes her back to
the first village and counts up the dead—eight
there was. For each dead man Dravot pours a

little milk on the ground and waves his arms like a whirligig, and " That's all right," says he.   Then he and Carnehan takes the big boss of each village by the arm and walks them down into the valley, and shows them how to scratch a line with a spear right down the valley, and gives each a sod of turf from both sides of the line.   Then all the people comes down and shouts like the devil and all, and Dravot says — " Go and dig the land, and be fruitful and multiply," which they did, though they didn't understand.   Then we asks the names of things in their lingo—bread and water and fire and idols and such, and Dravot leads the priest of each village up to the idol, and says he must sit there and judge the people, and if anything goes wrong he is to be shot.

'Next week they was all turning up the land in the valley as quiet as bees and much prettier, and the priests heard all the complaints and told Dravot in dumb show what it was about.   " That's just the beginning," says Dravot.   " They think we're Gods."   He and Carnehan picks out twenty good men and shows them how to click off a rifle, and form fours, and advance in line, and they was very pleased to do so, and clever to see the hang of it.   Then he takes out his pipe and his baccy-pouch and leaves one at one village, and one at the other, and off we two goes to see what was to be done in the next valley.   That was all rock, and there was a little village there, and Carnehan says— " Send 'em to the old valley to plant," and takes 'em there, and gives 'em some land that wasn't took before.   They were a poor lot, and we blooded 'em with a kid before letting 'em into the new Kingdom. That was to impress the people, and then they settled down quiet, and Carnehan went back to Dravot who had got into another valley, all snow and ice and most mountaineous. There was no people there and the Army got afraid, so Dravot shoots one of them, and goes on till he finds some people in a village, and the Army explains that unless the people wants to be killed they had better not shoot their little matchlocks; for they had matchlocks. We makes friends with the priest, and I stays there alone with two of the Army, teaching the men how to drill, and a thundering big Chief comes across the snow with kettle-drums and horns twanging, because he heard there was a new God kicking about. Carnehan sights for the brown of the men half a mile across the snow and wings one of them. Then he sends a message to the Chief that, unless he wished to be killed, he must come and shake hands with me and leave his arms behind. The Chief comes alone first, and Carnehan shakes hands with him and whirls his arms about, same as Dravot used, and very much surprised that Chief was, and strokes my eyebrows. Then Carnehan goes alone to the Chief, and asks him in dumb show if he had an enemy he hated. "I have," says the Chief. So Carnehan weeds out the pick of his men, and sets the two of the Army to show them drill, and at the end of two weeks the men can manœuvre about as well as Volunteers. So he marches with the Chief to a great big plain on the top of a mountain, and the Chief's men rushes into a village and takes it;

we three Martinis firing into the brown of the enemy. So we took that village too, and I gives the Chief a rag from my coat and says, " Occupy till I come " ; which was scriptural. By way of a reminder, when me and the Army was eighteen hundred yards away, I drops a bullet near him standing on the snow, and all the people falls flat on their faces. Then I sends a letter to Dravot wherever he be by land or by sea.'

At the risk of throwing the creature out of train I interrupted—' How could you write a letter up yonder ? '

' The letter ?—Oh !—The letter ! Keep looking at me between the eyes, please. It was a string-talk letter, that we'd learned the way of it from a blind beggar in the Punjab.'

I remember that there had once come to the office a blind man with a knotted twig and a piece of string which he wound round the twig according to some cipher of his own. He could, after the lapse of days or hours, repeat the sentence which he had reeled up. He had reduced the alphabet to eleven primitive sounds, and tried to teach me his method, but I could not understand.

' I sent that letter to Dravot,' said Carnehan ; ' and told him to come back because this Kingdom was growing too big for me to handle, and then I struck for the first valley, to see how the priests were working. They called the village we took along with the Chief, Bashkai, and the first village we took, Er-Heb. The priests at Er-Heb was doing all right, but they had a lot of pending cases about land to show me, and some men from another village had been firing arrows at night. I went out and looked for that village, and fired four rounds at it from a thousand yards. That used all the cartridges I cared to spend, and I waited for Dravot, who had been away two or three months, and I kept my people quiet.

'One morning I heard the devil's own noise of drums and horns, and Dan Dravot marches down the hill with his Army and a tail of hundreds of men, and, which was the most amazing, a great gold crown on his head. "My Gord, Carnehan," says Daniel, "this is a tremenjus business, and we've got the whole country as far as it's worth having. I am the son of Alexander by Queen Semiramis, and you're my younger brother and a God too! It's the biggest thing we've ever seen. I've been marching and fighting for six weeks with the Army, and every footy little village for fifty miles has come in rejoiceful; and more than that, I've got the key of the whole show, as you'll see, and I've got a crown for you! I told 'em to make two of 'em at a place called Shu, where the gold lies in the rock like suet in mutton. Gold I've seen, and turquoise I've kicked out of the cliffs, and there's garnets in the sands of the river, and here's a chunk of amber that a man brought me. Call up all the priests and, here, take your crown."

'One of the men opens a black hair bag, and I slips the crown on. It was too small and too heavy, but I wore it for the glory. Hammered gold it was—five pound weight, like a hoop of a barrel.

'"Peachey," says Dravot, "we don't want to

fight no more. The Craft's the trick, so help me ! "
and he brings forward that same Chief that I left at
Bashkai — Billy Fish we called him afterwards,
because he was so like Billy Fish that drove the big
tank-engine at Mach on the Bolan in the old days.
"Shake hands with him," says Dravot, and I shook
hands and nearly dropped, for Billy Fish gave me
the Grip. I said nothing, but tried him with the
Fellow Craft Grip. He answers all right, and I
tried the Master's Grip, but that was a slip. "A
Fellow Craft he is ! " I says to Dan. "Does he
know the word ? "—" He does," says Dan, "and all
the priests know. It's a miracle ! The Chiefs and
the priests can work a Fellow Craft Lodge in a way
that's very like ours, and they've cut the marks on
the rocks, but they don't know the Third Degree,
and they've come to find out. It's Gord's Truth.
I've known these long years that the Afghans knew
up to the Fellow Craft Degree, but this is a miracle.
A God and a Grand-Master of the Craft am I, and
a Lodge in the Third Degree I will open, and we'll
raise the head priests and the Chiefs of the villages."

' " It's against all the law," I says, " holding a
Lodge without warrant from any one ; and you
know we never held office in any Lodge."

' " It's a master-stroke o' policy," says Dravot.
" It means running the country as easy as a four-
wheeled bogie on a down grade. We can't stop to
inquire now, or they'll turn against us. I've forty
Chiefs at my heel, and passed and raised according
to their merit they shall be. Billet these men on
the villages, and see that we run up a Lodge of some
kind. The temple of Imbra will do for the Lodge-

room.   The women must make aprons as you show
them.   I'll hold a levee of Chiefs to-night and Lodge
to-morrow."

' I was fair run off my legs, but I wasn't such a
fool as not to see what a pull this Craft business
gave us.   I showed the priests' families how to make
aprons of the degrees, but for Dravot's apron the
blue border and marks was made of turquoise lumps
on white hide, not cloth.   We took a great square
stone in the temple for the Master's chair, and little
stones for the officers' chairs, and painted the black
pavement with white squares, and did what we could
to make things regular.

' At the levee which was held that night on the
hillside with big bonfires, Dravot gives out that him
and me were Gods and sons of Alexander, and Past
Grand-Masters in the Craft, and was come to make
Kafiristan a country where every man should eat in
peace and drink in quiet, and specially obey us.
Then the Chiefs come round to shake hands, and
they were so hairy and white and fair it was just
shaking hands with old friends.   We gave them
names according as they was like men we had
known in India—Billy Fish, Holly Dilworth, Pikky
Kergan, that was Bazar-master when I was at
Mhow, and so on, and so on.

' *The* most amazing miracles was at Lodge next
night.   One of the old priests was watching us con-
tinuous, and I felt uneasy, for I knew we'd have to
fudge the Ritual, and I didn't know what the men
knew.   The old priest was a stranger come in from
beyond the village of Bashkai.   The minute Dravot
puts on the Master's apron that the girls had made

for him, the priest fetches a whoop and a howl, and tries to overturn the stone that Dravot was sitting on. " It's all up now," I says. " That comes of meddling with the Craft without warrant ! " Dravot never winked an eye, not when ten priests took and tilted over the Grand-Master's chair—which was to say the stone of Imbra. The priests begins rubbing the bottom end of it to clear away the black dirt, and presently he shows all the other priests the Master's Mark, same as was on Dravot's apron, cut into the stone. Not even the priests of the temple of Imbra knew it was there. The old chap falls flat on his face at Dravot's feet and kisses 'em. " Luck again," says Dravot, across the Lodge to me ; " they say it's the missing Mark that no one could understand the why of. We're more than safe now." Then he bangs the butt of his gun for a gavel and says : " By virtue of the authority vested in me by my own right hand and the help of Peachey, I declare myself Grand-Master of all Freemasonry in Kafiristan in this the Mother Lodge o' the country, and King of Kafiristan equally with Peachey ! " At that he puts on his crown and I puts on mine—I was doing Senior Warden—and we opens the Lodge in most ample form. It was a amazing miracle ! The priests moved in Lodge through the first two degrees almost without telling, as if the memory was coming back to them. After that, Peachey and Dravot raised such as was worthy—high priests and Chiefs of far-off villages. Billy Fish was the first, and I can tell you we scared the soul out of him. It was not in any way according to Ritual, but it served our turn. We didn't raise more than ten of the biggest men, because we didn't want to make the Degree common. And they was clamouring to be raised.

' " In another six months," says Dravot, " we'll hold another Communication, and see how you are working." Then he asks them about their villages, and learns that they was fighting one against the other, and were sick and tired of it. And when they wasn't doing that they was fighting with the Mohammedans. " You can fight those when they come into our country," says Dravot. " Tell off every tenth man of your tribes for a Frontier guard, and send two hundred at a time to this valley to be drilled. Nobody is going to be shot or speared any more so long as he does well, and I know that you won't cheat me, because you're white people—sons of Alexander—and not like common, black Mohammedans. You are *my* people, and by God," says he, running off into English at the end—" I'll make a damned fine Nation of you, or I'll die in the making ! "

' I can't tell all we did for the next six months, because Dravot did a lot I couldn't see the hang of, and he learned their lingo in a way I never could. My work was to help the people plough, and now and again go out with some of the Army and see what the other villages were doing, and make 'em throw rope-bridges across the ravines which cut up the country horrid. Dravot was very kind to me, but when he walked up and down in the pine wood pulling that bloody red beard of his with both fists I knew he was thinking plans I could not advise about, and I just waited for orders.

'But Dravot never showed me disrespect before the people. They were afraid of me and the Army, but they loved Dan. He was the best of friends with the priests and the Chiefs ; but any one could come across the hills with a complaint, and Dravot would hear him out fair, and call four priests together and say what was to be done. He used to call in Billy Fish from Bashkai, and Pikky Kergan from Shu, and an old Chief we called Kafuzelum—it was like enough to his real name—and hold councils with 'em when there was any fighting to be done in small villages. That was his Council of War, and the four priests of Bashkai, Shu, Khawak, and Madora was his Privy Council. Between the lot of 'em they sent me, with forty men and twenty rifles and sixty men carrying turquoises, into the Ghorband country to buy those hand-made Martini rifles, that come out of the Amir's workshops at Kabul, from one of the Amir's Herati regiments that would have sold the very teeth out of their mouths for turquoises.

'I stayed in Ghorband a month, and gave the Governor there the pick of my baskets for hush-money, and bribed the Colonel of the regiment some more, and, between the two and the tribespeople, we got more than a hundred hand-made Martinis, a hundred good Kohat Jezails that'll throw to six hundred yards, and forty man-loads of very bad ammunition for the rifles. I came back with what I had, and distributed 'em among the men that the Chiefs sent in to me to drill. Dravot was too busy to attend to those things, but the old Army that we first made helped me, and we turned out five hundred men that could drill, and two hundred that knew how to hold arms pretty straight. Even those cork-screwed, hand-made guns was a miracle to them. Dravot talked big about powder-shops and factories, walking up and down in the pine wood when the winter was coming on.

'"I won't make a Nation," says he. "I'll make an Empire! These men aren't niggers; they're English! Look at their eyes—look at their mouths. Look at the way they stand up. They sit on chairs in their own houses. They're the Lost Tribes, or something like it, and they've grown to be English. I'll take a census in the spring if the priests don't get frightened. There must be a fair two million of 'em in these hills. The villages are full o' little children. Two million people—two hundred and fifty thousand fighting men—and all English! They only want the rifles and a little drilling. Two hundred and fifty thousand men, ready to cut in on Russia's right flank when she tries for India! Peachey, man," he says, chewing his beard in great hunks, "we shall be Emperors—Emperors of the Earth! Rajah Brooke will be a suckling to us. I'll treat with the Viceroy on equal terms. I'll ask him to send me twelve picked English—twelve that I know of—to help us govern a bit. There's Mackray, Sergeant-pensioner at Segowli—many's the good dinner he's given me, and his wife a pair of trousers. There's Donkin, the Warder of Toung-hoo Jail; there's hundreds that I could lay my hand on if I was in India. The Viceroy shall do it for me. I'll send a man through in the spring for those men, and I'll write for a dispensation from the Grand Lodge for what I've done as Grand-Master. That—and all the Sniders that'll be thrown out when the native troops in India take up the Martini. They'll be worn smooth, but they'll do for fighting in these hills. Twelve English, a hundred thousand Sniders run through the Amir's country in driblets—I'd be content with twenty thousand in one year—and we'd be an Empire. When everything was shipshape, I'd hand over the crown—this crown I'm wearing now —to Queen Victoria on my knees, and she'd say : ' Rise up, Sir Daniel Dravot.' Oh, it's big ! It's big, I tell you ! But there's so much to be done in every place—Bashkai, Khawak, Shu, and every-where else."

' " What is it ? " I says. " There are no more men coming in to be drilled this autumn. Look at those fat, black clouds. They're bringing the snow."

' " It isn't that," says Daniel, putting his hand very hard on my shoulder ; " and I don't wish to say anything that's against you, for no other living man would have followed me and made me what I am as you have done. You're a first-class Com-mander-in-Chief, and the people know you ; but— it's a big country, and somehow you can't help me, Peachey, in the way I want to be helped."

' " Go to your blasted priests, then ! " I said, and I was sorry when I made that remark, but it did hurt me sore to find Daniel talking so superior when I'd drilled all the men, and done all he told me.

' " Don't let's quarrel, Peachey," says Daniel without cursing. " You're a King too, and the half of this Kingdom is yours ; but can't you see, Peachey, we want cleverer men than us now—three or four of 'em, that we can scatter about for our Deputies. It's a hugeous great State, and I can't always tell the right thing to do, and I haven't time for all I want to do, and here's the winter coming on and all." He put half his beard into his mouth, all red like the gold of his crown.

' " I'm sorry, Daniel," says I. " I've done all I could. I've drilled the men and shown the people how to stack their oats better ; and I've brought in those tinware rifles from Ghorband—but I know what you're driving at. I take it Kings always feel oppressed that way."

' " There's another thing too," says Dravot, walking up and down. " The winter's coming and these people won't be giving much trouble, and if they do we can't move about. I want a wife."

' " For Gord's sake leave the women alone ! " I says. " We've both got all the work we can, though I *am* a fool. Remember the Contrack, and keep clear o' women."

' " The Contrack only lasted till such time as we was Kings ; and Kings we have been these months past," says Dravot, weighing his crown in his hand. " You go get a wife too, Peachey—a nice, strappin', plump girl that'll keep you warm in the winter. They're prettier than English girls, and we can take the pick of 'em. Boil 'em once or twice in hot water and they'll come out like chicken and ham."

' " Don't tempt me ! " I says. " I will not have any dealings with a woman not till we are a dam' side more settled than we are now. I've been doing the work o' two men, and you've been doing the work o' three. Let's lie off a bit, and see if we can get some better tobacco from Afghan country and run in some good liquor ; but no women."

' " Who's talking o' *women* ? " says Dravot. " I said *wife*—a Queen to breed a King's son for the King. A Queen out of the strongest tribe, that'll make them your blood-brothers, and that'll lie by your side and tell you all the people thinks about you and their own affairs. That's what I want."

' " Do you remember that Bengali woman I kept at Mogul Serai when I was a plate-layer ? " says I. " A fat lot o' good she was to me. She taught me the lingo and one or two other things ; but what happened ? She ran away with the Station-master's servant and half my month's pay. Then she turned up at Dadur Junction in tow of a half-caste, and had the impidence to say I was her husband—all among the drivers in the running-shed too ! "

' " We've done with that," says Dravot ; " these women are whiter than you or me, and a Queen I will have for the winter months."

' " For the last time o' asking, Dan, do *not*," I says. " It'll only bring us harm. The Bible says that Kings ain't to waste their strength on women, 'specially when they've got a new raw Kingdom to work over."

' " For the last time of answering I will," said Dravot, and he went away through the pine-trees looking like a big red devil, the sun being on his crown and beard and all.

'But getting a wife was not as easy as Dan thought. He put it before the Council, and there was no answer till Billy Fish said that he'd better ask the girls. Dravot damned them all round. "What's wrong with me?" he shouts, standing by the idol Imbra. "Am I a dog or am I not enough of a man for your wenches? Haven't I put the shadow of my hand over this country? Who stopped the last Afghan raid?" It was me really, but Dravot was too angry to remember. "Who bought your guns? Who repaired the bridges? Who's the Grand-Master of the sign cut in the stone?" says he, and he thumped his hand on the block that he used to sit on in Lodge, and at Council, which opened like Lodge always. Billy Fish said nothing and no more did the others. "Keep your hair on, Dan," said I; "and ask the girls. That's how it's done at Home, and these people are quite English."

' " The marriage of the King is a matter of State," says Dan, in a white-hot rage, for he could feel, I hope, that he was going against his better mind. He walked out of the Council-room, and the others sat still, looking at the ground.

' " Billy Fish," says I to the Chief of Bashkai, "what's the difficulty here? A straight answer to a true friend."

' " You know," says Billy Fish. " How should a man tell you who knows everything? How can daughters of men marry Gods or Devils ? It's not proper."

' I remembered something like that in the Bible ; but if, after seeing us as long as they had, they still believed we were Gods, it wasn't for me to undeceive them.

' " A God can do anything," says I. " If the King is fond of a girl he'll not let her die."— "She'll have to," said Billy Fish. " There are all sorts of Gods and Devils in these mountains, and now and again a girl marries one of them and isn't seen any more. Besides, you two know the Mark cut in the stone. Only the Gods know that. We thought you were men till you showed the sign of the Master."

' I wished then that we had explained about the loss of the genuine secrets of a Master-Mason at the first go-off; but I said nothing. All that night there was a blowing of horns in a little dark temple half-way down the hill, and I heard a girl crying fit to die. One of the priests told us that she was being prepared to marry the King.

' " I'll have no nonsense of that kind," says Dan. " I don't want to interfere with your customs, but I'll take my own wife."—" The girl's a little bit afraid," says the priest. " She thinks she's going to die, and they are a-heartening of her up down in the temple."

' " Hearten her very tender, then," says Dravot, " or I'll hearten you with the butt of a gun so you'll never want to be heartened again." He licked his lips, did Dan, and stayed up walking about more than half the night, thinking of the wife that he was going to get in the morning. I wasn't any means comfortable, for I knew that dealings with a woman in foreign parts, though you was a crowned King twenty times over, could not but be risky. I got up very early in the morning while Dravot was asleep, and I saw the priests talking together in whispers, and the Chiefs talking together too, and they looked at me out of the corners of their eyes.

' " What is up, Fish ? " I say to the Bashkai man, who was wrapped up in his furs and looking splendid to behold.

' " I can't rightly say," says he ; " but if you can make the King drop all this nonsense about marriage, you'll be doing him and me and yourself a great service."

' " That I do believe," says I. ' But sure, you know, Billy, as well as me, having fought against and for us, that the King and me are nothing more than two of the finest men that God Almighty ever made. Nothing more, I do assure you."

' " That may be," says Billy Fish, " and yet I should be sorry if it was." He sinks his head upon his great fur cloak for a minute and thinks. " King," says he, " be you man or God or Devil, I'll stick by you to-day. I have twenty of my men with me, and they will follow me. We'll go to Bashkai until the storm blows over."

' A little snow had fallen in the night, and everything was white except the greasy fat clouds that blew down and down from the north. Dravot came out with his crown on his head, swinging his arms and stamping his feet, and looking more pleased than Punch.

' " For the last time, drop it, Dan," says I in a whisper, " Billy Fish here says that there will be a row."

' " A row among my people ! " says Dravot. " Not much. Peachey, you're a fool not to get a wife too. Where's the girl ? " says he with a voice as loud as the braying of a jackass. " Call up all the Chiefs and priests, and let the Emperor see if his wife suits him."

' There was no need to call any one. They were all there leaning on their guns and spears round the clearing in the centre of the pine wood. A lot of priests went down to the little temple to bring up the girl, and the horns blew fit to wake the dead. Billy Fish saunters round and gets as close to Daniel as he could, and behind him stood his twenty men with matchlocks. Not a man of them under six feet. I was next to Dravot, and behind me was twenty men of the regular Army. Up comes the girl, and a strapping wench she was, covered with silver and turquoises, but white as death, and looking back every minute at the priests.

' " She'll do," said Dan, looking her over. " What's to be afraid of, lass ? Come and kiss me." He puts his arm round her. She shuts her eyes, gives a bit of a squeak, and down goes her face in the side of Dan's flaming red beard.

' " The slut's bitten me ! " says he, clapping his hand to his neck, and, sure enough, his hand was red with blood. Billy Fish and two of his match-lock-men catches hold of Dan by the shoulders and drags him into the Bashkai lot, while the priests howls in their lingo—" Neither God nor Devil but a man ! " I was all taken aback, for a priest cut at me in front, and the Army behind began firing into the Bashkai men.

' " God A'mighty ! " says Dan.   " What is the meaning o' this ? "

' " Come back !   Come away ! " says Billy Fish. " Ruin and Mutiny is the matter.   We'll break for Bashkai if we can."

' I tried to give some sort of orders to my men —the men o' the regular Army—but it was no use, so I fired into the brown of 'em with an English Martini and drilled three beggars in a line.   The valley was full of shouting, howling creatures, and every soul was shrieking, " Not a God nor a Devil but only a man ! "   The Bashkai troops stuck to Billy Fish all they were worth, but their match-locks wasn't half as good as the Kabul breech-loaders, and four of them dropped.   Dan was bellowing like a bull, for he was very wrathy ; and Billy Fish had a hard job to prevent him running out at the crowd.

' " We can't stand," says Billy Fish.   " Make a run for it down the valley !   The whole place is against us."   The matchlock-men ran, and we went down the valley in spite of Dravot.   He was swearing horrible and crying out he was a King. The priests rolled great stones on us, and the regular Army fired hard, and there wasn't more than six men, not counting Dan, Billy Fish, and Me, that came down to the bottom of the valley alive.

' Then they stopped firing and the horns in

the temple blew again. "Come away—for God's sake come away!" says Billy Fish. "They'll send runners out to all the villages before ever we get to Bashkai. I can protect you there, but I can't do anything now."

'My own notion is that Dan began to go mad in his head from that hour. He stared up and down like a stuck pig. Then he was all for walking back alone and killing the priests with his bare hands; which he could have done. "An Emperor am I," says Daniel, "and next year I shall be a Knight of the Queen."

'"All right, Dan," says I; "but come along now while there's time."

'"It's your fault," says he, "for not looking after your Army better. There was mutiny in the midst, and you didn't know—you damned engine-driving, plate-laying, missionary's-pass-hunting hound!" He sat upon a rock and called me every foul name he could lay tongue to. I was too heart-sick to care, though it was all his foolishness that brought the smash.

'"I'm sorry, Dan," says I, "but there's no accounting for natives. This business is our Fifty-Seven. Maybe we'll make something out of it yet, when we've got to Bashkai."

'"Let's get to Bashkai, then," says Dan, "and, by God, when I come back here again I'll sweep the valley so there isn't a bug in a blanket left!"

'We walked all that day, and all that night Dan was stumping up and down on the snow, chewing his beard and muttering to himself.

'"There's no hope o' getting clear," said Billy

Fish. " The priests will have sent runners to the villages to say that you are only men. Why didn't you stick on as Gods till things was more settled ? I'm a dead man," says Billy Fish, and he throws himself down on the snow and begins to pray to his Gods.

' Next morning we was in a cruel bad country —all up and down, no level ground at all, and no food either. The six Bashkai men looked at Billy Fish hungry-way as if they wanted to ask something, but they said never a word. At noon we came to the top of a flat mountain all covered with snow, and when we climbed up into it, behold, there was an Army in position waiting in the middle !

' " The runners have been very quick," says Billy Fish, with a little bit of a laugh. " They are waiting for us."

' Three or four men began to fire from the enemy's side, and a chance shot took Daniel in the calf of the leg. That brought him to his senses. He looks across the snow at the Army, and sees the rifles that we had brought into the country.

' " We're done for," says he. " They are Englishmen, these people,—and it's my blasted nonsense that has brought you to this. Get back, Billy Fish, and take your men away ; you've done what you could, and now cut for it. Carnehan," says he, " shake hands with me and go along with Billy. Maybe they won't kill you. I'll go and meet 'em alone. It's me that did it. Me, the King ! "

' " Go ! " says I. " Go to Hell, Dan ! I'm

with you here. Billy Fish, you clear out, and we two will meet those folk."

' " I'm a Chief," says Billy Fish, quite quiet. "I stay with you. My men can go."

' The Bashkai fellows didn't wait for a second word, but ran off, and Dan and Me and Billy Fish walked across to where the drums were drumming and the horns were horning. It was cold—awful cold. I've got that cold in the back of my head now. There's a lump of it there.'

The punkah-coolies had gone to sleep. Two kerosene lamps were blazing in the office, and the perspiration poured down my face and splashed on the blotter as I leaned forward. Carnehan was shivering, and I feared that his mind might go. I wiped my face, took a fresh grip of the piteously mangled hands, and said : ' What happened after that ? '

The momentary shift of my eyes had broken the clear current.

' What was you pleased to say ? ' whined Carnehan. ' They took them without any sound. Not a little whisper all along the snow, not though the King knocked down the first man that set hand on him—not though old Peachey fired his last cartridge into the brown of 'em. Not a single solitary sound did those swines make. They just closed up tight, and I tell you their furs stunk. There was a man called Billy Fish, a good friend of us all, and they cut his throat, Sir, then and there, like a pig ; and the King kicks up the bloody snow and says : " We've had a dashed fine run for our money. What's coming next ? " But

Peachey, Peachey Taliaferro, I tell you, Sir, in confidence as betwixt two friends, he lost his head, Sir. No, he didn't neither. The King lost his head, so he did, all along o' one of those cunning rope-bridges. Kindly let me have the paper-cutter, Sir. It tilted this way. They marched him a mile across that snow to a rope-bridge over a ravine with a river at the bottom. You may have seen such. They prodded him behind like an ox. "Damn your eyes!" says the King. "D'you suppose I can't die like a gentleman?" He turns to Peachey—Peachey that was crying like a child. "I've brought you to this, Peachey," says he. "Brought you out of your happy life to be killed in Kafiristan, where you was late Commander-in-Chief of the Emperor's forces. Say you forgive me, Peachey."—"I do," says Peachey. "Fully and freely do I forgive you, Dan."—"Shake hands, Peachey," says he. "I'm going now." Out he goes, looking neither right nor left, and when he was plumb in the middle of those dizzy dancing ropes—"Cut, you beggars," he shouts; and they cut, and old Dan fell, turning round and round and round, twenty thousand miles, for he took half an hour to fall till he struck the water, and I could see his body caught on a rock with the gold crown close beside.

'But do you know what they did to Peachey between two pine-trees? They crucified him, Sir, as Peachey's hand will show. They used wooden pegs for his hands and his feet; and he didn't die. He hung there and screamed, and they took him down next day, and said it was a miracle that he wasn't dead. They took him down—poor old Peachey that hadn't done them any harm—that hadn't done them any——'

He rocked to and fro and wept bitterly, wiping his eyes with the back of his scarred hands and moaning like a child for some ten minutes.

'They was cruel enough to feed him up in the temple, because they said he was more of a God than old Daniel that was a man. Then they turned him out on the snow, and told him to go home, and Peachey came home in about a year, begging along the roads quite safe; for Daniel Dravot he walked before and said : " Come along, Peachey. It's a big thing we're doing." The mountains they danced at night, and the mountains they tried to fall on Peachey's head, but Dan he held up his hand, and Peachey came along bent double. He never let go of Dan's hand, and he never let go of Dan's head. They gave it to him as a present in the temple, to remind him not to come again, and though the crown was pure gold, and Peachey was starving, never would Peachey sell the same. You knew Dravot, Sir ! You knew Right Worshipful Brother Dravot ! Look at him now !'

He fumbled in the mass of rags round his bent waist ; brought out a black horsehair bag embroidered with silver thread, and shook therefrom on to my table—the dried, withered head of Daniel Dravot ! The morning sun that had long been paling the lamps struck the red beard and blind sunken eyes ; struck, too, a heavy circlet of gold studded with raw turquoises, that Carnehan placed tenderly on the battered temples.

'You be'old now,' said Carnehan, 'the Emperor in his 'abit as he lived—the King of Kafiristan with his crown upon his head. Poor old Daniel that was a monarch once!'

I shuddered, for, in spite of defacements manifold, I recognised the head of the man of Marwar Junction. Carnehan rose to go. I attempted to stop him. He was not fit to walk abroad. 'Let me take away the whisky, and give me a little money,' he gasped. 'I was a King once. I'll go to the Deputy Commissioner and ask to set in the Poorhouse till I get my health. No, thank you, I can't wait till you get a carriage for me. I've urgent private affairs—in the south—at Marwar.'

He shambled out of the office and departed in the direction of the Deputy Commissioner's house. That day at noon I had occasion to go down the blinding hot Mall, and I saw a crooked man crawling along the white dust of the roadside, his hat in his hand, quavering dolorously after the fashion of street-singers at Home. There was not a soul in sight, and he was out of all possible ear-shot of the houses. And he sang through his nose, turning his head from right to left :—

> 'The Son of Man goes forth to war,
>   A golden crown to gain ;
> His blood-red banner streams afar—
>   Who follows in his train ?'

I waited to hear no more, but put the poor wretch into my carriage and drove him off to the nearest missionary for eventual transfer to the

Asylum.   He repeated the hymn twice while he was with me whom he did not in the least recognise, and I left him singing it to the missionary.

Two days later I inquired after his welfare of the Superintendent of the Asylum.

'He was admitted suffering from sunstroke. He died early yesterday morning,' said the Superintendent.   'Is it true that he was half an hour bareheaded in the sun at mid-day?'

'Yes,' said I, 'but do you happen to know if he had anything upon him by any chance when he died?'

'Not to my knowledge,' said the Superintendent.

And there the matter rests.

WEE WILLIE WINKIE

AND OTHER STORIES

Wee Willie Winkie

An officer and a gentleman

His full name was Percival William Williams, but he picked up the other name in a nursery-book, and that was the end of the christened titles. His mother's *ayah* called him Willie-*Baba*, but as he never paid the faintest attention to anything that the *ayah* said, her wisdom did not help matters.

His father was the Colonel of the 195th, and as soon as Wee Willie Winkie was old enough to understand what Military Discipline meant, Colonel Williams put him under it. There was no other way of managing the child. When he was good for a week, he drew good-conduct pay ; and when he was bad, he was deprived of his good-conduct stripe. Generally he was bad, for India offers many chances of going wrong to little six-year-olds.

Children resent familiarity from strangers, and Wee Willie Winkie was a very particular child. Once he accepted an acquaintance, he was graciously pleased to thaw. He accepted Brandis, a subaltern of the 195th, on sight. Brandis was having tea at the Colonel's, and Wee Willie Winkie entered

strong in the possession of a good-conduct badge
won for not chasing the hens round the compound.
He regarded Brandis with gravity for at least ten
minutes, and then delivered himself of his opinion.

'I like you,' said he slowly, getting off his chair
and coming over to Brandis. 'I like you. I shall
call you Coppy, because of your hair. Do you
mind being called Coppy? It is because of ve hair,
you know.'

Here was one of the most embarrassing of Wee
Willie Winkie's peculiarities. He would look at a
stranger for some time, and then, without warning
or explanation, would give him a name. And
the name stuck. No regimental penalties could
break Wee Willie Winkie off this habit. He lost
his good-conduct badge for christening the Commissioner's wife 'Pobs'; but nothing that the
Colonel could do made the Station forego the nick-
name, and Mrs. Collen remained 'Pobs' till the
end of her stay. So Brandis was christened
'Coppy,' and rose, therefore, in the estimation of
the regiment.

If Wee Willie Winkie took an interest in any
one, the fortunate man was envied alike by the
mess and the rank and file. And in their envy
lay no suspicion of self-interest. 'The Colonel's
son' was idolised on his own merits entirely. Yet
Wee Willie Winkie was not lovely. His face was
permanently freckled, as his legs were permanently
scratched, and in spite of his mother's almost
tearful remonstrances he had insisted upon having
his long yellow locks cut short in the military
fashion. 'I want my hair like Sergeant Tummil's,'

said Wee Willie Winkie, and, his father abetting, the sacrifice was accomplished.

Three weeks after the bestowal of his youthful affections on Lieutenant Brandis—henceforward to be called 'Coppy' for the sake of brevity—Wee Willie Winkie was destined to behold strange things and far beyond his comprehension.

Coppy returned his liking with interest. Coppy had let him wear for five rapturous minutes his own big sword—just as tall as Wee Willie Winkie. Coppy had promised him a terrier puppy; and Coppy had permitted him to witness the miraculous operation of shaving. Nay, more—Coppy had said that even he, Wee Willie Winkie, would rise in time to the ownership of a box of shiny knives, a silver soap-box, and a silver-handled 'sputter-brush,' as Wee Willie Winkie called it. Decidedly, there was no one except his father, who could give or take away good-conduct badges at pleasure, half so wise, strong, and valiant as Coppy with the Afghan and Egyptian medals on his breast. Why, then, should Coppy be guilty of the un-manly weakness of kissing—vehemently kissing—a 'big girl,' Miss Allardyce to wit? In the course of a morning ride Wee Willie Winkie had seen Coppy so doing, and, like the gentleman he was, had promptly wheeled round and cantered back to his groom, lest the groom should also see.

Under ordinary circumstances he would have spoken to his father, but he felt instinctively that this was a matter on which Coppy ought first to be consulted.

'Coppy, shouted Wee Willie Winkie, reining

up outside that subaltern's bungalow early one morning—'I want to see you, Coppy!'

'Come in, young 'un,' returned Coppy, who was at early breakfast in the midst of his dogs. 'What mischief have you been getting into now?'

Wee Willie Winkie had done nothing notoriously bad for three days, and so stood on a pinnacle of virtue.

'*I've* been doing nothing bad,' said he, curling himself into a long chair with a studious affectation of the Colonel's languor after a hot parade. He buried his freckled nose in a tea-cup and, with eyes staring roundly over the rim, asked: 'I say, Coppy, is it pwoper to kiss big girls?'

'By Jove! You're beginning early. Who do you want to kiss?'

'No one. My muvver's always kissing me if I don't stop her. If it isn't pwoper, how was you kissing Major Allardyce's big girl last morning, by ve canal?'

Coppy's brow wrinkled. He and Miss Allardyce had with great craft managed to keep their engagement secret for a fortnight. There were urgent and imperative reasons why Major Allardyce should not know how matters stood for at least another month, and this small marplot had discovered a great deal too much.

'I saw you,' said Wee Willie Winkie calmly. 'But ve *sais* didn't see. I said, "*Hut jao!*"'

'Oh, you had that much sense, you young Rip,' groaned poor Coppy, half amused and half angry. 'And how many people may you have told about it?'

'Only me myself. You didn't tell when I twied to wide ve buffalo ven my pony was lame ; and I fought you wouldn't like.'

'Winkie,' said Coppy enthusiastically, shaking the small hand, ' you're the best of good fellows. Look here, you can't understand all these things. One of these days—hang it, how can I make you see it !—I'm going to marry Miss Allardyce, and then she'll be Mrs. Coppy, as you say. If your young mind is so scandalised at the idea of kissing big girls, go and tell your father.'

'What will happen ? ' said Wee Willie Winkie, who firmly believed that his father was omnipotent.

'I shall get into trouble,' said Coppy, playing his trump card with an appealing look at the holder of the ace.

'Ven I won't,' said Wee Willie Winkie briefly. 'But my faver says it's un-man-ly to be always kissing, and I didn't fink *you'd* do vat, Coppy.'

'I'm not always kissing, old chap. It's only now and then, and when you're bigger you'll do it too. Your father meant it's not good for little boys.'

'Ah !' said Wee Willie Winkie, now fully enlightened. 'It's like ve sputter-brush ? '

'Exactly,' said Coppy gravely.

'But I don't fink I'll ever want to kiss big girls, nor no one, 'cept my muvver. And I *must* vat, you know.'

There was a long pause, broken by Wee Willie Winkie.

'Are you fond of vis big girl, Coppy ? '

'Awfully ! ' said Coppy.

'Fonder van you are of Bell or ve Butcha—or me?'

'It's in a different way,' said Coppy. 'You see, one of these days Miss Allardyce will belong to me, but you'll grow up and command the Regiment and—all sorts of things. It's quite different, you see.'

'Very well,' said Wee Willie Winkie, rising. 'If you're fond of ve big girl I won't tell any one. I must go now.'

Coppy rose and escorted his small guest to the door, adding—'You're the best of little fellows, Winkie. I tell you what. In thirty days from now you can tell if you like—tell any one you like.'

Thus the secret of the Brandis-Allardyce engagement was dependent on a little child's word. Coppy, who knew Wee Willie Winkie's idea of truth, was at ease, for he felt that he would not break promises. Wee Willie Winkie betrayed a special and unusual interest in Miss Allardyce, and, slowly revolving round that embarrassed young lady, was used to regard her gravely with unwinking eye. He was trying to discover why Coppy should have kissed her. She was not half so nice as his own mother. On the other hand, she was Coppy's property, and would in time belong to him. Therefore it behoved him to treat her with as much respect as Coppy's big sword or shiny pistol.

The idea that he shared a great secret in common with Coppy kept Wee Willie Winkie unusually virtuous for three weeks. Then the

Old Adam broke out, and he made what he called a ' camp-fire ' at the bottom of the garden. How could he have foreseen that the flying sparks would have lighted the Colonel's little hay-rick and consumed a week's store for the horses? Sudden and swift was the punishment—deprivation of the good-conduct badge and, most sorrowful of all, two days' confinement to barracks — the house and verandah—coupled with the withdrawal of the light of his father's countenance.

He took the sentence like the man he strove to be, drew himself up with a quivering under-lip, saluted, and, once clear of the room, ran to weep bitterly in his nursery—called by him ' my quarters.' Coppy came in the afternoon and attempted to console the culprit.

' I'm under awwest,' said Wee Willie Winkie mournfully, ' and I didn't ought to speak to you.'

Very early the next morning he climbed on to the roof of the house—that was not forbidden—and beheld Miss Allardyce going for a ride.

' Where are you going? ' cried Wee Willie Winkie.

' Across the river,' she answered, and trotted forward.

Now the cantonment in which the 195th lay was bounded on the north by a river—dry in the winter. From his earliest years, Wee Willie Winkie had been forbidden to go across the river, and had noted that even Coppy—the almost almighty Coppy —had never set foot beyond it. Wee Willie Winkie had once been read to, out of a big blue book, the history of the Princess and the Goblins

—a most wonderful tale of a land where the Goblins were always warring with the children of men until they were defeated by one Curdie. Ever since that date it seemed to him that the bare black and purple hills across the river were inhabited by Goblins, and, in truth, every one had said that there lived the Bad Men. Even in his own house the lower halves of the windows were covered with green paper on account of the Bad Men who might, if allowed clear view, fire into peaceful drawing-rooms and comfortable bedrooms. Certainly, beyond the river, which was the end of all the Earth, lived the Bad Men. And here was Major Allardyce's big girl, Coppy's property, preparing to venture into their borders ! What would Coppy say if anything happened to her ? If the Goblins ran off with her as they did with Curdie's Princess ? She must at all hazards be turned back.

The house was still. Wee Willie Winkie reflected for a moment on the very terrible wrath of his father ; and then—broke his arrest ! It was a crime unspeakable. The low sun threw his shadow, very large and very black, on the trim garden-paths, as he went down to the stables and ordered his pony. It seemed to him in the hush of the dawn that all the big world had been bidden to stand still and look at Wee Willie Winkie guilty of mutiny. The drowsy *sais* gave him his mount, and, since the one great sin made all others insignificant, Wee Willie Winkie said that he was going to ride over to Coppy Sahib, and went out at a foot-pace, stepping on the soft mould of the flower-borders.

The devastating track of the pony's feet was the last misdeed that cut him off from all sympathy of Humanity. He turned into the road, leaned forward, and rode as fast as the pony could put foot to the ground in the direction of the river.

But the liveliest of twelve-two ponies can do little against the long canter of a Waler. Miss Allardyce was far ahead, had passed through the crops, beyond the Police-posts, when all the guards were asleep, and her mount was scattering the pebbles of the river-bed as Wee Willie Winkie left the cantonment and British India behind him. Bowed forward and still flogging, Wee Willie Winkie shot into Afghan territory, and could just see Miss Allardyce, a black speck, flickering across the stony plain. The reason of her wandering was simple enough. Coppy, in a tone of too-hastily-assumed authority, had told her overnight that she must not ride out by the river. And she had gone to prove her own spirit and teach Coppy a lesson.

Almost at the foot of the inhospitable hills, Wee Willie Winkie saw the Waler blunder and come down heavily. Miss Allardyce struggled clear, but her ankle had been severely twisted, and she could not stand. Having fully shown her spirit, she wept, and was surprised by the apparition of a white, wide-eyed child in khaki, on a nearly spent pony.

'Are you badly, badly hurted ?' shouted Wee Willie Winkie, as soon as he was within range. 'You didn't ought to be here.'

'I don't know,' said Miss Allardyce ruefully,

ignoring the reproof. 'Good gracious, child, what
are *you* doing here ? '

'You said you was going acwoss ve wiver,'
panted Wee Willie Winkie, throwing himself off
his pony. 'And nobody—not even Coppy—must
go acwoss ve wiver, and I came after you ever so
hard, but you wouldn't stop, and now you've
hurted yourself, and Coppy will be angwy wiv me,
and—I've bwoken my awwest! I've bwoken my
awwest ! '

The future Colonel of the 195th sat down and
sobbed. In spite of the pain in her ankle the girl
was moved.

'Have you ridden all the way from cantonments,
little man ? What for ? '

'You belonged to Coppy. Coppy told me so ! '
wailed Wee Willie Winkie disconsolately. 'I saw
him kissing you, and he said he was fonder of you
van Bell or ve Butcha or me. And so I came.
You must get up and come back. You didn't
ought to be here. Vis is a bad place, and I've
bwoken my awwest.'

'I can't move, Winkie,' said Miss Allardyce,
with a groan. 'I've hurt my foot. What shall I
do ? '

She showed a readiness to weep anew, which
steadied Wee Willie Winkie, who had been brought
up to believe that tears were the depth of unmanli-
ness. Still, when one is as great a sinner as Wee
Willie Winkie, even a man may be permitted to
break down.

'Winkie,' said Miss Allardyce, 'when you've
rested a little, ride back and tell them to send out

something to carry me back in. It hurts fearfully.'

The child sat still for a little time and Miss Allardyce closed her eyes; the pain was nearly making her faint. She was roused by Wee Willie Winkie tying up the reins on his pony's neck and setting it free with a vicious cut of his whip that made it whicker. The little animal headed towards the cantonments.

'Oh, Winkie, what are you doing?'

'Hush!' said Wee Willie Winkie. 'Vere's a man coming—one of ve Bad Men. I must stay wiv you. My faver says a man must *always* look after a girl. Jack will go home, and ven vey'll come and look for us. Vat's why I let him go.'

Not one man but two or three had appeared from behind the rocks of the hills, and the heart of Wee Willie Winkie sank within him, for just in this manner were the Goblins wont to steal out and vex Curdie's soul. Thus had they played in Curdie's garden—he had seen the picture—and thus had they frightened the Princess's nurse. He heard them talking to each other, and recognised with joy the bastard Pushto that he had picked up from one of his father's grooms lately dismissed. People who spoke that tongue could not be the Bad Men. They were only natives after all.

They came up to the boulders on which Miss Allardyce's horse had blundered.

Then rose from the rock Wee Willie Winkie, child of the Dominant Race, aged six and three-quarters, and said briefly and emphatically ' *Jao !* ' The pony had crossed the river-bed.

The men laughed, and laughter from natives was the one thing Wee Willie Winkie could not tolerate. He asked them what they wanted and why they did not depart. Other men with most evil faces and crooked-stocked guns crept out of the shadows of the hills, till, soon, Wee Willie Winkie was face to face with an audience some twenty strong. Miss Allardyce screamed.

'Who are you?' said one of the men.

'I am the Colonel Sahib's son, and my order is that you go at once. You black men are frightening the Miss Sahib. One of you must run into cantonments and take the news that the Miss Sahib has hurt herself, and that the Colonel's son is here with her.'

'Put our feet into the trap?' was the laughing reply. 'Hear this boy's speech!'

'Say that I sent you—I, the Colonel's son. They will give you money.'

'What is the use of this talk? Take up the child and the girl, and we can at least ask for the ransom. Ours are the villages on the heights,' said a voice in the background.

These *were* the Bad Men—worse than Goblins —and it needed all Wee Willie Winkie's training to prevent him from bursting into tears. But he felt that to cry before a native, excepting only his mother's *ayah*, would be an infamy greater than any mutiny. Moreover, he, as future Colonel of the 195th, had that grim regiment at his back.

'Are you going to carry us away?' said Wee Willie Winkie, very blanched and uncomfortable.

'Yes, my little *Sahib Bahadur*,' said the tallest of the men, 'and eat you afterwards.'

'That is child's talk,' said Wee Willie Winkie. 'Men do not eat men.'

A yell of laughter interrupted him, but he went on firmly—'And if you do carry us away, I tell you that all my regiment will come up in a day and kill you all without leaving one. Who will take my message to the Colonel Sahib?'

Speech in any vernacular—and Wee Willie Winkie had a colloquial acquaintance with three— was easy to the boy who could not yet manage his 'r's' and 'th's' aright.

Another man joined the conference, crying : 'O foolish men! What this babe says is true. He is the heart's heart of those white troops. For the sake of peace let them go both, for if he be taken, the regiment will break loose and gut the valley. *Our* villages are in the valley, and we shall not escape. That regiment are devils. They broke Khoda Yar's breastbone with kicks when he tried to take the rifles ; and if we touch this child they will fire and rape and plunder for a month, till nothing remains. Better to send a man back to take the message and get a reward. I say that this child is their God, and that they will spare none of us, nor our women, if we harm him.'

It was Din Mahommed, the dismissed groom of the Colonel, who made the diversion, and an angry and heated discussion followed. Wee Willie Winkie, standing over Miss Allardyce, waited the upshot. Surely his 'wegiment,' his own 'wegiment,' would not desert him if they knew of his extremity.

. . . . .

The riderless pony brought the news to the 195th, though there had been consternation in the Colonel's household for an hour before. The little beast came in through the parade-ground in front of the main barracks, where the men were settling down to play Spoil-five till the afternoon. Devlin, the Colour-Sergeant of E Company, glanced at the empty saddle and tumbled through the barrack-rooms, kicking up each Room Corporal as he passed. 'Up, ye beggars! There's something happened to the Colonel's son,' he shouted.

'He couldn't fall off! S'elp me, 'e *couldn't* fall off,' blubbered a drummer-boy. 'Go an' hunt acrost the river. He's over there if he's anywhere, an' maybe those Pathans have got 'im. For the love o' Gawd don't look for 'im in the nullahs! Let's go over the river.'

'There's sense in Mott yet,' said Devlin. 'E Company, double out to the river—sharp!'

So E Company, in its shirt-sleeves mainly, doubled for the dear life, and in the rear toiled the perspiring Sergeant, adjuring it to double yet faster. The cantonment was alive with the men of the 195th hunting for Wee Willie Winkie, and the Colonel finally overtook E Company, far too exhausted to swear, struggling in the pebbles of the river-bed.

Up the hill under which Wee Willie Winkie's Bad Men were discussing the wisdom of carrying off the child and the girl, a look-out fired two shots.

'What have I said?' shouted Din Mahommed. 'There is the warning! The *pulton* are out already and are coming across the plain! Get away! Let us not be seen with the boy.'

The men waited for an instant, and then, as another shot was fired, withdrew into the hills, silently as they had appeared.

'The wegiment is coming,' said Wee Willie Winkie confidently to Miss Allardyce, 'and it's all wight. Don't cwy!'

He needed the advice himself, for ten minutes later, when his father came up, he was weeping bitterly with his head in Miss Allardyce's lap.

And the men of the 195th carried him home with shouts and rejoicings; and Coppy, who had ridden a horse into a lather, met him, and, to his intense disgust, kissed him openly in the presence of the men.

But there was balm for his dignity. His father assured him that not only would the breaking of arrest be condoned, but that the good-conduct badge would be restored as soon as his mother could sew it on his blouse-sleeve. Miss Allardyce had told the Colonel a story that made him proud of his son.

'She belonged to you, Coppy,' said Wee Willie Winkie, indicating Miss Allardyce with a grimy forefinger. 'I *knew* she didn't ought to go acwoss ve wiver, and I knew ve wegiment would come to me if I sent Jack home.'

'You're a hero, Winkie,' said Coppy—'a *pukka* hero!'

'I don't know what vat means,' said Wee Willie Winkie, 'but you mustn't call me Winkie any no more.   I'm Percival Will'am Will'ams.'

And in this manner did Wee Willie Winkie enter into his manhood.

Baa Baa, Black Sheep

Baa Baa, Black Sheep,
Have you any wool?
Yes, Sir, yes, Sir, three bags full.
One for the Master, one for the Dame—
None for the Little Boy that cries down the lane.
Nursery Rhyme.

THE FIRST BAG

When I was in my father's house, I was in a better place

THEY were putting Punch to bed—the *ayah* and the *hamal* and Meeta, the big *Surti* boy, with the red and gold turban. Judy, already tucked inside her mosquito-curtains, was nearly asleep. Punch had been allowed to stay up for dinner. Many privileges had been accorded to Punch within the last ten days, and a greater kindness from the people of his world had encompassed his ways and works, which were mostly obstreperous. He sat on the edge of his bed and swung his bare legs defiantly.

'Punch-*baba* going to bye-lo?' said the *ayah* suggestively.

'No,' said Punch. 'Punch-*baba* wants the story about the Ranee that was turned into a tiger.

Meeta must tell it, and the *hamal* shall hide behind the door and make tiger-noises at the proper time.'

'But Judy-*baba* will wake up,' said the *ayah*.

'Judy-*baba* is waked,' piped a small voice from the mosquito-curtains. 'There was a Ranee that lived at Delhi. Go on, Meeta,' and she fell fast asleep again while Meeta began the story.

Never had Punch secured the telling of that tale with so little opposition. He reflected for a long time. The *hamal* made the tiger-noises in twenty different keys.

''Top!' said Punch authoritatively. 'Why doesn't Papa come in and say he is going to give me *put-put?*'

'Punch-*baba* is going away,' said the *ayah*. 'In another week there will be no Punch-*baba* to pull my hair any more.' She sighed softly, for the boy of the household was very dear to her heart.

'Up the Ghauts in a train?' said Punch, standing on his bed. 'All the way to Nassick where the Ranee-Tiger lives?'

'Not to Nassick this year, little Sahib,' said Meeta, lifting him on his shoulder. 'Down to the sea where the cocoa-nuts are thrown, and across the sea in a big ship. Will you take Meeta with you to *Belait?*'

'You shall all come,' said Punch, from the height of Meeta's strong arms. 'Meeta and the *ayah* and the *hamal* and Bhini-in-the-Garden, and the salaam-Captain-Sahib-snake-man.'

There was no mockery in Meeta's voice when he replied—'Great is the Sahib's favour,' and laid the little man down in the bed, while the *ayah*, sitting in the moonlight at the doorway, lulled him to sleep with an interminable canticle such as they sing in the Roman Catholic Church at Parel. Punch curled himself into a ball and slept.

Next morning Judy shouted that there was a rat in the nursery, and thus he forgot to tell her the wonderful news. It did not much matter, for Judy was only three and she would not have understood. But Punch was five ; and he knew that going to England would be much nicer than a trip to Nassick.

.   .   .   .   .

Papa and Mamma sold the brougham and the piano, and stripped the house, and curtailed the allowance of crockery for the daily meals, and took long counsel together over a bundle of letters bearing the Rocklington postmark.

' The worst of it is that one can't be certain of anything,' said Papa, pulling his moustache. 'The letters in themselves are excellent, and the terms are moderate enough.'

' The worst of it is that the children will grow up away from me,' thought Mamma ; but she did not say it aloud.

' We are only one case among hundreds,' said Papa bitterly. 'You shall go Home again in five years, dear.'

' Punch will be ten then — and Judy eight. Oh, how long and long and long the time will be ! And we have to leave them among strangers.'

' Punch is a cheery little chap. He's sure to make friends wherever he goes.'

' And who could help loving my Ju ? '

They were standing over the cots in the nursery late at night, and I think that Mamma was crying softly.   After Papa had gone away, she knelt down by the side of Judy's cot.   The *ayah* saw her and put up a prayer that the *memsahib* might never find the love of her children taken away from her and given to a stranger.

Mamma's own prayer was a slightly illogical one.   Summarised it ran : ' Let strangers love my children and be as good to them as I should be, but let *me* preserve their love and their con-fidence for ever and ever.   Amen.'   Punch scratched himself in his sleep, and Judy moaned a little.

Next day they all went down to the sea, and there was a scene at the Apollo Bunder when Punch discovered that Meeta could not come too, and Judy learned that the *ayah* must be left behind.   But Punch found a thousand fascinating things in the rope, block, and steam-pipe line on the big P. and O. Steamer long before Meeta and the *ayah* had dried their tears.

' Come back, Punch-*baba*,' said the *ayah*.

' Come back,' said Meeta, ' and be a *Burra Sahib* ' (a big man).

' Yes,' said Punch, lifted up in his father's arms to wave good-bye.   ' Yes, I will come back, and I will be a *Burra Sahib Bahadur !* ' (a very big man indeed).

At the end of the first day Punch demanded to be set down in England, which he was certain must be close at hand.   Next day there was a merry breeze, and Punch was very sick. 'When I come back to Bombay,' said Punch on his recovery, 'I will come by the road—in a broom-*gharri*. This is a very naughty ship.'

The Swedish boatswain consoled him, and he modified his opinions as the voyage went on. There was so much to see and to handle and ask questions about that Punch nearly forgot the *ayah* and Meeta and the *hamal*, and with difficulty remembered a few words of the Hindustani once his second-speech.

But Judy was much worse. The day before the steamer reached Southampton, Mamma asked her if she would not like to see the *ayah* again. Judy's blue eyes turned to the stretch of sea that had swallowed all her tiny past, and she said : '*Ayah !* What *ayah ?* '

Mamma cried over her and Punch marvelled. It was then that he heard for the first time Mamma's passionate appeal to him never to let Judy forget Mamma. Seeing that Judy was young, ridiculously young, and that Mamma, every evening for four weeks past, had come into the cabin to sing her and Punch to sleep with a mysterious rune that he called 'Sonny, my soul,' Punch could not understand what Mamma meant. But he strove to do his duty ; for, the moment Mamma left the cabin, he said to Judy : 'Ju, you bemember Mamma ? '

' 'Torse I do,' said Judy.

' Then *always* bemember Mamma, 'r else I won't give you the paper ducks that the red-haired Captain Sahib cut out for me.'

So Judy promised always to 'bemember Mamma.'

Many and many a time was Mamma's command laid upon Punch, and Papa would say the same thing with an insistence that awed the child.

'You must make haste and learn to write, Punch,' said Papa, 'and then you'll be able to write letters to us in Bombay.'

'I'll come into your room,' said Punch, and Papa choked.

Papa and Mamma were always choking in those days. If Punch took Judy to task for not 'bemembering,' they choked. If Punch sprawled on the sofa in the Southampton lodging-house and sketched his future in purple and gold, they choked; and so they did if Judy put up her mouth for a kiss.

Through many days all four were vagabonds on the face of the earth—Punch with no one to give orders to, Judy too young for anything, and Papa and Mamma grave, distracted, and choking.

'Where,' demanded Punch, wearied of a loathsome contrivance on four wheels with a mound of luggage atop—'*where* is our broom-*gharri*? This thing talks so much that *I* can't talk. Where is our *own* broom-*gharri*? When I was at Bandstand before we comed away, I asked Inverarity Sahib why he was sitting in it, and he said it was his own. And I said, "I will *give* it you"—I like Inverarity Sahib—and I said, "Can you put your legs through the pully-wag loops by the windows?" And Inverarity Sahib said No, and laughed. *I* can

put my legs through the pully-wag loops. I can
put my legs through *these* pully-wag loops. Look !
Oh, Mamma's crying again ! I didn't know I
wasn't not to do *so*.'

Punch drew his legs out of the loops of the
four-wheeler : the door opened and he slid to the
earth, in a cascade of parcels, at the door of an
austere little villa whose gates bore the legend
' Downe Lodge.' Punch gathered himself together
and eyed the house with disfavour. It stood on a
sandy road, and a cold wind tickled his knicker-
bockered legs.

' Let us go away,' said Punch. ' This is not a
pretty place.'

But Mamma and Papa and Judy had left the
cab, and all the luggage was being taken into the
house. At the doorstep stood a woman in black,
and she smiled largely, with dry chapped lips.
Behind her was a man, big, bony, gray, and lame
as to one leg—behind him a boy of twelve, black-
haired and oily in appearance. Punch surveyed the
trio, and advanced without fear, as he had been
accustomed to do in Bombay when callers came and
he happened to be playing in the verandah.

' How do you do ? ' said he. ' I am Punch.'
But they were all looking at the luggage—all
except the gray man, who shook hands with Punch,
and said he was ' a smart little fellow.' There was
much running about and banging of boxes, and
Punch curled himself up on the sofa in the dining-
room and considered things.

' I don't like these people,' said Punch. ' But
never mind. We'll go away soon. We have

always went away soon from everywhere. I wish
we was gone back to Bombay *soon*.'

The wish bore no fruit. For six days Mamma
wept at intervals, and showed the woman in black
all Punch's clothes—a liberty which Punch resented.
'But p'raps she's a new white *ayah*,' he thought.
'I'm to call her Antirosa, but she doesn't call *me*
Sahib. She says just Punch,' he confided to Judy.
' What is Antirosa ? '

Judy didn't know. Neither she nor Punch had
heard anything of an animal called an aunt. Their
world had been Papa and Mamma, who knew everything, permitted everything, and loved everybody—
even Punch when he used to go into the garden at
Bombay and fill his nails with mould after the
weekly nail-cutting, because, as he explained between two strokes of the slipper to his sorely-tried
Father, his fingers 'felt so new at the ends.'

In an undefined way Punch judged it advisable to
keep both parents between himself and the woman
in black and the boy in black hair. He did not
approve of them. He liked the gray man, who had
expressed a wish to be called 'Uncleharri.' They
nodded at each other when they met, and the gray
man showed him a little ship with rigging that took
up and down.

'She is a model of the *Brisk*—the little *Brisk*
that was sore exposed that day at Navarino.' The
gray man hummed the last words and fell into a
reverie. ' I'll tell you about Navarino, Punch, when
we go for walks together ; and you mustn't touch
the ship, because she's the *Brisk*.'

Long before that walk, the first of many, was

taken, they roused Punch and Judy in the chill dawn of a February morning to say Good-bye ; and of all people in the wide earth to Papa and Mamma —both crying this time. Punch was very sleepy and Judy was cross.

'Don't forget us,' pleaded Mamma. 'Oh, my little son, don't forget us, and see that Judy remembers too.'

'I've told Judy to bemember,' said Punch, wriggling, for his father's beard tickled his neck, 'I've told Judy—ten—forty—'leven thousand times. But Ju's so young—quite a baby—isn't she ? '

'Yes,' said Papa, 'quite a baby, and you must be good to Judy, and make haste to learn to write and—and—and——'

Punch was back in his bed again. Judy was fast asleep, and there was the rattle of a cab below. Papa and Mamma had gone away. Not to Nassick ; that was across the sea. To some place much nearer, of course, and equally of course they would return. They came back after dinner-parties, and Papa had come back after he had been to a place called 'The Snows,' and Mamma with him, to Punch and Judy at Mrs. Inverarity's house in Marine Lines. Assuredly they would come back again. So Punch fell asleep till the true morning, when the black-haired boy met him with the information that Papa and Mamma had gone to Bombay, and that he and Judy were to stay at Downe Lodge 'for ever.' Antirosa, tearfully appealed to for a contradiction, said that Harry had spoken the truth, and that it behoved Punch

to fold up his clothes neatly on going to bed.
Punch went out and wept bitterly with Judy, into
whose fair head he had driven some ideas of the
meaning of separation.

When a matured man discovers that he has been
deserted by Providence, deprived of his God, and
cast without help, comfort, or sympathy, upon a
world which is new and strange to him, his despair,
which may find expression in evil-living, the writing
of his experiences, or the more satisfactory diversion
of suicide, is generally supposed to be impressive.
A child, under exactly similar circumstances as far
as its knowledge goes, cannot very well curse God
and die.   It howls till its nose is red, its eyes are
sore, and its head aches.   Punch and Judy, through
no fault of their own, had lost all their world.
They sat in the hall and cried ; the black-haired
boy looking on from afar.

The model of the ship availed nothing, though
the gray man assured Punch that he might pull the
rigging up and down as much as he pleased ; and
Judy was promised free entry into the kitchen.
They wanted Papa and Mamma gone to Bombay
beyond the seas, and their grief while it lasted was
without remedy.

When the tears ceased the house was very still.
Antirosa had decided that it was better to let the
children ' have their cry out,' and the boy had gone
to school.   Punch raised his head from the floor
and sniffed mournfully.   Judy was nearly asleep.
Three short years had not taught her how to bear
sorrow with full knowledge.   There was a distant,
dull boom in the air—a repeated heavy thud.

Punch knew that sound in Bombay in the Monsoon. It was the sea—the sea that must be traversed before any one could get to Bombay.

'Quick, Ju!' he cried, 'we're close to the sea. I can hear it! Listen! That's where they've went. P'raps we can catch them if we was in time. They didn't mean to go without us. They've only forgot.'

'Iss,' said Judy. 'They've only forgotted. Less go to the sea.'

The hall-door was open and so was the garden-gate.

'It's very, very big, this place,' he said, looking cautiously down the road, 'and we will get lost; but *I* will find a man and order him to take me back to my house—like I did in Bombay.'

He took Judy by the hand, and the two ran hatless in the direction of the sound of the sea. Downe Villa was almost the last of a range of newly-built houses running out, through a field of brick-mounds, to a heath where gypsies occasionally camped and where the Garrison Artillery of Rock-lington practised. There were few people to be seen, and the children might have been taken for those of the soldiery who ranged far. Half an hour the wearied little legs tramped across heath, potato-patch, and sand-dune.

'I'se so tired,' said Judy, 'and Mamma will be angry.'

'Mamma's *never* angry. I suppose she is waiting at the sea now while Papa gets tickets. We'll find them and go along with them. Ju, you mustn't sit down. Only a little more and we'll come to

the sea.   Ju, if you sit down I'll *thmack* you !' said
Punch.

They climbed another dune, and came upon the
great gray sea at low tide.   Hundreds of crabs
were scuttling about the beach, but there was no
trace of Papa and Mamma, not even of a ship upon
the waters— nothing but sand and mud for miles
and miles.

And 'Uncleharri' found them by chance—very
muddy and very forlorn—Punch dissolved in tears,
but trying to divert Judy with an 'ickle trab,' and
Judy wailing to the pitiless horizon for 'Mamma,
Mamma !'—and again 'Mamma !'

The Second Bag

Ah, well-a-day, for we are souls bereaved !
Of all the creatures under Heaven's wide scope
We are most hopeless, who had once most hope,
And most beliefless, who had most believed.
The City of Dreadful Night.

ALL this time not a word about Black Sheep.   He
came later, and Harry the black-haired boy was
mainly responsible for his coming.

Judy—who could help loving little Judy ?—
passed, by special permit, into the kitchen and
thence straight to Aunty Rosa's heart.   Harry was
Aunty Rosa's one child, and Punch was the extra
boy about the house.   There was no special place
for him or his little affairs, and he was forbidden
to sprawl on sofas and explain his ideas about the

manufacture of this world and his hopes for his future. Sprawling was lazy and wore out sofas, and little boys were not expected to talk. They were talked to, and the talking to was intended for the benefit of their morals. As the unquestioned despot of the house at Bombay, Punch could not quite understand how he came to be of no account in this his new life.

Harry might reach across the table and take what he wanted ; Judy might point and get what she wanted. Punch was forbidden to do either. The gray man was his great hope and stand-by for many months after Mamma and Papa left, and he had forgotten to tell Judy to ' bemember Mamma.'

This lapse was excusable, because in the interval he had been introduced by Aunty Rosa to two very impressive things—an abstraction called God, the intimate friend and ally of Aunty Rosa, generally believed to live behind the kitchen-range because it was hot there—and a dirty brown book filled with unintelligible dots and marks. Punch was always anxious to oblige everybody. He therefore welded the story of the Creation on to what he could recollect of his Indian fairy tales, and scandalised Aunty Rosa by repeating the result to Judy. It was a sin, a grievous sin, and Punch was talked to for a quarter of an hour. He could not understand where the iniquity came in, but was careful not to repeat the offence, because Aunty Rosa told him that God had heard every word he had said and was very angry. If this were true why didn't God come and say so, thought Punch, and dismissed the matter from his mind. Afterwards he learned to know the Lord as the only thing in the world more awful than Aunty Rosa—as a Creature that stood in the background and counted the strokes of the cane.

But the reading was, just then, a much more serious matter than any creed. Aunty Rosa sat him upon a table and told him that A B meant ab.

'Why?' said Punch. 'A is a and B is bee. *Why* does A B mean ab?'

'Because I tell you it does,' said Aunty Rosa, 'and you've got to say it.'

Punch said it accordingly, and for a month, hugely against his will, stumbled through the brown book, not in the least comprehending what it meant. But Uncle Harry, who walked much and generally alone, was wont to come into the nursery and suggest to Aunty Rosa that Punch should walk with him. He seldom spoke, but he showed Punch all Rocklington, from the mud-banks and the sand of the back-bay to the great harbours where ships lay at anchor, and the dock-yards where the hammers were never still, and the marine-store shops, and the shiny brass counters in the Offices where Uncle Harry went once every three months with a slip of blue paper and received sovereigns in exchange; for he held a wound-pension. Punch heard, too, from his lips the story of the battle of Navarino, where the sailors of the Fleet, for three days afterwards, were deaf as posts and could only sign to each other. 'That was because of the noise of the guns,' said Uncle Harry, 'and I have got the wadding of a bullet somewhere inside me now.'

Punch regarded him with curiosity. He had not the least idea what wadding was, and his notion of a bullet was a dockyard cannon-ball bigger than his own head. How could Uncle Harry keep a cannon-ball inside him? He was ashamed to ask, for fear Uncle Harry might be angry.

Punch had never known what anger—real anger —meant until one terrible day when Harry had taken his paint-box to paint a boat with, and Punch had protested. Then Uncle Harry had appeared on the scene and, muttering something about 'strangers' children,' had with a stick smitten the black-haired boy across the shoulders till he wept and yelled, and Aunty Rosa came in and abused Uncle Harry for cruelty to his own flesh and blood, and Punch shuddered to the tips of his shoes. 'It wasn't my fault,' he explained to the boy, but both Harry and Aunty Rosa said that it was, and that Punch had told tales, and for a week there were no more walks with Uncle Harry.

But that week brought a great joy to Punch.

He had repeated till he was thrice weary the statement that 'the Cat lay on the Mat and the Rat came in.'

'Now I can truly read,' said Punch, 'and now I will never read anything in the world.'

He put the brown book in the cupboard where his school-books lived and accidentally tumbled out a venerable volume, without covers, labelled *Sharpe's Magazine*. There was the most portentous picture of a griffin on the first page, with verses below. The griffin carried off one sheep a

day from a German village, till a man came with a
'falchion' and split the griffin open.   Goodness
only knew what a falchion was, but there was the
Griffin, and his history was an improvement upon
the eternal Cat.

'This,' said Punch, 'means things, and now I
will know all about everything in all the world.'
He read till the light failed, not understanding a
tithe of the meaning, but tantalised by glimpses of
new worlds hereafter to be revealed.

'What is a "falchion"?   What is a "e-wee
lamb"?   What is a "base *uss*urper"?   What is
a "verdant me-ad"?' he demanded with flushed
cheeks, at bedtime, of the astonished Aunty Rosa.

'Say your prayers and go to sleep,' she replied,
and that was all the help Punch then or afterwards
found at her hands in the new and delightful
exercise of reading.

'Aunty Rosa only knows about God and things
like that,' argued Punch.   'Uncle Harry will tell
me.'

The next walk proved that Uncle Harry could
not help either ; but he allowed Punch to talk,
and even sat down on a bench to hear about the
Griffin.   Other walks brought other stories as
Punch ranged farther afield, for the house held
large store of old books that no one ever opened
—from *Frank Fairlegh* in serial numbers, and the
earlier poems of Tennyson, contributed anony-
mously to *Sharpe's Magazine*, to '62 Exhibition
Catalogues, gay with colours and delightfully
incomprehensible, and odd leaves of *Gulliver's
Travels*.

As soon as Punch could string a few pot-hooks together he wrote to Bombay, demanding by return of post 'all the books in all the world.' Papa could not comply with this modest indent, but sent *Grimm's Fairy Tales* and a Hans Andersen. That was enough. If he were only left alone Punch could pass, at any hour he chose, into a land of his own, beyond reach of Aunty Rosa and her God, Harry and his teasements, and Judy's claims to be played with.

'Don't disturve me, I'm reading. Go and play in the kitchen,' grunted Punch. 'Aunty Rosa lets *you* go there.' Judy was cutting her second teeth and was fretful. She appealed to Aunty Rosa, who descended on Punch.

'I was reading,' he explained, 'reading a book I *want* to read.'

'You're only doing that to show off,' said Aunty Rosa. 'But we'll see. Play with Judy now, and don't open a book for a week.'

Judy did not pass a very enjoyable playtime with Punch, who was consumed with indignation. There was a pettiness at the bottom of the prohibition which puzzled him.

'It's what I like to do,' he said, 'and she's found out that and stopped me. Don't cry, Ju— it wasn't your fault—*please* don't cry, or she'll say I made you.'

Ju loyally mopped up her tears, and the two played in their nursery, a room in the basement and half underground, to which they were regularly sent after the mid-day dinner while Aunty Rosa slept. She drank wine—that is to say, something

from a bottle in the cellaret—for her stomach's
sake, but if she did not fall asleep she would sometimes come into the nursery to see that the children
were really playing.   Now bricks, wooden hoops,
ninepins, and chinaware cannot amuse for ever,
especially when all Fairyland is to be won by the
mere opening of a book, and, as often as not,
Punch would be discovered reading to Judy or
telling her interminable tales.   That was an offence
in the eyes of the law, and Judy would be whisked
off by Aunty Rosa, while Punch was left to play
alone, 'and be sure that I hear you doing it.'

It was not a cheering employ, for he had to
make a playful noise.   At last, with infinite craft,
he devised an arrangement whereby the table could
be supported as to three legs on toy bricks, leaving
the fourth clear to bring down on the floor.   He
could work the table with one hand and hold a
book with the other.   This he did till an evil day
when Aunty Rosa pounced upon him unawares
and told him that he was 'acting a lie.'

'If you're old enough to do that,' she said—
her temper was always worst after dinner—'you're
old enough to be beaten.'

'But—I'm—I'm not a animal!' said Punch
aghast.   He remembered Uncle Harry and the
stick, and turned white.   Aunty Rosa had hidden
a light cane behind her, and Punch was beaten
then and there over the shoulders.   It was a revela-
tion to him.   The room-door was shut, and he was
left to weep himself into repentance and work out
his own gospel of life.

Aunty Rosa, he argued, had the power to beat

him with many stripes. It was unjust and cruel, and Mamma and Papa would never have allowed it. Unless perhaps, as Aunty Rosa seemed to imply, they had sent secret orders. In which case he was abandoned indeed. It would be discreet in the future to propitiate Aunty Rosa, but, then, again, even in matters in which he was innocent, he had been accused of wishing to 'show off.' He had 'shown off' before visitors when he had attacked a strange gentleman—Harry's uncle, not his own—with requests for information about the Griffin and the falchion, and the precise nature of the Tilbury in which Frank Fairlegh rode—all points of paramount interest which he was bursting to understand. Clearly it would not do to pretend to care for Aunty Rosa.

At this point Harry entered and stood afar off, eyeing Punch, a dishevelled heap in the corner of the room, with disgust.

'You're a liar—a young liar,' said Harry, with great unction, 'and you're to have tea down here because you're not fit to speak to us. And you're not to speak to Judy again till Mother gives you leave. You'll corrupt her. You're only fit to associate with the servant. Mother says so.'

Having reduced Punch to a second agony of tears, Harry departed upstairs with the news that Punch was still rebellious.

Uncle Harry sat uneasily in the dining-room. 'Damn it all, Rosa,' said he at last, 'can't you leave the child alone? He's a good enough little chap when I meet him.'

'He puts on his best manners with you, Henry,'

said Aunty Rosa, 'but I'm afraid, I'm very much afraid, that he is the Black Sheep of the family.'

Harry heard and stored up the name for future use. Judy cried till she was bidden to stop, her brother not being worth tears ; and the evening concluded with the return of Punch to the upper regions and a private sitting at which all the blind-ing horrors of Hell were revealed to Punch with such store of imagery as Aunty Rosa's narrow mind possessed.

Most grievous of all was Judy's round-eyed reproach, and Punch went to bed in the depths of the Valley of Humiliation. He shared his room with Harry and knew the torture in store. For an hour and a half he had to answer that young gentleman's questions as to his motives for telling a lie, and a grievous lie, the precise quantity of punishment inflicted by Aunty Rosa, and had also to profess his deep gratitude for such religious instruction as Harry thought fit to impart.

From that day began the downfall of Punch, now Black Sheep.

'Untrustworthy in one thing, untrustworthy in all,' said Aunty Rosa, and Harry felt that Black Sheep was delivered into his hands. He would wake him up in the night to ask him why he was such a liar.

'I don't know,' Punch would reply.

'Then don't you think you ought to get up and pray to God for a new heart ?'

'Y-yess.'

'Get out and pray, then !' And Punch would get out of bed with raging hate in his heart against all the world, seen and unseen. He was always tumbling into trouble. Harry had a knack of cross-examining him as to his day's doings, which seldom failed to lead him, sleepy and savage, into half-a-dozen contradictions—all duly reported to Aunty Rosa next morning.

'But it *wasn't* a lie,' Punch would begin, charging into a laboured explanation that landed him more hopelessly in the mire. 'I said that I didn't say my prayers *twice* over in the day, and *that* was on Tuesday. *Once* I did. I *know* I did, but Harry said I didn't,' and so forth, till the tension brought tears, and he was dismissed from the table in disgrace.

'You usen't to be as bad as this,' said Judy, awe-stricken at the catalogue of Black Sheep's crimes. 'Why are you so bad now?'

'I don't know,' Black Sheep would reply. 'I'm not, if I only wasn't bothered upside down. I knew what I *did*, and I want to say so; but Harry always makes it out different somehow, and Aunty Rosa doesn't believe a word I say. Oh, Ju! don't *you* say I'm bad too.'

'Aunty Rosa says you are,' said Judy. 'She told the Vicar so when he came yesterday.'

'Why does she tell all the people outside the house about me? It isn't fair,' said Black Sheep. 'When I was in Bombay, and was bad—*doing* bad, not made-up bad like this—Mamma told Papa, and Papa told me he knew, and that was all. *Outside* people didn't know too—even Meeta didn't know.'

'I don't remember,' said Judy wistfully. 'I

was all little then.   Mamma was just as fond of you as she was of me, wasn't she?'

'Course she was.   So was Papa.   So was everybody.'

'Aunty Rosa likes me more than she does you. She says that you are a Trial and a Black Sheep, and I'm not to speak to you more than I can help.'

'Always?   Not outside of the times when you mustn't speak to me at all?'

Judy nodded her head mournfully.   Black Sheep turned away in despair, but Judy's arms were round his neck.

'Never mind, Punch,' she whispered.   'I *will* speak to you just the same as ever and ever. You're my own own brother though you are— though Aunty Rosa says you're bad, and Harry says you are a little coward.   He says that if I pulled your hair hard, you'd cry.'

'Pull, then,' said Punch.

Judy pulled gingerly.

'Pull harder—as hard as you can !   There !   I don't mind how much you pull it *now*.   If you'll speak to me same as ever I'll let you pull it as much as you like—pull it out if you like.   But I know if Harry came and stood by and made you do it I'd cry.'

So the two children sealed the compact with a kiss, and Black Sheep's heart was cheered within him, and by extreme caution and careful avoidance of Harry he acquired virtue, and was allowed to read undisturbed for a week.   Uncle Harry took him for walks, and consoled him with rough tenderness, never calling him Black Sheep.   'It's good for you, I suppose, Punch,' he used to say. 'Let us sit down. I'm getting tired.' His steps led him now not to the beach, but to the Cemetery of Rocklington, amid the potato-fields. For hours the gray man would sit on a tombstone, while Black Sheep would read epitaphs, and then with a sigh would stump home again.

'I shall lie there soon,' said he to Black Sheep, one winter evening, when his face showed white as a worn silver coin under the light of the lych-gate. 'You needn't tell Aunty Rosa.'

A month later he turned sharp round, ere half a morning walk was completed, and stumped back to the house. 'Put me to bed, Rosa,' he muttered. 'I've walked my last. The wadding has found me out.'

They put him to bed, and for a fortnight the shadow of his sickness lay upon the house, and Black Sheep went to and fro unobserved. Papa had sent him some new books, and he was told to keep quiet. He retired into his own world, and was perfectly happy. Even at night his felicity was unbroken. He could lie in bed and string himself tales of travel and adventure while Harry was downstairs.

'Uncle Harry's going to die,' said Judy, who now lived almost entirely with Aunty Rosa.

'I'm very sorry,' said Black Sheep soberly. 'He told me that a long time ago.'

Aunty Rosa heard the conversation. 'Will nothing check your wicked tongue?' she said angrily. There were blue circles round her eyes.

Black Sheep retreated to the nursery and read

Cometh up as a Flower with deep and uncomprehending interest.   He had been forbidden to open it on account of its 'sinfulness,' but the bonds of the Universe were crumbling, and Aunty Rosa was in great grief.

'I'm glad,' said Black Sheep.   'She's unhappy now.   It wasn't a lie, though.   *I* knew.   He told me not to tell.'

That night Black Sheep woke with a start. Harry was not in the room, and there was a sound of sobbing on the next floor.   Then the voice of Uncle Harry, singing the song of the Battle of Navarino, came through the darkness :—

> 'Our vanship was the Asia—
> The Albion and Genoa!'

'He's getting well,' thought Black Sheep, who knew the song through all its seventeen verses. But the blood froze at his little heart as he thought.   The voice leapt an octave, and rang shrill as a boatswain's pipe :—

> 'And next came on the lovely Rose,
> The Philomel, her fire-ship, closed,
> And the little Brisk was sore exposed
> That day at Navarino.'

'That day at Navarino, Uncle Harry!' shouted Black Sheep, half wild with excitement and fear of he knew not what.

A door opened, and Aunty Rosa screamed up the staircase : 'Hush!   For God's sake hush, you little devil.   Uncle Harry is *dead!*'

The Third Bag

Journeys end in lovers' meeting,
Every wise man's son doth know.

' I WONDER what will happen to me now,' thought
Black Sheep, when semi-pagan rites peculiar to the
burial of the Dead in middle-class houses had been
accomplished, and Aunty Rosa, awful in black
crape, had returned to this life. ' I don't think I've
done anything bad that she knows of. I suppose
I will soon. She will be very cross after Uncle
Harry's dying, and Harry will be cross too. I'll
keep in the nursery.'

Unfortunately for Punch's plans, it was decided
that he should be sent to a day-school which Harry
attended. This meant a morning walk with Harry,
and perhaps an evening one ; but the prospect of
freedom in the interval was refreshing. ' Harry'll
tell everything I do, but I won't do anything,' said
Black Sheep. Fortified with this virtuous resolu-
tion, he went to school only to find that Harry's
version of his character had preceded him, and that
life was a burden in consequence. He took stock
of his associates. Some of them were unclean,
some of them talked in dialect, many dropped
their h's, and there were two Jews and a negro,
or some one quite as dark, in the assembly.
' That's a *hubshi*,' said Black Sheep to himself.
' Even Meeta used to laugh at a *hubshi*. I don't
think this is a proper place.' He was indignant
for at least an hour, till he reflected that any
expostulation on his part would be by Aunty Rosa

construed into 'showing off,' and that Harry
would tell the boys.

'How do you like school?' said Aunty Rosa
at the end of the day.

'I think it is a very nice place,' said Punch
quietly.

'I suppose you warned the boys of Black Sheep's
character?' said Aunty Rosa to Harry.

'Oh yes,' said the censor of Black Sheep's morals.
'They know all about him.'

'If I was with my father,' said Black Sheep,
stung to the quick, 'I shouldn't *speak* to those
boys. He wouldn't let me. They live in shops.
I saw them go into shops—where their fathers
live and sell things.'

'You're too good for that school, are you?'
said Aunty Rosa, with a bitter smile. 'You ought
to be grateful, Black Sheep, that those boys speak
to you at all. It isn't every school that takes little
liars.'

Harry did not fail to make much capital out
of Black Sheep's ill-considered remark; with the
result that several boys, including the *hubshi*,
demonstrated to Black Sheep the eternal equality
of the human race by smacking his head, and
his consolation from Aunty Rosa was that it
'served him right for being vain.' He learned,
however, to keep his opinions to himself, and by
propitiating Harry in carrying books and the like
to get a little peace. His existence was not too
joyful. From nine till twelve he was at school,
and from two to four, except on Saturdays. In
the evenings he was sent down into the nursery

to prepare his lessons for the next day, and every night came the dreaded cross-questionings at Harry's hand. Of Judy he saw but little. She was deeply religious—at six years of age Religion is easy to come by—and sorely divided between her natural love for Black Sheep and her love for Aunty Rosa, who could do no wrong.

The lean woman returned that love with interest, and Judy, when she dared, took advantage of this for the remission of Black Sheep's penalties. Failures in lessons at school were punished at home by a week without reading other than school-books, and Harry brought the news of such a failure with glee. Further, Black Sheep was then bound to repeat his lessons at bedtime to Harry, who generally succeeded in making him break down, and consoled him by gloomiest forebodings for the morrow. Harry was at once spy, practical joker, inquisitor, and Aunty Rosa's deputy executioner. He filled his many posts to admiration. From his actions, now that Uncle Harry was dead, there was no appeal. Black Sheep had not been permitted to keep any self-respect at school : at home he was, of course, utterly discredited, and grateful for any pity that the servant girls—they changed frequently at Downe Lodge because they, too, were liars—might show. 'You're just fit to row in the same boat with Black Sheep,' was a sentiment that each new Jane or Eliza might expect to hear, before a month was over, from Aunty Rosa's lips; and Black Sheep was used to ask new girls whether they had yet been compared to him. Harry was ' Master

Harry' in their mouths; Judy was officially 'Miss Judy'; but Black Sheep was never anything more than Black Sheep *tout court.*

As time went on and the memory of Papa and Mamma became wholly overlaid by the unpleasant task of writing them letters, under Aunty Rosa's eye, each Sunday, Black Sheep forgot what manner of life he had led in the beginning of things. Even Judy's appeals to 'try and remember about Bombay' failed to quicken him.

'I can't remember,' he said. 'I know I used to give orders and Mamma kissed me.'

'Aunty Rosa will kiss you if you are good,' pleaded Judy.

'Ugh! I don't want to be kissed by Aunty Rosa. She'd say I was doing it to get something more to eat.'

The weeks lengthened into months, and the holidays came; but just before the holidays Black Sheep fell into deadly sin.

Among the many boys whom Harry had incited to 'punch Black Sheep's head because he daren't hit back,' was one more aggravating than the rest, who, in an unlucky moment, fell upon Black Sheep when Harry was not near. The blows stung, and Black Sheep struck back at random with all the power at his command. The boy dropped and whimpered. Black Sheep was astounded at his own act, but, feeling the unresisting body under him, shook it with both his hands in blind fury and then began to throttle his enemy; meaning honestly to slay him. There was a scuffle, and Black Sheep was torn off the body by Harry and some colleagues, and cuffed home tingling but exultant. Aunty Rosa was out : pending her arrival, Harry set himself to lecture Black Sheep on the sin of murder—which he described as the offence of Cain.

'Why didn't you fight him fair? What did you hit him when he was down for, you little cur?'

Black Sheep looked up at Harry's throat and then at a knife on the dinner-table.

'I don't understand,' he said wearily. 'You always set him on me and told me I was a coward when I blubbed. Will you leave me alone until Aunty Rosa comes in? She'll beat me if you tell her I ought to be beaten ; so it's all right.'

'It's all wrong,' said Harry magisterially. 'You nearly killed him, and I shouldn't wonder if he dies.'

'Will he die?' said Black Sheep.

'I daresay,' said Harry, 'and then you'll be hanged, and go to Hell.'

'All right,' said Black Sheep, picking up the table-knife. 'Then I'll kill *you* now. You say things and do things and—and *I* don't know how things happen, and you never leave me alone—and I don't care *what* happens!'

He ran at the boy with the knife, and Harry fled upstairs to his room, promising Black Sheep the finest thrashing in the world when Aunty Rosa returned. Black Sheep sat at the bottom of the stairs, the table-knife in his hand, and wept for that he had not killed Harry. The servant-girl came up from the kitchen, took the knife away, and consoled him. But Black Sheep was beyond consolation. He would be badly beaten by Aunty Rosa; then there would be another beating at Harry's hands; then Judy would not be allowed to speak to him; then the tale would be told at school, and then—

There was no one to help and no one to care, and the best way out of the business was by death. A knife would hurt, but Aunty Rosa had told him, a year ago, that if he sucked paint he would die. He went into the nursery, unearthed the now disused Noah's Ark, and sucked the paint off as many animals as remained. It tasted abominable, but he had licked Noah's Dove clean by the time Aunty Rosa and Judy returned. He went upstairs and greeted them with: 'Please, Aunty Rosa, I believe I've nearly killed a boy at school, and I've tried to kill Harry, and when you've done all about God and Hell, will you beat me and get it over?'

The tale of the assault as told by Harry could only be explained on the ground of possession by the Devil. Wherefore Black Sheep was not only most excellently beaten, once by Aunty Rosa and once, when thoroughly cowed down, by Harry, but he was further prayed for at family prayers, together with Jane who had stolen a cold rissole from the pantry, and snuffled audibly as her sin was brought before the Throne of Grace. Black Sheep was sore and stiff but triumphant. He would die that very night and be rid of them all. No, he would ask for no forgiveness from Harry, and at bed-time would stand no questioning at

Harry's hands, even though addressed as 'Young Cain.'

'I've been beaten,' said he, 'and I've done other things. I don't care what I do. If you speak to me to-night, Harry, I'll get out and try to kill you. Now you can kill me if you like.'

Harry took his bed into the spare room, and Black Sheep lay down to die.

It may be that the makers of Noah's Arks know that their animals are likely to find their way into young mouths, and paint them accordingly. Certain it is that the common, weary next morning broke through the windows and found Black Sheep quite well and a good deal ashamed of himself, but richer by the knowledge that he could, in extremity, secure himself against Harry for the future.

When he descended to breakfast on the first day of the holidays, he was greeted with the news that Harry, Aunty Rosa, and Judy were going away to Brighton, while Black Sheep was to stay in the house with the servant. His latest outbreak suited Aunty Rosa's plans admirably. It gave her good excuse for leaving the extra boy behind. Papa in Bombay, who really seemed to know a young sinner's wants to the hour, sent, that week, a package of new books. And with these, and the society of Jane on board-wages, Black Sheep was left alone for a month.

The books lasted for ten days. They were eaten too quickly in long gulps of twelve hours at a time. Then came days of doing absolutely nothing, of dreaming dreams and marching imaginary

armies up and downstairs, of counting the number
of banisters, and of measuring the length and
breadth of every room in handspans—fifty down
the side, thirty across, and fifty back again.   Jane
made many friends, and, after receiving Black
Sheep's assurance that he would not tell of her
absences, went out daily for long hours.   Black
Sheep would follow the rays of the sinking sun
from the kitchen to the dining-room and thence
upward to his own bedroom until all was gray
dark, and he ran down to the kitchen fire and
read by its light.   He was happy in that he was left
alone and could read as much as he pleased.   But,
later, he grew afraid of the shadows of window-
curtains and the flapping of doors and the creaking
of shutters.   He went out into the garden, and
the rustling of the laurel-bushes frightened him.

He was glad when they all returned—Aunty
Rosa, Harry, and Judy—full of news, and Judy
laden with gifts.   Who could help loving loyal
little Judy?   In return for all her merry babble-
ment, Black Sheep confided to her that the distance
from the hall-door to the top of the first landing
was exactly one hundred and eighty-four handspans.   He had found it out himself.

Then the old life recommenced ; but with a
difference, and a new sin.   To his other iniquities
Black Sheep had now added a phenomenal clumsi-
ness—was as unfit to trust in action as he was in
word.   He himself could not account for spilling
everything he touched, upsetting glasses as he put
his hand out, and bumping his head against doors
that were manifestly shut.   There was a gray haze

upon all his world, and it narrowed month by month, until at last it left Black Sheep almost alone with the flapping curtains that were so like ghosts, and the nameless terrors of broad daylight that were only coats on pegs after all.

Holidays came and holidays went, and Black Sheep was taken to see many people whose faces were all exactly alike ; was beaten when occasion demanded, and tortured by Harry on all possible occasions ; but defended by Judy through good and evil report, though she hereby drew upon herself the wrath of Aunty Rosa.

The weeks were interminable, and Papa and Mamma were clean forgotten. Harry had left school and was a clerk in a Banking-Office. Freed from his presence, Black Sheep resolved that he should no longer be deprived of his allowance of pleasure-reading. Consequently when he failed at school he reported that all was well, and conceived a large contempt for Aunty Rosa as he saw how easy it was to deceive her. 'She says I'm a little liar when I don't tell lies, and now I do, she doesn't know,' thought Black Sheep. Aunty Rosa had credited him in the past with petty cunning and stratagem that had never entered into his head. By the light of the sordid knowledge that she had revealed to him he paid her back full tale. In a household where the most innocent of his motives, his natural yearning for a little affection, had been interpreted into a desire for more bread and jam, or to ingratiate himself with strangers and so put Harry into the background, his work was easy. Aunty Rosa could penetrate certain kinds of hypocrisy, but not all. He set his child's wits against hers and was no more beaten. It grew monthly more and more of a trouble to read the school-books, and even the pages of the open-print story-books danced and were dim. So Black Sheep brooded in the shadows that fell about him and cut him off from the world, inventing horrible punishments for 'dear Harry,' or plotting another line of the tangled web of deception that he wrapped round Aunty Rosa.

Then the crash came and the cobwebs were broken. It was impossible to foresee everything. Aunty Rosa made personal inquiries as to Black Sheep's progress and received information that startled her. Step by step, with a delight as keen as when she convicted an underfed housemaid of the theft of cold meats, she followed the trail of Black Sheep's delinquencies. For weeks and weeks, in order to escape banishment from the book-shelves, he had made a fool of Aunty Rosa, of Harry, of God, of all the world! Horrible, most horrible, and evidence of an utterly depraved mind.

Black Sheep counted the cost. 'It will only be one big beating and then she'll put a card with "Liar" on my back, same as she did before. Harry will whack me and pray for me, and she will pray for me at prayers and tell me I'm a Child of the Devil and give me hymns to learn. But I've done all my reading and she never knew. She'll say she knew all along. She's an old liar too,' said he.

For three days Black Sheep was shut in his

own bedroom — to prepare his heart. 'That means two beatings. One at school and one here. *That* one will hurt most.' And it fell even as he thought. He was thrashed at school before the Jews and the *hubshi* for the heinous crime of carrying home false reports of progress. He was thrashed at home by Aunty Rosa on the same count, and then the placard was produced. Aunty Rosa stitched it between his shoulders and bade him go for a walk with it upon him.

'If you make me do that,' said Black Sheep very quietly, 'I shall burn this house down, and perhaps I'll kill you. I don't know whether I *can* kill you—you're so bony—but I'll try.'

No punishment followed this blasphemy, though Black Sheep held himself ready to work his way to Aunty Rosa's withered throat, and grip there till he was beaten off. Perhaps Aunty Rosa was afraid, for Black Sheep, having reached the Nadir of Sin, bore himself with a new recklessness.

In the midst of all the trouble there came a visitor from over the seas to Downe Lodge, who knew Papa and Mamma, and was commissioned to see Punch and Judy. Black Sheep was sent to the drawing-room and charged into a solid tea-table laden with china.

'Gently, gently, little man,' said the visitor, turning Black Sheep's face to the light slowly. 'What's that big bird on the palings?'

'What bird?' asked Black Sheep.

The visitor looked deep down into Black Sheep's eyes for half a minute, and then said suddenly: 'Good God, the little chap's nearly blind!'

It was a most business-like visitor. He gave orders, on his own responsibility, that Black Sheep was not to go to school or open a book until Mamma came home. 'She'll be here in three weeks, as you know of course,' said he, 'and I'm Inverarity Sahib. I ushered you into this wicked world, young man, and a nice use you seem to have made of your time. You must do nothing whatever. Can you do that?'

'Yes,' said Punch in a dazed way. He had known that Mamma was coming. There was a chance, then, of another beating. Thank Heaven, Papa wasn't coming too. Aunty Rosa had said of late that he ought to be beaten by a man.

For the next three weeks Black Sheep was strictly allowed to do nothing. He spent his time in the old nursery looking the broken toys, for all of which account must be rendered to Mamma. Aunty Rosa hit him over the hands if even a wooden boat were broken. But that sin was of small importance compared to the other revelations, so darkly hinted at by Aunty Rosa. 'When your Mother comes, and hears what I have to tell her, she may appreciate you properly,' she said grimly, and mounted guard over Judy lest that small maiden should attempt to comfort her brother, to the peril of her soul.

And Mamma came—in a four-wheeler—fluttered with tender excitement. Such a Mamma! She was young, frivolously young, and beautiful, with delicately-flushed cheeks, eyes that shone like stars, and a voice that needed no appeal of outstretched arms to draw little ones to her heart. Judy ran straight to her, but Black Sheep hesitated. Could this wonder be 'showing off'? She would not put out her arms when she knew of his crimes. Meantime was it possible that by fondling she wanted to get anything out of Black Sheep? Only all his love and all his confidence; but that Black Sheep did not know. Aunty Rosa withdrew and left Mamma, kneeling between her children, half laughing, half crying, in the very hall where Punch and Judy had wept five years before.

'Well, chicks, do you remember me?'

'No,' said Judy frankly, 'but I said, "God bless Papa and Mamma" ev'vy night.'

'A little,' said Black Sheep. 'Remember I wrote to you every week, anyhow. That isn't to show off, but 'cause of what comes afterwards.'

'What comes after? What should come after, my darling boy?' And she drew him to her again. He came awkwardly, with many angles. 'Not used to petting,' said the quick Mother-soul. 'The girl is.'

'She's too little to hurt any one,' thought Black Sheep, 'and if I said I'd kill her, she'd be afraid. I wonder what Aunty Rosa will tell.'

There was a constrained late dinner, at the end of which Mamma picked up Judy and put her to bed with endearments manifold. Faithless little Judy had shown her defection from Aunty Rosa already. And that lady resented it bitterly. Black Sheep rose to leave the room.

'Come and say good-night,' said Aunty Rosa, offering a withered cheek.

'Huh!' said Black Sheep. 'I never kiss you,

and I'm not going to show off. Tell that woman what I've done, and see what she says.'

Black Sheep climbed into bed feeling that he had lost Heaven after a glimpse through the gates. In half an hour 'that woman' was bending over him. Black Sheep flung up his right arm. It wasn't fair to come and hit him in the dark. Even Aunty Rosa never tried that. But no blow followed.

'Are you showing off? I won't tell you anything more than Aunty Rosa has, and *she* doesn't know everything,' said Black Sheep as clearly as he could for the arms round his neck.

'Oh, my son—my little, little son! It was my fault—*my* fault, darling—and yet how could we help it? Forgive me, Punch.' The voice died out in a broken whisper, and two hot tears fell on Black Sheep's forehead.

'Has she been making you cry too?' he asked. 'You should see Jane cry. But you're nice, and Jane is a Born Liar—Aunty Rosa says so.'

'Hush, Punch, hush! My boy, don't talk like that. Try to love me a little bit—a little bit. You don't know how I want it. Punch-*baba*, come back to me! I am your Mother—your own Mother—and never mind the rest. I know—yes, I know, dear. It doesn't matter now. Punch, won't you care for me a little?'

It is astonishing how much petting a big boy of ten can endure when he is quite sure that there is no one to laugh at him. Black Sheep had never been made much of before, and here was this beautiful woman treating him—Black Sheep, the

Child of the Devil and the inheritor of undying flame—as though he were a small God.

'I care for you a great deal, Mother dear,' he whispered at last, 'and I'm glad you've come back; but are you sure Aunty Rosa told you everything?'

'Everything. What *does* it matter? But——' the voice broke with a sob that was also laughter —'Punch, my poor, dear, half-blind darling, don't you think it was a little foolish of you?'

'*No*. It saved a lickin'.'

Mamma shuddered and slipped away in the darkness to write a long letter to Papa. Here is an extract :—

. . . Judy is a dear, plump little prig who adores the woman, and wears with as much gravity as her religious opinions—only eight, Jack !—a venerable horse-hair atrocity which she calls her Bustle ! I have just burnt it, and the child is asleep in my bed as I write. She will come to me at once. Punch I cannot quite understand. He is well nourished, but seems to have been worried into a system of small deceptions which the woman magnifies into deadly sins. Don't you recollect our own upbringing, dear, when the Fear of the Lord was so often the beginning of falsehood ? I shall win Punch to me before long. I am taking the children away into the country to get them to know me, and, on the whole, I am content, or shall be when you come home, dear boy, and then, thank God, we shall be all under one roof again at last !

Three months later, Punch, no longer Black Sheep, has discovered that he is the veritable owner of a real, live, lovely Mamma, who is also a sister, comforter, and friend, and that he must protect her till the Father comes home. Deception does not suit the part of a protector, and, when one can do anything without question, where is the use of deception?

'Mother would be awfully cross if you walked through that ditch,' says Judy, continuing a conversation.

'Mother's never angry,' says Punch. 'She'd just say, "You're a little *pagal*;" and that's not nice, but I'll show.'

Punch walks through the ditch and mires himself to the knees. 'Mother, dear,' he shouts, 'I'm just as dirty as I can pos-*sib*-ly be!'

'Then change your clothes as quickly as you pos-*sib*-ly can!' Mother's clear voice rings out from the house. 'And don't be a little *pagal!*'

'There! 'Told you so,' says Punch. 'It's all different now, and we are just as much Mother's as if she had never gone.'

Not altogether, O Punch, for when young lips have drunk deep of the bitter waters of Hate, Suspicion, and Despair, all the Love in the world will not wholly take away that knowledge; though it may turn darkened eyes for a while to the light, and teach Faith where no Faith was.

His Majesty the King

Where the word of a King is, there is power : And who may say unto him—What doest thou ?

'YETH ! And Chimo to sleep at ve foot of ve bed, and ve pink pikky-book, and ve bwead— 'cause I will be hungwy in ve night—and vat's all, Miss Biddums. And now give me one kiss and I'll go to sleep.—So! Kite quiet. Ow ! Ve pink pikky-book has slidded under ve pillow and ve bwead is cwumbling ! Miss Biddums ! Miss *Bid*-dums ! I'm *so* uncomfy ! Come and tuck me up, Miss Biddums.'

His Majesty the King was going to bed ; and poor, patient Miss Biddums, who had advertised herself humbly as a 'young person, European, accustomed to the care of little children,' was forced to wait upon his royal caprices. The going to bed was always a lengthy process, because His Majesty had a convenient knack of forgetting which of his many friends, from the *mehter's* son to the Commissioner's daughter, he had prayed for, and, lest the Deity should take offence, was used to toil through his little prayers, in all reverence, five times in one evening. His Majesty

the King believed in the efficacy of prayer as devoutly as he believed in Chimo the patient spaniel,
or Miss Biddums, who could reach him down his
gun—'with cursuffun caps—*reel* ones'—from the
upper shelves of the big nursery cupboard.

At the door of the nursery his authority
stopped. Beyond lay the empire of his father and
mother—two very terrible people who had no time
to waste upon His Majesty the King. His voice
was lowered when he passed the frontier of his
own dominions, his actions were fettered, and his
soul was filled with awe because of the grim man
who lived among a wilderness of pigeon-holes and
the most fascinating pieces of red tape, and the
wonderful woman who was always getting into or
stepping out of the big carriage.

To the one belonged the mysteries of the
'*duftar*-room,' to the other the great, reflected
wilderness of the 'Memsahib's room,' where the
shiny, scented dresses hung on pegs, miles and
miles up in the air, and the just-seen plateau of
the toilet-table revealed an acreage of speckly
combs, broidered 'hanafitch-bags,' and 'white-
headed' brushes.

There was no room for His Majesty the King
either in official reserve or worldly gorgeousness.
He had discovered that, ages and ages ago—
before even Chimo came to the house, or Miss
Biddums had ceased grizzling over a packet of
greasy letters which appeared to be her chief treasure
on earth. His Majesty the King, therefore, wisely
confined himself to his own territories, where only
Miss Biddums, and she feebly, disputed his sway.

From Miss Biddums he had picked up his simple theology and welded it to the legends of gods and devils that he had learned in the servants' quarters.

To Miss Biddums he confided with equal trust his tattered garments and his more serious griefs. She would make everything whole. She knew exactly how the Earth had been born, and had reassured the trembling soul of His Majesty the King that terrible time in July when it rained continuously for seven days and seven nights, and—there was no Ark ready and all the ravens had flown away ! She was the most powerful person with whom he was brought into contact—always excepting the two remote and silent people beyond the nursery door.

How was His Majesty the King to know that, six years ago, in the summer of his birth, Mrs. Austell, turning over her husband's papers, had come upon the intemperate letter of a foolish woman who had been carried away by the silent man's strength and personal beauty ? How could he tell what evil the overlooked slip of notepaper had wrought in the mind of a desperately jealous wife ? How could he, despite his wisdom, guess that his mother had chosen to make of it excuse for a bar and a division between herself and her husband, that strengthened and grew harder to break with each year ; that she, having unearthed this skeleton in the cupboard, had trained it into a household God which should be about their path and about their bed, and poison all their ways ?

These things were beyond the province of His

Majesty the King. He only knew that his father
was daily absorbed in some mysterious work for a
thing called the *Sirkar*, and that his mother was the
victim alternately of the *Nautch* and the *Burrak-
hana*. To these entertainments she was escorted
by a Captain-Man for whom His Majesty the King
had no regard.

'He *doesn't* laugh,' he argued with Miss Biddums, who would fain have taught him charity.
'He only makes faces wiv his mouf, and when he
wants to o-muse me I am *not* o-mused.' And His
Majesty the King shook his head as one who knew
the deceitfulness of this world.

Morning and evening it was his duty to salute
his father and mother—the former with a grave
shake of the hand, and the latter with an equally
grave kiss. Once, indeed, he had put his arms
round his mother's neck, in the fashion he used
towards Miss Biddums. The openwork of his
sleeve-edge caught in an earring, and the last stage
of His Majesty's little overture was a suppressed
scream and summary dismissal to the nursery.

'It is w'ong,' thought His Majesty the King, 'to
hug Memsahibs wiv fings in veir ears. I will
amember.' He never repeated the experiment.

Miss Biddums, it must be confessed, spoilt him
as much as his nature admitted, in some sort of
recompense for what she called 'the hard ways of
his Papa and Mamma.' She, like her charge, knew
nothing of the trouble between man and wife—the
savage contempt for a woman's stupidity on the
one side, or the dull, rankling anger on the other.
Miss Biddums had looked after many little children

in her time, and served in many establishments. Being a discreet woman, she observed little and said less, and, when her pupils went over the sea to the Great Unknown, which she, with touching confidence in her hearers, called 'Home,' packed up her slender belongings and sought for employment afresh, lavishing all her love on each successive batch of ingrates.   Only His Majesty the King had repaid her affection with interest ; and in his uncomprehending ears she had told the tale of nearly all her hopes, her aspirations, the hopes that were dead, and the dazzling glories of her ancestral home in '*Cal*cutta, close to Wellington Square.'

Everything above the average was in the eyes of His Majesty the King 'Calcutta good.'   When Miss Biddums had crossed his royal will, he reversed the epithet to vex that estimable lady, and all things evil were, until the tears of repentance swept away spite, 'Calcutta bad.'

Now and again Miss Biddums begged for him the rare pleasure of a day in the society of the Commissioner's child—the wilful four-year-old Patsie, who, to the intense amazement of His Majesty the King, was idolised by her parents. On thinking the question out at length, by roads unknown to those who have left childhood behind, he came to the conclusion that Patsie was petted because she wore a big blue sash and yellow hair.

This precious discovery he kept to himself. The yellow hair was absolutely beyond his power, his own tousled wig being potato-brown; but something might be done towards the blue sash. He tied a large knot in his mosquito-curtains in order to remember to consult Patsie on their next meeting. She was the only child he had ever spoken to, and almost the only one that he had ever seen. The little memory and the very large and ragged knot held good.

'Patsie, lend me your blue wiband,' said His Majesty the King.

'You'll bewy it,' said Patsie doubtfully, mindful of certain atrocities committed on her doll.

'No, I won't—twoofanhonour. It's for me to wear.'

'Pooh!' said Patsie. 'Boys don't wear sa-ashes. Zey's only for dirls.'

'I didn't know.' The face of His Majesty the King fell.

'Who wants ribands? Are you playing horses, chickabiddies?' said the Commissioner's wife, stepping into the verandah.

'Toby wanted my sash,' explained Patsie.

'I don't now,' said His Majesty the King hastily, feeling that with one of these terrible 'grown-ups' his poor little secret would be shamelessly wrenched from him, and perhaps—most burning desecration of all—laughed at.

'I'll give you a cracker-cap,' said the Commissioner's wife. 'Come along with me, Toby, and we'll choose it.'

The cracker-cap was a stiff, three-pointed vermilion-and-tinsel splendour. His Majesty the King fitted it on his royal brow. The Commissioner's wife had a face that children instinctively trusted, and her action, as she adjusted the toppling middle spike, was tender.

'Will it do as well?' stammered His Majesty the King.

'As what, little one?'

'As ve wiban?'

'Oh, quite. Go and look at yourself in the glass.'

The words were spoken in all sincerity, and to help forward any absurd 'dressing-up' amusement that the children might take into their minds. But the young savage has a keen sense of the ludicrous. His Majesty the King swung the great cheval-glass down, and saw his head crowned with the staring horror of a fool's cap—a thing which his father would rend to pieces if it ever came into his office. He plucked it off, and burst into tears.

'Toby,' said the Commissioner's wife gravely, 'you shouldn't give way to temper. I am very sorry to see it. It's wrong.'

His Majesty the King sobbed inconsolably, and the heart of Patsie's mother was touched. She drew the child on to her knee. Clearly it was not temper alone.

'What is it, Toby? Won't you tell me? Aren't you well?'

The torrent of sobs and speech met, and fought for a time, with chokings and gulpings and gasps. Then, in a sudden rush, His Majesty the King was delivered of a few inarticulate sounds, followed by the words—'Go a—way you—dirty—little debbil!'

'Toby! What do you mean?'

'It's what he'd say. I *know* it is! He said vat when vere was only a little, little eggy mess, on my t-t-unic ; and he'd say it again, and laugh, if I went in wif vat on my head.'

' Who would say that ? '

' M-m-my Papa ! And I fought if I had ve blue wiban, he'd let me play in ve waste-paper basket under ve table.'

' *What* blue riband, childie ? '

' Ve same vat Patsie had—ve big blue wiban w-w-wound my t-t-tummy ! '

' What is it, Toby ? There's something on your mind. Tell me all about it, and perhaps I can help.'

' Isn't anyfing,' sniffed His Majesty, mindful of his manhood, and raising his head from the motherly bosom upon which it was resting. ' I only fought vat you—you petted Patsie 'cause she had ve blue wiban, and—and if I'd had ve blue wiban too, m-my Papa w-would pet me.'

The secret was out, and His Majesty the King sobbed bitterly in spite of the arms around him and the murmur of comfort on his heated little forehead.

Enter Patsie tumultuously, embarrassed by several lengths of the Commissioner's pet *mahseer*-rod. ' Tum along, Toby ! Zere's a *chu-chu* lizard in ze *chick*, and I've told Chimo to watch him till we tum. If we poke him wiz zis his tail will go *wiggle-wiggle* and fall off. Tum along ! I can't weach.'

' I'm comin',' said His Majesty the King, climbing down from the Commissioner's wife's knee after a hasty kiss.

Two minutes later, the *chu-chu* lizard's tail was

wriggling on the matting of the verandah, and the children were gravely poking it with splinters from the *chick*, to urge its exhausted vitality into 'just one wiggle more, 'cause it doesn't hurt *chu-chu*.'

The Commissioner's wife stood in the doorway and watched—'Poor little mite! A blue sash—— and my own precious Patsie! I wonder if the best of us, or we who love them best, ever understood what goes on in their topsy-turvy little heads.'

She went indoors to devise a tea for His Majesty the King.

'Their souls aren't in their tummies at that age in this climate,' said the Commissioner's wife, 'but they are not far off. I wonder if I could make Mrs. Austell understand. Poor little fellow!'

With simple craft, the Commissioner's wife called on Mrs. Austell and spoke long and lovingly about children; inquiring specially for His Majesty the King.

'He's with his governess,' said Mrs. Austell, and the tone showed that she was not interested.

The Commissioner's wife, unskilled in the art of war, continued her questionings. 'I don't know,' said Mrs. Austell. 'These things are left to Miss Biddums, and, of course, she does not ill-treat the child.'

The Commissioner's wife left hastily. The last sentence jarred upon her nerves. 'Doesn't *ill-treat* the child! As if that were all! I wonder what Tom would say if I only "didn't ill-treat" Patsie!'

Thenceforward, His Majesty the King was an honoured guest at the Commissioner's house, and the chosen friend of Patsie, with whom he blundered into as many scrapes as the compound and the servants' quarters afforded. Patsie's Mamma was always ready to give counsel, help, and sympathy, and, if need were and callers few, to enter into their games with an *abandon* that would have shocked the sleek-haired subalterns who squirmed painfully in their chairs when they came to call on her whom they profanely nicknamed ' Mother Bunch.'

Yet, in spite of Patsie and Patsie's Mamma, and the love that these two lavished upon him, His Majesty the King fell grievously from grace, and committed no less a sin than that of theft—unknown, it is true, but burdensome.

There came a man to the door one day, when His Majesty was playing in the hall and the bearer had gone to dinner, with a packet for His Majesty's Mamma. And he put it upon the hall-table, and said that there was no answer, and departed.

Presently, the pattern of the dado ceased to interest His Majesty, while the packet, a white, neatly-wrapped one of fascinating shape, interested him very much indeed. His Mamma was out, so was Miss Biddums, and there was pink string round the packet. He greatly desired pink string. It would help him in many of his little businesses— the haulage across the floor of his small cane-chair, the torturing of Chimo, who could never understand harness—and so forth. If he took the string it would be his own, and nobody would be any the wiser. He certainly could not pluck up sufficient courage to ask Mamma for it. Wherefore, mounting upon a chair, he carefully untied the string and, behold, the stiff white paper spread out in four

directions, and revealed a beautiful little leather
box with gold lines upon it! He tried to replace
the string, but that was a failure. So he opened
the box to get full satisfaction for his iniquity, and
saw a most beautiful Star that shone and winked,
and was altogether lovely and desirable.

'Vat,' said His Majesty meditatively, 'is a
'parkle cwown, like what I will wear when I go to
heaven. I will wear it on my head—Miss Biddums
says so. I would like to wear it *now*. I would
like to play wiv it. I will take it away and play
wiv it, very careful, until Mamma asks for it. I
fink it was bought for me to play wiv—same as my
cart.'

His Majesty the King was arguing against his
conscience, and he knew it, for he thought immediately after : 'Never mind, I will keep it to play wiv
until Mamma says where is it, and then I will say—
" I tookt it and I am sorry." I will not hurt it
because it is a 'parkle cwown. But Miss Biddums
will tell me to put it back. I will not show it to
Miss Biddums.'

If Mamma had come in at that moment all
would have gone well. She did not, and His
Majesty the King stuffed paper, case, and jewel
into the breast of his blouse and marched to the
nursery.

'When Mamma asks I will tell,' was the salve
that he laid upon his conscience. But Mamma
never asked, and for three whole days His Majesty
the King gloated over his treasure. It was of no
earthly use to him, but it was splendid, and, for
aught he knew, something dropped from the

heavens themselves. Still Mamma made no inquiries, and it seemed to him, in his furtive peeps, as though the shiny stones grew dim. What was the use of a 'parkle cwown if it made a little boy feel all bad in his inside? He had the pink string as well as the other treasure, but greatly he wished that he had not gone beyond the string. It was his first experience of iniquity, and it pained him after the flush of possession and secret delight in the ' 'parkle cwown ' had died away.

Each day that he delayed rendered confession to the people beyond the nursery doors more impossible. Now and again he determined to put himself in the path of the beautifully-attired lady as she was going out, and explain that he and no one else was the possessor of a ' 'parkle cwown,' most beautiful and quite uninquired for. But she passed hurriedly to her carriage, and the opportunity was gone before His Majesty the King could draw the deep breath which clinches noble resolve. The dread secret cut him off from Miss Biddums, Patsie, and the Commissioner's wife, and—doubly hard fate—when he brooded over it Patsie said, and told her mother, that he was cross.

The days were very long to His Majesty the King, and the nights longer still. Miss Biddums had informed him, more than once, what was the ultimate destiny of ' fieves,' and when he passed the interminable mud flanks of the Central Jail, he shook in his little strapped shoes.

But release came after an afternoon spent in playing boats by the edge of the tank at the bottom of the garden. His Majesty the King went to tea, and, for the first time in his memory, the meal revolted him. His nose was very cold, and his cheeks were burning hot. There was a weight about his feet, and he pressed his head several times to make sure that it was not swelling as he sat.

'I feel vevy funny,' said His Majesty the King, rubbing his nose. 'Vere's a buzz-buzz in my head.'

He went to bed quietly. Miss Biddums was out and the bearer undressed him.

The sin of the ' 'parkle cwown' was forgotten in the acuteness of the discomfort to which he roused after a leaden sleep of some hours. He was thirsty, and the bearer had forgotten to leave the drinking-water. 'Miss Biddums! Miss Biddums! I'm so kirsty!'

No answer. Miss Biddums had leave to attend the wedding of a Calcutta schoolmate. His Majesty the King had forgotten that.

'I want a dwink of water,' he cried, but his voice was dried up in his throat. 'I want a dwink! Vere is ve glass?'

He sat up in bed and looked round. There was a murmur of voices from the other side of the nursery door. It was better to face the terrible unknown than to choke in the dark. He slipped out of bed, but his feet were strangely wilful, and he reeled once or twice. Then he pushed the door open and staggered—a puffed and purple-faced little figure—into the brilliant light of the dining-room full of pretty ladies.

'I'm vevy hot! I'm vevy uncomfitivle,' moaned

His Majesty the King, clinging to the portière, 'and vere's no water in ve glass, and I'm *so* kirsty. Give me a dwink of water.'

An apparition in black and white—His Majesty the King could hardly see distinctly—lifted him up to the level of the table, and felt his wrists and forehead. The water came, and he drank deeply, his teeth chattering against the edge of the tumbler. Then every one seemed to go away—every one except the huge man in black and white, who carried him back to his bed ; the mother and father following. And the sin of the ' 'parkle cwown' rushed back and took possession of the terrified soul.

' I'm a fief! ' he gasped. ' I want to tell Miss Biddums vat I'm a fief. Vere is Miss Biddums ? '

Miss Biddums had come and was bending over him. ' I'm a fief,' he whispered. ' A fief—like ve men in ve pwison. But I'll tell now. I tookt—I tookt ve 'parkle cwown when ve man that came left it in ve hall. I bwoke ve paper and ve little bwown box, and it looked shiny, and I tookt it to play wif, and I was afwaid. It's in ve dooly-box at ve bottom. No one *never* asked for it, but I was afwaid. Oh, go an' get ve dooly-box ! '

Miss Biddums obediently stooped to the lowest shelf of the *almirah* and unearthed the big paper box in which His Majesty the King kept his dearest possessions. Under the tin soldiers, and a layer of mud pellets for a pellet-bow, winked and blazed a diamond star, wrapped roughly in a half-sheet of notepaper whereon were a few words.

Somebody was crying at the head of the bed, and

a man's hand touched the forehead of His Majesty the King, who grasped the packet and spread it on the bed.

'Vat is ve 'parkle cwown,' he said, and wept bitterly ; for now that he had made restitution he would fain have kept the shining splendour with him.

'It concerns you too,' said a voice at the head of the bed. 'Read the note. This is not the time to keep back anything.'

The note was curt, very much to the point, and signed by a single initial. '*If you wear this to-morrow night I shall know what to expect.*' The date was three weeks old.

A whisper followed, and the deeper voice returned : 'And you drifted as far apart as *that !* I think it makes us quits now, doesn't it ? Oh, can't we drop this folly once and for all ? Is it worth it, darling ?'

'Kiss me too,' said His Majesty the King dreamily. 'You isn't *vevy* angwy, is you ?'

The fever burned itself out, and His Majesty the King slept.

When he waked, it was in a new world— peopled by his father and mother as well as Miss Biddums; and there was much love in that world and no morsel of fear, and more petting than was good for several little boys. His Majesty the King was too young to moralise on the uncertainty of things human, or he would have been impressed with the singular advantages of crime—ay, black sin. Behold, he had stolen the ''parkle cwown,' and his reward was Love, and the right to play in the waste - paper basket under the table 'for always.'

.   .   .   .   .

He trotted over to spend an afternoon with Patsie, and the Commissioner's wife would have kissed him.   'No, not vere,' said His Majesty the King, with superb insolence, fencing one corner of his mouth with his hand.   'Vat's my Mamma's place—vere *she* kisses me.'

'Oh!' said the Commissioner's wife briefly. Then to herself : 'Well, I suppose I ought to be glad for his sake.   Children are selfish little grubs and—I've got my Patsie.'

The Drums of the Fore and Aft

In the Army List they still stand as 'The Fore
and Fit Princess Hohenzollern-Sigmaringen-
Auspach's Merthyr-Tydfilshire Own Royal Loyal
Light Infantry, Regimental District 329A,' but
the Army through all its barracks and canteens
knows them now as the 'Fore and Aft.' They
may in time do something that shall make their
new title honourable, but at present they are
bitterly ashamed, and the man who calls them
'Fore and Aft' does so at the risk of the head
which is on his shoulders.

Two words breathed into the stables of a certain
Cavalry Regiment will bring the men out into the
streets with belts and mops and bad language ; but
a whisper of 'Fore and Aft' will bring out this
regiment with rifles.

Their one excuse is that they came again and
did their best to finish the job in style. But for a
time all their world knows that they were openly
beaten, whipped, dumb-cowed, shaking, and afraid.
The men know it ; their officers know it ; the
Horse Guards know it, and when the next war
comes the enemy will know it also. There are

two or three regiments of the Line that have a black mark against their names which they will then wipe out ; and it will be excessively inconvenient for the troops upon whom they do their wiping.

The courage of the British soldier is officially supposed to be above proof, and, as a general rule, it is so. The exceptions are decently shovelled out of sight, only to be referred to in the freshest of unguarded talk that occasionally swamps a Messtable at midnight. Then one hears strange and horrible stories of men not following their officers, of orders being given by those who had no right to give them, and of disgrace that, but for the standing luck of the British Army, might have ended in brilliant disaster. These are unpleasant stories to listen to, and the Messes tell them under their breath, sitting by the big wood fires, and the young officer bows his head and thinks to himself, please God, his men shall never behave unhandily.

The British soldier is not altogether to be blamed for occasional lapses ; but this verdict he should not know. A moderately intelligent General will waste six months in mastering the craft of the particular war that he may be waging ; a Colonel may utterly misunderstand the capacity of his regiment for three months after it has taken the field ; and even a Company Commander may err and be deceived as to the temper and temperament of his own handful : wherefore the soldier, and the soldier of to-day more particularly, should not be blamed for falling back. He should be shot or hanged afterwards—to encourage the others ; but he should not be vilified in newspapers, for that is want of tact and waste of space.

He has, let us say, been in the service of the Empress for, perhaps, four years. He will leave in another two years. He has no inherited morals, and four years are not sufficient to drive toughness into his fibre, or to teach him how holy a thing is his Regiment. He wants to drink, he wants to enjoy himself—in India he wants to save money—and he does not in the least like getting hurt. He has received just sufficient education to make him understand half the purport of the orders he receives, and to speculate on the nature of clean, incised, and shattering wounds. Thus, if he is told to deploy under fire preparatory to an attack, he knows that he runs a very great risk of being killed while he is deploying, and suspects that he is being thrown away to gain ten minutes' time. He may either deploy with desperate swiftness, or he may shuffle, or bunch, or break, according to the discipline under which he has lain for four years.

Armed with imperfect knowledge, cursed with the rudiments of an imagination, hampered by the intense selfishness of the lower classes, and unsupported by any regimental associations, this young man is suddenly introduced to an enemy who in eastern lands is always ugly, generally tall and hairy, and frequently noisy. If he looks to the right and the left and sees old soldiers—men of twelve years' service, who, he knows, know what they are about —taking a charge, rush, or demonstration without embarrassment, he is consoled and applies his shoulder to the butt of his rifle with a stout heart.

His peace is the greater if he hears a senior, who has taught him his soldiering and broken his head on occasion, whispering : ' They'll shout and carry on like this for five minutes. Then they'll rush in, and then we've got 'em by the short hairs ! '

But, on the other hand, if he sees only men of his own term of service turning white and playing with their triggers, and saying : ' What the Hell's up now ? ' while the Company Commanders are sweating into their sword-hilts and shouting : ' Front-rank, fix bayonets. Steady there—steady ! Sight for three hundred—no, for five ! Lie down, all ! Steady ! Front-rank kneel ! ' and so forth, he becomes unhappy ; and grows acutely miserable when he hears a comrade turn over with the rattle of fire-irons falling into the fender, and the grunt of a pole-axed ox. If he can be moved about a little and allowed to watch the effect of his own fire on the enemy he feels merrier, and may be then worked up to the blind passion of fighting, which is, contrary to general belief, controlled by a chilly Devil and shakes men like ague. If he is not moved about, and begins to feel cold at the pit of the stomach, and in that crisis is badly mauled, and hear orders that were never given, he will break, and he will break badly ; and of all things under the light of the Sun there is nothing more terrible than a broken British regiment. When the worst comes to the worst and the panic is really epidemic, the men must be e'en let go, and the Company Commanders had better escape to the enemy and stay there for safety's sake. If they can be made to come again they are not pleasant men to meet ; because they will not break twice.

About thirty years from this date, when we have succeeded in half-educating everything that wears trousers, our Army will be a beautifully unreliable machine. It will know too much and it will do too little. Later still, when all men are at the mental level of the officer of to-day it will sweep the earth. Speaking roughly, you must employ either black-guards or gentlemen, or, best of all, blackguards commanded by gentlemen, to do butcher's work with efficiency and despatch. The ideal soldier should, of course, think for himself—the *Pocket-book* says so. Unfortunately, to attain this virtue he has to pass through the phase of thinking of himself, and that is misdirected genius. A blackguard may be slow to think for himself, but he is genuinely anxious to kill, and a little punishment teaches him how to guard his own skin and perforate another's. A powerfully prayerful Highland Regiment, officered by rank Presbyterians, is, perhaps, one degree more terrible in action than a hard-bitten thousand of irresponsible Irish ruffians led by most improper young un-believers. But these things prove the rule—which is that the midway men are not to be trusted alone. They have ideas about the value of life and an up-bringing that has not taught them to go on and take the chances. They are carefully unprovided with a backing of comrades who have been shot over, and until that backing is re-introduced, as a great many Regimental Commanders intend it shall be, they are more liable to disgrace themselves than the size of the Empire or the dignity of the Army allows.

Their officers are as good as good can be, because their training begins early, and God has arranged that a clean-run youth of the British middle classes shall, in the matter of backbone, brains, and bowels, surpass all other youths. For this reason a child of eighteen will stand up, doing nothing, with a tin sword in his hand and joy in his heart until he is dropped. If he dies, he dies like a gentleman. If he lives, he writes Home that he has been 'potted,' 'sniped,' 'chipped,' or 'cut over,' and sits down to besiege Government for a wound-gratuity until the next little war breaks out, when he perjures himself before a Medical Board, blarneys his Colonel, burns incense round his Adjutant, and is allowed to go to the Front once more.

Which homily brings me directly to a brace of the most finished little fiends that ever banged drum or tootled fife in the Band of a British Regiment. They ended their sinful career by open and flagrant mutiny and were shot for it. Their names were Jakin and Lew—Piggy Lew—and they were bold, bad drummer-boys, both of them frequently birched by the Drum-Major of the Fore and Aft.

Jakin was a stunted child of fourteen, and Lew was about the same age. When not looked after, they smoked and drank. They swore habitually after the manner of the Barrack-room, which is cold-swearing and comes from between clinched teeth ; and they fought religiously once a week. Jakin had sprung from some London gutter and may or may not have passed through Dr. Barnardo's hands ere he arrived at the dignity of drummer-boy. Lew could remember nothing except the regiment and

the delight of listening to the Band from his earliest
years. He hid somewhere in his grimy little soul
a genuine love for music, and was most mistakenly
furnished with the head of a cherub : insomuch that
beautiful ladies who watched the Regiment in church
were wont to speak of him as a ' darling.' They
never heard his vitriolic comments on their manners
and morals, as he walked back to barracks with the
Band and matured fresh causes of offence against
Jakin.

The other drummer-boys hated both lads on
account of their illogical conduct. Jakin might be
pounding Lew, or Lew might be rubbing Jakin's
head in the dirt, but any attempt at aggression on
the part of an outsider was met by the combined
forces of Lew and Jakin ; and the consequences were
painful. The boys were the Ishmaels of the corps,
but wealthy Ishmaels, for they sold battles in alternate
weeks for the sport of the barracks when they were
not pitted against other boys ; and thus amassed
money.

On this particular day there was dissension in the
camp. They had just been convicted afresh of
smoking, which is bad for little boys who use plug-
tobacco, and Lew's contention was that Jakin had
' stunk so 'orrid bad from keepin' the pipe in pocket,'
that he and he alone was responsible for the birching
they were both tingling under.

' I tell you I 'id the pipe back o' barracks,' said
Jakin pacifically.

' You're a bloomin' liar,' said Lew without
heat.

' You're a bloomin little barstard,' said Jakin,

strong in the knowledge that his own ancestry was unknown.

Now there is one word in the extended vocabulary of barrack-room abuse that cannot pass without comment. You may call a man a thief and risk nothing. You may even call him a coward without finding more than a boot whiz past your ear, but you must not call a man a bastard unless you are prepared to prove it on his front teeth.

'You might ha' kep' that till I wasn't so sore,' said Lew sorrowfully, dodging round Jakin's guard.

'I'll make you sorer,' said Jakin genially, and got home on Lew's alabaster forehead. All would have gone well and this story, as the books say, would never have been written, had not his evil fate prompted the Bazar-Sergeant's son, a long, employless man of five-and-twenty, to put in an appearance after the first round. He was eternally in need of money, and knew that the boys had silver.

'Fighting again,' said he. 'I'll report you to my father, and he'll report you to the Colour-Sergeant.'

'What's that to you?' said Jakin with an unpleasant dilation of the nostrils.

'Oh! nothing to *me*. You'll get into trouble, and you've been up too often to afford that.'

'What the Hell do you know about what we've done?' asked Lew the Seraph. '*You* aren't in the Army, you lousy, cadging civilian.'

He closed in on the man's left flank.

'Jes' 'cause you find two gentlemen settlin' their

diff'rences with their fistes you stick in your ugly nose where you aren't wanted. Run 'ome to your 'arf-caste slut of a Ma—or we'll give you what-for,' said Jakin.

The man attempted reprisals by knocking the boys' heads together. The scheme would have succeeded had not Jakin punched him vehemently in the stomach, or had Lew refrained from kicking his shins. They fought together, bleeding and breathless, for half an hour, and, after heavy punishment, triumphantly pulled down their opponent as terriers pull down a jackal.

'Now,' gasped Jakin, 'I'll give you what-for.' He proceeded to pound the man's features while Lew stamped on the outlying portions of his anatomy. Chivalry is not a strong point in the composition of the average drummer-boy. He fights, as do his betters, to make his mark.

Ghastly was the ruin that escaped, and awful was the wrath of the Bazar-Sergeant. Awful, too, was the scene in Orderly-room when the two reprobates appeared to answer the charge of half-murdering a 'civilian.' The Bazar-Sergeant thirsted for a criminal action, and his son lied. The boys stood to attention while the black clouds of evidence accumulated.

'You little devils are more trouble than the rest of the Regiment put together,' said the Colonel angrily. 'One might as well admonish thistledown, and I can't well put you in cells or under stoppages. You must be birched again.'

'Beg y' pardon, Sir. Can't we say nothin' in our own defence, Sir?' shrilled Jakin.

'Hey! What? Are you going to argue with *me*?' said the Colonel.

'No, Sir,' said Lew. 'But if a man come to you, Sir, and said he was going to report you, Sir, for 'aving a bit of a turn-up with a friend, Sir, an' wanted to get money out o' *you*, Sir——'

The Orderly-room exploded in a roar of laughter. 'Well?' said the Colonel.

'That was what that measly *jarnwar* there did, Sir, and 'e'd 'a' *done* it, Sir, if we 'adn't prevented 'im. We didn't 'it 'im much, Sir. 'E 'adn't no manner o' right to interfere with us, Sir. I don't mind bein' birched by the Drum-Major, Sir, nor yet reported by *any* Corp'ral, but I'm—but I don't think it's fair, Sir, for a civilian to come an' talk over a man in the Army.'

A second shout of laughter shook the Orderly-room, but the Colonel was grave.

'What sort of characters have these boys?' he asked of the Regimental Sergeant-Major.

'Accordin' to the Bandmaster, Sir,' returned that revered official—the only soul in the regiment whom the boys feared—'they do everything *but* lie, Sir.'

'Is it like we'd go for that man for fun, Sir?' said Lew, pointing to the plaintiff.

'Oh, admonished — admonished!' said the Colonel testily, and when the boys had gone he read the Bazar-Sergeant's son a lecture on the sin of unprofitable meddling, and gave orders that the Bandmaster should keep the Drums in better discipline.

'If either of you comes to practice again with so

much as a scratch on your two ugly little faces,'
thundered the Bandmaster, 'I'll tell the Drum-
Major to take the skin off your backs. Understand that, you young devils.'

Then he repented of his speech for just the
length of time that Lew, looking like a Seraph in
red worsted embellishments, took the place of one
of the trumpets—in hospital—and rendered the
echo of a battle-piece. Lew certainly was a musician,
and had often in his more exalted moments expressed a yearning to master every instrument of
the Band.

'There's nothing to prevent your becoming a
Bandmaster, Lew,' said the Bandmaster, who had
composed waltzes of his own, and worked day and
night in the interests of the Band.

'What did he say?' demanded Jakin after
practice.

''Said I might be a bloomin' Bandmaster, an'
be asked in to 'ave a glass o' sherry-wine on Mess-
nights.'

'Ho! 'Said you might be a bloomin' non-
combatant, did 'e! That's just about wot 'e
would say. When I've put in my boy's service
—it's a bloomin' shame that doesn't count for
pension—I'll take on as a privit. Then I'll be a
Lance in a year—knowin' what I know about the
ins an' outs o' things. In three years I'll be a
bloomin' Sergeant. I won't marry then, not I!
I'll 'old on and learn the orf'cers' ways an' apply
for exchange into a reg'ment that doesn't know
all about me. Then I'll be a bloomin' orf'cer.
Then I'll ask you to 'ave a glass o' sherry-wine,

Mister Lew, an' you'll bloomin' well 'ave to stay in the hanty-room while the Mess-Sergeant brings it to your dirty 'ands.'

' 'S'pose I'm going to be a Bandmaster? Not I, quite. I'll be a orf'cer too. There's nothin' like taking to a thing an' stickin' to it, the Schoolmaster says. The reg'ment don't go 'ome for another seven years. I'll be a Lance then or near to.'

Thus the boys discussed their futures, and conducted themselves piously for a week. That is to say, Lew started a flirtation with the Colour-Sergeant's daughter, aged thirteen—'not,' as he explained to Jakin, 'with any intention o' matrimony, but by way o' keepin' my 'and in.' And the black-haired Cris Delighan enjoyed that flirtation more than previous ones, and the other drummerboys raged furiously together, and Jakin preached sermons on the dangers of 'bein' tangled along o' petticoats.'

But neither love nor virtue would have held Lew long in the paths of propriety had not the rumour gone abroad that the Regiment was to be sent on active service, to take part in a war which, for the sake of brevity, we will call 'The War of the Lost Tribes.'

The barracks had the rumour almost before the Mess-room, and of all the nine hundred men in barracks not ten had seen a shot fired in anger. The Colonel had, twenty years ago, assisted at a Frontier expedition; one of the Majors had seen service at the Cape; a confirmed deserter in E Company had helped to clear streets in Ireland; but that was all. The Regiment had been put by

for many years. The overwhelming mass of its
rank and file had from three to four years' service;
the non-commissioned officers were under thirty
years old ; and men and sergeants alike had forgotten to speak of the stories written in brief upon
the Colours — the New Colours that had been
formally blessed by an Archbishop in England ere
the Regiment came away.

They wanted to go to the Front—they were
enthusiastically anxious to go—but they had no
knowledge of what war meant, and there was none
to tell them. They were an educated regiment, the
percentage of school-certificates in their ranks was
high, and most of the men could do more than
read and write. They had been recruited in loyal
observance of the territorial idea ; but they themselves had no notion of that idea. They were
made up of drafts from an over-populated manu-
facturing district. The system had put flesh and
muscle upon their small bones, but it could not
put heart into the sons of those who for genera-
tions had done overmuch work for over-scanty
pay, had sweated in drying-rooms, stooped over
looms, coughed among white-lead, and shivered
on lime-barges. The men had found food and
rest in the Army, and now they were going to
fight 'niggers'—people who ran away if you
shook a stick at them. Wherefore they cheered
lustily when the rumour ran, and the shrewd,
clerkly non-commissioned officers speculated on
the chances of batta and of saving their pay. At
Headquarters men said : 'The Fore and Fit have
never been under fire within the last generation.

Let us, therefore, break them in easily by setting them to guard lines of communication.' And this would have been done but for the fact that British Regiments were wanted — badly wanted — at the Front, and there were doubtful Native Regiments that could fill the minor duties. 'Brigade 'em with two strong Regiments,' said Headquarters. 'They may be knocked about a bit, but they'll learn their business before they come through. Nothing like a night-alarm and a little cutting-up of stragglers to make a Regiment smart in the field. Wait till they've had half-a-dozen sentries' throats cut.'

The Colonel wrote with delight that the temper of his men was excellent, that the Regiment was all that could be wished, and as sound as a bell. The Majors smiled with a sober joy, and the sub-alterns waltzed in pairs down the Mess-room after dinner, and nearly shot themselves at revolver-practice. But there was consternation in the hearts of Jakin and Lew. What was to be done with the Drums? Would the Band go to the Front? How many of the Drums would accompany the Regiment?

They took counsel together, sitting in a tree and smoking.

'It's more than a bloomin' toss-up they'll leave us be'ind at the Depot with the women. You'll like that,' said Jakin sarcastically.

''Cause o' Cris, y' mean? Wot's a woman, or a 'ole bloomin' depot o' women, 'longside o' the chanst of field-service? You know I'm as keen on goin' as you,' said Lew.

' 'Wish I was a bloomin' bugler,' said Jakin sadly. ' They'll take Tom Kidd along, that I can plaster a wall with, an' like as not they won't take us.'

' Then let's go an' make Tom Kidd so bloomin' sick 'e can't bugle no more. You 'old 'is 'ands an' I'll kick him,' said Lew, wriggling on the branch.

' That ain't no good neither. We ain't the sort o' characters to presoom on our rep'tations—they're bad. If they leave the Band at the Depot we don't go, and no error *there*. If they take the Band we may get cast for medical unfitness. Are you medical fit, Piggy ? ' said Jakin, digging Lew in the ribs with force.

' Yus,' said Lew with an oath. ' The Doctor says your 'eart's weak through smokin' on an empty stummick. Throw a chest an' I'll try yer.'

Jakin threw out his chest, which Lew smote with all his might. Jakin turned very pale, gasped, crowed, screwed up his eyes, and said—' That's all right.'

' You'll do,' said Lew. ' I've 'eard o' men dying when you 'it 'em fair on the breastbone.'

' Don't bring us no nearer goin', though,' said Jakin. ' Do you know where we're ordered ? '

' Gawd knows, an' 'E won't split on a pal. Somewheres up to the Front to kill Paythans—hairy big beggars that turn you inside out if they get 'old o' you. They say their women are good-looking, too.'

' Any loot ? ' asked the abandoned Jakin.

' Not a bloomin' anna, they say, unless you dig

up the ground an' see what the niggers 'ave 'id.
They're a poor lot.' Jakin stood upright on the
branch and gazed across the plain.

'Lew,' said he, 'there's the Colonel coming.
'Colonel's a good old beggar. Let's go an' talk to
'im.'

Lew nearly fell out of the tree at the audacity
of the suggestion. Like Jakin he feared not God,
neither regarded he Man, but there are limits even
to the audacity of drummer-boy, and to speak to
a Colonel was——

But Jakin had slid down the trunk and doubled
in the direction of the Colonel. That officer was
walking wrapped in thought and visions of a C.B.—
yes, even a K.C.B., for had he not at command
one of the best Regiments of the Line—the Fore
and Fit? And he was aware of two small boys
charging down upon him. Once before it had
been solemnly reported to him that 'the Drums
were in a state of mutiny,' Jakin and Lew being
the ringleaders. This looked like an organised
conspiracy.

The boys halted at twenty yards, walked to the
regulation four paces, and saluted together, each as
well-set-up as a ramrod and little taller.

The Colonel was in a genial mood; the boys
appeared very forlorn and unprotected on the
desolate plain, and one of them was handsome.

'Well!' said the Colonel, recognising them.
'Are you going to pull me down in the open?
I'm sure I never interfere with you, even though'
—he sniffed suspiciously—'you have been
smoking.'

It was time to strike while the iron was hot. Their hearts beat tumultuously.

'Beg y' pardon, Sir,' began Jakin. 'The Reg'ment's ordered on active service, Sir?'

'So I believe,' said the Colonel courteously.

'Is the Band goin', Sir?' said both together. Then, without pause, 'We're goin', Sir, ain't we?'

'You!' said the Colonel, stepping back the more fully to take in the two small figures. 'You! You'd die in the first march.'

'No, we wouldn't, Sir. We can march with the Reg'ment anywheres—p'rade an' anywhere else,' said Jakin.

'If Tom Kidd goes 'e'll shut up like a clasp-knife,' said Lew. 'Tom 'as very-close veins in both 'is legs, Sir.'

'Very how much?'

'Very-close veins, Sir. That's why they swells after long p'rade, Sir. If 'e can go, we can go, Sir.'

Again the Colonel looked at them long and intently.

'Yes, the Band is going,' he said as gravely as though he had been addressing a brother officer. 'Have you any parents, either of you two?'

'No, Sir,' rejoicingly from Lew and Jakin. 'We're both orphans, Sir. There's no one to be considered of on our account, Sir.'

'You poor little sprats, and you want to go up to the Front with the Regiment, do you? Why?'

'I've wore the Queen's Uniform for two years,' said Jakin. 'It's very 'ard, Sir, that a man don't get no recompense for doin' of 'is dooty, Sir.'

'An'—an' if I don't go, Sir,' interrupted Lew,

'the Bandmaster 'e says 'e'll catch an' make a bloo—
a blessed musician o' me, Sir. Before I've seen
any service, Sir.'

The Colonel made no answer for a long time.
Then he said quietly : ' If you're passed by the
Doctor I daresay you can go. I shouldn't smoke
if I were you.'

The boys saluted and disappeared. The Colonel
walked home and told the story to his wife, who
nearly cried over it. The Colonel was well pleased.
If that was the temper of the children, what would
not the men do?

Jakin and Lew entered the boys' barrack-room
with great stateliness, and refused to hold any conversation with their comrades for at least ten
minutes. Then, bursting with pride, Jakin drawled :
' I've bin intervooin' the Colonel. Good old beggar
is the Colonel. Says I to 'im, " Colonel," says I,
" let me go to the Front, along o' the Reg'ment."—
" To the Front you shall go," says 'e, " an' I only
wish there was more like you among the dirty little
devils that bang the bloomin' drums." Kidd, if
you throw your 'courtrements at me for tellin' you
the truth to your own advantage, your legs'll
swell.'

None the less there was a Battle-Royal in the
barrack-room, for the boys were consumed with
envy and hate, and neither Jakin nor Lew behaved
in conciliatory wise.

' I'm goin' out to say adoo to my girl,' said
Lew, to cap the climax. ' Don't none o' you touch
my kit because it's wanted for active service ; me
bein' specially invited to go by the Colonel.'

He strolled forth and whistled in the clump of trees at the back of the Married Quarters till Cris came to him, and, the preliminary kisses being given and taken, Lew began to explain the situation.

'I'm goin' to the Front with the Reg'ment,' he said valiantly.

'Piggy, you're a little liar,' said Cris, but her heart misgave her, for Lew was not in the habit of lying.

'Liar yourself, Cris,' said Lew, slipping an arm round her. 'I'm goin'. When the Reg'ment marches out you'll see me with 'em, all galliant and gay. Give us another kiss, Cris, on the strength of it.'

'If you'd on'y a-stayed at the Depot—where you *ought* to ha' bin—you could get as many of 'em as—as you dam please,' whimpered Cris, putting up her mouth.

'It's 'ard, Cris. I grant you it's 'ard. But what's a man to do? If I'd a-stayed at the Depot, you wouldn't think anything of me.'

'Like as not, but I'd 'ave you with me, Piggy. An' all the thinkin' in the world isn't like kissin'.'

'An' all the kissin' in the world isn't like 'avin' a medal to wear on the front o' your coat.'

'*You* won't get no medal.'

'Oh yus, I shall though. Me an' Jakin are the only acting-drummers that'll be took along. All the rest is full men, an' we'll get our medals with them.'

'They might ha' taken anybody but you, Piggy. You'll get killed—you're so venturesome. Stay

with me, Piggy darlin', down at the Depot, an' I'll
love you true, for ever.'

'Ain't you goin' to do that *now*, Cris? You
said you was.'

'O' course I am, but th' other's more comfortable. Wait till you've growed a bit, Piggy. You
aren't no taller than me now.'

'I've bin in the Army for two years an' I'm not
goin' to get out of a chanst o' seein' service, an'
don't you try to make me do so. I'll come back,
Cris, an' when I take on as a man I'll marry you—
marry you when I'm a Lance.'

'Promise, Piggy?'

Lew reflected on the future as arranged by Jakin
a short time previously, but Cris's mouth was very
near to his own.

'I promise, s'elp me Gawd!' said he.

Cris slid an arm round his neck.

'I won't 'old you back no more, Piggy. Go
away an' get your medal, an' I'll make you a new
button-bag as nice as I know how,' she whispered.

'Put some o' your 'air into it, Cris, an' I'll keep
it in my pocket so long's I'm alive.'

Then Cris wept anew, and the interview ended.
Public feeling among the drummer-boys rose to
fever pitch and the lives of Jakin and Lew became
unenviable. Not only had they been permitted to
enlist two years before the regulation boy's age—
fourteen—but, by virtue, it seemed, of their extreme
youth, they were allowed to go to the Front—
which thing had not happened to acting-drummers
within the knowledge of boy. The Band which
was to accompany the Regiment had been cut down

to the regulation twenty men, the surplus returning to the ranks. Jakin and Lew were attached to the Band as supernumeraries, though they would much have preferred being Company buglers.

' 'Don't matter much,' said Jakin, after the medical inspection. ' Be thankful that we're 'lowed to go at all. The Doctor 'e said that if we could stand what we took from the Bazar-Sergeant's son we'd stand pretty nigh anything.'

' Which we will,' said Lew, looking tenderly at the ragged and ill-made housewife that Cris had given him, with a lock of her hair worked into a sprawling ' L ' upon the cover.

' It was the best I could,' she sobbed. ' I wouldn't let mother nor the Sergeants' tailor 'elp me. Keep it always, Piggy, an' remember I love you true.'

They marched to the railway station, nine hundred and sixty strong, and every soul in cantonments turned out to see them go. The drummers gnashed their teeth at Jakin and Lew marching with the Band, the married women wept upon the platform, and the Regiment cheered its noble self black in the face.

' A nice level lot,' said the Colonel to the Second-in-Command as they watched the first four companies entraining.

' Fit to do anything,' said the Second-in-Command enthusiastically. ' But it seems to me they're a thought too young and tender for the work in hand. It's bitter cold up at the Front now.'

' They're sound enough,' said the Colonel. ' We must take our chance of sick casualties.'

So they went northward, ever northward, past droves and droves of camels, armies of camp followers, and legions of laden mules, the throng thickening day by day, till with a shriek the train pulled up at a hopelessly-congested junction where six lines of temporary track accommodated six forty-waggon trains ; where whistles blew, Babus sweated, and Commissariat officers swore from dawn till far into the night amid the wind-driven chaff of the fodder-bales and the lowing of a thousand steers.

'Hurry up—you're badly wanted at the Front,' was the message that greeted the Fore and Aft, and the occupants of the Red Cross carriages told the same tale.

''Tisn't so much the bloomin' fightin',' gasped a headbound trooper of Hussars to a knot of admiring Fore and Afts. ''Tisn't so much the bloomin' fightin', though there's enough o' that. It's the bloomin' food an' the bloomin' climate. Frost all night 'cept when it hails, and biling sun all day, and the water stinks fit to knock you down. I got my 'ead chipped like a egg ; I've got pneumonia too, an' my guts is all out o' order. 'Tain't no bloomin' picnic in those parts, I can tell you.'

'Wot are the niggers like ?' demanded a private.

'There's some prisoners in that train yonder. Go an' look at 'em. They're the aristocracy o' the country. The common folk are a dashed sight uglier. If you want to know what they fight with, reach under my seat an' pull out the long knife that's there.'

They dragged out and beheld for the first time
the grim, bone-handled, triangular Afghan knife.
It was almost as long as Lew.

'That's the thing to jint ye,' said the trooper
feebly. 'It can take off a man's arm at the
shoulder as easy as slicing butter. I halved the
beggar that used that 'un, but there's more of his
likes up above. They don't understand thrustin',
but they're devils to slice.'

The men strolled across the tracks to inspect
the Afghan prisoners. They were unlike any
'niggers' that the Fore and Aft had ever met—
these huge, black-haired, scowling sons of the Beni-
Israel. As the men stared the Afghans spat freely
and muttered one to another with lowered eyes.

'My eyes! Wot awful swine!' said Jakin,
who was in the rear of the procession. 'Say, old
man, how you got *puckrowed*, eh? *Kiswasti* you
wasn't hanged for your ugly face, hey?'

The tallest of the company turned, his leg-irons
clanking at the movement, and stared at the boy.
'See!' he cried to his fellows in Pushto. 'They
send children against us. What a people, and
what fools!'

'*Hya!*' said Jakin, nodding his head cheerily.
'You go down-country. *Khana* get, *peenikapanee*
get—live like a bloomin' Raja *ke marfik*. That's
a better *bandobust* than baynit get it in your
innards. Good-bye, ole man. Take care o' your
beautiful figure-'ed, an' try to look *kushy*.'

The men laughed and fell in for their first
march, when they began to realise that a soldier's
life was not all beer and skittles. They were much

impressed with the size and bestial ferocity of the niggers whom they had now learned to call 'Paythans,' and more with the exceeding discomfort of their own surroundings. Twenty old soldiers in the corps would have taught them how to make themselves moderately snug at night, but they had no old soldiers, and, as the troops on the line of march said, 'they lived like pigs.' They learned the heart-breaking cussedness of camp-kitchens and camels and the depravity of an E. P. tent and a wither-wrung mule. They studied animalculæ in water, and developed a few cases of dysentery in their study.

At the end of their third march they were disagreeably surprised by the arrival in their camp of a hammered iron slug which, fired from a steady rest at seven hundred yards, flicked out the brains of a private seated by the fire. This robbed them of their peace for a night, and was the beginning of a long-range fire carefully calculated to that end. In the daytime they saw nothing except an unpleasant puff of smoke from a crag above the line of march. At night there were distant spurts of flame and occasional casualties, which set the whole camp blazing into the gloom and, occasionally, into opposite tents. Then they swore vehemently, and vowed that this was magnificent but not war.

Indeed it was not. The Regiment could not halt for reprisals against the sharpshooters of the countryside. Its duty was to go forward and make connection with the Scotch and Gurkha troops with which it was brigaded. The Afghans knew this, and knew too, after their first tentative shots, that they were dealing with a raw regiment. Thereafter they devoted themselves to the task of keeping the Fore and Aft on the strain. Not for anything would they have taken equal liberties with a seasoned corps—with the wicked little Gurkhas, whose delight it was to lie out in the open on a dark night and stalk their stalkers— with the terrible, big men dressed in women's clothes, who could be heard praying to their God in the night-watches, and whose peace of mind no amount of 'sniping' could shake—or with those vile Sikhs, who marched so ostentatiously unprepared, and who dealt out such grim reward to those who tried to profit by that unpreparedness. This white regiment was different—quite different It slept like a hog, and, like a hog, charged in every direction when it was roused. Its sentries walked with a footfall that could be heard for a quarter of a mile ; would fire at anything that moved—even a driven donkey—and when they had once fired, could be scientifically 'rushed' and laid out a horror and an offence against the morning sun. Then there were camp-followers who straggled and could be cut up without fear. Their shrieks would disturb the white boys, and the loss of their services would inconvenience them sorely.

Thus, at every march, the hidden enemy became bolder and the regiment writhed and twisted under attacks it could not avenge. The crowning triumph was a sudden night-rush ending in the cutting of many tent-ropes, the collapse of the sodden canvas, and a glorious knifing of the men who struggled and kicked below. It was a great deed, neatly carried out, and it shook the already shaken nerves of the Fore and Aft. All the courage that they had been required to exercise up to this point was the 'two o'clock in the morning courage;' and, so far, they had only succeeded in shooting their comrades and losing their sleep.

Sullen, discontented, cold, savage, sick, with their uniforms dulled and unclean, the Fore and Aft joined their Brigade.

'I hear you had a tough time of it coming up,' said the Brigadier. But when he saw the hospital-sheets his face fell.

'This is bad,' said he to himself. 'They're as rotten as sheep.' And aloud to the Colonel—'I'm afraid we can't spare you just yet. We want all we have, else I should have given you ten days to recover in.'

The Colonel winced. 'On my honour, Sir,' he returned, 'there is not the least necessity to think of sparing us. My men have been rather mauled and upset without a fair return. They only want to go in somewhere where they can see what's before them.'

'Can't say I think much of the Fore and Fit,' said the Brigadier in confidence to his Brigade-Major. 'They've lost all their soldiering, and, by the trim of them, might have marched through the country from the other side. A more fagged-out set of men I never put eyes on.'

'Oh, they'll improve as the work goes on. The parade gloss has been rubbed off a little, but they'll put on field polish before long,' said the Brigade-

Major. 'They've been mauled, and they quite
don't understand it.'

They did not. All the hitting was on one
side, and it was cruelly hard hitting with accessories
that made them sick. There was also the real
sickness that laid hold of a strong man and dragged
him howling to the grave. Worst of all, their
officers knew just as little of the country as the
men themselves, and looked as if they did. The
Fore and Aft were in a thoroughly unsatisfactory
condition, but they believed that all would be well
if they could once get a fair go-in at the enemy.
Pot-shots up and down the valleys were unsatisfactory, and the bayonet never seemed to get a
chance. Perhaps it was as well, for a long-limbed
Afghan with a knife had a reach of eight feet, and
could carry away lead that would disable three
Englishmen.

The Fore and Fit would like some rifle-practice
at the enemy—all seven hundred rifles blazing
together. That wish showed the mood of the
men.

The Gurkhas walked into their camp, and in
broken, barrack-room English strove to fraternise
with them; offered them pipes of tobacco and
stood them treat at the canteen. But the Fore
and Aft, not knowing much of the nature of the
Gurkhas, treated them as they would treat any
other ' niggers,' and the little men in green trotted
back to their firm friends the Highlanders, and
with many grins confided to them : ' That dam
white regiment no dam use. Sulky—ugh! Dirty
—ugh! Hya, any tot for Johnny ?' Whereat

the Highlanders smote the Gurkhas as to the head, and told them not to vilify a British Regiment, and the Gurkhas grinned cavernously, for the Highlanders were their elder brothers and entitled to the privileges of kinship. The common soldier who touches a Gurkha is more than likely to have his head sliced open.

Three days later the Brigadier arranged a battle according to the rules of war and the peculiarity of the Afghan temperament. The enemy were massing in inconvenient strength among the hills, and the moving of many green standards warned him that the tribes were 'up' in aid of the Afghan regular troops. A squadron and a half of Bengal Lancers represented the available Cavalry, and two screw-guns borrowed from a column thirty miles away, the Artillery at the General's disposal.

'If they stand, as I've a very strong notion that they will, I fancy we shall see an infantry fight that will be worth watching,' said the Brigadier. 'We'll do it in style. Each regiment shall be played into action by its Band, and we'll hold the Cavalry in reserve.'

'For *all* the reserve?' somebody asked.

'For all the reserve; because we're going to crumple them up,' said the Brigadier, who was an extraordinary Brigadier, and did not believe in the value of a reserve when dealing with Asiatics. Indeed, when you come to think of it, had the British Army consistently waited for reserves in all its little affairs, the boundaries of Our Empire would have stopped at Brighton beach.

That battle was to be a glorious battle.

The three regiments debouching from three separate gorges, after duly crowning the heights above, were to converge from the centre, left, and right upon what we will call the Afghan army, then stationed towards the lower extremity of a flat-bottomed valley. Thus it will be seen that three sides of the valley practically belonged to the English, while the fourth was strictly Afghan property. In the event of defeat the Afghans had the rocky hills to fly to, where the fire from the guerilla tribes in aid would cover their retreat. In the event of victory these same tribes would rush down and lend their weight to the rout of the British.

The screw-guns were to shell the head of each Afghan rush that was made in close formation, and the Cavalry, held in reserve in the right valley, were to gently stimulate the break-up which would follow on the combined attack. The Brigadier, sitting upon a rock overlooking the valley, would watch the battle unrolled at his feet. The Fore and Aft would debouch from the central gorge, the Gurkhas from the left, and the Highlanders from the right, for the reason that the left flank of the enemy seemed as though it required the most hammering. It was not every day that an Afghan force would take ground in the open, and the Brigadier was resolved to make the most of it.

'If we only had a few more men,' he said plaintively, 'we could surround the creatures and crumple 'em up thoroughly. As it is, I'm afraid we can only cut them up as they run. It's a great pity.'

The Fore and Aft had enjoyed unbroken peace for five days, and were beginning, in spite of dysentery, to recover their nerve. But they were not happy, for they did not know the work in hand, and had they known, would not have known how to do it. Throughout those five days in which old soldiers might have taught them the craft of the game, they discussed together their misadventures in the past—how such an one was alive at dawn and dead ere the dusk, and with what shrieks and struggles such another had given up his soul under the Afghan knife. Death was a new and horrible thing to the sons of mechanics who were used to die decently of zymotic disease ; and their careful conservation in barracks had done nothing to make them look upon it with less dread.

Very early in the dawn the bugles began to blow, and the Fore and Aft, filled with a misguided enthusiasm, turned out without waiting for a cup of coffee and a biscuit ; and were rewarded by being kept under arms in the cold while the other regiments leisurely prepared for the fray. All the world knows that it is ill taking the breeks off a Highlander. It is much iller to try to make him stir unless he is convinced of the necessity for haste.

The Fore and Aft waited, leaning upon their rifles and listening to the protests of their empty stomachs. The Colonel did his best to remedy the default of lining as soon as it was borne in upon him that the affair would not begin at once, and so well did he succeed that the coffee was just ready when—the men moved off, their Band leading.

Even then there had been a mistake in time, and the Fore and Aft came out into the valley ten minutes before the proper hour. Their Band wheeled to the right after reaching the open, and retired behind a little rocky knoll still playing while the regiment went past.

It was not a pleasant sight that opened on the uninstructed view, for the lower end of the valley appeared to be filled by an army in position—real and actual regiments attired in red coats, and—of this there was no doubt—firing Martini-Henry bullets which cut up the ground a hundred yards in front of the leading company. Over that pock-marked ground the regiment had to pass, and it opened the ball with a general and profound courtesy to the piping pickets ; ducking in perfect time, as though it had been brazed on a rod. Being half-capable of thinking for itself, it fired a volley by the simple process of pitching its rifle into its shoulder and pulling the trigger. The bullets may have accounted for some of the watchers on the hillside, but they certainly did not affect the mass of enemy in front, while the noise of the rifles drowned any orders that might have been given.

'Good God ! ' said the Brigadier, sitting on the rock high above all. 'That regiment has spoilt the whole show. Hurry up the others, and let the screw-guns get off.'

But the screw-guns, in working round the heights, had stumbled upon a wasp's nest of a small mud fort which they incontinently shelled at eight hundred yards, to the huge discomfort of the occupants, who were unaccustomed to weapons of such devilish precision.

The Fore and Aft continued to go forward, but with shortened stride. Where were the other regiments, and why did these niggers use Martinis? They took open order instinctively, lying down and firing at random, rushing a few paces forward and lying down again, according to the regulations. Once in this formation, each man felt himself desperately alone, and edged in towards his fellow for comfort's sake.

Then the crack of his neighbour's rifle at his ear led him to fire as rapidly as he could—again for the sake of the comfort of the noise. The reward was not long delayed. Five volleys plunged the files in banked smoke impenetrable to the eye, and the bullets began to take ground twenty or thirty yards in front of the firers, as the weight of the bayonet dragged down and to the right arms wearied with holding the kick of the leaping Martini. The Company Commanders peered helplessly through the smoke, the more nervous mechanically trying to fan it away with their helmets.

'High and to the left!' bawled a Captain till he was hoarse. 'No good! Cease firing, and let it drift away a bit.'

Three and four times the bugles shrieked the order, and when it was obeyed the Fore and Aft looked that their foe should be lying before them in mown swaths of men. A light wind drove the smoke to leeward, and showed the enemy still in position and apparently unaffected. A quarter of a ton of lead had been buried a furlong in front of them, as the ragged earth attested.

That was not demoralising to the Afghans, who have not European nerves. They were waiting for the mad riot to die down, and were firing quietly into the heart of the smoke. A private of the Fore and Aft spun up his company shrieking with agony, another was kicking the earth and gasping, and a third, ripped through the lower intestines by a jagged bullet, was calling aloud on his comrades to put him out of his pain. These were the casualties, and they were not soothing to hear or see. The smoke cleared to a dull haze.

Then the foe began to shout with a great shouting, and a mass—a black mass—detached itself from the main body, and rolled over the ground at horrid speed. It was composed of, perhaps, three hundred men, who would shout and fire and slash if the rush of their fifty comrades who were determined to die carried home. The fifty were Ghazis, half-maddened with drugs and wholly mad with religious fanaticism. When they rushed the British fire ceased, and in the lull the order was given to close ranks and meet them with the bayonet.

Any one who knew the business could have told the Fore and Aft that the only way of dealing with a Ghazi rush is by volleys at long ranges ; because a man who means to die, who desires to die, who will gain heaven by dying, must, in nine cases out of ten, kill a man who has a lingering prejudice in favour of life. Where they should have closed and gone forward, the Fore and Aft opened out and skirmished, and where they should have opened out and fired, they closed and waited.

A man dragged from his blankets half awake and unfed is never in a pleasant frame of mind. Nor does his happiness increase when he watches the whites of the eyes of three hundred six-foot fiends upon whose beards the foam is lying, upon whose tongues is a roar of wrath, and in whose hands are yard-long knives.

The Fore and Aft heard the Gurkha bugles bringing that regiment forward at the double, while the neighing of the Highland pipes came from the left. They strove to stay where they were, though the bayonets wavered down the line like the oars of a ragged boat. Then they felt body to body the amazing physical strength of their foes ; a shriek of pain ended the rush, and the knives fell amid scenes not to be told. The men clubbed together and smote blindly—as often as not at their own fellows. Their front crumpled like paper, and the fifty Ghazis passed on ; their backers, now drunk with success, fighting as madly as they.

Then the rear-ranks were bidden to close up, and the subalterns dashed into the stew—alone. For the rear-rank had heard the clamour in front, the yells and the howls of pain, and had seen the dark stale blood that makes afraid. They were not going to stay. It was the rushing of the camps over again. Let their officers go to Hell, if they chose ; they would get away from the knives.

'Come on !' shrieked the subalterns, and their men, cursing them, drew back, each closing into his neighbour and wheeling round.

Charteris and Devlin, subalterns of the last company, faced their death alone in the belief that their men would follow.

' You've killed me, you cowards,' sobbed Devlin and dropped, cut from the shoulder-strap to the centre of the chest, and a fresh detachment of his men retreating, always retreating, trampled him under foot as they made for the pass whence they had emerged.

> I kissed her in the kitchen and I kissed her in the hall.
> Child'un, child'un, follow me !
> Oh Golly, said the cook, is he gwine to kiss us all ?
> Halla—Halla—Halla—Hallelujah !

The Gurkhas were pouring through the left gorge and over the heights at the double to the invitation of their Regimental Quick-step. The black rocks were crowned with dark green spiders as the bugles gave tongue jubilantly :—

> In the morning ! In the morning *by* the bright light !
> When Gabriel blows his trumpet in the morning !

The Gurkha rear-companies tripped and blundered over loose stones. The front-files halted for a moment to take stock of the valley and to settle stray boot-laces. Then a happy little sigh of contentment soughed down the ranks, and it was as though the land smiled, for behold there below was the enemy, and it was to meet them that the Gurkhas had doubled so hastily. There was much enemy. There would be amusement. The little men hitched their *kukris* well to hand, and gaped expectantly at their officers as terriers grin ere the stone is cast for them to fetch. The

Gurkhas' ground sloped downward to the valley, and they enjoyed a fair view of the proceedings. They sat upon the boulders to watch, for their officers were not going to waste their wind in assisting to repulse a Ghazi rush more than half a mile away. Let the white men look to their own front.

'Hi! yi!' said the Subadar-Major, who was sweating profusely. 'Dam fools yonder, stand close-order! This is no time for close order, it is the time for volleys. Ugh!'

Horrified, amused, and indignant, the Gurkhas beheld the retirement of the Fore and Aft with a running chorus of oaths and commentaries.

'They run! The white men run! Colonel Sahib, may *we* also do a little running?' murmured Runbir Thappa, the Senior Jemadar.

But the Colonel would have none of it. 'Let the beggars be cut up a little,' said he wrathfully. ''Serves 'em right. They'll be prodded into facing round in a minute.' He looked through his field-glasses, and caught the glint of an officer's sword.

'Beating 'em with the flat—damned conscripts! How the Ghazis are walking into them!' said he.

The Fore and Aft, heading back, bore with them their officers. The narrowness of the pass forced the mob into solid formation, and the rear-rank delivered some sort of a wavering volley. The Ghazis drew off, for they did not know what reserves the gorge might hide. Moreover, it was never wise to chase white men too far. They returned as wolves return to cover, satisfied with the slaughter that they had done, and only stopping

to slash at the wounded on the ground. A quarter
of a mile had the Fore and Aft retreated, and
now, jammed in the pass, was quivering with pain,
shaken and demoralised with fear, while the officers,
maddened beyond control, smote the men with the
hilts and the flats of their swords.

'Get back! Get back, you cowards—you
women! Right about face—column of companies,
form—you hounds!' shouted the Colonel, and the
subalterns swore aloud. But the Regiment wanted
to go—to go anywhere out of the range of those
merciless knives. It swayed to and fro irresolutely
with shouts and outcries, while from the right the
Gurkhas dropped volley after volley of cripple-
stopper Snider bullets at long range into the mob
of the Ghazis returning to their own troops.

The Fore and Aft Band, though protected from
direct fire by the rocky knoll under which it had
sat down, fled at the first rush. Jakin and Lew
would have fled also, but their short legs left them
fifty yards in the rear, and by the time the Band
had mixed with the regiment, they were painfully
aware that they would have to close in alone and
unsupported.

'Get back to that rock,' gasped Jakin. 'They
won't see us there.'

And they returned to the scattered instruments
of the Band, their hearts nearly bursting their ribs.

'Here's a nice show for *us*,' said Jakin, throwing
himself full length on the ground. 'A bloomin'
fine show for British Infantry! Oh, the devils!
They've gone an' left us alone here! Wot'll we
do?'

Lew took possession of a cast-off water bottle, which naturally was full of canteen rum, and drank till he coughed again.

'Drink,' said he shortly. 'They'll come back in a minute or two—you see.'

Jakin drank, but there was no sign of the regiment's return. They could hear a dull clamour from the head of the valley of retreat, and saw the Ghazis slink back, quickening their pace as the Gurkhas fired at them.

'We're all that's left of the Band, an' we'll be cut up as sure as death,' said Jakin.

'I'll die game, then,' said Lew thickly, fumbling with his tiny drummer's sword. The drink was working on his brain as it was on Jakin's.

' 'Old on! I know something better than fightin',' said Jakin, 'stung by the splendour of a sudden thought' due chiefly to rum. 'Tip our bloomin' cowards yonder the word to come back. The Paythan beggars are well away. Come on, Lew! We won't get hurt. Take the fife an' give me the drum. The Old Step for all your bloomin' guts are worth! There's a few of our men coming back now. Stand up, ye drunken little defaulter. By your right—quick march!'

He slipped the drum-sling over his shoulder, thrust the fife into Lew's hand, and the two boys marched out of the cover of the rock into the open, making a hideous hash of the first bars of the 'British Grenadiers.'

As Lew had said, a few of the Fore and Aft were coming back sullenly and shamefacedly under the stimulus of blows and abuse ; their red coats shone at the head of the valley, and behind them were wavering bayonets. But between this shattered line and the enemy, who with Afghan suspicion feared that the hasty retreat meant an ambush, and had not moved therefore, lay half a mile of level ground dotted only by the wounded.

The tune settled into full swing and the boys kept shoulder to shoulder, Jakin banging the drum as one possessed. The one fife made a thin and pitiful squeaking, but the tune carried far, even to the Gurkhas.

'Come on, you dogs!' muttered Jakin to himself. 'Are we to play forhever?' Lew was staring straight in front of him and marching more stiffly than ever he had done on parade.

And in bitter mockery of the distant mob, the old tune of the Old Line shrilled and rattled :—

> Some talk of Alexander,
>   And some of Hercules ;
> Of Hector and Lysander,
>   And such great names as these !

There was a far-off clapping of hands from the Gurkhas, and a roar from the Highlanders in the distance, but never a shot was fired by British or Afghan. The two little red dots moved forward in the open parallel to the enemy's front.

> But of all the world's great heroes
>   There's none that can compare,
> With a tow-row-row-row-row-row,
>   To the British Grenadier !

The men of the Fore and Aft were gathering thick at the entrance to the plain. The Brigadier on the heights far above was speechless with rage.

Still no movement from the enemy.   The day stayed to watch the children.

Jakin halted and beat the long roll of the Assembly, while the fife squealed despairingly.

'Right about face! Hold up, Lew, you're drunk,' said Jakin.   They wheeled and marched back :—

> Those heroes of antiquity
>> Ne'er saw a cannon-ball,
> Nor knew the force o' powder,

'Here they come!' said Jakin. 'Go on, Lew' :—

> To scare their foes withal !

The Fore and Aft were pouring out of the valley. What officers had said to men in that time of shame and humiliation will never be known ; for neither officers nor men speak of it now.

' They are coming anew !' shouted a priest among the Afghans. ' Do not kill the boys ! Take them alive, and they shall be of our faith.'

But the first volley had been fired, and Lew dropped on his face. Jakin stood for a minute, spun round and collapsed, as the Fore and Aft came forward, the curses of their officers in their ears, and in their hearts the shame of open shame.

Half the men had seen the drummers die, and they made no sign. They did not even shout. They doubled out straight across the plain in open order, and they did not fire.

'This,' said the Colonel of Gurkhas, softly, ' is the real attack, as it should have been delivered. Come on, my children.'

' Ulu-lu-lu-lu !' squealed the Gurkhas, and came

down with a joyful clicking of *kukris*—those vicious Gurkha knives.

On the right there was no rush. The Highlanders, cannily commending their souls to God (for it matters as much to a dead man whether he has been shot in a Border scuffle or at Waterloo), opened out and fired according to their custom, that is to say, without heat and without intervals, while the screw-guns, having disposed of the impertinent mud fort aforementioned, dropped shell after shell into the clusters round the flickering green standards on the heights.

'Charrging is an unfortunate necessity,' murmured the Colour-Sergeant of the right company of the Highlanders. 'It makes the men sweer so, but I am thinkin' that it will come to a charrge if these black devils stand much longer. Stewarrt, man, you're firing into the eye of the sun, and he'll not take any harm for Government ammuneetion. A foot lower and a great deal slower! What are the English doing? They're very quiet there in the centre. Running again?'

The English were not running. They were hacking and hewing and stabbing, for though one white man is seldom physically a match for an Afghan in a sheepskin or wadded coat, yet, through the pressure of many white men behind, and a certain thirst for revenge in his heart, he becomes capable of doing much with both ends of his rifle. The Fore and Aft held their fire till one bullet could drive through five or six men, and the front of the Afghan force gave on the volley. They then selected their men, and slew them with deep gasps and short hacking coughs, and groanings of leather belts against strained bodies, and realised for the first time that an Afghan attacked is far less formidable than an Afghan attacking : which fact old soldiers might have told them.

But they had no old soldiers in their ranks.

The Gurkhas' stall at the bazar was the noisiest, for the men were engaged—to a nasty noise as of beef being cut on the block—with the *kukri*, which they preferred to the bayonet ; well knowing how the Afghan hates the half-moon blade.

As the Afghans wavered, the green standards on the mountain moved down to assist them in a last rally. This was unwise. The Lancers chafing in the right gorge had thrice despatched their only subaltern as galloper to report on the progress of affairs. On the third occasion he returned, with a bullet-graze on his knee, swearing strange oaths in Hindustani, and saying that all things were ready. So that Squadron swung round the right of the Highlanders with a wicked whistling of wind in the pennons of its lances, and fell upon the remnant just when, according to all the rules of war, it should have waited for the foe to show more signs of wavering.

But it was a dainty charge, deftly delivered, and it ended by the Cavalry finding itself at the head of the pass by which the Afghans intended to retreat ; and down the track that the lances had made streamed two companies of the Highlanders, which was never intended by the Brigadier. The new development was successful. It detached the enemy from his base as a sponge is torn from a rock, and left him ringed about with fire in that pitiless plain. And as a sponge is chased round the bath-tub by the hand of the bather, so were the Afghans chased till they broke into little detachments much more difficult to dispose of than large masses.

'See!' quoth the Brigadier. 'Everything has come as I arranged. We've cut their base, and now we'll bucket 'em to pieces.'

A direct hammering was all that the Brigadier had dared to hope for, considering the size of the force at his disposal; but men who stand or fall by the errors of their opponents may be forgiven for turning Chance into Design. The bucketing went forward merrily. The Afghan forces were upon the run—the run of wearied wolves who snarl and bite over their shoulders. The red lances dipped by twos and threes, and, with a shriek, up rose the lance-butt, like a spar on a stormy sea, as the trooper cantering forward cleared his point. The Lancers kept between their prey and the steep hills, for all who could were trying to escape from the valley of death. The Highlanders gave the fugitives two hundred yards' law, and then brought them down, gasping and choking, ere they could reach the protection of the boulders above. The Gurkhas followed suit; but the Fore and Aft were killing on their own account, for they had penned a mass of men between their bayonets and a wall of rock, and the flash of the rifles was lighting the wadded coats.

'We cannot hold them, Captain Sahib!' panted

a Ressaldar of Lancers. 'Let us try the carbine. The lance is good, but it wastes time.'

They tried the carbine, and still the enemy melted away—fled up the hills by hundreds when there were only twenty bullets to stop them. On the heights the screw-guns ceased firing—they had run out of ammunition—and the Brigadier groaned, for the musketry fire could not sufficiently smash the retreat. Long before the last volleys were fired the doolies were out in force looking for the wounded.. The battle was over, and, but for want of fresh troops, the Afghans would have been wiped off the earth. As it was they counted their dead by hundreds, and nowhere were the dead thicker than in the track of the Fore and Aft.

But the Regiment did not cheer with the Highlanders, nor did they dance uncouth dances with the Gurkhas among the dead. They looked under their brows at the Colonel as they leaned upon their rifles and panted.

'Get back to camp, you. Haven't you disgraced yourself enough for one day! Go and look to the wounded. It's all you're fit for,' said the Colonel. Yet for the past hour the Fore and Aft had been doing all that mortal commander could expect. They had lost heavily because they did not know how to set about their business with proper skill, but they had borne themselves gallantly, and this was their reward.

A young and sprightly Colour-Sergeant, who had begun to imagine himself a hero, offered his water-bottle to a Highlander, whose tongue was black with thirst. 'I drink with no cowards,' answered the youngster huskily, and, turning to a Gurkha, said, 'Hya, Johnny! Drink water got it?' The Gurkha grinned and passed his bottle. The Fore and Aft said no word.

They went back to camp when the field of strife had been a little mopped up and made presentable, and the Brigadier, who saw himself a Knight in three months, was the only soul who was complimentary to them. The Colonel was heart-broken, and the officers were savage and sullen.

'Well,' said the Brigadier, 'they are young troops of course, and it was not unnatural that they should retire in disorder for a bit.'

'Oh, my only Aunt Maria!' murmured a junior Staff Officer. 'Retire in disorder! It was a bally run!'

'But they came again, as we all know,' cooed the Brigadier, the Colonel's ashy-white face before him, 'and they behaved as well as could possibly be expected. Behaved beautifully, indeed. I was watching them. It's not a matter to take to heart, Colonel. As some German General said of his men, they wanted to be shooted over a little, that was all.' To himself he said—'Now they're blooded I can give 'em responsible work. It's as well that they got what they did. 'Teach 'em more than half-a-dozen rifle flirtations, that will— later—run alone and bite. Poor old Colonel, though.'

All that afternoon the heliograph winked and flickered on the hills, striving to tell the good news to a mountain forty miles away. And in the evening there arrived, dusty, sweating, and sore, a misguided Correspondent who had gone out to assist at a trumpery village-burning, and who had read off the message from afar, cursing his luck the while.

' Let's have the details somehow—as full as ever you can, please. It's the first time I've ever been left this campaign,' said the Correspondent to the Brigadier, and the Brigadier, nothing loath, told him how an Army of Communication had been crumpled up, destroyed, and all but annihilated by the craft, strategy, wisdom, and foresight of the Brigadier.

But some say, and among these be the Gurkhas who watched on the hillside, that that battle was won by Jakin and Lew, whose little bodies were borne up just in time to fit two gaps at the head of the big ditch-grave for the dead under the heights of Jagai.

THE END